RIDDLE CHILD

RIDDLE CHILD

Annelie Botes

VIKING
an imprint of
PENGUIN BOOKS

VIKING

Published by the Penguin Group
80 Strand, London WC2R 0RL, England
Penguin Putnam Inc, 375 Hudson Street, New York, New York 10014, USA
Penguin Books Australia Ltd, 250 Camberwell Road, Camberwell,
Victoria 3124, Australia
Penguin Books Canada Ltd, 10 Alcorn Avenue, Toronto, Ontario,
Canada M4V 3B2
Penguin Books (NZ) Ltd, Cnr Rosedale and Airborne Roads, Albany,
Auckland, New Zealand
Penguin Books India (Pvt) Ltd, 11 Community Centre, Panchsheel Park,
New Delhi – 110 017 India
Penguin Books (South Africa) (Pty) Ltd, 24 Sturdee Avenue, Rosebank,
Johannesburg 2196, South Africa

Penguin Books (South Africa) (Pty) Ltd, Registered Offices:
Second Floor, 90 Rivonia Road, Sandton 2196, South Africa

First published in Afrikaans as *Raaiselkind* by Tafelberg Publishers, 2001
First published in English by Penguin Books (South Africa) (Pty) Ltd 2003

ISBN 0 670 04792 9

Typeset by CJH Design in 11/13 point Galliard
Cover design: Flame Design
Printed and bound by Interpak Books, Pietermaritzburg

Heed those with troubled minds
For they have strange wisdom

Wall inscription, Nineveh 6 BC

Acknowledgements

With respect and appreciation to:

Quest School in Port Elizabeth, where the scales fell from my eyes
Professional people who shifted forbidden boundaries
The staff at Mount Road police station who tolerated me
Dianne Beukes-Jesson who illuminated the riddle for me
Lynn Wood for allowing me to touch Vanessa's life
Alida and Brent who will haunt me for ever
Michael MacGregor for allowing me to step ashore on his lonely
　　island
Hannelie Bakker for her brilliant knowledge of the law
Johann Nel for precious midnight conversations
Nelene de Beer for lending me her thesis
André Louw for the silver sound of the harp, and for solid faith
Captain Elsabé Munro for bringing me tea in the prison cell
Superintendent Henry Trytsman for walking the gateways of hell
　　with me
My editor Pam Thornley, who was my angel of goodness
The prison walls where my graffiti is carved
And all those who carried me over the finishing line

*To all those who have been given the task
of steering a riddle child through life*

1

THE CEMENT FLOOR OF THE bathroom is like a block of ice under her bare feet. The cold shoots up through her calves into her knees. Bewildered, she looks down at her own pearly white body, and then at the woman detective standing next to the basin with her hands clasped behind her back. From the corner of her eye she catches a glimpse of a small, square, frosted glass window above the toilet.

It is too small and too high. Even if she could escape through there, she could never run naked through the city streets. Moreover, it was a long way home; she would have to keep to the bushes on the side of the road to get there undetected. And when she eventually arrived home after two or three days, they'd be waiting for her, because they know she has nowhere else to go.

Perhaps she could leave the road before she reached the town, and hide in the mountains on Gunter's farm. Live off the veld. Somewhere in the mountain thickets she would find a cave or an overhanging krantz where she could shelter from the bitter cold of winter. Perhaps go down the mountain at night to fetch a blanket and cough medicine from Gunter. He wouldn't tell anyone she was hiding in the mountains.

No. She wouldn't know which berries and veld fruits were edible and which were poisonous. And what if she was too scared to go down the mountain to Gunter's house in the dark, or if she caught pneumonia in the damp kloofs? No. They'd be watching Gunter's homestead. Probably use police dogs to track her down.

What about Miriam's house in the township? Surely no one would come looking for her in the little woodshed behind the chicken run. No. The township had too many eyes, and Miriam could get into trouble because of her.

No. It would be stupid to try to escape. Sooner or later they would find her.

Besides, there is no need for her to hide. She knows that the detective thinks she drowned Alexander. Why else would they have arrested her and brought her here for questioning; why else keep digging into the past?

They were wrong. Alexander was her flesh and blood. Even though he was autistic, he was her child. An uncontrollable child, wild, and ruled by neurosis and ritual.

But she would never have harmed him.

'Squat,' the woman says, retreating a step, and staring unflinchingly at her.

Squat? Has the woman lost her mind? She doesn't answer, but remains standing.

'Please, Mrs Dorfling.'

She must not give in. 'But I'm naked. I can't . . . I mean . . .'

The woman steps closer. 'I have to search you for dangerous objects, Mrs Dorfling, that's all.'

'But you have searched me already,' she pleads, spreading her palms. 'I'm naked, what can I hide?'

'This is normal procedure. You'd be surprised if you knew where desperate women hide dangerous objects to use later as weapons or to try to escape. Now, please squat, Mrs Dorfling.'

For an eternity, it seems, they size each other up. Then, slowly, she squats. Humiliated. Stripped of dignity. As the tips of her fingers touch the ice-cold bathroom floor, a rattling cough shakes her body. In trying to control the muscles of her bladder, she loses her balance. The coughing brings tears to her eyes, blurring her vision. Through the film of tears she notices the shoes and legs of the woman coming closer.

'Get up and get dressed. Whatever might have been hidden inside would have fallen out by now. Remove your shoelaces so that they can be added to the inventory of your belongings.'

'You are humiliating me terribly. How would you like to squat and have a complete stranger look between your legs?'

2

'It's my job, Mrs Dorfling, something I do every day.' Impassively, without even raising her voice. 'If there's trouble later because you had hidden something inside, I would be accountable.'

2

THE MORNING IS STILL PITCH DARK and it is bitterly cold. It's hard to get out from under the warm blankets.

She must get ready. The truck going to the *grootkerk* in the kloof won't wait for her. For a long time she's wanted to go to the *grootkerk* back in the kloof, to bow down before the Lord. There are many things she has to confess to Him. Tonight, at the preparatory service, she needs to find peace in her heart. Tomorrow is Sunday, *Nagmaal* Sunday. Time to level her sins before she returns to her township house.

She lifts the blanket covering the kneading bowl and pushes the sleeves of the blue jersey, which she inherited when Master Dawid died, up above her elbows. Dips her knuckles in the saucer of melted butter to knead down the bread dough.

She has stomach cramps.

Heaven knows, since she woke up this morning her insides have not felt quite right. It's the sort of feeling that makes her feel faint.

It is an omen. No doubt about it.

Long ago, when her mother was still alive, she had told her that some people are born with second sight in their stomachs. And that second sight in the stomach is more significant than being born with a caul. There had been many strange deaths in the township, and each time her stomach had warned her long before the tragedy struck. Like the time Aunt Maria's Manny died, choking on a shirt button. And when Sina's third illegitimate child slipped and drowned in a pool of water only two fingers deep.

She'd rather not think about all the times the angel of death had spoken loudly to her. It was bad for her head, as well as her stomach.

'Miriam!' Jeremiah calls from the back room. 'Is the coffee ready yet?'

She ignores him. Lazy bastard, Jeremiah. Lies with his backside under the warm bedclothes while she struggles outside in the piercing cold wind with her arthritic legs to fetch kindling from the woodshed. While she kneads down the dough, greases the bread pans, struggles with the smoky damp wood fire. And she will probably also have to help Jeremiah into his pants before she gets on the truck for the journey to the *grootkerk* in the kloof.

Again her stomach turns. Perhaps she should go to the privy. No, it's not that kind of stomach turn.

It is different.

The Lord must look after Miss Ingrid and Lexi this weekend, till Monday morning when she'll be back at work. And Jeremiah, too, so that he doesn't let the bread dough rise too high or leave it in the oven until it's rock hard. Let him be good to her chickens too, and let him keep his hands off the eggs of her nesting hens.

And bless the *grootkerk*.

3

GOD OF ALL gods.

Is there anything left inside her? All that she ever was or could have been has died. Slowly and laboriously, over nine wretched years. Cell by cell. Tissue sloughing off, bit by bit. What Alexander hadn't chiselled off during the nine years, the townsfolk had destroyed.

Now Alexander is dead.

If she hadn't picked up his limp little body from the bath with her own hands and stared into the stillness of his blue eyes, she wouldn't have believed it.

What will she do when they realise that she's innocent and they take her back to town?

Town. A place of rejection and animosity. Where there is no one on whose door she can knock, no friend at whose kitchen table she can sit and weep about the loss of her child. As surely as God is alive, the townsfolk will carry on gossiping and speculating. The only person in town who cares about her and Alexander is Miriam. Mother hen who sheltered them under her protective brown wings, wherever and whenever she could. Has anyone thought of telling Miriam about this terrible thing that has happened? No, Miriam is not at home this weekend. When she took Miriam home after work on Friday she had told her that early on Saturday morning she was taking a truck to the kloof to celebrate the *Nagmaal* service with her in-laws. It will take time for the news to reach the kloof.

Apart from Miriam, there is only one other human being who ever got close to her soul.

Gunter.

Yet close as he was to her, he remained inaccessible. Man with the quiet, brown eyes that revealed everything, yet said nothing. Man who walked towards her with the saddle on his shoulder to saddle the gentle old horse for Alexander, the tinkling sound of stirrups filling the air while he worked silently. Patches of perspiration staining the back of his khaki shirt. Wiping the dust from his forehead with the back of his sunburnt hand. Taking his pocket knife out and cleaning the blade on his trousers. Man with whom she had so often sat on the kraal wall, the smell of bruised camphor bush drifting on the breeze around them.

'You must take better care of Alexander's feet, Ingrid,' he said, kneeling with the pocket knife in his hand next to Alexander who was lying on his back in the straw in the shed. 'Just look at the thorns and festering sores.'

She was tired that day. Dawid's death still weighed on her mind. No one in town looked her in the eye, nor could she have met their gaze if they had. Because she was afraid of what might be hidden in their eyes.

'Oh, Gunter, he's not even aware of the thorns in his feet.'

'He might step on something rusty and get blood poisoning. You have to take better care of his feet, Ingrid. Or teach him to wear shoes.'

'He refuses to wear shoes, and it's hard trying to take care of his feet because he kicks me in my face.'

Gunter fiddled with the knife without looking up at her. 'Then why does he lie still when I remove the thorns?'

'Because you are not me. He fights me all the time.'

He gestured to the tin of milk ointment on the gatepost. 'Stop talking nonsense and pass me the ointment so that I can rub it into his feet.'

Every Sunday when she took Alexander to ride and Gunter approached with the saddle and bridle, Alexander would willingly lie down on his back on the straw. It was as if he understood that he would only be able to ride after Gunter had scraped his feet clean and rubbed in the milk ointment. He never kicked or growled at Gunter. For those few peaceful minutes she could cut herself off from Alexander and leave him in the safety of Gunter's hands.

At first she was nervous when Alexander swung from the horse's mane or pulled back her lips and scratched on her teeth. Or when he lay on the ground and hoisted himself on to his shoulders and pummelled her stomach with his feet. Every time Alexander moved behind the horse and hung from her tail, she would watch anxiously for the slightest movement from the horse.

'I'm uneasy when he lies between the horse's legs. She might step on him or kick him.'

'Lucy won't kick or step on him. She knows him and she understands.'

'How can you say the horse understands? She hasn't got eyes under her stomach to see where Alexander is.'

'Don't worry, Ingrid. Lucy won't step on him.'

She would watch the man sitting hunched over the child's feet, patiently digging out thorns, removing every bit of dead skin, rubbing the oily liniment into every cut and sore.

Why had God given her an autistic child? She often asked the question silently while she sat on the kraal wall. How could she love and comfort him when he always pushed her away and growled at her? He neither heeded nor seemed to understand her. Looked right through her as if she did not exist.

She never found any answers.

Yet she could sense God in the smell of straw and horse and stable and ointment. In peacefully watching Gunter and Alexander. Even if that was the only memory she'd ever have of Gunter, it was better than nothing.

Would the news of Alexander's death have spread like wildfire? Had it reached Gunter's ears? Would he come looking for her and find that the house was locked?

'Walk ahead of me.' The woman prods her in the back.

Down the passage. Up the stairs. Past closed doors. Back to where the man with the jet black eyes is waiting for her at his desk. Ready to break her down. Systematically. God, she is tired. She cannot cope with his broad red face with the hair protruding from his nostrils. If only he would leave her alone for an hour. To weep for Alexander; to be alone with the image of her dead child hanging limp in her arms. To recall how she had laid him on the bed and placed her mouth over his to blow life back into his body. How she had called and called to him. How she kept trying to blow life into his mouth. But his eyes had stared unblinkingly into hers.

Ever since the man and woman had walked into her house earlier that afternoon, he had not left her alone for a second. Kept on asking questions. Incessantly. And every question seemed to indicate that he was convinced that *she* had drowned Alexander. Why should he consider her a suspect? Why didn't he ask about all the times she had protected Alexander like a tigress from the townsfolk? The years during which she had loved him unconditionally. How she would sit by his bed at night, gently rubbing the soles of his feet with a shoebrush while he slept. On her knees playing with him in his tablecloth house. Giving him milk coffee when he hid, hunched up, in the broom cupboard. The years during which she had torn herself apart searching for answers. On the verge of bankruptcy, she continued endlessly seeing one doctor after another, hoping for solutions. Her odyssey in her battered old car searching for help and knowledge. How she travelled home alone at night, through dangerous kudu territory, after yet another futile doctor's appointment. Why didn't he give her a chance to tell how she had teetered on the brink of insanity because nobody could give her answers.

But those weren't the things he was questioning her about.

If she had known that they would come back to interrogate her once more, she would never have taken the sleeping pill. Then she would not be fighting a debilitating drowsiness.

'Hurry up,' the woman says and prods her in the small of her back.

Their footsteps echo through the Saturday afternoon desolation of the Murder and Robbery building. A little further down the passage a pool of light spills from an open office door. She doesn't have the strength to defend herself against the man's accusations yet again. But at least the office won't be as cold as the bathroom where she had to stand naked with her arms above her head.

Perhaps they will take her home now.

No, she must not raise her hopes.

If they were planning to send her home, they would not have searched her so thoroughly. She vaguely remembers the man saying something about detaining her for questioning for forty-eight hours. Somewhere in those forty-eight hours she has to be allowed to sleep and bath and eat. What if they put her in a cell for forty-eight hours? And what if the man is never convinced of her innocence?

'I'd advise you to cooperate with Colonel Herselman. Don't make things difficult for yourself,' the woman says behind her. 'The Colonel is not a patient man; nor is he a compassionate man.

Many suspects regret afterwards that they did not cooperate from the very beginning . . .'

'Please,' and she stops in her tracks in the badly lit passage so that the woman almost bumps into her, turns and begs. 'Can't I go home? I am incredibly tired. I've hardly slept at all for the past two weeks. You are making a terrible mistake in accusing me . . .'

'We're not accusing you, Mrs Dorfling, we're questioning you.'

God almighty. Please make the woman listen to her and take her home. If the silence and emptiness of the house become unbearable, she can drive out to Gunter's farm. Sit alone on the kraal wall; the winter wind nipping at her cheeks; search for God in the familiar smell of the stable.

'How can I be a suspect? Surely you realise that you're making a mistake . . .'

'Mrs Dorfling, your child's death was definitely not an accident.'

'How can you say that? You weren't there . . .'

'Exactly. But the post-mortem report indicates that something abnormal happened. It's our job to find out what.'

She has to convince the woman. She wants to sleep in her own bed tonight. 'What do you mean by "abnormal"?'

'That is what we want to find out from you, Mrs Dorfling.'

The woman takes her by the elbow, pushes her in the back with her other hand. 'You can tell your story to Colonel Herselman. Let's go.'

'Please, I . . .'

'Walk, Mrs Dorfling.'

She walks.

Because she has no choice.

How do you describe nine years of torture and hell? But the detective does not want to hear about her hell. All he is interested in is finding a way to prove her guilt. When she is quiet, trying to organise the chaos in her mind, he pushes her for an answer. Then he destroys her answers one after the other with yet another clever question.

And another.

And another.

Until she thinks her brain will splinter into a thousand pieces.

The townsfolk never showed concern for Alexander. They treated his existence like a contagious disease. Ran away, turned their backs, looked the other way. Never-ending quarantine. Perhaps they would have understood better if she could have labelled his condition much earlier on: Alexander is autistic. Somewhere in his genes the attributes of love and conscience had been short circuited.

But she could not, because she did not know. By the time she found out, the barriers were there. When eventually she could name the disorder, nobody was interested. They just fled from Alexander's bizarre behaviour. Clutched their ornaments and cats and children and pot plants to their breasts before he could destroy them.

Gunter never asked about her private life. Perhaps if he had, it would have helped. Because then she might have been able to sit on the kraal wall with him and gradually make some sense of the chaos. The answers and events might have registered more clearly in her mind. But Gunter was not the type to dig into her soul. Quite the opposite. Sometimes they hardly spoke. Often they just sat on the kraal wall, watching Lucy walk in circles with Alexander on her back. Always the same route. Sometimes Alexander would slowly bend forward and fall asleep on her back. Then Lucy would stop and stand with her head hanging; not moving until Gunter lifted the sleeping child from her back. While she watched Alexander and the horse on their circular route, she often wished that she too could do what Lucy did: carry Alexander until he slept; understand the complexity of his distorted world.

'Gunter, how does Lucy know Alexander is asleep? I mean, she's just an animal.'

He smiled at her, his brown eyes warm. 'Animals are not like people, Ingrid.'

'Do you think Lucy has a soul like a human being?'

'Who knows? She knows instinctively when Alexander is asleep. And if she has instincts, she must have a soul.'

'What if animals really have souls . . .?'

'Don't go there, Ingrid. Questions like that don't have answers.'

He knew that somehow she needed to work through the soul of the horse to find her own; perhaps his as well. Some Sundays he would look at her like an explorer trying to discover the paths of her mind; silently searching for ravines and bridges; roundabout routes and shortcuts. Sometimes she yearned for him to look at her like a man, to love her. With his heart and his body. To lift her from the kraal wall and hold her close to his heart. Take her to his big white house with the green louvres and make her tea with warm milk; hold out his hands and say to her: come to me, Ingrid, let me show you the room and the bed where I sleep.

But he never did.

Throughout the many nights when Alexander pulled her through the house to close cupboard doors and realign carpets or turn off a dripping tap, she would cherish the hope that Gunter would one day love her.

This man is not like Gunter. He is sly, hard as a rock.

How old was your child, Mrs Dorfling? When last did you take him for a medical check-up? Has he seen a paediatrician? When last did *you* see a doctor or a psychologist? So, you *did* see a psychologist. Who did you see; when and why? Why did you stop the therapy? What do you think was the reason for your husband's suicide? When did you lie down on your bed, before or after daybreak? Were you really asleep, Mrs Dorfling? Where was the child at that time? Was he lying face down or face up in the water? What first aid measures did you apply? What do you mean, it was useless? How did he communicate with you for nine years if he couldn't speak? What exactly do you mean when you say the child could only make growling sounds?

The child.
Alexander.
What had they done to his frail little body during the autopsy? Why does she keep visualising a broken child with organs floating in the pit of his stomach? She wishes she could banish these images from her mind. They will drive her crazy. She didn't want to see him dead. Just as she wished she hadn't had to identify Dawid's body. That gruesome sight had scarred her for ever.

Let the man ask what he wants to and let it take him wherever he wants to go. She will stick to the truth to the very end. The truth as it is in her head. In spite of all that had been wrong, he was her child, and she had loved him in a way that was beyond normal understanding. Unpredictable Alexander, who charged at her without warning and scratched her face with his fingernails. Who knelt on the floor, rocking to and fro while he banged his head against her shins until they turned blue. Who sat on the piano stool from dawn to dusk, his face devoid of expression, rhythmically striking the black key of F-sharp with his middle finger. *Ta-tate-ta. Ta-tate-ta.* At night, a ghostly figure moving around the house with his chisel, hammering at the plaster on the walls until the bricks were exposed. Chipping and chipping and chipping. Until sunrise. Until the sun set again. Until it felt as if he was chipping right inside her skull.

Chip, chip, chip. Until there was not a single fibre of her being that had not been pulverised into nothingness. Incessantly, since he first discovered the chisel, for seven long years. Without the chisel ever becoming blunt.

The child.

Alexander.

4

'JEREMIAH,' SHE SAYS AS SHE puts the coffee mug on the window sill
next to the bed. 'Don't let the bread rise too high while you're
lazing in bed. When you see the dough reaching the top of the
bread pans you must put them in the oven.'

She knows she is wasting her breath. He always pretends to be
deaf. He knows that if he pays attention, he'll have to get up and
move his backside. And work has never been Jeremiah's strong
point. But when he has a bottle of wine to finish or a game of
dominoes to play, he's very eager. God knows, there have been
times when she felt like bashing his brains in with a pick handle.

'If the rain stops and the sun comes out, you must open the
chicken run. But if it starts raining again, you must put them back
in. And you had better bring in dry kindling for tomorrow. I don't
want to return to a smoke-filled house. After all, I'm going to the
grootkerk to cleanse my heart. So don't let me come back to an
argument about bread and kindling and chickens.'

He lies on the bed looking at her as if she has had too much to
drink. God help her the day she grabs Jeremiah and knocks some
sense into his head.

'Did you hear me, Jeremiah?'

'How could I not hear you? You're shouting in my face!'

'Just asking. And, Jeremiah, don't think I'm too stupid to see that some of the money in my sacred bottle has disappeared. That money was saved for missionary work and should have been taken to the *grootkerk* tomorrow. God will strike you down if you take His money to pay your domino debts.'

He turns on his side and pulls the blankets up around his neck. '*Jissus*, Miriam, just leave me alone!'

It's Jeremiah's way to *Jissus* at her when he's cornered. And he knows perfectly well that the name of Jesus is not to be used disrespectfully in her house. Tormenting her, that's all it is.

'God will punish you for taking His Son's name in vain.'

She must leave him alone before she bursts a blood vessel.

5

THE CRAMPED OFFICE AT Murder and Robbery smells of carbon paper and inkpads and cigarette butts. The window has been closed and the poor ventilation makes her nauseous and giddy.

When last did she eat? Yesterday morning? She can't remember. Yesterday seems light years away. Perhaps he'll give her coffee and a chair if her answers satisfy him. No, he won't. She has been giving him all the answers she knows and he is still not satisfied.

He looks up from the brown police docket. Taps on the desk with the pencil in his stubby fingers. *Ta-tate-ta, ta-tate-ta*. In God's name, stop it! she wants to shout. Don't drum the pencil the way Alexander played F-sharp!

'Mrs Dorfling,' and he puts the pencil down, leans back in the chair. 'Your child is dead and yet you show no grief.' He folds his hands behind his head and looks at her quizzically. 'Why not? After all, you are his mother.'

Dear God. If only she weren't so tired. 'You haven't given me the opportunity to mourn his death. How do you expect me . . .?'

His raised hand interrupts her in mid-sentence. 'No, Mrs Dorfling, I'm not just talking about now. When we arrived at your home this afternoon, I could see no sign that you had been weeping.' *Ta-tate-ta*. 'Tell me, are you really grieving?'

She is dizzy; her arms feel numb. 'I don't think I have any tears left to shed. The past nine years have made me hard. I cannot remember when last I cried . . . I want to, but I can't.'

Ta-tate-ta, ta-tate-ta.

The exhaustion of so many days with so little sleep, as well as the previous night when she hardly slept at all, is taking its toll. How long will she be able to stand? She shifts her weight from one foot to the other. An invisible hand tries to shut her eyes. She's going to fall asleep on her feet. Around her the office space and the man's face are being sucked up into a narrow tunnel. Her ears are ringing, his voice is distorting into a vague background noise.

'May I please have a chair? I'm tired and I had no sleep last night . . .'

Swiftly and brutally he attacks. 'Mrs Dorfling, you are contradicting yourself. Up to this point you've claimed that you were asleep when the child drowned. What's the truth?'

Trapped by a semantic quibble. 'I had just dozed off. It was too short to be regarded as sleep.'

'In your statement you said that you didn't know how long you slept. Now you say that it was short.'

'I . . . I . . . may I have a chair to sit down?'

He lays the pencil down on the docket, gets up and folds his arms. Paces up and down behind the desk. 'Let's start at the beginning, Mrs Dorfling. At the very beginning. And we'll start right at the beginning every time until you tell the truth.'

'I've been telling the truth all along.'

'I've looked at the facts, and I cannot believe you, Mrs Dorfling. And I'll keep asking until I get the whole truth from you.'

'Can I please go home to sleep before you continue?'

He ignores her. 'What do you think, Mrs Dorfling? How did the child land up in the bath full of water?'

Through the window she can see that evening is falling. And she is overcome by an overwhelming sense of helplessness. Because she realises that he is determined to go back to the very beginning yet again.

'He must have got into the bath by himself.'

'Did he usually get into the bath on his own?'

'No, I've already told you that he didn't like being bathed. I think he was afraid of being sucked down the plughole.'

He sits down, picks up the pencil. 'So he decided this morning, for the first time in his life, that he'd like to have a bath and got into the tub by himself?'

'That's the only explanation I can think of.'

'The detectives could find no sign of forced entry into your home, Mrs Dorfling. Nor were there any strange fingerprints. All the keys have been accounted for. Therefore one may assume that there was no unauthorised entry to your home and there was nobody but you who could have put the child in the bath.'

'He must have got into the bath by himself.'

He opens a drawer, takes out a yellow neon highlighter, underlines something in the docket. 'I can assure you, Mrs Dorfling, he did not.'

'I really don't understand how you can make such a statement. You weren't there. And I'm not going to let you intimidate me . . .'

'No, Mrs Dorfling,' and he rises so quickly that the chair falls over. 'I wasn't there and intimidation has nothing to do with it. An autopsy was performed. Autopsies don't lie, and Murder and Robbery isn't called in for petty crime.' He walks round the desk, stands close to her. 'What *really* happened this morning, Mrs Dorfling?'

She can't think straight. 'I don't know.'

He turns to the woman. 'Make a note that the suspect is unwilling to cooperate.'

From the corner of her eye she sees the woman writing something. Whether she wants to admit it or not, she is scared. Not of the truth, but of the unknown territory she finds herself in. 'May I please have a headache tablet?'

'Record her request,' he says to the woman. Then he turns to her again. 'It's against police regulations to supply medication during interrogation. Now, answer my question: what *really* happened to your child this morning?'

He's not going to stop. And her head is bursting. 'He drowned. I don't know more than that.'

'How did he get into the bath?'

She must think; try to reconstruct the events of last night exactly.

'Alexander was awake the whole night, chiselling at the plaster on the walls. He was covered in cheese spread and cement dust. His body was ice cold and I wanted to try and bath him and put him in my bed, hoping he would go to sleep.'

Her mouth is dry.

'I had run the bath, but he wouldn't get in until he had finished the jar of cheese spread. My feet ached and I went to lie down on the bed while he sat at the television set eating the cheese spread out of the jar. I didn't mean to fall asleep. When I woke up, I found him in the bath.'

Water. A chair. Please. Her legs and feet can't take it any more.

He moves out of her personal space; clasps his hands behind his back. With his head bent, he paces the office. Her skin prickles as he moves in behind her. And she knows: he is dangerous. Merciless. Clever. If there really is something incriminating in the autopsy report, she'll have to be strong or, as surely as God is alive, he'll break her in some devious way. She is the last person in the world who would ever have harmed Alexander.

Let them think what they like.

She would never have harmed him.

'You said the bath had already been run. Does that mean that you had turned off the taps before you fell asleep?'

'Yes, I did.'

'The passage was flooded, Mrs Dorfling. Who opened the taps again?'

'Alexander loved playing with taps. Perhaps he opened them himself.'

'His birth, Mrs Dorfling, was it a normal birth?'

'I said earlier that he was two weeks premature but everything else was normal.'

'He was born when you were thirty-three years old, ten years after your two older daughters were born. Did you really want this child?'

God knew how much she and Dawid had wanted a boy. Especially Dawid. He made no secret of it. When she fell pregnant, it was Dawid who spread the news.

As postmaster, he knew everyone in their small country town. Through his office window he could see when people came to fetch their mail and he always took the time to open the door on to the stoep and to make conversation with them. The post office stoep became a favourite meeting place. People liked Dawid and trusted him. He was always willing to give advice on hunting rifles, fishing tackle, tree houses. He loved spending time with his poker partners. Some Saturdays he would bet on the horses. From time to time he still played flank for the town's rugby team. He was an enthusiastic member of the golf club. Not a heavy drinker, not then. Fond of conversation and stories and jokes. His uninhibited laughter was infectious.

She had wanted to wait until the twelfth week of her pregnancy before telling anyone. But she knew Dawid would never be able to keep quiet until then. She did not really mind him telling, as she too was so happy about it. Teresa and Zettie were nine and eleven then, too young to be embarrassed by the prospect of a mother with a bulging tummy. They blurted it out at school, and before she reached her eighth week of pregnancy everybody in town knew. The clients at the bank where she worked enquired about the due date; whether she had any feelings about whether it was a boy or a girl. Many of the women brought her baby socks and crocheted bibs; gave advice on heartburn and stretch marks and breast feeding, while they watched the growing curve of her stomach.

'If you carry in your buttocks, like you do, it's a boy,' her next door neighbour Aunt Betty predicted when she brought over a basket of young gem squashes from her vegetable garden. 'Boys leave bad stretch marks on your thighs. At night you must rub your legs with lukewarm olive oil. Warm the bottle in boiling water . . .'

Miriam's Jeremiah walked all the way from the township to tell her that if it was a boy, he would teach him to build a racing cart from wire and how to drain the resin from a bluegum tree. And he would show him how to slaughter a chicken.

'And what if it's a girl, Jeremiah?'

He laughed timidly and scratched his head. 'No, *Jissus*, Miss Ingrid, then I don't know. Maybe Miriam can teach her to make mud cakes. Small round ones decorated with chinaberries, like the ones our township children make.'

Rosie, the cook at the school hostel and midwife to many township babies, brought her a bottle of buchu vinegar.

'It's for later on when your feet start swelling, Miss Ingrid. And you shouldn't sit on your haunches when you do the gardening, Miss Ingrid. Just the other morning when the township taxi passed your house on the way to the hostel, I saw you sitting on your haunches at the rose bed. Sitting like that can easily cause a miscarriage, Miss Ingrid. The Xhosa women taught me that you only sit like that when it's time to push. Then they squat in a corner or against a tree and, I'm telling you, Miss Ingrid, only two hard pushes and the baby slips out like a wet fish.'

Visitors came for tea; brought knitted baby clothes. She was often nauseous and suffered from heartburn, but she could not bear to miss the book club's monthly gathering or the weekly prayer meeting. The dominee and his wife paid a pastoral visit and the dominee read from the Bible about Abraham and Isaac and the sacrificial lamb. At the tennis club they joked that she was playing doubles and should be disqualified.

Everybody was happy for her and for Dawid.

After all, news about a *laatlam* was quite an event in the lives of the people in the small town. They were a close-knit community, tucked beneath the mountain that hovered watchfully over the town like a grandfather; dependent on one another's caring and compassion. And even though she and Dawid had only been living there for three years, they had been warmly accepted into the community. Dawid was elected to every committee and board, was part of every team and the life and soul of every party.

How absolutely normal they had been.

They had often gathered for a *braai*, hooked the caravan to the car and driven to the sea for weekends with Mirna and Lida and Hannah and their families. Her close friendships with Mirna and Lida and Hannah added value to her life, each in its unique way.

Mirna had inherited money. She had a beautiful thatched house set between the dense trees on the river bank. It had a serene garden with mossy stones, hidden footpaths laid with river stones wound through soft green carpets of peace-in-the-home. Bright red begonias flourished in the south-facing corners. Clumps of fern. Black lilies. The interior of the house was decorated in the style of a hunting lodge with earth colours creating an impression of straw and mud. There were rough hessian textures and scatter cushions decorated with animal skin motifs. Stuffed heads of buffalo and kudu were mounted on the mud-coloured walls. Cured zebra skins lay on the stone floors. It was always Mirna who was consulted about matters of style.

Lida lived in the square house opposite the bank. A remedial teacher at the school, she was the intellectual one in their circle. She had little interest in gardening or art or elegance. But she knew about politics and the stock market. And she was chairperson of the book club, an expert on writers and writing. An entire room in her house was filled with bookshelves. She was the first woman in the congregation to be elected to the Church Council.

Hannah was the spiritual one. A dreamer, her head forever filled with lingering tunes. She forgot to comb her hair in the morning; went to the shop barefoot wearing a bright-coloured skirt brushing her ankle rings. She made jam from rose petals, baked rye bread. Went digging for smooth clay to paint her door frames in ochre African patterns. Single-handedly put up a reed ceiling in her kitchen. She was always wanting to read poetry to them.

She often wondered how she had come to be embraced by this special circle of women. She, who possessed no brilliance; who was more than satisfied with her simple life with Dawid. Sitting at the kitchen table, balancing their budget. Sending the children to bed early and playing scrabble until midnight, a pot of coffee brewing on the hot plate. Going for a walk down the gravel road to cool off on sweltering summer nights. Pottering in the garden before sunset and picking bunches of sweetpeas to fill the house with the fragrance of spring.

Dawid loved his vegetable garden and Jeremiah often came on Saturdays to give him a hand. Thyme, parsnips, sage, mint, red chillies, garlic. In summer they planted rows and rows of runner beans. And in the coolness of the early morning, when the mountain was still just a dark shadow against the changing sky, she and Dawid and the girls picked the dew-covered beans from under the cool leaves. At night they would sit at the kitchen table slicing the beans, while Dawid told the girls stories about sea tortoises that could talk and water princesses with silver crowns decorated with scarlet rubies.

They did not have the faintest idea that the normality of their lives would soon disintegrate before their eyes. How could they have known?

The sonar showed a boy. Dawid's joy knew no limits. He put a notice on the wall above the mailboxes at the post office: *It's going to be a boy!* She too was overjoyed, especially for Dawid's sake.

'He must be named after my grandfather,' Dawid said while they were playing scrabble one Tuesday evening.

Dawid never went out on Tuesday evenings. It was a self-imposed rule. Monday and Thursday evenings were set aside for committee meetings. Wednesday and Friday evenings he spent at the golf club and with his poker friends. On Saturdays they drifted along on the social tide of the town.

'Alexander. Just that. No second names.' He moved the scrabble blocks round on the wooden holder. 'And you must promise me, Ingrid, that he won't be baptised in some kind of dress.'

'What if the sonar was wrong and it's a girl, Dawid?'

'Then we'll call her Alexandra. But it won't happen. I've seen the little spout with my own eyes.'

It was a relief when her maternity leave began. Despite the coolness of late autumn, her feet were swollen to her ankles. At night she got cramp in her calves; during the day her back troubled her and she was uncomfortable standing on her feet behind the cashier's counter at the bank all day long. The manager offered to let her work at the back of the office where she could sit at a desk, but she did not want to change her working routine.

'It's better to give birth with a clean house, Ingrid,' Aunt Betty said when she popped in with a plate of hot cinnamon pancakes. 'A woman's mind must not be divided by untidy cupboards and dirty curtains and an empty deep freeze when she arrives home from hospital with a new baby. Get everything in order before you go to the hospital.'

There were lots of tasks that she and Miriam had to finish before she could go to hospital with an easy mind. The linen cupboard had to be sorted out, the kitchen cupboards had to be scrubbed. Dawid still planned to paint the nursery and she had to make curtains. She slept restlessly, waking with every cramp and turn. Winter was slowly creeping in, and she longed to linger in bed in the mornings. Halfway through a working day, her feet painfully swollen, she longed to lie down for an hour. And she wanted to be kind to Dawid, for her attention would be divided after the baby's arrival.

But, most of all, she desperately needed a time of emotional rest before the birth. The pregnancy had drained her. Her body was not as young and strong as it had been with the girls. And unlike Teresa and Zettie, the baby was exceptionally restless, as if he was anxious to wrestle his way out. He nudged her stomach with his elbows and knees; kicked her bladder so that she started leaking.

The thought of friends giving her a foolish stork party hung like a sword over her head. She had long outgrown the time when eating raisins from a bowl of icing sugar was fun. And so it came as a tremendous relief when one day she came home from a visit to Old Doctor to find Mirna and Lida and Hannah had, instead of organising a stork party, washed and ironed all the curtains in the house. They had defrosted the deep freeze and filled it up with scones and cottage pies and muffins baked by the women of the congregation.

'We used Miriam's house key. We wanted to save you from a circus,' Hannah said.

The tears welled up in her eyes. 'Thank you, Hannah.'

Often she found herself dreading the birth. Wished she could just close her eyes and get it over painlessly and without effort.

'The baby is well positioned,' Old Doctor assured her. 'I think he might arrive a little bit earlier than we expect.'

Two weeks before the due date, she called Dawid at the golf club. It was after ten o'clock in the evening.

'My water has broken, Dawid, I think you should come home.'

She was thankful for the two weeks she would be spared. Her body was tired.

'Boys!' She could hear Dawid shouting above the background noise. 'Set up a round of drinks, I'm paying!'

She could picture the excitement on his face, innocent, almost childlike. There was nothing about Dawid that she would want to change. Notwithstanding his social life and committee meetings and poker friends, he was good to her and the children. A caring father to Teresa and Zettie. He fixed their bicycles, plaited their hair, put up a netball ring. Got up at night to switch on the bathroom light for them; went to the kitchen when they called for water. At bedtime they cuddled in his arms while he read them Bible stories. Together they turned the kitchen into chaos making pancakes. When they were running a fever, or had nightmares, they sought comfort by creeping into Dawid's side of the bed. When she wanted to attend the women's prayer meeting or visit Mirna or Lida or Hannah, he never grumbled. As long as she did not make any claims on his poker time.

She loved Dawid.

He loved her too.

'Are you having contractions yet?'

She wanted him to be with her. 'A little, but I think you should come home. I must still bath and pack my suitcase.'

At half past ten he was home. He helped to pack the suitcase and cleaned up the pool of water on the kitchen floor. Made her some tea and phoned Old Doctor. In the early hours of the morning when her contractions became intense, he went to fetch Miriam.

'You must stay with me until the very end, Dawid.'

'I will.' He held her to his chest so that the swollen bulge of her stomach pressed painfully against him. 'Everything will be fine, you'll see.' He stroked her hair tenderly. 'I love you, Ingrid.'

At thirteen minutes past six on a freezing winter's morning Alexander slipped from her with a piercing scream. He was perfect.

Dawid kissed the child's wrinkled face, ran his finger over the slimy hair and rested the tiny, naked, blood-wet bundle in the hollow of his neck. He looked at her over the tiny shoulder. And his stubbly cheeks were stained with tears and birth fluid.

'Yes, I did want Alexander.'

'And when the trouble started, did you still want him?'

'Yes, I did.'

Her feet are aching. Her mouth feels sticky. She regrets taking the sleeping pill.

'When did you first suspect that something was wrong with the child?'

6

SHE DUSTS THE LOOSE flour from the table and rinses the butter saucer with warm water. Heaven knows, her stomach feels as if it's turning inside out. Maybe she should have half a cup of coffee before she leaves for the kloof. No, that might make her late for the truck.

Funny how she had had the same sort of feeling in her guts that night, years ago, when Lexi was born. When Master Dawid knocked at the door during the early morning hours she was out of bed immediately. She had kept him waiting barely ten minutes while she dressed and combed her hair.

'Jeremiah,' she had said the previous evening after she had rounded up the chickens and locked the gate of the chicken run, 'tomorrow you must be my hands in the house while I am at work. Miss Ingrid's time is getting closer and the housework cannot pile up until then.'

There were many things that had to be done in her own house before Miss Ingrid's baby arrived. She had to clean every nook and cranny, hang the blankets in the sun. The wood stove had to be scrubbed and polished. There was a broken window in the dining room that let in a cold draught. It had to be fixed. And Jeremiah was a sluggish man. If she wanted the runner beans planted by

September, she had to plan ahead and prod him in June to start digging the beds and to cut reeds for the runners. If he was not complaining that his back was half broken, then he had dizziness in his head. Or he pretended to be crippled. Or deaf.

'You must go to the shop to buy putty and a window pane, Jeremiah. Steel wool to clean the stove as well. I'll leave the money in the Bible, at the Book of Judges.' It was her way to leave money in the Bible, the only way in which she could move Jeremiah to page through the Bible. 'Then you must . . .'

He shouted her down. 'Do you perhaps want *me* to scrub the stove?'

'Yes. Or does it look like I have two pairs of hands?'

'I am going to cure skins tomorrow, and when I have finished there . . .'

'Cure skins? You are lying in my face, Jeremiah! Don't take me for a fool! Surely you mean you're going down the street to sit at a five-gallon drum playing dominoes all day long. Don't even think about it, Jeremiah. Tomorrow you're going to buy steel wool and putty. And God help you if I come home and the stove isn't . . .'

'Oh, *Jissus*, Miriam. Why can't you scrub the stove yourself on Saturday? Stop being so bloody fidgety! One would swear that it's *you* who's having a baby!'

He knew very well that her Christian soul could not bear it when he used the name of God's Son profanely. But he kept taunting her, until her blood boiled. Because he knew that when she lost her temper she would tell him to his face that he was a useless and Godless creature. And that her own two hands were strong enough to do his share of the work too. He always tempted her into the sin of anger. And then he sat back with folded arms while she worked her backside off.

But that evening before Lexi was born, she wouldn't allow herself to be engulfed by Jeremiah's wickedness. Because at twilight that evening, when she turned the key in the door of the chicken run, she had a clear foreboding that something was wrong. It was as if Miss Ingrid was calling out in agony. Only one loud shout. When she turned around to see if Miss Ingrid was perhaps standing behind her, she saw Miss Ingrid's face drifting in the evening clouds. But where her eyes were supposed to be, there were only two milky marbles.

Dear God, she was frightened.

No sooner had she pulled the key out of the door, than the second sight in her stomach started speaking.

In the early evening she walked across the street to Aunt Maria's house to borrow a bundle of steel wool. And she did not go to bed that night until the stove was shining.

'I'm going now, Jeremiah, before I miss the truck. Don't forget my chickens.'

'You've said that a thousand times, Miriam! Go, I won't forget anything.' His voice is filled with impatience.

She leaves the candle stub burning on the table and puts her coat on. At the front gate she turns and goes back to Jeremiah, still lying in bed. 'Jeremiah, if it doesn't rain you must go up to Miss Ingrid's house. Check that everything is all right. And ask if Miss Ingrid is coping with Lexi.'

He snorts. 'You must be soft in the head, Miriam! Why should I walk all the way up there in this freezing cold?'

'I'll leave you some of the money from my sacred bottle in the Bible. At Ezekiel. But then you must swear that you will go to Miss Ingrid.'

'Rather put the money in front in the Bible. Then I'll go.'

In the candlelight she places the money at Ezekiel. Almost a quarter of the savings in her sacred bottle. God won't punish her. He knows that in some way it's for Miss Ingrid. And for Lexi.

Then she walks out the front door.

7

'ANSWER MY QUESTION, Mrs Dorfling.'

She must have fallen asleep.

'I cannot remember what you asked.'

'I asked: When did you first suspect that something was wrong with the child?'

She'd only been in hospital once before, when she had an asthma attack after accidentally inhaling insecticide from an aerosol. The hospital was homely and relaxed, no hard and fast rules about visiting hours. For the most part she could follow her own routine. Teresa and Zettie could come and go as they pleased.

For this reason, she had told Dawid long before the birth that she was going to stay in hospital for eight days after the baby was born. She needed time to rest. If she went home earlier she would be making endless cups of tea, entertaining visitors who came to see the baby. In hospital she would be able to read, sleep when her body felt the need for it, leave the baby to the care of the nursing staff. She could sit on the hospital stoep in the winter sun, listening to the starlings in the honeysuckle.

But the reality was not at all what she had planned.

On the morning of the second day Alexander started crying. Inceasingly, tearlessly. One moment she was paging quietly through a magazine, a polisher droning in the passage outside, teacups clattering in the distance. The next moment she was almost frightened out of her wits by a piercing scream from Alexander. When she bent over the cradle she could see that his face was red and his tongue was swollen in his mouth. He had managed to free his hands from the blankets, and was grabbing wildly at the air with his bony little fingers. Bewildered, she pressed the bell to call for help. Perhaps he was choking?

'Nothing to worry about,' the nurse said after picking him up and changing his nappy while he continued to scream non-stop. 'Perhaps the sound of the polisher frightened him. I'll tell them to turn it off. Put him in the bed with you. Perhaps he needs the warmth of your body.'

She put him in the bed, thinking he was going to scream until he lost his breath. Through the thin skin at his temples she could see a cobweb of tiny swollen veins. Small as he was, he was arching his body backwards, holding his neck stiff. All day long she rocked him, trying to comfort him. In vain. The nursing staff took over. Also in vain.

His crying had a strange undertone. It was not the usual sound of a baby's crying. A little voice inside her whispered that he was not crying because he was in pain, but because he was scared. She wrapped him in a flannel blanket, folding it around his head. She sat with him in a sunny corner on the hospital stoep. She dipped her little finger in a glass of water and held it to his lips. He sucked at her finger thirstily but carried on crying plaintively. No matter how hard she tried, she could not get him to take her breast.

After school Teresa and Zettie came to visit on their bicycles. After a short while they looked at each other uncertainly.

'Why is he crying like that?' Teresa asked.

'I don't know. Maybe he's in pain.'

They stayed for less than ten minutes before they fled from the piercing noise. Mirna and Lida and Hannah arrived with cheerful faces, but they stood in the doorway, staring.

'How long has he been crying like this?' Mirna asked, frowning.

'All day.'

'My goodness, Ingrid! Has Old Doctor checked on him yet?'

'Old Doctor is away for the day. He'll be back tonight. He'll come around as soon as he can. It might only be in the morning.'

They were uncomfortable. Couldn't hear each other speak. Hannah picked Alexander up and sat down at the foot of the bed, humming softly close to his ear while she rocked him. His crying intensified and he turned his head vigorously against her shoulder. Before long her friends made a feeble excuse about having to go to prepare for a meeting.

Dawid came to visit after work. The dominee and his wife brought a baby diary and a bunch of roses from the manse garden. Her colleagues came, and the bank manager's wife. Nobody could be heard above the crying of the child. At her wits' end, she asked the nursing staff to take the cradle out for a while.

'Cramps,' the nurse said when he was still screaming late that night.

'But surely cramps come and go; he's crying continuously.'

'It could be your milk.'

'What milk? He has sucked only a couple of drops of water from my finger today.'

He cried all night. At times the intensity of his crying subsided into a soft whimper, so that she thought he had fallen asleep. Then she tenderly wiped the sweat from his cheeks and upper lip. She leaned back against the pillows and dozed, a shallow half sleep, only to be shaken awake by yet another outburst.

Unlike Teresa and Zettie, who took her breast eagerly, he struggled as if her breast would smother him. She couldn't believe the strength in his tiny body. He refused the bottle too. Time and time again she dipped her little finger in a glass of water and held it to his lips, praying that he wouldn't choke when taking a breath for the next scream. It didn't seem possible, but his crying was even more intense when she bathed him. He arched his back so that his head and heels rested on the bed while she changed his nappy.

'You mustn't let his crying upset you too much, Ingrid,' Old Doctor attempted to comfort her when he examined the writhing baby. 'The more relaxed you are, the sooner he will calm down. You must remember that the process of being born was a shock to his system too. And shock could cause him to sleep all day long or, on the other hand, it could cause him to cry all day long.'

But from the way his fingers touched and examined the tiny body and the frown on his forehead while he pressed the stethoscope everywhere, she could sense that he was looking for something other than cramps.

'Why the hell is he crying like this?' Dawid asked when he came after work. Panic-stricken, he moved his weight from one foot to the other. 'Is he feeding?'

'A few drops from my finger, and only with a huge effort.'

'Perhaps he's cold?'

'With so many blankets on him? And a heater in the room. It's like a hothouse in here.'

'Then maybe he's too warm?'

'I don't know.'

'Let's switch the heater off. Then I'll pick him up. Maybe I can quieten him.'

But Dawid had no success. He left without the two of them exchanging more than a few meaningful sentences.

On the fifth day no visitors came and a numb melancholy took hold of her. When Old Doctor came on his rounds she asked him if she and the baby could be discharged. She was longing for her own room and bed and bathroom and teapot. And for Miriam. When Dawid came after work she packed her suitcase and they left with Alexander. It would be different at home. She would be able to follow her own routine without interference. Dawid would help her at night. And Miriam's instincts would guide them.

Miraculously, on the way home he stopped crying. One moment his voice was howling in the vacuum of the car; the next a disquieting silence fell over them. She swung around to see if he had stopped breathing. He lay there, dead still, his eyes open wide as if he had been startled by some distant sound. His eyes were too wide open for a newborn baby, and behind the grey-blue depths a mysterious light shone, as if he was looking at something exquisitely beautiful. Something that only he could see.

She knew that something in his eyes was wrong.

Something was terribly wrong.

She wouldn't tell Dawid, she decided.

'Thank heavens,' Dawid sighed. 'I hope his tantrum is over now. No normal person could tolerate that crying.'

It would be three and a half years before she could begin to understand the mysterious light in Alexander's eyes. And even then she could not understand it fully.

Autism.

Accursed illness.

'I began gradually to realise that something was wrong. It's so long ago, I can't remember exactly when I first noticed . . .' Her tongue feels heavy and thick on the floor of her mouth. The walls of the office seem to tilt; the man's face slips out of focus. 'When he was a baby he cried a lot.'

There's a bumblebee trapped in her brain. 'He was always a

tiny and fragile child, he ate very little.'

Saliva floods her mouth; she is nauseous. She looks at the woman sitting behind her and wants to stretch out her hand towards her. But the woman is looking down at the clipboard on her lap.

'Alexander was my first boy and . . . everybody said that boys were . . . more prone to . . . colic.'

Then her body starts tumbling. She's rudely brought to her senses when cold water dashes her face. She licks the wetness from her lips and opens her eyes. The woman is bending over her with a cup in her hand.

'Please, Mrs Dorfling,' the man says and sits down on the chair, planting his elbows on the desk, 'we need your cooperation.'

'I'm very tired.'

'You'll be given time to rest later, Mrs Dorfling. We are investigating the unnatural death of a child. A disabled child, moreover. In terms of the law this is a priority crime, and it's my job to . . .'

'A crime? Alexander drowned. How can that be a crime?'

'I assure you, Mrs Dorfling,' and he looks up, straight into her eyes, 'that he did *not* drown. And we have every reason to believe that you can explain what happened.'

How, *how* could they suspect her? She, who had spent every spare cent and every spare moment of her life on Alexander. Who loved him unconditionally, as far as he would allow her. How many nights had she followed him around the house while he hammered and hammered with his chisel? How many times had she grabbed the foot that kicked her in the face, kissing the sole again and again? *Don't, Xander, don't kick Mommy's face. It hurts, Xander. Look, Mommy bought you a new pair of socks. Blue ones. Especially for you. Give me your foot, Xander, let Mommy put your socks on.*

Merciful God, how was it possible that she could find herself cornered in an office in the Murder and Robbery Unit? Yesterday she was at work. Yesterday evening she phoned Gunter and asked if he would be willing to buy Lucy from her. And now, barely a few hours later, she is defending herself against accusations she doesn't understand.

'Please, I am exhausted, I can no longer think straight.'

'That's an old trick, Mrs Dorfling, many have tried it before. You won't get around me with that.'

'I swear.'

'Many others have sworn in this office before. Only to make a confession later. Some just take longer than others to get to that point.'

Endless questions.

He gives her no time to think before answering. Confuses her, jumps from one thing to another. She is drained. All she wants to do is go home and find shelter in her own bed; bury her face in the pillow and weep for nine years of sheer hell. For all that she had sacrificed, and not sacrificed. For Dawid, who could no longer see a purpose in life. For Alexander. Her child with the clear blue eyes whom she loved so desperately. Even though he never loved her.

And when her weeping subsides, she wants to drift off into a world of silence and tranquillity. Sleep, sleep, sleep. Perhaps she would go to Gunter and cry herself to sleep on the straw in the kraal. And when she wakes up, she'll tell Gunter that after all Alexander had been safer between the horse's feet than with his own mother. Gunter, she'll plead, help me climb on to the kraal wall so that I can see into the future. Take your pocket knife, Gunter, and cut away this heavy sense of guilt from my heart. And I ask you, Gunter, because I have no one else to turn to, to help me with money for Alexander's funeral.

Gunter will help her up on to the kraal wall and the future will lie clear in front of her. He'll place the money to cover the funeral costs in her hand. Because in his own way he loved Alexander. And because there had been a day when he washed and dried *her* feet. A day long ago when she had fallen asleep on the straw in the kraal and he had covered her with his jacket.

At some time or other the woman brings her a cup of water and a chair. A creaking old wooden chair with dilapidated legs. But she does not care if she stands or sits or lies down, or if the legs break off under her weight. Her resistance is at breaking point and the man's ceaseless talk is like a foreign language. His lips seem to move soundlessly; she cannot follow his questions and he has to keep repeating them.

'What is the time?' she asks when she notices through the window that it is pitch dark outside. Somewhere her sense of time has deserted her. It's Saturday, that she knows. Just yesterday she was seven hundred and ninety-two rand short at the cashier's counter. She can remember taking Miriam home, and afterwards she took Alexander to the hairdresser. Or is it Sunday now? Maybe Gunter doesn't know what has happened; maybe he's waiting for her and Alexander at the kraal. He'll realise that something is wrong if she doesn't turn up.

No, it's definitely Saturday. Because no night has passed since she lifted Alexander's body from the bath.

Endless questions.

Her weariness is so overwhelming that she feels no fear for the relentless tone of the man's voice. She couldn't care less if they put her behind bars for the rest of her life for a crime she has not committed. What difference will it make? For nine years she was locked up in a prison that Alexander had built around her. Brick by brick. Day after day. Night after night.

Windowless. Lightless. Loveless. No conscience.

No other prison could be more cruel.

Slowly, very slowly she leaves her body; slides into nothingness. Far away she hears the woman calling to her. *Mrs Dorfling! Mrs Dorfling!*

Oblivion.

She dives into cool water. Turns into a mermaid with a strong tail flipper. She swims away, going deeper and deeper, to a safe place where she can no longer see Alexander's blue eyes; a soundless vacuum where she can no longer remember Dawid's bitterness. A far-off place that Gunter has told her about. Where the key of F sharp stops its *ta-tate-ta*. Where the chisel becomes blunt and she no longer hears pieces of plaster thudding to the floor in the middle of the night.

She hears herself coughing.

But she's not sure whether the coughing is coming from *her* lungs.

FROM THE MOMENT SHE placed her two arthritic legs over the rails of
the truck this morning, she began to regret letting herself in for
this. She should have known it would turn out to be a drunken
madhouse. Every trip to the *grootkerk* is the same, over and over
again. She cannot understand what is wrong with her people's sense
of Christianity. It's a slap in God's face to get on to the truck with
such disorderly drunks, and to top it all, they know very well they're
on their way to attend a holy service with the purpose of levelling
their sins. But instead they stack new sins on their shoulders. No,
she should never have let herself make this trip to the kloof with a
bunch of polished heathens.

It's cold on the open truck. To shelter from the biting wind,
they huddle close together. Why has she forgotten to bring her
umbrella? But perhaps it's a good thing she has, since every freezing
soul would be trying to shelter under it. And besides, what if the
wind got under the umbrella and lifted her over the side of the
truck, umbrella and all?

The driver takes the bends at a speed which causes them to
tumble on top of one another. Heavens knows, she should have
stayed home with Jeremiah. It's because of this goddamned
drunken driver that the second sight in her stomach spoke to her
so clearly this morning. But she had closed her ears to the Voice.

What's more, she left months of savings from her sacred bottle behind for Jeremiah. Really, she doesn't know why she asked him to go up to Miss Ingrid's house. Because the premonitions in her stomach don't concern Miss Ingrid, they're about this truck driver. Today is the day they're all going to die.

'Do you have a match for me, Aunt Miriam?' one of the drunk youngsters asks.

It irritates her to death. 'You know I don't smoke. Would I carry matches on me for your convenience? And you had better plant your backside flat on this truck before you get thrown off.'

The words are barely out of her mouth when the driver takes a bend so fast that they all fall to one side, suitcases scattered between them. Fortunately, she saw the bend coming and anchored herself to the rail in time.

If a merciful God doesn't bless them today and take hold of the steering wheel Himself, they won't make it to the *grootkerk*. Why hadn't she simply gone behind the chicken run to offer up her prayers? After all, there's little difference between the church and the chicken run. But behind the chicken run her fate wouldn't be in the hands of a drunk man. And Jeremiah would have been only too eager to walk to town to buy a bottle of communion wine. Eager, too, to take communion with her. If that was the only way in which she could force God's voice into his head, she would leave him to celebrate communion until the bottle was empty. God would understand that she had no other way with Jeremiah.

And if she had stayed home, she could have given Miss Ingrid a helping hand. Even if it was just for an hour or two. All week she had noticed that something was wrong with Miss Ingrid, and it made her heart heavy. Miss Ingrid was so frail that the slightest breeze would blow her off her feet. There was not much food in the kitchen cupboards and Miss Ingrid was as thin as a rake. Just last week she had felt huge guilt when Miss Ingrid gave her a pocket of potatoes and a pumpkin and a large packet of sugar to take home. It was more than the entire contents of Miss Ingrid's kitchen cupboards. But Miss Ingrid insisted that she take the food, because meals were not regularly prepared in her house. And she's worried about Miss Ingrid's cough. It sounds like a tin filled with gravel.

God above knows that, if she's lucky enough to get to the *grootkerk* alive, she's going to talk seriously to Him about Miss Ingrid. Beg Him to spread His wings over Lexi too. He's had a runny nose for more than two weeks. He blows his nose in the palm of his hand and with his thumb and forefinger he makes snot bubbles which he holds against the sun. Laughs and laughs like a wound-up toy when the sunlight reflects all kinds of colours from the bubbles.

She's going to dedicate Miss Ingrid and Lexi to God from the deepest recesses of her heart. God will know how to pave the road ahead.

As the truck hurtles towards the next bend, she anchors her feet wide apart and grips the rail. God, please take over the steering wheel and get us safely around the bend, she prays, while the frightened bunch of people stagger to one side.

And please, don't let it rain. At least not until the truck has come to a complete stop in the churchyard.

9

DISORIENTATED, SHE WAKES up when the woman touches her shoulder. She's lying on a narrow wooden bench and the room around her is shrouded in shadow.

'I brought you something to eat.'

The strong smell of curry fills the air. Where is she? Only when the woman shuts and locks the barred door, does she realise that she's in a cell; that time has passed of which she can recall nothing. The wooden bench feels sticky under her fingertips. The musty darkness stinks of urine and vomit. Her mouth tastes of dust.

'You must eat quickly, Colonel Herselman is waiting for you,' says the woman through the barred door. Then she disappears.

Behind prison bars? Prison food? How did this happen?

Slowly it comes back to her that she walked here herself. The man was in front of her; the woman behind. The woman told the man they must make a note of her bad cough. The woman entered the cell with her, mentioning something about its being a temporary cell and that she could sleep for a while. Is it her imagination, or did she ask the woman for water?

It's like a nightmare welling up from her subconscious. When was it? An hour ago? Yesterday? Nobody brought the water. Did she dream that she heard the city traffic in the distance; the whistling of a train? And was she really sleeping with her head down, so that it felt as if the blood was ballooning in her brain?

She touches the enamel plate of food that the woman has left on the wooden bench. It's lukewarm. Her hunger is overwhelming. When last did she eat? Yesterday morning? Yes, during teatime at work, half a cheese sandwich. She picks up the enamel plate; puts it down again. No, she won't eat prison food. Not in this dim cell where she cannot see what she's eating, where the revolting smell of urine and vomit threatens to upset her stomach. Where previous prisoners have left crushed cigarette butts on the floor and written their names on the walls with their own excrement.

But her hunger remains overwhelming. Where is the knife and fork? She walks to the barred door and calls down the passage. Rests her forehead against the bars and hopes that someone will hear her calling and bring a knife and a fork. When the woman suddenly appears on the other side of the door, she retreats and starts coughing.

'Something wrong, Mrs Dorfling?'

'You forgot to bring me a knife and fork. Could I please . . .?'

'We did not forget, Mrs Dorfling. This is a temporary cell and no cutlery is supplied.'

'But . . . how must I . . .?'

'Use your hands, Mrs Dorfling.'

Wild child, who ate with his hands, sometimes not touching food for days, making her wonder what kept him alive. On other days he would devour mountains of food, three times the amount a grown-up could eat, until she thought his stomach would burst. He stuffed it in, smacked his lips, spat, messed. Had fits of giggles so that the food splattered in her face.

Cold pumpkin. Mashed bananas. Cheese spread.

That was all he ever wanted.

He was always suspicious of what was dished up on his plate. He sniffed at it, stuck his fingers into the mashed food searching for lumps; worked his fingers through the food like an earthworm crawling through mud. If she dared to dish up a single pea or a grain of rice or a crumb of minced meat, he lowered his head and growled like a dog smelling danger.

She could not remember how many plates he had broken in the past nine years. And he refused to eat from anything other than a white porcelain plate, and it had to be plain. No flowered edge or gold rim. There was a time when his plate breaking had her at her wits' end, and she bought white plastic plates. He spent days in the sandpit, battering the umpteenth plastic plate to pieces with a stone. She stopped buying plastic plates. It was senseless. She'd rather leap to catch the porcelain plate as he flung it at the kitchen wall.

At the age of six weeks he weighed less than he had at birth. Old Doctor was uneasy. Not so much because of her weekly visits and the ongoing complaints about which he could do little, but because she and Dawid could not get around to finding a suitable date to see a paediatrician. If Dawid wasn't testifying in court about the theft of the post office's delivery bicycle, it was open day at the school. Or Teresa and Zettie had to play a netball match in the neighbouring town. Or the school was planning a concert and the children had to rehearse day after day. Or it was time for the choir festival.

One day Rosie from the school hostel came and said there was someone in the township selling goat's milk. For two days it seemed as if the goat's milk was helping. It raised her hopes. On the third day Alexander started vomiting. Aunt Betty claimed that he was constipated, and smoothed a soap splinter which they pushed up his anus. Alexander's tummy started running terribly. He slept soundly and seemingly without cramps until the next morning. Again her hopes rose. But when she came back from the hairdresser, Miriam was walking up and down the street with the screaming child in the pushchair.

But each day she continued to believe that the next day would be better. Every time Alexander slept for longer than two hours it was as if heaven had descended. Every time he kept a spoonful of milk in his stomach, she thought it was the turning point. She did not have the emotional or physical strength to embark on a visit to a paediatrician. The truth was, she was scared. Why, she could not fathom. But she was dreadfully scared.

When she arrived at the surgery one morning Old Doctor was upset. Not just because she and Dawid had not been able to agree on a date, but because of the coin that Miriam attached to Alexander's navel with a plaster.

'Heavens, Miss Ingrid, Lexi is going to develop a ruptured navel. See how his navel bulges when he cries!' Miriam was anxious. 'We cannot ignore it! A ruptured navel isn't something that will ever heal by itself.'

'Miriam, the coin is dirty, we cannot stick it on to his navel . . .'

'Miss Ingrid, I know all about ruptured navels. Three of my children had the same thing. Back then, I used a half-a-crown. Nothing will happen to Lexi.'

Lexi. Miriam's term of endearment. Half speaking, half singing in a comforting voice. *Come here, Lexi. Take, Lexi. Don't do that, Lexi. Slow down, Lexi, slow down . . .*

To her he was Alexander. And later on Xander. The pet name with which she attempted to lure him from his distant world; which she hoped would make him love her and stop him kicking her in the face or hitting her shins with his head.

To Dawid he was just *the child*.

'Miriam,' she stared at the coin, on the verge of tears, 'what is wrong with him? Such a small baby doesn't know about being naughty, and he would surely not cry like this for nothing. Do you think he's in pain, or do you think he's hungry?'

'He must be hungry, Miss Ingrid, he's hardly drinking any milk.'

'But you can see for yourself that he doesn't want to.'

How many days and nights had she spent with him at her breast? But he wriggled and fought; turned his head away; bent his neck back. Until at last she felt like forcing his jaws open and squirting the milk down his throat until he drowned in it. Sometimes Dawid tried to feed him with a dropper, mostly unsuccessfully. He gave up hope and lost interest.

'If he refuses to drink, then he's not hungry,' Dawid said, putting his wallet in his pocket. He was going to play poker. 'When he's hungry, he'll drink.'

She was close to tears. The glazed expression in Dawid's eyes alarmed her. His cheeks were covered in stubble and his hair needed cutting. 'Dawid, I . . . I . . .'

'What?'

'It's just . . . No, never mind.'

He hesitated for a few seconds. 'I'm going to play poker. I'll see you later.' Apathetically, he kissed her on the forehead.

The only time Alexander ate anything worth mentioning was when Miriam sat with him in the dappled shade under the wild olive tree. She sang to him, over and over: *Gentle Jesus, meek and mild, look upon a little child* . . . She said Lexi liked the leaves because he stopped crying and fell asleep against her chest when he heard the leaves rustling in the breeze. But it was winter and there were not many warm days. She did not want him to catch cold.

'I'm at a loss, Miss Ingrid,' Miriam said timidly, stroking the coin with her forefinger. 'Maybe you must take him to the doctor again. Tell the doctor that if he can't make a plan about Lexi's navel, then it's only the two of us left to do the thinking.'

'I've taken him there so many times, the doctor can't find

anything wrong.'

Miriam shook her head. 'Then it's God's will, Miss Ingrid. It's a three-month wind that's bothering him. You'll see, at three months he's going to stop crying. We must just bear with him until then. And, Miss Ingrid, you mustn't forget to buy glycerine to remove the milk coating on his tongue.'

In time she felt like covering her ears when she heard the word *doctor*. Every time she sat in the crowded waiting room with the crying child on her lap, the misery grew in her. More and more. She had the urge to tie Alexander to her back and run away to a place where there were no other humans. Where he could cry endlessly and nobody would be tormented by it. If anyone had told her that such a place existed, she would have run to it.

The irritated expressions on the faces of other patients in the waiting room embarrassed her; the way they shifted around on their chairs, crossing and uncrossing their legs, vigorously turning the pages of their magazines while they glared at her and Alexander.

'I am really sorry,' she apologised.

They stared at her with sheep eyes. 'It's fine, we understand.'

But she could see that they did not understand at all. They fluttered their magazines as if they wanted to shake Alexander's crying off the pages. Eventually she chose to wait outside on the staircase where his wailing would not disturb them. It was easier to wrap him in an extra blanket and endure the cold wind until the receptionist called her.

One desperate day she told Miriam that the two of them had to join forces. Going to the doctor did not help. Rocking him made Alexander fight as if he was being smothered. And it was impossible to walk him in the pushchair all day and night, or sit under the wild olive tree for ever.

'There's an old woman in the township who knows how to brew dagga tea. Do you want me to get a bottle from her?'

Her mind was too weary to work out how they would get the dagga tea down Alexander's throat. 'Get a bottle, let's try it.'

'Then Miss Ingrid must give me some money. The old woman won't give me the dagga tea for nothing.'

Dagga tea. Rooibos tea. Mint tea. A quarter of a spoon of whisky and sugar water in a dropper. Tranquillising medicine. Hot-water bottle against his tummy. Suppositories. Colic medicine. There was nothing that she and Miriam had not pinned their hopes on.

'There is an Indian man in the township who drives out devils. Maybe Lexi is bewitched and the man must bury something in the garden. Last year he buried a plover's claws and red beak at some-one's house and that man was cured from fits, even to this day. If Miss Ingrid wants me to, I'll ask Jeremiah to go and see the man.'

She would surely have tried that too, except that Dawid would have killed her if he'd found out. 'No, rather not.'

When Alexander was nine weeks old, Old Doctor put his foot down: they had to see a paediatrician. Urgently. Because the baby was very underweight. There could be an obstruction in his windpipe, or a problem with his stomach valves. He guessed that the baby was having difficulty swallowing. And, no, it was not possible that the baby was crying just for the sake of it.

She was relieved to put her nameless fears and the home remedies and blind alleys aside and make an appointment to see the paediatrician

She and Dawid battled with Alexander that day. If she had known then how many times they would still endure the hell of visiting doctors, she would have turned back. Given up on doctors and answers and solutions. Just tried to survive from day to day, struggling and despairing, until she dropped dead from exhaustion and frustration.

But she did not know about the curse of autism then. She did not even know that it existed.

On an unexpectedly dry, hot day in late winter they set off for the paediatrician. A strong north wind threatened to blow the car off the road. As long as the car was moving, it was bearable because then Alexander was calm, as he was when Miriam walked him in the pushchair. But when they stopped under a tree at a picnic spot to eat the cheese sandwiches and meatballs Miriam had packed, the siren went off again.

'It seems to me he likes it when the car is moving,' she said in a flat voice as she opened the container with the food. 'The moment we stopped, he started crying again.'

Empty words; words almost beyond stupidity. As though Dawid could not reason it out for himself. Annoyed, he banged the coffee mug down on the bonnet of the car. His face darkened. She could see that he was trying to contain himself, biting back his words.

That day, while they were sitting under the shade of the tree, she became intensely aware of the growing rift between them. She yearned to reach out to him and plead for understanding for herself and for Alexander. For him, too. She wanted to comfort him with the promise that Alexander's crying would stop some time. But Dawid's whole being was clouded in bitter discontent, and she could not find the courage to offer him the little bit of strength that was left in her.

She closed the food container and they left.

'Damn it, Ingrid, I can't stand this any longer,' he said when they reached the outskirts of the city. 'My work is suffering, and I don't know what we're going to do when you're back at work after your maternity leave. Miriam is old, she cannot possibly keep up with the housework *and* look after the child. She might decide to retire, and then we'll really be in trouble.'

'Dawid, you know Miriam will never . . .'

'No, Ingrid, you're wrong! I don't know anything any more! If I can age like I have these last eight weeks, then I don't know what Miriam must feel like. After all, the child is not her flesh and blood.'

'Perhaps I should get Miriam some help with the washing and ironing. Just for a month or so, until Alexander is more settled. Miriam is sure to know of someone who's looking for a half-day job.'

'We are hardly making ends meet as it is! Zettie's talking about a school camp and Teresa's asked for a new tennis racket. Last month I didn't even hand in our pledge money to the church. And you talk about spending more money!'

She was uneasy about their money matters. Dawid's account was with a different bank, but she had signing powers. Perhaps she should ask for a statement and check if things were really as bad as Dawid claimed.

'I just thought that Miriam would appreciate extra help with . . .'

'It's a stupid thought! Forget it, Ingrid!'

She would have liked to tackle him about the money he squandered on poker, and point out that he was always generous about buying rounds of drinks at the golf club. But she kept her mouth shut because the day ahead of them was going to be long and tiring, and she lacked the emotional strength to survive another outburst so early in the day.

Better to create a buffer.

'Coffee?' She opened the thermos flask and balanced the coffee mug on her lap.

In reply, he changed gear quite unnecessarily and accelerated.

'I'm telling you, Ingrid, we're not leaving the paediatrician today without answers. I want to know exactly what is wrong with the child, and I want to know today!'

What could she say?

Everything Dawid said, she had been through a hundred times herself. Her inner turmoil was no less intense than his. If *he* could not tolerate the situation any longer, how could it be expected of *her*? At least he was at work during the day, and in the evenings he attended meetings and enjoyed a social life. She was on duty twenty-four hours a day. Without proper sleep; without answers. And a miserable support system. On top of everything, her belief in her ability to be a competent mother was fading by the day.

'Do you hear me, Ingrid?'

'Yes, Dawid, I hear you.'

'Have you got the letter from Old Doctor?'

'Yes, Dawid, I have.'

The paediatrician was not in the least perturbed by Alexander, as if he examined a screaming, writhing baby every day of his life. Ears, throat, stomach, urine, stool, lungs, fontanelle. He checked everything. When he had finished, he asked Dawid to wait in the passage with the screaming baby so that they could hear themselves speak.

He could find nothing to be concerned about, he announced. Physically the boy was healthy. Some children did have a tendency towards colic. It could be an allergy to milk. But since they had come such a long way, he was going to do a couple of additional tests as well.

They were sent from pillar to post through the hospital building. First floor for this. Second floor for that. X-rays on the third floor.

By mid-afternoon they were back in the doctor's rooms. Exhausted. Dawid's eyes were sunk in their sockets. She was hungry and thirsty. As if in a state of surrender, Alexander was sleeping on her lap, his arms spread.

'Take him off the breast,' the paediatrician advised. He pre-scribed soya milk and yet another kind of tranquillising syrup. He advised her to start with tiny portions of solid food to see if Alexander would gain weight.

She felt like crying and bursting into hysterical laughter simul-taneously. Solid food? And how would she get that into his stomach?

'If he doesn't gain weight within two weeks, you must bring him back,' the paediatrician said, tearing a prescription off the pad. Perhaps he noticed the anguish on her face. 'You must try to understand that making a final diagnosis is not so simple. If his condition doesn't improve we'll have to place him under observation for a couple of days.'

'I understand.'

But inside her there was nothing, nothing that could or even wanted to understand anything. Her hopes had turned to utter despair.

When the paediatrician's account arrived two weeks later, she wished she could hide it from Dawid. Or simply tear it up, burn it and reduce it to ashes.

'*Bliksem*, Ingrid, we were with the man for less than half an hour! How the hell can he send us such an astronomical account?'

'He's a paediatrician, Dawid. We have to accept that his consultation fees are more than . . .'

'Bloody arsehole! What did he do for the child? He fed us a lot of crap, that's all!'

She was afraid of Dawid's red-hot fury. 'Dawid, we had to start *somewhere* . . .'

He interrupted, pointing his finger at her. 'Ingrid, if you consider this account *somewhere* to start, and that's excluding the hospital account for the other tests, where is this going to end?'

'He said we must bring Alexander back for . . .'

His face red, he clenched his teeth. 'Take the child back for what?'

She had no answer.

Maybe it was the huge account, maybe it was the effort that had turned out to be fruitless, but in her mind she marked that day as the first time Dawid struck Alexander. Two hard smacks on his thin little thigh. She grabbed Alexander and ran outside to the wild olive tree. She sat with him in her arms in the shade, hoping his crying would subside as he watched the sun-speckled leaves dancing in the breeze.

He was ten weeks old.

And there, under the wild olive tree, as the late winter chill enfolded them, a strange tenderness and compassion awoke in her. Fragile child with the clear blue eyes. Riddle child who called and called, but no one understood his language. And she decided: even if it took her last ounce of energy, *she* would love him and *she* would make an effort to understand him. Even if no one else was willing to fight on his behalf, she would not push him aside.

She sat under the wild olive tree for a long time. Until her tears had dried and Alexander was sleeping in her arms. Gently, she stroked his eyebrows with the tip of her finger. He sighed in his sleep and her tears started again.

Nobody would be allowed to hurt him.

Because he was small.

And he couldn't fight back.

There were times when his crying subsided, fading into a soft plaintive lament. And sometimes, only sometimes, he fell into a dead sleep for many hours. It was as though his frail body was so drained of energy that he simply slipped into unconsciousness.

Exactly two years and two days after his birth Alexander stopped crying. Abruptly, on a Sunday morning. One moment he was sitting on a blanket on the stoep kicking, yelling, flapping his hands, knocking the bottle of cold milk coffee out of her hand. The next moment he was quiet, turning his head as if he was listening to something.

The quietness of the winter morning was filled with the echoing of church bells.

She stood next to him on the stoep, frozen, watching as his face filled with awe. His eyes expressed recognition and humanity. He turned his face towards her, looked her straight in the eye; leaned forward and stretched his fingers out to her. When she bent over to curl her fingers around his little hand, his lips silently said *mommy*.

Petrified, she watched him.

Then he turned his eyes away from hers and tilted his head to listen to the silvery sound of the church bells, his face beaming with joy. For one short moment he was not hiding on the secret island that only he knew about.

If she knew nothing else, she was sure in that moment that he recognised her as his mother.

She stood motionless until the church bells stopped ringing, overwhelmed by the palpable silence that pervaded the stoep and the house. In awe, she stared at the brightness in his clear blue eyes, the smile on his lips.

God, for those few seconds he was normal. For the first time in hundreds of days he opened the curtain just a little so that she could detect the human being hidden behind it.

Slowly, so as not to frighten him, she stepped back. In the kitchen she rested her head on her arms on the counter, and wept. Because for the very first time she was sure he was capable of laughter, and that he was not deaf. And that his lips could say *mommy*.

She walked to the bedroom to tell Dawid. But she could not wake him from his drunken sleep.

She presses her fingers together and scoops the curry in the plate, brings her hand to her mouth. Half the gravy lands on her tracksuit pants. She licks her fingers and attempts to wipe away the mess but it only spreads into a bigger mess. The curry is spicy and burns her mouth. But her hunger is stronger than her feelings of revulsion. She sticks her fingers into the plate again. Food is food. Eat faster. Don't chew, just swallow. She mustn't fiddle with her tongue, she might find a bone splinter or a sinew. Scoop, swallow, scoop, swallow.

Footsteps in the passage.

She must finish eating quickly, who knows when they'll give her food again. Later, when nobody is watching, she can pull her tracksuit pants towards her mouth and suck the curry stain clean. Or maybe they will allow her to use the bathroom.

Clanking of keys. Sound of metal on metal.

'Come, Colonel Herselman is waiting for you.'

'Could I please go to the bathroom?'

In the bathroom the woman will not allow her to close the door.

'Leave the door slightly open,' she commands.

The first thin trickle of urine brings tears of relief to her eyes. She forces every drop out, and longs for the protection and warmth of her own house. To be able to draw the curtains and lie down on her bed in the darkened room; to try to understand how she had managed to protect Alexander for nine long years, only to fall asleep during a moment of crisis.

No, she'd rather not go home, the silence will drive her insane. She'd rather go and sit on the kraal wall with Gunter. Or walk blindly into the mountains and never return. Walk and walk until the soles of her feet bleed; until she drops dead from fatigue and dehydration and sorrow. Until she sinks into a pitch-black well of nothingness where she can forget to remember Alexander.

Dear God, how is this possible? How could they have covered him with a blanket and pushed the trolley out her front door, as if being parted from her own flesh and blood did not matter to her?

Gone.

For ever.

Alexander always loved hiding in quiet, dark places. Under the beds, in the cupboards, curled up in the ragbox with his head covered, bundled up in the small cavity of the broom cupboard, his safe haven for so many years.

Stop thinking. Just stop thinking!

She unrolls the last few squares of toilet paper. When she flushes the toilet, the woman pushes the door wide open.

'Hurry up, we must go.'

She struggles at the washbasin. The hot water tap is tied with a piece of wire and there's no sense in trying to clean the curry stain with cold water. There is no towel and she dries her hands on her tracksuit pants.

'What is the time?'

'Twenty to nine.'

It's impossible.

'In the evening?'

'Yes. Hurry up, we must go.'

'How long did I sleep?'

'Less than an hour. Hurry up, Mrs Dorfling.'

What is an hour's sleep compared to nine years of sleep deprivation? Endless night hours during which Alexander woke her up time and time again. Took her by her pyjamas and pulled her through the chaotic house until she felt faint with fatigue. Switched the lights on and off, on and off, until the flashing felt like explosions in her eye sockets. Chipped away with the chisel, all night long, so that during the day the sound still echoed through her brain while she cashed cheques and weighed bags of coins.

'I . . . I . . .'

'Hurry up, Mrs Dorfling, Colonel Herselman is waiting.'

The chair has been removed. How long will she have to stand this time? The man sits at the desk, a pile of faxes stacked in front of him. Fleetingly, a few words on the fax on top of the pile register . . . *medico-legal post-mortem* . . .

'Did you sleep well?' He clasps his hands together and leans back in the chair. 'Pity we could not offer you more comfort.' He pulls the pile of faxes towards him, arranges it neatly. 'But console yourself with the thought that you won't have to sleep here tonight. We use the temporary cell at Murder and Robbery for short periods of solitary confinement only. Mostly to give people in custody time to come to their senses.'

Bewildered, she looks at him. 'Where am I going to sleep?'

'In the police cells.'

She gasps, and it feels as if her breath is hitting the bottom of her stomach. Merciful God, no. 'Does that mean I'm going to be locked up in gaol?'

'You could call it that. You are a suspect, Mrs Dorfling. There are many questions arising from the post-mortem that have to be cleared up. As long as you are a suspect and are detained for questioning, you will stay in the police cells. And we will not release you unless we are one hundred per cent satisfied with your answers.'

'How many times do I have to tell you: I had absolutely nothing to do with Alexander's . . .'

'No, Mrs Dorfling,' he interrupts her relentlessly. 'We suspect that you can give us many answers. We are detectives, we base our investigation on witnesses, post-mortems and hard facts. And there are too many aspects of this case that just don't add up.'

What on earth could be in the post-mortem report or in the faxes other than the fact that Alexander had drowned? Who had the man spoken to? And what could anybody have said to implicate her?

'May I please see the reports?'

He puts the faxes back in the docket and places his hand on it possessively. 'The contents of this docket are meant exclusively for the eyes of the investigating officer, Mrs Dorfling.'

'But surely I have a right to read them?'

'If you don't understand your rights, call a lawyer to assist you. We've already explained that to you.'

'I don't need a lawyer to assist me, because I have nothing to defend.'

'Your position is possibly worse than you think, Mrs Dorfling.' He turns to the woman. 'Captain,' he says and he starts to *ta-tate-ta* with the pencil on the desk again, 'make a note again, and add the time to it, that the suspect refuses legal assistance.'

She must stop fretting about reports and witnesses. Nothing anyone can say can possibly cast a shadow of doubt over her innocence. The truth is that Alexander's death was an unfortunate accident. The only mistake she made was to fall asleep while he was licking out the jar of cheese spread. And then tragedy struck. She must not allow herself to be threatened.

'You've been given time to rest and to think sensibly, Mrs Dorfling. Now we can continue.'

She must not let him find out that she has not been thinking at all; that instead she had slept the sleep of the dead, totally unaware of the stench rising from the floor, or the uncomfortable wooden bench.

He takes his pen and opens the docket. 'Autism is a lifelong disability, Mrs Dorfling. The past nine years could not have been easy for you.'

Is it possible that behind his hard exterior he is hiding a sense of compassion and understanding? Or is this a subtle tactic to soften her?'

'I don't deny it, they were nine difficult years.'

'Your parents, did you receive any support from them?'

'My parents died before I was married.'

'Any other family members on whose support you could rely?'

'I have a sister but she lives abroad and I never see her.'

'And your late husband's family?'

Heaven knows, she does not want to revisit those dreadful times. How they had left her in a desert of loneliness after Dawid's death. Never gave a penny to assist her. Never phoned on Teresa's or Zettie's birthdays. They were always intolerant of Alexander. Before Dawid died, they at least visited occasionally. Put earplugs in their ears to escape the hammering of the chisel. Locked the door of their bedroom so that Alexander could not slip in and destroy their possessions or plaster their walls and pyjamas with pumpkin, or flick the light-switch on and off.

A highly upset Miriam came to the bank one morning to tell her that the Old Missus had given Lexi a hiding with the wooden spoon because he refused to eat oat porridge. And the Old Master had put the ragbox on top of the cupboard and now Lexi had nowhere to sleep.

'Mother,' she had said that afternoon when she arrived home from work, 'Alexander doesn't eat oats. He doesn't eat food with lumps in it. And you have no right to give him a hiding when . . .'

'Oh? And *who* is supposed to give him a hiding then?'

'We don't know what's wrong with him, Mother, but we do know that he's different from other children.'

'It's because you don't punish him when he deserves it that he is such a naughty little brat. It's because you . . .'

Her heart was beating rapidly, a glow of red-hot anger spreading through her. 'Mother, let's understand each other: in this house only Dawid and I decide when Alexander deserves a hiding.'

Suddenly, everybody attacked her. Her in-laws, Dawid. In the background she heard the whistle of the afternoon train; Alexander yelled and started bashing his head against the passage wall. Afterwards she couldn't remember who said what. But they over-powered her like an army. If it hadn't been for Teresa and Zettie coming to her assistance, she would have had to face the onslaught on her own.

Long after everybody had gone to sleep that night, she was still walking the streets with Alexander in the pushchair, like a deaf-blind creature. She begged God to take them both away to a place where Alexander's weirdness would not matter. But she knew such a place did not exist.

'Mom?'

When she turned around Teresa was a few yards behind her in the dim light of the streetlamp. 'Let me push him for a while, Mom. You go to bed.'

Her eyes filled with tears as she looked at the barefoot child who had come to her support in the lonely night. She hugged Teresa's bony shoulders. 'I won't be able to sleep if I know you're out here alone.'

'You didn't even have supper tonight, Mom. Can I make you a sandwich and bring it to you?'

'That would be nice, my girl.'

'I hope granny and grandpa leave tomorrow, Mom.'

As Teresa walked off in the dark, she stared at the fragile child, wondering how on earth she could divide her time so that everyone close to her could be given their fair share of attention.

Apart from Dawid's funeral, she hadn't seen her in-laws since Alexander was between three and four years old. What was engraved in her memory though, was that they had known then that Alexander was autistic.

Dawid's parents had planned on staying for two weeks. But on the sixth day they left, bristling with indignation. *No one can stand this! It's a madhouse! Saying he's autistic is a pathetic excuse! It's because you don't punish him, and you allow him to have his way all the time! All he needs is a damn good hiding! We come to visit and to rest, and all we do is battle to protect our belongings and our sanity! Have you ever heard of a child being left alone during the night to chisel the plaster off the walls? Why should he be allowed to rule this household like a demon? He rants and raves and kicks you in the face! He eats with his hands like a savage! And you just let him do as he pleases!*

It felt as if a huge weight had been lifted from her shoulders when they finally left. But ironically their departure created an equally heavy burden. Because from that point on Dawid began to lose what was left of his reason. His animosity towards Alexander deepened. His drinking habits changed for the worse, the puffy skin on his face became a cobweb of tiny red veins. He refused to help Teresa and Zettie with their homework. He stopped going to church altogether. And his outpourings of hatred for the church began. He lay in front of the television every night, aloof from all that was happening around him. He often went to bed without bathing and she could smell the bitter reek of stale sweat on his body. Many mornings he went to work without shaving, and without thinking twice of wearing the previous day's wrinkled shirt and trousers.

'My husband's parents had distanced themselves. The last time I saw them or heard from them was at my husband's funeral.'

'Why was that, Mrs Dorfling?'

It upsets her to revive the old dispute.

'They could not abide Alexander. And I think they blamed me for my husband's death.'

He makes a note in the docket.

The aftertaste of the curry boils up from her stomach.

'Your religious denomination and the name and telephone number of the dominee?'

She stutters; wipes a strand of hair from her forehead and feels the cold skin of the palm of her hand against the bridge of her nose. 'In theory, I am a member of the Dutch Reformed Church.' She tries to suppress a coughing fit. 'But I've lost all contact with the church and the dominee. I don't know his telephone number.'

He peers at her distrustfully. 'Oh, come on, Mrs Dorfling! You live in a small town where everybody knows the telephone numbers of the doctor and dominee and lawyer and hospital by heart.'

Why won't he believe her? What makes him think that the dominee was tolerant of a maniacal child who disrupted every service by jumping on the pews, shouting and clapping his hands while the Ten Commandments were being read? Knocked the collection plate from the deacon's hand and giggled hysterically when the coins clattered to the floor?

What makes him think that *she* was immune to the congregation's aversion to her and Alexander? The frowns and expressions of disgust when she and Alexander entered the church and sat at the back. When she attempted to sit in the gallery, she encountered a notice on the staircase: *Choir members only.* Perhaps the organist thought Alexander might attack her.

The last wedge driven between her and the dominee was the result of his treatment of Dawid in the six months before his death. She had often wondered if Dawid would have jumped off the bridge if it hadn't been for the dominee's judgemental stance.

'It must be six years since I attended a church service. The mothers' room was not fit for use and when Alexander was older

I did not dare sit in the church with him.'

'Did your husband not sometimes take care of the child so that you could go to church?'

'No, my husband never took care of Alexander. The only time he helped was on Sundays when he took Alexander horse riding.'

Her eyes feel dry and gritty. Why is the man probing into her religious life? What can it possibly have to do with Alexander's death?

The man licks his middle finger and thumb and pulls a report from the stack of faxes. He reads, shakes his head. 'From the statement I have here, it seems you wanted to sell the horse, Mrs Dorfling? But we'll come back to that later. So . . . you claim that you haven't been to church for six years?'

So they had been to Gunter after all. Only he knew that she planned to sell Lucy in an attempt to salvage her job. Where else would she get the money to repay Friday's shortfall at the counter?

Stay calm. Don't let the man pick up her nervousness. Gunter knows what she needed the money for; he would have told them the truth.

'Yes.'

'Was your husband not buried from the church four years ago?'

Damn. She shouldn't answer without weighing her words carefully. This man is as sharp as a needle. 'No, my husband was cremated without a memorial service. I thought you were referring to an ordinary Sunday service.'

'Don't twist my words, Mrs Dorfling. Answer my questions, and tell the truth. If you say that you haven't been to church for six years,' and he thumps his fist on the desk, 'then that must be exactly what happened. Please give the details of your ward deacon and elder.'

Why is he questioning her about unimportant matters to which she can supply no clear answers? 'I have no idea who the church officials are. None of them have paid a visit to my house in many years, because they knew I could not afford a pledge.'

As if in a dream, she recalls the time that Dawid had taken back the envelope meant for their pledge, telling the dominee that giving was a two-way affair. Dawid was furious when he came home from the manse. He opened a bottle of brandy and took his bitterness and hatred out on her. Said he would not subsidise luxurious beach houses and overseas trips, while the congregation was trapped in an everlasting struggle to make ends meet.

'The last time a church elder visited my house was when my

husband died. And that particular man left town two years ago.'

'So, you have no contact with the church or any of its structures?'

God knows, there were times when she had longed to go to church. The yearning throbbed inside her like an open wound. To hear the deep bass notes of the organ; to see the soft light filtering through the stained-glass windows. To smell the sweetness of the communion wine; to take a tiny block of Hannah's home-made unleavened bread on her tongue and to ask for forgiveness for her sins.

Some nights while she watched over Alexander, she paged through her hymn book, filled with nostalgia for the past. Wept softly when she came upon forgotten dates and notes. *Zettie cut her first tooth. Finished knitting Dawid's cable jersey. Lida's confirmation as deaconess.*

Coffee stains, dried leaves from the mop tree that grew at the entrance to the churchyard. Sometimes she turned to old familiar hymns and hummed the tunes. And her mind went back to the times when her life had been serene. The times when she and Dawid and the girls went to Mirna's house for tea on Sundays after church and sat in the shade of a jacaranda tree, the lilac petals falling on their heads, enjoying their tea in peace. The times when she and Hannah stayed up until all hours of the night, painting tablecloths for the church fête. Aunt Betty, standing at her garden gate, waiting for them to give her a lift to church.

In pastures green; He leadeth me, the quiet waters by . . .

One day she sat on the kraal wall with Gunter, watching Lucy circling with Alexander on her back. It was a misty afternoon, the rain clouds hanging low.

The sombreness of the winter day resonated within her heart.

'Gunter,' she asked, 'who and what is the church?'

He clasped his hands between his knees, gazed into the grey mistiness for such a long time that she thought he wasn't going to reply.

'I cannot answer you, Ingrid, because I don't understand the church myself.'

'What *should* the church be?'

He stared into the distance. 'An instrument of God.'

As clear as if he was standing in front of her, she recalled the wrath and bitterness on Dawid's face the last time he had shown the dominee to the door.

'Which God, Gunter? Or which god?'

'It's complicated, Ingrid. Let's not try to reason it out. It's like a never-ending circle. Create your own church in your mind.'

'Why do you never go to church, Gunter?'

He jumped off the kraal wall and walked towards Lucy who had stopped with the sleeping child on her back. She followed him. 'Tell me the truth, Gunter: why do you never go to church?'

His eyes clouded. 'I am not a church man, that's all. But I am a man of God. The two concepts are often difficult to reconcile. Dawid and I talked about it a week before he died. Dawid had a terrible anger in him towards the community, but his anger towards the church was even greater. After what happened between him and the church one could hardly blame him. But it cost him dearly. Control your bitterness, Ingrid; and don't waste your mental energy. It's not worth it.' Gently, he pushed her out of his way and walked off to lift the sleeping child from the horse's back.

There was something incomprehensible about Dawid's emotions that only Gunter knew about. She would have liked to ask him about Dawid, but she lacked the courage. And even if she found answers to her questions, she could not pick Dawid up from the river-bed and put him together again.

The man's voice hits her eardrums like a whiplash.

'I asked you a question, Mrs Dorfling, and I'm waiting for a reply!'

'I'm sorry, but I cannot remember your question.'

He runs his fingers through his spiky hair. 'Please, Mrs Dorfling, don't try my patience too far.'

'I'm tired. I swear I cannot remember . . .'

'Have you cut the ties between yourself and the church?'

She meets his eyes. 'Yes, I have.'

'Any specific reason?'

'My husband and later I, too, had huge conflicts with the church.'

He notes it down, looks up again and fires another question at her. 'Did you use any special teaching methods or consult specialists to assist you in educating your child?'

Instinctively, she senses danger. In her dazed state she realises she must be careful not to give the impression that she had left Alexander to his own fate. Because she had not. 'Alexander was exempted from school. No one in the community was interested in helping. Maybe they didn't have the time, or maybe they simply lacked the knowledge, I don't know. He was extremely difficult and it took a lot of effort just to look after him, let alone teach him. He wasn't capable of learning. Apart from Gunter and Miriam and myself, nobody paid any attention to him.'

'And your two daughters?'

'When they were in primary school they sometimes played with him, if you could call it that. He didn't understand how to play. When they were in high school they helped when I forced them to. Nowadays they only come home during holidays and then they do help a bit. But they . . .'

'Half a minute ago you said that nobody except yourself and Miriam looked after him. Now you say that your daughters helped.'

'I think it's quite clear what I mean.'

He drums his fingertips on the desk. 'Mrs Dorfling, please understand me: in this investigation *I* will decide what is clear and what is not. Did your child attend pre-school? Did he go to Sunday school? Did he have playmates?'

The pulse in her neck throbs. 'How many times must I say it? Alexander was autistic. It seems you don't have the faintest idea what autism is.'

He gets up from the chair; starts circling around her again. 'Don't bother your brain about my knowledge of autism, Mrs Dorfling. I may appear stupid, but I am not. And don't try to avoid my question: was your child attending pre-school or involved with the church's . . .?'

'No.'

'So, I can conclude that you didn't make use of stimulating teaching methods?'

A heavy sigh escapes her. But it's as if the sound comes from someone else's lungs. 'You have it all wrong. It's just . . . we . . .'

He interrupts her. 'Earlier you said you had a small circle of friends . . .'

'Can we please finish with one question before jumping to the next? I can't think clearly when you keep changing direction all the time.'

'All my questions, Mrs Dorfling, will eventually form one picture: the death of your child, and the events that led up to it. I want the names of all your friends. Telephone numbers and addresses, too. Start with those who were closest to you. Every single one, don't leave anyone out.'

10

THERE'S A GREY CLOUD hanging low over the kloof.

If it starts raining now, it's going to cause big problems because the truck doesn't have a canopy. But getting drenched by the rain is not her greatest worry. Her greatest worry is the gravel road. It's already slippery from yesterday's showers. More rain today will mean the lives of all of them on the truck will be dangling by a very thin thread.

When the driver changes gear to climb the last steep stretch to the top of the kloof, the people hold on to their suitcases with one hand, and anchor themselves with the other. The children cling to their mothers' dresses and the mothers don't know whether to hold on to their children or on to the suitcases.

Crawling up the kloof in low gear is nothing. It's the steep downhill on the other side that's worrying her to death. Through the cab window she can see the driver closing his lips around the neck of a bottle. Head tilted backwards, he drinks and drinks, his Adam's apple bobbing up and down. He flings the bottle out the window and it splinters against the cliff face. There's naked fear on the people's faces now. The children's eyes bulge white in their sockets. To die of illness is one thing; to die at the hands of a drunken driver is another thing altogether.

'You must nip your cigarettes!' she shouts above the roar of the engine. 'If we crash and the petrol leaks out, we will be burnt to ashes!'

Silenced by fear, they put their cigarettes out. The children fling their arms around their mothers' legs. The old woman who lives in the house next to the pepper tree, and who weeps for two days on end every month when the full moon hangs in the dark night sky, wipes the tears from her cheeks.

Now she must take the lead. They must not attract fear out of the kloof. When you stare death in the eye you must stand with your feet firmly on the ground. You must ask God to be your armour and your strength. And to send you a host of angels. Then you must grab death by the throat and throttle it. To fight back is their only hope. They must sing. Many a time she's seen death shy away from a hallelujah song. If you sing all the verses over and over, the angel of death backs off. Because there's strong power woven into the words of a hallelujah song.

Like the time when the township children were playing in the reeds at the waterhole, and the puff adder bit Aunt Sophie's Johnny in the calf. He ran away yelling and was ash-white and stupid with shock when he eventually arrived in Aunt Sophie's kitchen. A festering, stinking wound developed on his calf. When they all thought God was coming to fetch Johnny to sit at His feet, they decided to take turns to sing next to Johnny's bed. The same song, over and over. *Lord, in this Thy mercy's day . . . Humbly at Thy feet we pray . . .*

Right through the day. Right through the night.

Two weeks later Johnny was playing in the street again.

She must start singing so that everybody will join in to keep the angel of death at bay. Her voice must rise above the noise of the engine. Then the people's fear will change into strength. And all the angels in the kloof will hear their plea and guide the truck safely through the kloof. Her voice trembles when she strikes the first note. *Hark! The herald angels sing . . . Peace on earth and mercy mild . . .*

At first they stare at her like a flock of frightened sheep just out of the dipping-pen. Then the youngster who asked her for matches joins in. Word for word he keeps up with her. His bass voice rises above the sound of the engine, and she notices the people's lips starting to move. Hesitantly, the children's fingers let go of their mothers' dresses. When they begin with verse three, she asks God to wipe out her sinful thoughts towards the wine-fly of a youngster. She would never have thought he would know the words of the first verse; let alone the rest.

Mild He lays His glory by . . . born that man no more may die . . .

She stops counting how many times they complete all the verses. All she knows for certain is that there is not a single angel in the whole kloof that did not come to their aid. Then she knows why she had to get on to the truck that morning. Because they would never have made it through the kloof without a hallelujah song.

When the steep descent lies safely behind them, and the white wall of the church becomes visible between the thorn trees in the distance, she hears Lexi calling her. It's so clear, it's as if he's standing right next to her.

Mimmi! Mimmi!

God of all men on earth, are her eyes playing tricks on her? Can it be true that Lexi is flying around the truck amongst the angels? Why do his eyes look so stone-dead in his head?

The words of the hallelujah song are frightened off her tongue. Jesus of Nazareth, please be with Miss Ingrid and with Lexi this weekend, she prays, and wipes the wind-tears from her eyes. It's a long time since they last baked a cake in Miss Ingrid's house, and maybe the baking pans have rusted. But on Monday, and not any other day, she'll bake a cake. But please, dear Jesus, watch over Miss Ingrid and Lexi until then.

11

THE DETAILS OF ALL her close friends. What can she say?

'Before Alexander was born, we had many friends and acquaint-ances, especially my husband. It's impossible to recall them all. But I had three special friends who were very close to me.'

'Start with the particulars of those three.'

An immeasurable sadness overcomes her. Mirna. Lida. Hannah. Loyal companions through thick and thin. How often had they gone shopping together in the nearest big town on Saturdays? Dyed one another's hair. Exchanged advice on choosing dress materials, then gathered at Mirna's house to cut out the garments on the huge yellowwood table. They had philosophised about raising children. Borrowed tampons from one another late at night. Organised stork parties. Sat around a kitchen table, drinking coffee, complaining of infections and mothers-in-law. They took care of one another's children. Served tea after Holy Communion. Baked their Christmas biscuits together. Loved and supported one another when the black cloak of depression afflicted one of them.

But Alexander's arrival damaged the bond. Strong bridges crumbled like dry sandcastles.

'They were like sisters to me. But after Alexander was born our friendship slowly disintegrated. At first I was sad, and angry too, but later on I realised it was only natural, in the circumstances.'

'Just give their names, addresses and telephone numbers.'

While she gives the details, she recalls their faces. Mirna bending over the bed of Inca lilies, her honey-brown hair tumbling forward. Lida standing at the material counter, calculating the length of fabric needed. Hannah, wearing a too-big woolly coat, sitting on the couch with her eyes closed, transported by the silver sounds of harp music.

And the memory brings pain.

Until that first spring, when Alexander was about three months old and she was still on maternity leave, a lot of friends visited her at home. But she could sense how they shrank from Alexander's penetrating screams, and she could hardly blame them. Now and again someone offered to hold him for a while, but they soon handed him back to her or Miriam. Occasionally, he was quiet for an hour or so, and she could pour the tea with less shaking of her hands.

'Bring him to me on Saturday,' Mirna had offered. 'I'll manage. After all, it's just for a few hours. You go and have a game of tennis.'

She did. When she went to fetch him at five o'clock, Mirna was sitting outside in the garden, pale as death, complaining about a throbbing headache.

Lida had said: 'I'll take care of him on Sunday while you go to church.'

When she arrived at Lida's house after the service, she found her sitting on a blanket under the peach tree, trying to pacify the writhing bundle. Her husband wanted to watch the cricket on television, she said timidly. She sent one of her children to make tea and bring it out to the garden.

Hannah said she would take care of Alexander during the prayer meeting because Dawid was out playing poker. She placed Alexander on a bed of pillows on the lounge floor and lit a row of candles on the mantelpiece; played Mozart's *Elvira Madigan* over and over.

'I don't think he listens to the music, Ingrid, but he notices the candles,' Hannah said when she fetched him after the prayer meeting. 'His eyes are so blank, Ingrid, so strange . . . '

It was true; her friends had reached out in the beginning.

In the weeks after she came home from hospital Aunt Betty often came over to bath Alexander, out of the simple kindness of her heart. She could see Aunt Betty was nervous, that she was exhausted afterwards. But her mouth was set in a determined line: she wouldn't let a baby's wilfulness get her down.

'Babies tend to arch their backs when they have worms, Ingrid dear,' she said, the nappy pin between her pinched lips as she struggled to pull the long-sleeved vest over Alexander's head. 'There's an itching in their stomachs. Have you tried castor oil?'

She was annoyed. 'He can't have worms, Aunt Betty, he doesn't eat solid food. Where would he get worms from?'

'You must take him to another doctor, Ingrid dear. Old Doctor has never been good at diagnosis. If you read the certificates hanging above his desk, you will see that he trained back in the sixties.'

'But he has had so much experience.'

'Nevertheless, I think you should get a second opinion. We're in the year 2000, and Old Doctor still believes in sweet oil and navel belts. His home remedies are definitely not going to cure your child, Ingrid dear.'

Her neck flushed with annoyance. 'What do you mean by *cure*? Alexander isn't sick.'

'Good gracious me, Ingrid dear, a healthy child wouldn't cry like this! It's obvious there's something wrong with him.'

Her tongue felt dry and paralysed. 'Aunt Betty, please don't interfere . . .'

'I'm still convinced that he has worms.'

As fond as she was of Aunt Betty, she could feel the blood rushing to her head. 'And I think you are talking absolute nonsense!'

'Goodness, Ingrid dear, how can you . . .?'

'For God's sake, Aunt Betty! Everybody makes me feel as if I neglect Alexander! You are all driving me insane with your ridiculous remedies and solutions. One would almost swear you'd never heard a baby cry! Why don't all you busybodies leave me and my child alone!'

'Goodness, Ingrid dear, we don't mean to . . .'

'I don't care what you mean! I'm sick and tired of know-alls giving me advice!'

The rising shrillness of her voice fused with Alexander's deafening screams. Aunt Betty looked uncomfortable; then she folded the towel and put the baby cream away. 'I'm going now, Ingrid dear, let me know if you need help.'

'I don't need anything, Aunt Betty! Except silence and privacy!'

That night, while she sat in the kitchen with the crying baby so that Dawid could get some sleep, she felt terrible because she had been so rude to Aunt Betty, of all people. But her nerves were at breaking point, and she couldn't cope with Alexander *and* with a bunch of uninformed advisers.

Aunt Betty never came to bath Alexander again.

On the Sunday that he was christened there weren't enough chairs for all the visitors who came to the house for tea after church. She and Miriam had started baking on the Friday morning, and she was grateful for Miriam's expertise. She could tell at a glance when the dough was too soft or the tart crust too crumbly.

All her colleagues were there; old friends from caravanning days, bank clients, the elder and the deacon of their ward. Children were running through the house, bouncing a ball on the stoep. She found herself regretting not having the christening tea in the church hall. The chaos in the house and Alexander's persistent crying threatened to drive her insane.

In church Alexander had squealed like a stuck pig, but Miriam was waiting in the vestry to take him home in the pushchair after the ceremony. Miriam would also boil the water for tea and warm the quiches and cut the *melktert*.

The christening tea was a fiasco. Worse, perhaps, for her than for the guests. The more people tried to pick Alexander up and cuddle him, the more vehemently he protested. It was as though with every intake of breath he was trying to say: *Don't touch me; don't come near me! Leave me, go away!*

Dawid and the men gathered under a tree in the garden, drinking beer. Afterwards she couldn't remember if they had had anything to eat. She had the awful feeling all along that Dawid was embarrassed by Alexander's bizarre behaviour.

But the one image of the church ceremony that was engraved in her mind, was that of Dawid taking his handkerchief out, mopping the sweat on his forehead, while he watched the thrashing child out of the corner of his eye. And when he was supposed to answer 'yes' out loud, he could only nod his head.

Poor Miriam ran between the kitchen and the dining room with clean cups and cake forks and serviettes. There was no time for her to take Alexander and escape to the wild olive tree for a few minutes of peace and calm. And she was alone with the chaos around her, and the turmoil inside her. She tried to conceal her panic and desperation behind a bright smile. But her heart yearned to chase the chattering women from her house and push Alexander into Dawid's arms; tell him to drive around with the child for an hour so that she could sleep.

'Angry little man,' one woman remarked, passing the squirming child to another pair of hands. 'He put dominee off completely this morning.'

'Yes,' someone else said in an insincere attempt to pacify the child, 'little men with such strong voices often turn out to be great speakers.'

She wanted to laugh hysterically; tell the woman she was talking rubbish. Dawid! Dawid! she shouted silently. Come and help me, Dawid, before I lose my sanity! But she knew he wouldn't come to her rescue. Not even if she stood next to him under the tree and shouted the words in his face.

'Has Miss Ingrid had a cup of tea?' Miriam whispered.

'Not yet.'

'I'll bring Miss Ingrid some. Then I'm going to leave everything just as it is and go sit outside with Lexi. One can see he doesn't like a crowd around him. Then Miss Ingrid can have some time to sit down and have a cup of tea with the visitors.'

On that christening day, surrounded by a crowd of garrulous women who had no idea of the fatigue of her body and mind, a strong aversion to the child came over her. She wanted to tell Miriam: take him and throw him over the edge of the earth. Put him down under a bush and leave him to die. Do with him whatever you want.

Just never bring him home again.

'There's no one else whose particulars I can give. Only Miriam's.'

'It's my duty to question your friends, Mrs Dorfling. Their statements could be to your advantage.' *Ta-tate-ta.* 'Or do they perhaps know something that you don't want them to tell me?'

'I no longer have close friends, it's as simple as that.'

'And this Gunter, is he not a close friend?'

She is alarmed. What do they know about Gunter? What has Gunter told them about their conversations on the kraal wall? The times when she unburdened pent-up sorrow and anger. No, Gunter would never betray her. Never. If she could be sure of anything, it was that Gunter would never betray her.

Gunter never visited her at her house. He did all his business in the city and hardly ever came to town. A loner, Gunter. Had it not been for Dawid, who wrote off one of his poker friends' debts in exchange for a horse, she would probably never have known Gunter. Dawid reasoned that Gunter's farm was the closest place to town where the horse could be kept, and asked Gunter if he would be willing to stable the horse. And to give a hand with the saddling.

They became like blood brothers, Dawid and Gunter. Gunter's farm was about the only place Dawid went to in the year before his death. It was Gunter who found Dawid's car in the dense bushes near the bridge on that tragic Monday morning. And it was Gunter who knocked at her door with the shocking news.

No, Gunter could not be counted as a close friend. They must leave him out of the matter.

'My child's horse was stabled on his farm. On Sundays I took him there to ride. That's all.'

'All, Mrs Dorfling? Are you absolutely sure?'

She swallows. 'Yes.'

'Why was his telephone number written on the notebook next to the telephone?'

Is the man actually trying to establish a connection between the sale of Lucy and Alexander's death?

'I don't know his telephone number by heart. I wrote it down after looking it up in the directory.'

Ta-tate-ta with the pencil on the cover of the docket. 'When did you phone him, and why?'

'I phoned him on Friday evening, to . . . to . . .' Will she be incriminating herself?

'You are going to lie yourself into a corner, Mrs Dorfling. Don't do it. We'll come back to that question later.' He leans forward in his chair, pulls the docket closer. 'Let me ask you once again,' he says in a measured tone, 'the names of all your intimate friends, Mrs Dorfling. And those of your late husband, too.'

Her patience gives out and she storms at him, pounding her forefinger at his chest. 'I don't have close friends! Or do you want me to invent names and telephone numbers that don't exist?' She gasps for breath and simultaneously tries to stifle the coughing fit that threatens to explode from her lips. She hears herself yelling at the man as though someone else has taken over her body. Vaguely, she's aware of the woman moving behind her. Then the man takes hold of her arm, bends it behind her back. Slowly, slowly, down, down. Until the pain forces her to her knees.

'Mrs Dorfling, if you shout and threaten me, I will retaliate. You might regret your behaviour later on.'

She tries to wrench free from his grip, but a sharp pain shoots through her shoulder. Slowly, he lets go of her arm and turns to the woman. 'Make a note that the suspect is behaving aggressively. Fill out the prisoner's possessions register, I want to leave within twenty minutes. The sooner we get her to the police cells, the better.'

Fingerprints. Palm prints. Thumb prints. Sides of her hands. A cracked splinter of soap to try to wash off the black ink. They walk through the bare passages, back to the stuffy office. The woman empties the contents of her handbag on the desk; lists every single item.

'Check the list.'

Brush, hand-mirror. Lipstick. Receipt for the telephone account. Identity document. Cheque book and the numbers of the cheques. Credit card and its expiry date. Pen. Tampons. Two headache tablets. Four peppermints. Creased tissues. The woman counts every cent in her purse. Then she zips open the small first-aid bag that she carries with her everywhere she goes.

'And this?' With raised eyebrows, the woman holds up the syringe and the ampoule containing the sedative.

12

THE DRIVER HOLDS THE steering wheel with his knees and unscrews another bottle of wine. Thank the Lord, she can already see the white wall of the church in the distance. Before the wine fogs his brain too much, they should be there. It will be good to free her mind of this damned driver. Of Miss Ingrid and Lexi, too. The people must carry on singing by themselves now.

She wonders if Jeremiah has baked the bread properly. Will he have remembered to butter the upper crust to make it soft? Otherwise he'll strew the kitchen floor with crumbs when he cuts through the hard crust. And she hopes he doesn't forget to let her chickens out. They're not used to being cooped up in the chicken run all day long. It gets on their nerves and they lay fewer eggs when they're confined. Jeremiah can be a very absent-minded man. For all she knows, he might leave the chickens to their own fate until she gets home tomorrow evening.

'It's because you poison yourself with all kinds of strange brews that you have so little brain left,' she told him the previous week when he came home from the shop with a packet of brown bread flour. She wanted to bake sugar cakes, and it's no use trying to bake sugar cakes with brown bread flour.

'As God is my witness, Jeremiah, one morning you're going to wake up with nothing left in your skull. It's time you bend down before the Lord and beg His forgiveness.'

'Oh, *Jissus*, Miriam, there's nothing wrong with my brain! You'd better watch out that too much Christianity doesn't cause your brain to burst at the seams.'

'Why did you buy brown bread flour? I told you to buy cake flour!'

'The shop was sold out of cake flour.'

'You're lying, Jeremiah! Where's the change?'

He turned his pockets out, threw a couple of coins on the table. More than five rand short. The angel of goodness who flies around her every day helped her to keep her mouth shut. Because if she had given him a piece of her mind there and then, it would have made his ancestors turn in their graves.

Jeremiah can lie like a trooper. And he thinks she's too stupid to know when he's spinning her a tall story. She knows he's going to squander the money that she left at the Book of Ezekiel on sinful things. Heaven knows, she has a hard time with Jeremiah. For more than thirty years she's been dragging him through life. She cannot even ask him to go to town for a packet of yeast with an easy mind.

Of course she could go to town herself, but her legs are not strong any more. When she gets back from town the arthritic pains are shooting right up into her hip joints. And after all, why can't Jeremiah lift his backside and do the shopping? If he's not playing dominoes, he's just sitting in the sun against the front wall of the house, chasing flies from his face. Smoking, chatting to everyone who passes by. Too lazy to work. He doesn't lift a finger to train the runner beans up the reeds, or to collect the day's eggs from the nests. Let alone chop the firewood. Truly, the day you marry a man, you marry endless troubles, too. It was true what her mother had told her long ago: if you play with dung, you mustn't complain if your hands stink.

But Jeremiah had been a handsome man when he was young. Pearly white teeth; strong shoulders. He had a good job at the furniture factory and brought home enough money every month to compensate for any defects. She had paid little attention to her mother's warnings.

'He has a sly way of looking back over his shoulder,' her mother had warned her, 'as if he fears that someone is following him. And his eyes don't look straight. You're taking on trouble, Miriam.'

She wouldn't listen. Now she was stuck with him.

70

But back then the evangelist said that marriage is for better or for worse. She should have asked him what to do when one experienced only the worse. Four children she had borne for Jeremiah. Five, if she included Little Leth who died young. Katrien came first, and she was an easy child. Level-headed. The best educated of all four of her children. Never had an illegitimate child. She had worn a delicate white dress of layered honeycomb cotton the day she got married, with a thickly pleated veil that swung below her buttocks. They had even hired the white church's organist to play the dilapidated church organ at the brown people's church in the township. Katrien entered on the tune of the wedding march, the one that starts with the many similar notes. For many years she's held a steady job at Miss Mari's hairdressing salon. Katrien always claims that she can cut and perm just as well as Miss Mari. If it wasn't for the money that Katrien set aside each month for her parents, she wouldn't have been able to sew all the patches of her life together into one useful blanket.

Then came Izak and Evert and Joseph.

Cut from the same cloth as their father. They had inherited his bad habits of lying and looking over the shoulder, always off work with one-day sicknesses. If it wasn't an aching head that threatened to burst, it was a tight chest. Or toothache. Or a running stomach. All the while the actual problem was that they had hangovers.

Tomorrow, before she lifts the communion cup to her lips, she's going to talk seriously to God about her three sinful sons. Especially about Evert. Any day now his wife will be giving birth, and she told Jeremiah she can smell trouble coming. Before long, Evert will land in gaol. Because hardly a day passes when mutton isn't served at his table. Since when can Evert afford to eat mutton every day? And that while he's wearing worn shoes, and begging money off her to buy a pocket of potatoes. And to add to her worries, there are rumours in town that the detectives from the stock theft unit are paying informers large sums of money for information.

'I'm telling you, Jeremiah, I see big trouble coming with Evert,' she said, turning the lamp wick up so she could see to slice the bread nice and thin.

'And how can you see that, Miriam?' he asked, chewing. He always eats all the food that she brings from Miss Ingrid's house, without any sign of shame or guilt. As though he owned the plate of food. He always pushed the lettuce aside; said he was not a rabbit or a chicken. And he always complained about the small piece of meat: 'Or can *you* perhaps see it with the God-given second sight in your stomach?'

She asked the angel of goodness to help her guard her tongue. Better not to pick a scrap with him, because she wanted to ask him to collect some of the rooster's tail feathers and tie them in bundles for Lexi. Lexi would sit in one spot for hours, as quiet as a mouse, trying to pull the greasy threads of the tail feathers apart. Then she could finish the ironing and polish the brassware.

The driver holds the wine bottle out to the man in the passenger seat. Hardly two fingers left. But at least they're near the end of this terrifying journey. She can already see the rooster on the steeple of the church.

This afternoon she wants to keep to herself at Jeremiah's people's place. Lock the door of the room and make a list in her mind of all those people that she wants to dedicate to the Lord's mercy. It would be best to start with Evert. Because there is much about Evert that she has to lay before His feet.

Barely a month ago she was deeply ashamed of her own flesh and blood. Evert and a crowd of others had gone by truck to attend a funeral at Master Siegfried's farm. It turned into a weekend of merrymaking. They took along gallons of wine. Guitars, too. One would never think they were supposed to be paying their last respects to a dead man.

When the funeral was about to start, the rain came down. It was slippery and muddy around the grave. And Evert's foot slipped on the edge of the grave. He landed on the lid of the coffin, crushing the wreath of white chrysanthemums. And Aunt Maria, who made all the wreaths for the township people, had paid a fortune at the florist for the white chrysanthemums. Afterwards she heard from Aunt Maria how the other funeral-goers had struggled to lift Evert from the grave. They were all drunk, and they trampled the area around the grave into a sea of mud that was as slippery as butter. According to Aunt Maria, there were eventually three of them in the grave, and the wreath was completely destroyed. Aunt Maria's brother had to fetch a rope from Master Siegfried to pull the bunch of noisy drunkards from the grave.

In spite of her aching legs, she walked over to Evert's house that Monday afternoon after work. He was in bed with stomach cramps.

'Evert,' she said, and she knew from the expression on his face that he was going to wipe his boots on her, 'you're a grown man.

But I'm warning you today: I'll take a strap and give you the thrashing of your life.'

'It'll take more than Ma to give me a thrashing.'

She breathed deeply. She didn't want Evert's anger to become her anger. 'Why did you fall into the grave on Saturday? Were you drunk?'

He snorted at her in contempt. 'Drunk? Who says I was drunk?'

She breathed again. 'Evert, don't take me for a baboon. I'm your mother and I'm telling you straight to your face that you fell into the grave for no other reason but that you were drunk.'

'And I'm telling you, Ma, it was not because I was drunk, it was out of compassion.'

Imagine, compassion. She zipped her lips, because she was close to having a stroke out of anger at his arrogance.

It will be best if she starts her prayers with Evert, while her mind is still fresh.

The driver slams on the brakes at the turn-off to the church. She lifts her eyes to the clouds and thanks the angels who brought them here safely. When the angels take hands to fly back to the kloof, she notices Lexi amongst them again. If it weren't for the uncombed hair at the back of his head, she wouldn't have recognised him.

13

THE WOMAN EXAMINES the syringe, sniffs at it.

'Mrs Dorfling, I asked you: what is this?'

Since Alexander's birth, and especially after he was able to move around the house on his own, she had been a light sleeper, always aware of his movements around the dark house throughout the night. Sometimes she stayed up with him, as long as she could endure it. But in the end it turned her into a zombie.

The first time she had a deficit when she cashed up, and felt like a thief, she made up her mind: at bedtime she would put her guilty feelings aside and go to bed. Even if it meant Alexander's ghostly figure roamed the house while everyone else was sleeping. Neither physically nor emotionally could she afford to stay up watching him night after night. She had to be able to concentrate every day on working with large sums of money at the bank. But sound, dreamless sleep was impossible for her. All night, every night, she was vaguely alert to what was happening in the house. Sometimes she woke Dawid and asked him to check on Alexander.

'Leave him, let him do as he bloody well pleases,' Dawid mumbled. 'I can't get up every five minutes to spy on him.'

She was close to tears. 'Please, Dawid, I have a job, too. I . . . I . . .' The stillborn sentence hung in the air. He ignored her. Turned over and fell asleep immediately.

Some time after Alexander's second birthday an unusual sound woke her in the early hours of the morning. Alarmed, she sat up, running her fingers through her hair. She listened. What kind of sound was that? Was Alexander asleep? Why was the house as quiet as the grave? Day was already breaking; why was he not chipping with his chisel? She got up quietly, so as not to disturb Dawid.

She found Alexander lying on the kitchen floor, his head next to the cat's bowl, a ring of foam around his lips. His fists were clenched, his body arched and stiff; his eyes turned back. Oh, my God, he's choking on the cat's milk was the first thought to flash through her mind.

'Dawid!' she yelled through the quiet house. 'Dawid! Help me, Dawid!'

Her first instinct was to splash cold water on his face. But she was frozen with shock.

'Dawid!'

She sank to her knees, touched the wooden body with her fingertips. 'Xander! Look at Mommy, Xander!'

Dizzy with sleep, Dawid staggered into the kitchen in his underpants. 'What the hell is going on?'

'Help me, Dawid!'

Dawid was suddenly awake. And terrified. 'Oh, my God, Ingrid! The child is having a fit!'

She dialled the hospital's number with trembling hands, while Dawid tried to push his fingers between the child's clenched jaws. Teresa and Zettie stood in the kitchen door, their eyes as wide as saucers. It'll be fine, it'll be fine, she said rushing past them. There was no time to dress or comb her hair. She searched frantically for the car keys, grabbed the little wooden body; raced to the hospital.

There was a whirlwind of busy white uniforms.

The sister on night duty took one look at Alexander. 'Epileptic seizure,' she said. Then her experienced hands took over.

Dawid whispered that they should move aside. With one hand he held her shoulder, with the other he wiped the tears from her cheeks. It was a small gesture of comfort. 'Everything's going to be fine, the sister is with him.' He held her against him and patted her back.

She prayed. She had the urge to weep out loud. Weep and weep until the tightness in her eased. But the tears were buried too deep inside her, in a distant place that she had forgotten about. She looked at her brittle child's ash-white face and knew that she couldn't give him what he begged for. Not because she didn't want to, but because she didn't understand what it was that he wanted. She didn't know if she would ever understand his mysterious language. Because his isolated island was forbidden to her; he wouldn't even allow her to explore its outer edges.

While she wondered whether God really existed, Alexander's hands and back relaxed, his eyes became normal. His tiny chest stopped heaving. He sighed like someone who was utterly exhausted.

'It's over now,' the sister said. 'He'll sleep. Nothing to worry about. You can go home. It'll be best if you leave him here until Old Doctor comes on his morning rounds.'

A tiny bundle in the huge white hospital bed. A human being who seemed to be completely different from all other humans. And yet as human as any. How could she leave him alone in the white bed and go home? 'I'd rather stay with him until Old Doctor arrives.'

'There's nothing you can do for him, Ingrid. I gave him a Valium injection, he'll sleep for a long time. An epileptic seizure is exhausting. Rather go home and get an hour's sleep. I'll phone you when he wakes up, or as soon as Old Doctor has examined him.'

'Maybe I should stay just a little longer. He will be hysterical when he wakes up and everything around him is strange and . . .'

Long after he had been stabilised and was sleeping like a wax doll, she stood in her pyjamas in the hospital room, her teeth chattering with cold and shock. Dawid stood at the foot of the bed watching the sleeping child, his fingers creasing the white bed-spread. He walked round the bed and tucked the sheets in behind Alexander's neck and back. Then he went to her and took her face in his hands; a handful of warmth on her cold skin. He suggested that they should go home.

'Good God, Ingrid, what a shock that gave me,' he said when they arrived home.

'Me too.'

'Make us some coffee, Ingrid, I'm stiff with cold.'

First she looked into Teresa and Zettie's room. They were fast asleep, as though immune to the drama that had taken place around them. She squatted between their beds and while she watched their innocent sleeping faces a deep empathy for them took hold of her. If *she* could understand nothing, how could *they* understand? She got up and tucked the blankets in at Teresa's feet, closed the door. Went to the kitchen. Boiled water for coffee; heated the milk. She turned around with the coffee mugs. Dawid was sitting at the kitchen table, his face in his hands, weeping soundlessly, the tears running through the dark hair of his forearms.

'Dawid?'

When he looked up at her, the wet pools of his eyes held a silent plea. She put the coffee mugs down and went to him, pulled his head gently against her stomach. He clung to her in desperation, his shoulders jerking, the choking sound of a man's weeping coming from deep within him. She stroked his back with her hand, trying to soothe him with a strength that came from God knows where.

'I'm tired to death, Ingrid.' His breath was warm against her stomach. 'Tired of trying to cope and tired of being rejected. Fed up with struggling with money and doctors. I can't live with this child any longer. God knows, Ingrid, I can't. If only I could . . . If only . . .' and he clung to her. 'I think I'm losing my mind, Ingrid.'

She was overcome by hopelessness. What would happen if Dawid left her and the children? Or if Alexander never got any better? Or when they reached a point where they had no more money or credit? What would happen if the medical aid fund refused to keep paying for Alexander's medication?

But she wanted to hide her anxiety from Dawid. 'Don't upset yourself, Dawid, one day there will . . .'

Without warning, he wrenched himself free from her arms and banged his fist on the kitchen table, knocking the sugar bowl flying in an outburst of wild rage. 'One day? What do you mean by *one day*? If *one day* is in any way like today, I'd prefer it never to come!' He grabbed the cloth with which she was trying to wipe the sugar from her hands and crumpled it up between his shaking fingers. 'Do you hear me, Ingrid? Before *one day* comes, as God is my witness, I'll shoot myself!'

It's hard when your husband weeps like a child and you don't know where to turn. You want him to take the crumbs of comfort that you are offering him. You hold him against your own warmth until his anger subsides and your own shivering body becomes still. Not because you feel stronger than him, but because you know you can fight harder for survival than he can.

'Go back to bed, Dawid, I'll wake you up when the hospital phones.'

Long after he had gone back to bed, she recalled the fragility of his bony shoulders under her fingertips. And her instincts warned her to hide the revolver. Her thoughts scared her. She longed to phone Lida or Hannah or Mirna. To tell them how frightened she was when she found Alexander next to the cat's bowl. To ask them if they know anything about epilepsy. To tell them how Dawid had sat at the kitchen table, weeping. How he walked back to the bedroom, hunched, crushing the strewn sugar under his shoes, walking over the scattered shards on the floor like a blind man. To ask them the safest place to hide the revolver.

But she knew the bridges had been burnt.

She wrapped the revolver in plastic and hid it between the spare pillows high up in the linen cupboard.

After that night she always carried the emergency kit with the sedative and the syringe in her handbag. Everywhere. Dawid put his kit in his trousers pocket when they went out. Initially he did so with the utmost aversion; later with resignation, as though it was a wallet or a handkerchief. An extra kit was kept in the side pocket of the pushchair. Miriam and Teresa and Zettie knew that a spare kit was also kept next to the bread bin.

How clearly she recalled the scorching summer afternoon when she arrived home from work to find Teresa sitting cross-legged on the kitchen floor with Alexander sleeping beside her. Head in her hands, she was sobbing, her shoulders jerking convulsively. The empty syringe lay next to her. When Teresa lifted her face from her hands, her eyes were swollen and red; her neck wet with sweat.

'I can't do this, Mom, I can't! I told you that long ago!'

She didn't know what to say. She pulled Alexander's pants up and carried him to her bed. As she covered him with the bedspread, she remembered that it was pension day and that Miriam had asked if she could go with Jeremiah to fetch his pension, so that he did not squander it. She felt that her life was slipping from her hands uncontrollably.

She went back to the kitchen. She knew that Teresa would be waiting to be comforted.

'Teresa . . .?'

'I promise you, Mom, next time I'll just leave him to . . . to . . .' Her shoulders started jerking again; she covered her face, the hair at the back of her neck was damp with sweat.

She sat down next to her and pulled her steaming body towards her. She held her; rocked her. Heard herself singing a nursery rhyme from Teresa's childhood. After a while the steady rhythm of her breathing told her that she had fallen asleep against her shoulder. What she later recalled most clearly of that day on the kitchen floor was the worn condition of Teresa's netball shoes.

No one outside the walls of their home knew how to use the syringe and the Valium. Why would she have explained it to anyone else? Those who had once been part of her support system had sailed away to less troubled waters. Only Miriam remained.

Because she could no longer count on Dawid.

While Alexander was asleep, her subconscious was always on guard. Because experience had taught her that when he was drifting in a state of slumber the epilepsy monster could grab him without warning and turn his eyes back.

'It's the fits,' Miriam had said.

'No, Miriam, it's called epilepsy.'

'When my children were growing up, we just called it fits. But if Miss Ingrid calls it by another name that's fine, and I'll use the syringe as you have shown me. And, Miss Ingrid, maybe it'd be a good thing if you bought us a bottle of strengthening drops.'

Subconsciously, they all listened for the frightening gasp that announced an epileptic seizure. A time bomb waiting to explode when least expected.

Make sure that the tongue is not blocking the airway. Loosen all clothing, especially in the neck area. Remove all objects that could cause injury. Draw the Valium up in the syringe and wait for five minutes. If the seizure continues, administer the full ampoule per rectum.

If only she could find the words to explain to the disrespectful woman how she and Dawid had often been frightened out of their senses. Miriam and Teresa and Zettie, too. Drawing the Valium up with trembling hands; removing Alexander's pants from his tiny buttocks. Would the woman then perhaps understand their fear, their dread?

'It's Alexander's epilepsy medication,' she tells the woman. 'Why are you listing my possessions?'

The woman writes without looking up. 'Because they must be handed back to you eventually.'

'Where are you taking me?'

'To the police cells.'

Fear makes her nauseous. Dear God, is the woman serious? Should she consider speaking to a lawyer? No, it's an unnecessary expense. Surely they will soon take her home. She must just stick to the truth.

'To the police cells? But I have done nothing . . .'

'We have a case to solve, Mrs Dorfling, and we have the right to detain you for forty-eight hours for questioning before we decide whether or not to charge you.'

She clutches at any little straw. 'I have to make funeral arrangements and . . .'

'The funeral arrangements will be handled for you.'

She keeps clutching. 'My daughters are on their way home.'

'We will arrange that they have a key to the house. Please stand up straight against the opposite wall, hands to your sides.'

A board is hung around her neck. Click. She is commanded to turn sideways. Click. The board is taken off. Before the woman puts it down, she catches sight of the ominous words written on it in black felt pen: *Case number 526 . . . Ingrid Dorfling . . . Murder . . .*

Something inside her snaps like a dry branch. But somehow she stays on her feet, tearless. Because in the past nine years she's become as hard as stone.

'Let's go. Colonel Herselman is in a hurry. Lace up your shoes if you want to, but you'll have to loosen them again when we get to the police cells.'

'I'll leave them.'

'Hold your hands together for the handcuffs.'

No. No.

'Please, don't. I'll keep my hands on my lap the whole time. Please . . .'

'Unfortunately the law doesn't allow detainees to be transported unless they are handcuffed.'

'Please, I beg you . . .'

'Believe me, Mrs Dorfling, there's nothing I can do to change the law. Hold your hands out, please.'

Cold metal against her skin. The click as the handcuffs lock is like the chains of nine years finally closing in on her.

Nine years.

Manifested in one short sickening click.

She walks down the passage with flapping shoes. Picks up the stale smell of her own sweat. Gets into the back of the police car with the woman. And she knows: the same God who gave Alexander to her on a cold winter's night has determined the course of her life. A path which she could never have imagined.

This night, too.

And tomorrow.

And all the days of her life.

'I don't know why God gave Alexander to me,' she had once said to Gunter. They were sitting on the straw bales beneath the kraal wall, sheltering from the cold south wind. 'Why an *autistic* child? God knew very well that I lived in a place where there were no specialised facilities. Why did He make me travel from doctor to doctor for three and a half years before spelling out my fate in the form of a vague diagnosis?'

He was a soundboard against whom she could convert her thoughts; lift the paper-thin layer of powerless frustration within her.

'Ingrid, why don't you ask the bank manager to help you get a transfer to a city? Pack up, and move where there are facilities and therapists and a school for autistic children. It would make things so much easier if . . .'

'It's impossible.'

'Why is it impossible?'

The most important impossibility she dared not tell him: I'm staying here, Gunter, because you are here. Because Sundays have become the beginning and end of my life, my entire horizon. I love you, Gunter. I cannot leave you and the kraal wall.

But even if Gunter and the kraal wall had never existed, there were too many obstacles. Miriam. Where would she ever find someone like Miriam again? What sort of house could she buy in a city with the miserable amount she would get for her neglected *platteland* house? An apartment or a semi-detached house would be out of the question with Alexander. What time would she have to leave for work in the mornings, and what time would she get home? Who would take Alexander to school and bring him back? Even if he could travel by school bus, who would take care of him until she got home in the afternoons? Where would she find the money to pay his school fees and bus fares? Where would she begin to search for him if he wandered off?

'My circumstances are too complicated for me to think of moving. I just wish I could understand why God in His wisdom gave me an autistic child . . .'

They sat quietly for a long time, watching Lucy complete her slow, wide circles. Gunter took his jacket off and hung the warmth of his body around her shoulders. The coarse material smelled of the man and of soil and straw, and the lingering odour brought a simultaneous feeling of paralysis and security. She had to swallow her tears down.

'What makes you so sure it was God who gave him to you,

Ingrid? All too often and all too easily people drag in God's intentions when things go wrong as a way of escaping their own share in their sadness.'

'Who gave Alexander to me then?'

'I don't know. All I know is that God is not the great chastiser.' He bent forward to pick up a small round stone, rolled it on the palm of his hand with his forefinger. 'We sow our own land, Ingrid.'

His words shocked her. Surely, she has misunderstood him. 'Do you mean I deserve a child like Alexander; that I have reaped what I sowed?'

'Not literally. I've told you before, Ingrid, don't question me about God. My knowledge of Him is inadequate. Here, take,' and he opened his fingers and put the little stone in her hand. 'Put the stone in a safe place, then ask the stone your questions every day. If you ask often enough, and listen carefully, you will find answers.'

In a strange way it was reassuring to watch him sitting on the straw bale, hands folded under his chin, eyes staring into the distance. He was the only person in the world whom she would trust for answers. Who else could she trust? The one time in her life that she had trusted the dominee with her deepest secrets, he turned his evil power against Dawid.

'Why do you give me a stone when I'm looking for answers?'

'The answers are inside the stone, Ingrid. You must find them. And that could take a lifetime.'

'The Bible says you shouldn't give someone a stone when he asks for bread.'

He turned, lifted his foot on to the straw bale. 'The bread is inside the stone, Ingrid, like God is inside you. The Bible also says: knock, and the door shall be opened to you. Let it be, Ingrid. Throw the stone away if you don't want it.'

She had put the little stone in an oyster shell on the window sill in the bathroom. Sometimes she put it in her mouth while she was praying in the bath. *Lead us not into temptation, but deliver us from evil.*

When they release her today she is going to tell Gunter that stones cannot speak.

Despite the burning sensation where the handcuffs chafe the flesh of her wrists, she falls asleep in the car. She dreams that Alexander is alone in the dark house with his chisel. But tonight he's not chipping the plaster. Tonight he sits hunched up in the broom cupboard, licking out the jar of cheese spread. Suddenly he drops the jar on the wooden floor of the cupboard with a thud, and covers his ears when the midnight train rattles past.

She wakes up, her mind foggy and clouded, when they stop at a traffic light. Her head is throbbing and her eyes feel as if they are bulging from their sockets. When did she last sleep properly? Thursday night? Wednesday night? She cannot remember that far back. And it's Saturday night already. If they don't give her a chance to sleep, the man is going to shatter her emotionally.

What's going to happen to her tonight? It's ludicrous to think they are actually going to lock her up in a cell. Or is this a dirty trick the man is playing to break her down the way *he* prefers to do it? How can she convince him that Alexander's death was nobody's fault? God knows, she never intended to fall asleep. She did run the bath water, yes, and it was a mistake. If she had known she would fall asleep, she would never have opened the taps.

She would not have.

How could Alexander have died before he got into the bath? If the man is really going to charge her with murder, she will be left with no option but to find legal assistance. But where? And who? Will a stranger take her word that she will pay him later?

She turns to the woman next to her. 'I have a splitting headache. Do you perhaps have a headache tablet?'

'No. We'll make a note of your request at the charge office.'

Charge office.

'I don't want to go to the charge office. I'd rather go home.'

The woman sighs, looks away. 'Mrs Dorfling, I've told you over and over that we are investigating a case of murder. You are a suspect, and . . .'

'And I've told you over and over that I would never drown my own child.'

'The findings in the autopsy report make it clear that he did not drown. And unfortunately that is not the only suspicion.'

She jerks upright, painfully aware of the handcuffs cutting into her flesh. 'What other suspicions can you have?'

'Get yourself a lawyer, Mrs Dorfling, he will go through the autopsy report and advise you.'

Dejected, her shoulders slump. She must stop upsetting herself. Just answer their questions. Stay awake, be consistent. Think before she speaks. Falling asleep from exhaustion cannot be construed as murder. They *will* let her go home tonight. Nine years of hell cannot end like this.

If only something would release the tears inside her. Perhaps the man thinks that her lack of tears is evidence of her guilt.

But at the same time she knows that the place where her tears and emotions should be no longer exists. Alexander killed it.

Alexander.

Lonely child on a lonely island.

A hiding place where light and sound and colour could not hurt him. Where the shadows of faces and hands and bodies did not threaten him. Where he could isolate himself in his deaf-mute world, visiting the mainland for short periods only to listen to the ringing of the church bells. King of his island where no one was admitted. Where warmth and conscience had never existed, not even for one second. How fiercely she had fought to get through to him. If she could do nothing else but explore the coastline of his island it would have brought some sweetness to her life. She would have stayed up all night with him; played ring-a-rosy until she panted like a dog. Scratched his tiny back until he fell asleep. Removed every single thorn from his feet with her fingers. Sat with him in his tablecloth house until her back ached.

Anything, God, anything.

But he pushed her away, growled at her, kicked her in the face, bit her hands. Pulled away when she wanted to kiss or comfort him. Scuttled off and covered himself in the ragbox when she wanted to bath him. Knocked the white porcelain plate from the table if she dared dish up a single grain of rice.

No one else existed in the isolation of his glass bubble. To the very end he allowed no one to step across the boundary of his island. The only people who ever came near to setting foot ashore were Miriam and Gunter. To Gunter, he gave his feet, fleeting moments of tender touch, sometimes slavish obedience. To Miriam, he gave much more. He allowed her to sit with him on her lap under the wild olive tree; to rock him while she sang to him. *Gentle Jesus, meek and mild . . . Give a little child a place . . .*

Lonely child trying to survive in an upside down world filled with frightening throat gasps and F-sharps and flapping hands. Misty eyes looking right through her as if she was a window pane. Seeking sanctuary in the ragbox or the broom cupboard. What inaudible message was caught up in the north wind that made him run around the house like a lunatic? What strange music was hidden in the song of the south wind that made him climb into the pine trees in the schoolyard to listen to it?

Lonely child.

Upside down world.

Merciful God, she would never have run the bath water.

One stifling hot Sunday afternoon while Dawid was sleeping spread-eagled on his back on their bed, she walked into Alexander's room with a bottle of cold milk coffee. He was cutting his first tooth and had a middle ear infection. He was feverish and miserable and, as always, refused to take the antibiotics. He knocked the teaspoon away so that the medicine spilled all over her blouse.

She did not know why she still bothered to order medicine from the chemist, or why she still took him to Old Doctor, for he was terrified of the surgery. Even though Old Doctor spoke gently and tried to calm him with a toy or a sweet, it made no impression on him. The moment she flicked on the indicator to turn into the street where the surgery was, he began wriggling in his car seat. And it took holding on for dear life when he detected the smell of the surgery. He screamed blue murder and hit Old Doctor in the face, especially if there was an injection needle in sight.

Yet she always went back. What else could she do? Because Old Doctor was kind to her, in spite of everything. He always gave her the last appointment of the day so she wouldn't be rushed. Alexander would curl up into a tiny bundle under the fish tank while she and Old Doctor talked. Later, after the diagnosis had been made, he often gave her copies of articles from medical publications; information on new medication; told her about a documentary video.

Old Doctor. Heart of gold. But old. Once she asked him to give a talk on autism at the Ladies' Club, to try to improve their understanding.

'My dear Ingrid,' and he shook his head compassionately, 'my knowledge is too poor. I have to admit: you, who live with autism every day probably know far more about the condition than I do. These mysterious behaviour-related diseases are something that still baffle the medical world. Sometimes we strike it lucky, mostly we don't. But why don't you give the talk yourself?'

She did.

Only a few people attended. Nobody asked questions. Just stared at her until she felt like someone begging for sympathy. Afterwards, they handed her a bunch of Mirna's Inca lilies. And that was it.

When Alexander had a middle ear infection he was more aggressive than usual, as if it was the only language in which he could relate his pain to her. Sometimes she was stunned by the imbalance in his development: why could he roll, but not sit? Why could he growl, but not laugh?

At such times, he rolled wildly into the corner of the cot, growling when she approached to pick him up or change his nappy. Bathing him was almost impossible. To get him to eat was completely impossible. Five, six days would pass without him swallowing even a morsel of pumpkin, cheese spread or mashed banana. But he loved cold coffee, strong, with lots of milk, so at least she could stir the antibiotic into the coffee, a little at a time, so that he wouldn't pick up the taste of medicine.

That swelteringly hot Sunday her energy was sapped. It was the end of February, financial year-end for many bank clients. Time-consuming tax information had to be compiled. The staff struggled to keep up with the workload. Everyone was irritable. If it wasn't the computer system packing up, then it was someone wanting to make an investment three minutes before closing time. Or needing information that had to be dug out of the archives. She worked late on the Friday evening, trying to catch up with the backlog. She couldn't expect Miriam to postpone her weekend off again. Miriam was probably more worn out than she was.

Why did Alexander have to choose *that* time to cut his first tooth, she wondered as she separated the soiled notes from the clean ones. The heat was debilitating, her feet were swollen, her body sticky. A minute before closing time the church clerk came in to bank the Women's League quarterly street collection. Three bags of coins. She felt like yelling with frustration.

'I must call it a day and go home,' she hinted to the accountant when it was late and Dawid had already phoned twice to ask when she was going to come home. He grumbled that it was Friday evening; he had planned to play poker, and was definitely not going to babysit all evening. Then he slammed the phone down.

Their relationship was going downhill faster than she could handle. She could no longer deny it. There was a tense atmosphere in the house. They picked on each other, exchanged accusations. Shouted at the girls over trivial issues like lunch boxes and unwashed hair and school books that had to be covered, as if it was their fault that Alexander blew everyone's routine out the window.

There were days when she wished she could push Alexander back into her body and never give birth to him. Or bang his head against the wall in the hope that something might slip into gear. More than once she was on the point of telling Miriam to ask

Jeremiah to bring along the Indian man from the township. Let him bury a dead leguaan under the kitchen floor, anything, as long as there was a chance it might help.

'We all want to go home,' the accountant replied.

When she arrived home at nine o'clock, Dawid was drunk. Paralytic. The kitchen was in chaos with dirty dishes, knives smeared with syrup, empty milk cartons, crumbs. Smelly nappies on the bedroom floor. Teresa and Zettie were sitting in front of the television, faces expressionless, pretending not to notice their staggering father. Alexander lay in the corner of the playpen, screaming, his thin fingers grasping at the air, as if reaching for something only he could see.

'What bloody time is this to come home?' Dawid snapped at her.

From the corner of her eye she could see Teresa and Zettie moving closer together on the couch. If she could pick them up there and then and put them down in a better place in the world, she would. But she couldn't.

'I asked you: is this the time to . . .?'

Lightning flashed in her brain. She clenched her teeth to stop herself flying at him. 'I was working, Dawid. You *know* it's the end of the financial year and we are very busy.'

'Work, you say, work? What about your home and your children? And that screaming brat,' and he pointed at the playpen. 'Who do you think must look after him? You knew damn well I was playing poker tonight!'

Breathe, stay calm. Consider Teresa and Zettie. 'Please, Dawid, be reasonable. We were terribly busy and I can't just rush out of the bank and leave everyone else to . . .'

'You know the bloody child is sick, but you give Miriam the weekend off and leave this madhouse to me! You know bloody well I play poker on Friday evenings!'

She longed to get into a bath and go to bed. 'I am here now. Stop bitching and go play poker if you want to.'

'This time of night! Poker's arse!'

She forgot she was trying to watch her words. 'You're too drunk to hold the cards in any case.'

Bloodshot eyes glared at her, fists opening and closing as the anger welled up in him. 'Look here, Ingrid, you'd better shut that child up,' he hissed, 'or I'll go crazy and strangle him!'

She was too tired to argue. 'Then, go crazy and strangle him! But take care that I don't go crazy before you do!'

She turned on her heel, threw her handbag down. Picked Alexander up out of the playpen. Dumped him in the pushchair and walked aimlessly into the hot night. She hoped God would send a truck to run over both of them. So that they would be out of everyone's way. Up and down the street with the pushchair. Until her legs felt weak and she didn't know if she was walking or floating. Later she sat down with her back against a tree trunk and moved the pushchair to and fro with her foot. Sang him a lullaby, over and over.

They slept under the tree until daybreak; until the buzz of mosquitoes woke her.

Dawid left in a huff for golf on the Saturday, without saying goodbye. He came home late that evening and slumped down next to her without bathing or brushing his teeth. All night she could smell the stale sweat on his body. On the Sunday morning he didn't get up to take Teresa and Zettie to Sunday School. She had to cope on her own.

God knows how.

And yet, angry as she was, she felt sorry for him. How could she understand what was going on inside Dawid's head? How pleased he had been when the scan showed it was a boy. How excitedly he had helped to pack her suitcase for the hospital. Supported her throughout the birth. Had held the wet baby against his cheek. Who was *she* to judge if she herself felt the urge to bash Alexander's head against the wall?

When she walked into Alexander's room that Sunday afternoon with the bottle of cold coffee containing his medicine he was kneeling in the cot, his cheek buried in the pillow. And he was rocking. Forwards, backwards. Forwards, backwards. Seemingly unaware of anything around him. He just rocked and rocked while his soft laments slowly died away.

She stood like stone with the bottle in her hand. Merciful Father, this was not normal. Teresa and Zettie had never done this. What was he doing? She called him. He didn't react. She called again. Bent over the edge of the cot and shook the bottle near his face. He seemed to register nothing.

She sank to her knees and clicked her fingers in front of his eyes.

Rock, rock, rock.

Forwards, backwards, forwards, backwards.

'Xander? Look, Mommy brought you some coffee, Xander . . .'

No reaction. She pressed her face against the railings of the cot and blew in his face. He did not even blink his eyes. Nothingness in the blue irises, as if they were covered with a hazy membrane. Far away on his remote island. His soundless island. Where the reality of wind and sun and shadow didn't exist.

Rock, rock, rock.

She put her hand through the railings, and laid the bottle of coffee down next to his hand. Then she retreated slowly, her eyes fixed on the child as he rocked on his knees, a deaf-mute. And her thoughts paralysed her. Something was wrong with Alexander. Dreadfully wrong. And it had nothing to do with middle ear infection or fever or cutting teeth.

She went to their room and looked at the sleeping Dawid. She stood for a long time, until her blouse was wet with tears and pins and needles tingled in her calves. In his sleep, Dawid licked his dry lips and turned over; curled himself into a foetal position, his hands tucked between his thighs. She pulled the blanket over him, because he seemed cold, despite the summer heat. She wished he would open his eyes and look at her; invite her to lie with him under the blanket so that they could comfort each other.

But he slept the sleep of the dead.

On the Monday she didn't want to go to work. Even though there was nothing she could do for Alexander, she just wanted to be close to him. To try to persuade him to eat something or fall asleep with her. She wanted to ask Miriam to make meatballs and sweet potatoes and yellow rice and brown pudding with custard, so that when Dawid came home for lunch, the house would smell of food.

'Stay at home? What for?' Dawid asked as he knotted his tie in front of the bathroom mirror.

'I am sick with worry, Dawid. Alexander hasn't eaten for days, and he's feverish and . . .'

He shifted the knot neatly and took the aftershave out of the bathroom cabinet. 'He'll eat when he's hungry. And you *do* have medicine.'

She moved closer and put her arms around him, pressing her cheek against his back. His shirt smelled of sun and ironing. I love you, Dawid, she wanted to say, and I need you. But her breath echoed soundlessly against his shirt. She started sobbing uncontrollably, holding tightly on to him until her ribs ached. She wanted to tell him about Alexander's rocking, but she couldn't get the words out of her mouth.

'For goodness sake, Ingrid,' and he loosened the hands clasped around his waist and looked at her in the mirror. 'I must go to work and I'm already late, and now my shirt is soaked! Pull yourself together! You can't keep on staying off work to . . .'

She threw her arms around him again. She would beg if she had to. 'Dawid, listen to me. Please. There's something terribly wrong with Alexander. We cannot go on like this. Our lives are falling apart. You *must* help me, Dawid, you must *please* help me to . . .'

'What must I help you with, Ingrid?' He put the aftershave away, slammed the door of the bathroom cabinet. 'I'm sick and tired as it is! My life is just as buggered up as yours. Do you want me to go even further into the red, or waste more petrol going to listen to another quack's nonsense?'

'I beg you, Dawid.'

Again, he loosened her arms and pushed her aside. 'I must go, otherwise I'll be late. Stay at home if you want to. Until Friday, or until the end of the month. But don't come crying to me if you get fired.'

She watched the car as it disappeared down the street. And a dark well of despair grew inside her.

The bank manager said it was inconvenient to have to put someone else on counter duty at such short notice. But he understood and she could take a day's leave.

Thank you. Thank you.

When the surgery opened, she was there. Why, she wasn't sure. But for the umpteenth time since Alexander's birth, she was at a dead end. Thank goodness it was early and the surgery was still empty. She slumped into the riempie chair opposite Old Doctor's desk with Alexander on her lap. How she hated that chair. And the smell of illness and medicine too.

Old Doctor looked at Alexander's file and he asked how he could help.

'There's something terribly wrong, Doctor.'

'This is your third child, Ingrid,' he said, trying to press the stethoscope on to the squirming little body. 'You know that children have their own ways and means of attracting attention and entertaining themselves.'

'I know, but his eyes were . . .' Suddenly her tongue refused to form the words. *Doctor, is Alexander perhaps mentally retarded?*

She could not utter the question.

'Maybe he was sleepy, Ingrid. Or maybe the rocking helped to soothe his earache.'

It was a small solace with which she could kill the devil in her mind. 'You're probably right, Doctor.'

Fifteen minutes later she left with yet another prescription for antibiotics and pain medicine, and with the deeply disturbing feeling that she was a pathetic mother. If she could have dropped dead right there in front of the surgery with Alexander in her arms, she would willingly have done so. Yet, she knew she was not a bad mother. There was something wrong with Alexander that couldn't be detected with a stethoscope or an X-ray.

Or perhaps Old Doctor was right? Perhaps Alexander *was* rocking to ease his pain?

No.

Her maternal instincts would never lie to her. Old Doctor could say what he liked, *she* knew there was something wrong. Because Alexander was her own flesh and blood.

For most of the nine years she saw a lot of blood. Fresh red blood. Dry brown blood. Alexander's blood. On the walls, the furniture, his hands. On the old hairdryer that he pulled behind him like a pet dog. On everything.

Self-mutilation.

'How could anyone find pleasure in hurting himself?' she asked Gunter on a Sunday when he sat, his back to her, cleaning the soles of Alexander's feet. 'It's totally against human nature.'

The hand holding the knife froze. 'How does he do it, Ingrid, and who says he gets pleasure from it?'

'If you watched him, you'd *have* to believe that he gets pleasure from it. His eyes shine and he flaps his hands faster than ever. It's as if a diabolical energy is radiating from him.'

The words flowed from her mouth. The relief of speaking out loud to *someone*. The years of bottled-up emotions becoming sounds.

'He does it with anything and everything he can get hold of. Cupboard doors, door frames, the cheese grater, the can opener. Stones, bottle tops. You should have seen what his tongue looked like after he cut it with the kitchen scissors last week. His mouth and chest and the front of his pants were covered in blood. And he was extremely excited about it.'

Gunter took the other foot. 'You mustn't leave things lying around . . .'

'I *do* watch him, but he's quick and sly. Besides, cupboard doors and door frames don't lie around. It doesn't matter *where* we hide the grater or the can opener, he goes through everything and he knows exactly which key fits where. And sometimes he spends hours licking metal objects.'

Suddenly, she remembered the day she told Mirna about Alexander's licking habit. And she recalled how Mirna had frowned in disgust. She did not even say thank you for the strawberries she'd brought her. Would not invite her further than the front door of her palace. Offered her a chair on the stoep. She was probably scared that Alexander would break things.

She didn't want to burden Gunter with her sorrow. But something in her felt safe, because she knew he wouldn't frown at her with disgust on his face.

'For all I know, he swallows the nails and screws.'

Gunter dipped his finger in the milk ointment and rubbed it in circles on Alexander's chapped heels. 'He could have an iron deficiency, that's why he sucks his own blood. Ask the doctor to prescribe an iron supplement.'

She wanted to laugh hysterically. 'And then *you'll* try and get it down his throat?'

'Get something in liquid form and mix it into his cooldrink.'

'He doesn't drink cooldrink. Never ever.'

'Put it in his food, or let the doctor inject him regularly.'

'Do you *know* how acute his senses of smell and taste are, Gunter? I'd have to force his jaws apart to get something in against his will. And if you want to see him go berserk, just bring an injection needle near him. Tell me, Gunter, what do *you* think goes on inside Alexander's head?'

He continued to rub. Wiped the blade of his pocket knife. Put more milk ointment on his finger. 'Honestly, Ingrid, I don't know. Why don't you ask a psychologist?'

Soundlessly, she slid off the kraal wall. She walked up to him, where he was kneeling next to Alexander. Until she was close enough to touch his back; to see each dark hair on his forearm; the cuticles of his thumb nails; the movement of his back muscles under his khaki shirt. When she put her hands on his back, he did not even look up. Just stopped rubbing Alexander's foot. Sat dead still. As if he had heard her feet on the straw long before she got to him.

'Gunter?'

Slowly, he put Alexander's foot down on the straw. 'What is wrong, Ingrid?'

'It's, it's . . .'

She sank down on her knees next to him. Pressed her forearms and face against his back. And cried. About everything. Everything that was, everything that had ever been. Everything still to come. About that which she understood, and that which only God understood. But what made her cry most of all was when Gunter put his hand over his shoulder and folded his fingers over her arm. Soothed her shoulder, her forearm. Until her crying subsided and the cool afternoon breeze swept over them. When she lifted her head from the wet patch on his khaki shirt, he loosened his fingers from her arm, picked up the sleeping child and carried him to the car without saddling Lucy.

Gunter's back. His fingers on her shoulder. That was how she would always remember that Sunday afternoon.

Merciful Saviour, she prayed that night while she sat cross-legged and half-asleep on the floor, watching Alexander stand on a dining room chair with the chisel. Chopping and chopping at the plaster until he reached raw brick. Please, help me not to destroy Gunter with the fire burning within me. Because then my hell on earth would become his too.

What if he also jumped from a bridge and left her alone with Alexander?

Later, she would ask many questions about self-mutilation. About hand flapping and sun watching and blood sucking. And many other things. She asked Old Doctor, the specialists at the children's hospital; her own clinical psychologist. And God.

Fruitless.

Nobody could give her answers.

14

WHEN THE TRUCK COMES to a screeching halt under the pepper tree at the church, everyone rushes towards the railings to climb off. She wipes the dampness from the corners of her eyes. They could all have died today had God not been watching over them. Glory to Him. She would rather not think about what could have happened if He had not put His hands over those of that damned wine-fly of a driver. All He must do now, is send the angels to guide them back to town tomorrow. And listen to her prayers about Evert. She must pray for Evert first, while her pleas are still strong. Because Evert, like this no-good drunken truck driver, is walking along a path to hell.

'Can I help Aunt Miriam?' asks the youngster who had earlier asked her for matches. 'I'll carry Aunt Miriam's suitcase, if you like.'

She puts out her hand hesitantly. 'Thank you. For the suitcase, and because you helped to lead the singing. The Lord will remember you for that.' Then she walks over to where the unconcerned driver stands lighting a cigarette. Just looking at his bloodshot eyes makes the anger well up in her. 'Have you gone stone mad?'

He shrugs his shoulders contemptuously. 'What does Aunt Miriam mean?'

'You know damn well what I mean. Speeding through the kloof like a maniac when you're drunk as a skunk, without thinking of the people's lives you hold in your irresponsible hands!'

'Me? Drunk? Since when?' He blows the smoke into her face.

'Yes, you! I'm telling you today: I'm not putting my foot back on this truck tomorrow, not with you behind the steering wheel . . .'

'Don't talk crap to me, Aunt Miriam.' It's clear that the last bottle of wine has gone right to his head. 'I don't let anyone make accusations against me! Just because Aunt Miriam works with a crazy child all day, you shouldn't think that I'm also crazy!'

The angel of goodness grabs her hand to prevent her from picking up a stone and bashing it against his head.

When she turns around and walks to where the youngster is waiting with her suitcase, she remembers that she didn't tell Miss Ingrid that she used up the medicine for Lexi's fits on Thursday. Never mind, Miss Ingrid will notice. And even if she doesn't, there's always an extra supply in her handbag.

'Yes, you can go ahead and put my suitcase down,' and she gestures for him to go along to Jeremiah's people. She wants to walk at her own pace. To think. She doesn't want anyone talking around her ears. 'I'll come along slowly.'

15

THE LAST THING SHE recalls is a street vendor trying to sell the man something through the car window at a traffic light. Then she dozes off. She dreams Dawid is holding her by her hair and swinging her like a pendulum over the side of the bridge.

Wider, wider. And the wider the pendulum swings, the louder Dawid screams at her to shut the child's mouth. And if she doesn't listen, he will let her fall.

I will try, Dawid! I will try!

I'm finished! he screams. I'm way beyond crazy!

Please, Dawid, please . . .

For five years you've been saying that you'll try!

I'll try harder, Dawid. I swear to God I will!

His insane laugh echoes through the kloof. Then he opens his fingers. She tumbles with outstretched arms into the depths, the wind pulling at her cheeks. A wingless bird. Far above her she hears Dawid laughing like a madman.

The stony river-bed does not get any closer.

She falls and falls.

And Dawid laughs and laughs.

She wakes when the woman slams the car door. Where are they? What day is it? When she moves, the handcuffs cut into her flesh.

The woman opens the back door and an ice cold wind blows against her sleepy body.

'Get out, Mrs Dorfling, we're at the charge office.'

She remains motionless. Each step from here on will be a step closer to hell. Why does she dream so often that Dawid is throwing her from a bridge? After all, Alexander was his child, too. But she shouldn't try to analyse it. Not now.

'Get out, Mrs Dorfling.'

She sits still.

Suddenly, the man is next to her. His fingers close over her upper arm and he forces her out of the car. 'Don't dawdle, Mrs Dorfling, it won't get you anywhere. If we say get out,' and his stale breath is in her face, 'then you get out.'

Her legs tremble. The cough rattles in her chest. 'I want to go home, please.'

'Walk,' and he sends her around the car.

No, he is not going to force her across this border. For nine long years she was a problem case to doctors and psychologists. Dawid's punchbag. The church's lost sheep. A social misfit. She is *not* a murderer or a bandit.

Her heart pounds in her throat, her head throbs. Around her the darkness melts into thousands of shimmering stipples of light that flash through her tired brain. She must get hold of a lawyer before she sets foot in here.

'May I please use your mobile phone to call a lawyer?'

'Walk. You can make a call from the official telephone inside.'

God will help her to walk.

She walks.

A bunch of drunkards are huddled together in the narrow passage at the entrance to the charge office. The floor is strewn with cigarette butts. The stench of urine emerges from the public toilets. A loud-mouthed prostitute makes her way from one drunkard to another shaking her finger in their faces; inciting them to stand up for their rights.

'If there are no buttons on your pants, you *don't* take your belts off! You are not clowns who have to walk around with your pants hanging around your ankles.'

'Stand still!' a policewoman commands, rubber baton in her hand. 'Stand in a row against the wall, and keep quiet!'

The prostitute speaks out again. 'Standing naked in front of a woman is your human right! Naked in front of the police is a disgrace you don't have to put up with!'

The policewoman grabs the prostitute's arm and twists it behind her back. 'Stand against the wall!'

'Go crap on your auntie's head! Don't try to violate my rights!'

The baton strikes the prostitute on the shoulder. Suddenly, everyone scurries for a place against the wall.

She is anxious in the midst of the crowd scuttling around her, doesn't know whether to give way. She worms her way to one side so that no one is touching her.

'You too,' and the policewoman points straight at her.

Bewildered, she presses her back against the cold wall. A barefoot drunk is standing next to her, his jersey full of pulled threads and holes. Raw flesh is visible in a cut across his eyebrow. He bends down to pull his pants up, mumbles something about a belt and human rights and being naked in front of the law.

'What are you in for?' He leans towards her and she smells his acid breath.

She stares at him. In? What does he mean? Before she has time to think, the woman takes her by her sleeve and directs her to where the man is sitting with a police constable who is writing in a big book.

'Come, sign,' and the woman shoves a sticky pen in her hand.

'Sign? What for?'

'For your possessions which will be placed in safe keeping, and to testify that you have no complaints or injuries, and that you understand your rights.'

'What rights?'

'The rights I read you this afternoon when you were taken into custody.'

This afternoon. So long ago.

She can't remember that they read her her rights.

She can vaguely remember the woman reading something. Legal-sounding words, of which she took in very little. Nothing could have shocked her more than when the woman told her to hold out her hands to be handcuffed.

Handcuffed? In her own home? She hid her hands behind her back and retreated to the furthest corner of the kitchen. 'You have no reason to do this.'

The woman came closer with the open cuffs, the man covering her. 'Don't make matters worse.' Cold, businesslike. 'Resisting arrest will compel us to use force. Please hold out your hands, Mrs Dorfling.'

Over her dead body.

She pressed herself further into the corner. The man moved behind the woman and scratched in the rubbish bin, unmoved by her fear. He slammed the lid down, and held up an empty pill container.

'Who took these pills?'

'I did.'

'How many?'

'Two.'

'What for?'

'Because I had a headache.'

The two of them had caught her off guard at a time when she was weak. A snail without a shell. She didn't register anything clearly; only remembered the stillness of Alexander's sharp blue eyes, the wet patch where she had placed him on the bed.

The whole morning had buzzed with strangers in and around the house. First the local police. Then the ambulance staff. Grey blanket over the little body on the stainless steel trolley. They did not even grant her one final moment to be alone with him. Just to smooth his fringe and to straighten his twisted shirt. A tearless sadness throbbed in her chest; she didn't want them to take him away. All she wanted to do was to take the past nine years and change them. For Dawid. For Teresa and Zettie. For Alexander. But all she could do was stand dumbly, watching the ambulance man pushing nine years of sorrow out the door on a trolley.

'Where are you taking him?' she asked.

'To the hospital, for a death certificate. And from there to the police mortuary for the autopsy.' He did not even look up; just pushed the trolley out the front door.

'Autopsy? Why?' They must not mutilate him. 'You know he drowned . . .'

He lifted the trolley over the threshold. 'With any unnatural death there has to be an autopsy, Madam.'

After they left, the inspectors from the detective branch arrived.

'The police have been here already,' she said. 'The ambulance left long ago.'

The man spoke politely. Not like the Colonel who arrived later that afternoon. 'Because your child died of unnatural causes, Madam, we have to examine the scene. Just routine. We won't be long.'

They investigated every window pane and doorknob; checked every key in the house. Made notes of everything lying on the floor. Took photos from every conceivable angle. Rummaged through the medicine cabinet and the fridge, in Alexander's toy box. Sniffed at the half-eaten jar of cheese spread. Pressed the redial button on the phone and got through to the ambulance. Asked her whose number was written on the notebook next to the telephone. She told them it was a farmer she had called about something. Asked if she was having repairs done on the inside walls. No? Why had the plaster been chipped off? She told the detective about the chisel, but he looked at her in total disbelief and took a photo of the chisel. He asked what had happened to the pelmet, why was it lying on the floor?

'Alexander climbed up the curtains when the train passed, and pulled the pelmet off the wall.'

He made notes.

'And all these feathers?'

She told them about the pillow that Alexander had cut open with the scissors. She said nothing of all the other pillows he'd cut up before. How he charged through the house, throwing the feathers up in the air and dancing while they rained down on him. Then, captivated for hours, he would struggle to remove the down from his sticky fingers. She would spare herself the useless explanations; he wouldn't understand about a child who ran through the house with feathered fingers, looking like an upside down bantam chick. Who ran and ran, without ever becoming tired.

They stayed a long time, inspecting every inch of the house. When they left she was grateful to be alone for the first time since the morning. A snail without a shell who had at last found a little protection. She thought for a while. Made tea. Toast. But she couldn't eat anything. She went to Alexander's room and sat on the edge of the cold bed.

She searched for tears. Searched for *something*.

But she found nothing.

She roamed through the disorderly house and couldn't imagine where to start tidying up, or even if she had the energy to try. Maybe she should call Aunt Betty. Or phone Mirna or Lida or Hannah and tell them Alexander was dead. Ask if they would please come and help her.

Help with what?

She took the cold tea to the kitchen table and sat down. Her throat was dry. She didn't want to think about hard reality, would rather wipe it out of her mind. She rinsed the cup and turned it over on the drying rack. Started sorting out the chaos in the house.

Don't think, keep moving. A damp cloth to collect the scattered feathers. Fold the bundle of curtains. Find a broom for the pieces of plaster. A towel to soak up the water on the carpet. She picked up a bundle of wet toilet paper. Wiped the streaks of cheese spread off the television screen. Hung the wet bedding on which she had placed his body this morning on the washing line. Put away the Lego pieces. Gathered the shredded magazines.

She stepped over things blindly. Tried to cut herself off from everything. Put the kettle on for coffee, but realised that she had used the last bit of milk in her tea. Switched it off again. Lifted the lid of the piano and looked at the F-sharp key, dented and played to death. Picked up the chisel and pressed its cold metal against her cheek.

She wished the tears would come. But they didn't. She listened to the deafening silence in the house and all she could hear was the ticking of the wall clock. She didn't know what to do with her heartache. It was a nameless heartache. Something was gone. And although she might not have wanted that something, she also did not want it to be gone.

She must go to the township to tell Miriam before she heard from someone else. Because Alexander was her heart's child. *Be careful at the stove, Lexi. Come, let's go buy bananas, Lexi. Listen, Lexi, there comes the ice cream cart.* Singing while she hung up the washing and he played with the dry leaves in the wind, crushing them between his fingers and throwing the bits up into the air. Then giggling as they rained down on his head. Singing the first verse again. *Gentle Jesus, meek and mild, look upon this little child . . . It's too cold outside here, Lexi, fetch your puzzles, let's build.*

No, Miriam won't be at home. She said she was going to celebrate *Nagmaal* with her in-laws in the kloof.

She must phone Teresa and Zettie. It's Saturday, will they be at the college hostel? Maybe it would be better to phone the college social worker and ask him to tell them. She might burst into tears when she heard their voices. But she didn't have a clue how to get hold of the college social worker. Teresa and Zettie wouldn't get hysterical. Alexander wasn't a brother they could love; quite the contrary. Each time they wanted to pick him up or feed or bath him, he fought them. Hit them, scratched them, bit them, kicked them.

Blood of their blood, yes, but that was where it ended. No devotion. They had had to put up with too much from him. He broke their toys and, later, their girl-things and make-up. Scribbled on their bedroom walls. Tore pages from their school books. Chipped away at the walls at night so that they could not sleep. Tapped on the F-sharp key while they were studying for exams. Hammered on their closed bedroom doors; kicked and banged when they refused to open them.

Before Alexander was born they had many friends. Birthday parties with balloons and colourful birthday cakes. Friends sleeping over. They played house under the overhanging branches of the puzzle bush in the back garden. Sneaked her make-up from her vanity case and pretended to be ladies. Staged the Seven Dwarfs on the stoep. But the flow of playmates dried up like mist in the morning sun, and there were no boyfriends when they were in their teens. Because their house was a disgrace. Chipped plaster. Pumpkin splashes on the walls. Mashed banana thrown at the ceiling. It was a madhouse filled with screaming. And they had no money to buy CDs and trendy clothes like their friends.

They were stigmatised, like lepers. Just like Dawid and her.

And as time went by, they grew apart from her too. They spoke to Miriam about matters which they should have come to her about. They believed they were loved less than Alexander. Why does Alexander always come first, Mom? Why is he allowed to ruin the house, but at the same time you freak out when my drawers are untidy? I failed my geography test, Mom. I couldn't study properly, because Alexander . . . One day Zettie had held out her needlework basket in despair, stamping her feet in sheer frustration. Look, Mom, Alexander has cut my cushion cover to shreds! I've been working on it since the second term, and the needlework teacher is going to bite my head off. Or: These torn pages were my assignment on birds, Mom. Do you know how much time I spent in the library researching this? Then there was a project on cotton growing that was plastered with pumpkin.

'Zettie, you know you shouldn't leave your things lying around.'

'But I did *not*, Mom, they were on my desk!'

'I'll help you make a new cushion cover before Friday, I promise.'

Tears streaming down her cheeks, Zettie unexpectedly came up to her and put her arms around her tightly. 'On your word of honour . . .?'

'Yes.'

She worked throughout the night. When Friday came, the cushion cover was done. But the teacher phoned to say it was obviously not Zettie's work, and that it was not permitted for mothers to do their daughters' needlework. Zettie had to start from scratch. All on her own.

After Dawid died, the distance between her and her daughters increased. They were fourteen and sixteen then. And no matter what Dawid had been, he was theirs. A small patch of shade in which they could shelter. At least he wasn't a submissive slave to Alexander's wilfulness. He supported them at netball matches. Attended the prize-giving ceremony just to see them receive certificates for a hundred per cent annual school attendance.

Dear God, what a gulf Dawid's death had created between them. They never hugged her, or told her about their schooldays. Never offered to make her a cup of tea. Remained behind the closed doors of their rooms all evening. What should have been normal conversation about hairstyles or lingerie or study plans, turned into arguments and accusations.

'I wish I was dead! Or that Alexander was dead!'

'Goodness, Zettie, how can you say such a terrible thing?'

'Because it's the truth, Mom! It's his fault Dad died! Because if he hadn't committed suicide, he would have drunk himself to death. Why can't you put Alexander in an institution so that we can have peace in this house?'

'You *know* there are no suitable institutions in this country. Alexander cannot be blamed for *every* . . .'

'We're in the year 2000, Mom! Are there really no institutions, or are you just ignoring the possibility? And if they *did* exist, would you put him there?'

'I can assure you, Zettie, there are no institutions for autists in this country. And Alexander cannot help being autistic. If *I* don't protect him and stand up for him . . .'

'Well, don't ever expect me to! You sacrifice everything for him, and Teresa and I mean nothing to you! Nothing, Mom, *nothing*!'

'That's not true, Zettie. It's just that . . .'

'I'm not going to listen to the same old story again, Mom!'

Her heart was torn. What could she do? God, what? Sometimes she yearned for them to be grown up so they could escape and create their own peaceful homes far away from Alexander.

That night she took the Bible from the bottom drawer of Dawid's desk. She sat with it on her knees on the dining room floor while Alexander ran through the house flicking the light-switches on and off. She searched for the story of Solomon who had told the two women to divide the child in two. She couldn't find it. And she had no idea how to divide herself so that she could give everyone she loved a fair share.

It was late when she fell asleep on the dining room carpet. She woke at sunrise. Alexander was on his knees next to her, rocking, his cheek pressed against the carpet. He rocked and rocked, staring unblinkingly at the framed picture of Dawid, while his spittle gathered in a tiny pool at the corner of his mouth.

She got up slowly and went to the kitchen to boil the last four eggs to make sandwiches for Teresa and Zettie's lunch boxes.

There had not been many times after Dawid's death when she could offer them anything of value. But at least she had been able to show them the bank's approval of their study loans in black and white. God alone knew how she would repay the loans. Her only consolation was that she was well used to struggling.

It was her duty to phone to tell them what had happened.

'Mom?' There was a tense silence. Teresa sounded out of breath. Perhaps she had run to the phone. 'Could you start again, Mom? I don't think I'm understanding you clearly.'

She started again, incoherently rattling off the details. Said that no arrangements had been made yet, her mind was still too chaotic.

'I'll tell Zettie, Mom. She went to the city library, but she should be back any moment. Are you all right, Mom? Sure? I'll phone you back in a little while.'

She waited. Made some bitter black tea. Searched in her handbag for the car keys. Took two headache tablets. Threw the empty container into the dustbin. Switched on the familiar Baroque music; switched it off again. She never wanted to hear Vivaldi's *Four Seasons* again. Never. Gunter told her to play Baroque music to Alexander. She must phone Gunter. No, she'd wait until her headache was better. Perhaps she should sleep for a while, and go to the farm in the afternoon.

The house was silent. She walked through the pool of water on the bathroom floor to wash her hands and face. Stared mindlessly at the framed photograph of Dawid and wondered if he knew. What if there really was a great beyond where people could recognise one another? Would Dawid get the fright of his life when Alexander walked in? Or would Dawid be in a different eternity? Would God allow Alexander to play with feathers and stones and leaves for hours on end? Or give him an indestructible chisel to ruin heaven? Would there be a wild olive tree, and a sweet voice to sing *Gentle Jesus meek and mild*?

'Do you believe in heaven and hell?' she asked Gunter one Sunday afternoon while he was removing a spike-thorn from the thick flesh of Alexander's heel.

He did not answer. Sometimes, especially in the beginning, he did that. As if he hadn't heard her. The next Sunday she would ask the same question again. And the next Sunday. Until eventually he answered.

On the fourth Sunday that she asked the question, he answered. 'If you mean, is hell a physical place of fire, with a demon wielding a pitchfork, and heaven a place with streets of gold and angels playing harps, then, no, Ingrid, I don't believe in it.'

'Why not?'

'It's illogical. Heaven and hell are here,' and he pointed to his head. 'God is not a remote God guarding an unknown territory, Ingrid. God lives inside you and me, and all men on earth.'

'According to the dominee . . .'

He did not give her the chance to complete her sentence. 'Then you must rather ask the dominee. He'll know the answers. Some dominees pretend to know God better than He knows Himself.'

He got up and fetched the equipment to saddle Lucy. His determined strides told her that he was upset.

'Why are you angry, Gunter?'

'Because I allow you to lure me into discussions like these.'

She walked around the horse to face him, tangled her fingers in the horse's mane. 'I don't mean to lure you into anything, Gunter. I'm searching, and I trust your opinion. That's all.'

He lifted Alexander on to Lucy and gave the horse a light flick on the buttocks. 'I am also searching, Ingrid,' he said after they had sat down on the straw bales. 'And I don't want to confuse or mislead you.'

When the breeze came up and the late afternoon carried the scent of cow's milk and camphor bush, she and Alexander went home.

'We're leaving this afternoon, Mom,' Teresa said when she phoned back. 'Zettie has a netball match and must find a replacement. As soon as that's done, we'll leave. If the car doesn't give trouble we should be home shortly after twelve o'clock tonight. You must go to bed, Mom, just leave the house key on the window sill. And don't worry about money, Mom. Zettie has enough on her bank card for petrol.'

'Teresa, if you and Zettie don't feel like . . . I mean . . . I just thought I should let you know.'

'We both want to come, Mom, honestly. After all, Alexander was . . . he was . . .' Her voice broke. 'I promise you, Mom, we *want* to come.'

She said goodbye and stood motionless at the telephone. She felt disorientated. Suddenly she was overcome by an urge to go to Aunt Betty. To put her head on Aunt Betty's shoulder; feel the warmth of another human being's hands. But her courage failed her because the bond of understanding between her and Aunt Betty had been severed a long time ago. The only way she knew Aunt Betty was aware of her existence, was when she threw back the green apricots that Alexander had picked and thrown over the fence. Or when she sent an account for the repair of the windows that Alexander had broken.

Perhaps she should phone the bank manager and ask for a few days' leave. To bury her child. The impossible child who had elicited so many reprimands from him. Because the counter did not balance; because she was asleep on her feet when she was supposed to be concentrating.

He drowned in the bath, this morning.

Maybe he'd ask her where she's going to get the money for the funeral, because he knew her account was overdrawn beyond the permitted limit.

No, she wouldn't phone the bank manager.

She wouldn't phone anybody. Nor would she tidy up the house. Or think. Or go next door to Aunt Betty. She wouldn't send a message to Miriam. She would close the curtains and put an extra blanket on the bed and try to warm her frozen body. She would sleep. When she woke up and regained her senses she would think about the funeral.

She scratched in the medicine cabinet to see if there were any of the sleeping pills that Old Doctor had prescribed for her after Dawid's death. There were. She swallowed one. Went to the toilet. Closed the curtains. Pulled the blanket up over her shoulders. The flannelette pillow case was soft against her cheek. Her tired body sank into the mattress. Slowly, softly she drifted off. To a place where reality didn't exist.

She was fast asleep when a persistent knocking on the front door woke her. Her head was throbbing and she felt confused. Was it day or night? She stumbled out of bed and slipped on her tracksuit pants.

It was the man and the woman. He held out his police identity card. 'Colonel Herselman, Murder and Robbery Squad. May we please come in?'

Not for a moment had she imagined they would come back to question her again. Everything she could possibly say had been said. Maybe, she thought dully, they had come to take more photographs or to assist with arrangements. Perhaps even offer emotional support. What if they asked her to go to the mortuary to identify the body? Like Dawid?

No. *No*.

She was reluctant to let them in, because the sleeping pill had blunted her senses; she couldn't think straight. She stood in the doorway, shivering with cold. 'Is there anything I can help you with?'

'Can we come inside? We are investigating a . . .'

'I am sorry but it is not convenient right now.' Her legs and arms were covered in goosebumps; her teeth chattered. 'Tomorrow morning would be better. I need to sleep right now.' She stepped forward to close the door.

'Mrs Dorfling,' and the man put his foot on the threshold, 'I'm afraid this cannot wait until tomorrow morning. We need to question you in connection with the death of . . .'

'Tomorrow morning at ten o'clock would be fine,' she said and started closing the door.

She was shocked when the man quickly moved his shiny sharp-pointed brown shoe over the threshold and forced the door open. Pushed her aside and stepped in as if he owned the house. His body language expressed a self-righteousness that struck her like an iron fist.

'The detectives questioned me this morning.'

'We need to question you again, Mrs Dorfling.'

Coffee. She needed coffee. The world was spinning and swirling around her. 'There's no milk, but can I make you some coffee?'

He put his mobile phone, a docket and a bunch of keys down on the table. With his back to her, he spoke. 'No, thank you. This is not a social visit, Mrs Dorfling, it's an official interrogation.'

What more could they want to know? Alexander was dead and there was nothing she could do to change it. Nor could they.

'My son drowned in the bath this morning, and I don't feel capable of talking to anyone right now. Emotionally, I am confused and . . .'

'Confused? You seem half asleep to me.'

A dark threat lurked in his voice. What was he implying?

'I've already told you: they questioned me this morning. They searched the house and took photos of . . .' A coughing fit sent a sharp pain through her shoulders. 'I'm exhausted and sick with bronchitis, and I didn't have any sleep last night . . .'

Abruptly, he interrupted; said something about her right to remain silent and to consult a lawyer; that anything she said could be used against her in a court of law.

Dumbstruck, she stared at him. What was the real reason behind their visit? 'I have done nothing I need to keep silent about, or about which I need to consult a lawyer. Besides, I don't have the money for a lawyer.'

'You have a right to legal assistance; the state will provide a lawyer.'

She couldn't believe what was happening. Were they going to charge her with negligence because she fell asleep? If she explained how little sleep she had had over the last few days, surely they would be understanding? 'No, thank you, it's not necessary.'

Bluntly, he told the woman to make a note of her refusal. 'The choice is yours, Mrs Dorfling. But don't say afterwards that you haven't been properly informed. Captain, read her rights to her and get her to sign.'

God knows, he was merciless. Delved and dug into her private life. She clenched her teeth trying not to collapse from exhaustion. His persistent and deliberate questions indicated that he knew what autism was. And with every question he asked she realised that they definitely did not regard Alexander's death as an accident. The man said something about a crime against a child receiving priority; about evidence from the post-mortem that contradicted what she had told them.

Something was horribly wrong. Her stomach knotted. What did they actually want from her?

At what time did you go to bed last night? I didn't. I was up all night, because Alexander was up all night. He was difficult to handle when it rained.

What do you mean by difficult to handle? He behaved like a trapped animal. It was the sound of the rain on the roof that made him like that.

Isn't it abnormal for a boy of nine to be scared of the rain on the roof? Yes, but it was normal for Alexander because he was autistic. I have said that in my statement.

What degree of autism? Classical autist.

Any obsessions? Briefly, please. He was fanatical about tearing paper; he played with feathers, chiselled the plaster off the walls, always went through doorways backwards, hated the sound of plastic bags. Do you want to know about all of them, because there are many more?

How did you communicate with him if he couldn't talk? We did not communicate. He ignored me. The only time he took any notice of me was when he pulled me by my clothes or by the hand to where he wanted me to go.

Did he react to sign language? No.

When was he diagnosed? He was three and a half.

Who made the diagnosis? A medical team at the Children's Hospital in Cape Town.

Did you employ any specific approach or teaching method? I tried but it simply didn't work.

Why not? I don't know. He couldn't be taught, that's all. After my husband died I struggled to keep body and soul together. I couldn't carry on spending money and time on fruitless efforts. In the statement I made this morning, you'll have seen that I have two older daughters to think of as well. And I have a fulltime job.

Who took care of the child during the day while you were at work? Miriam.

For how long has she been working for you? About thirteen years.

Her full name and residential address, please. Miriam Slangveld, 23 North Extension.

What type of medication was your child using? There were many kinds. The bottles are in the medicine cabinet. But he stopped using most of them a long time ago.

Do you believe that there is a connection between your child's autism and your husband's death? It's hard to say, but after Alexander was born my husband's whole personality changed – for the worse.

Who has keys to the house? Only me. There is a spare set which Miriam occasionally uses. It's hanging on the key-rack, I showed it to the police this morning.

Who have you spoken to since this morning? Only to the police and to my elder daughter.

Not to the dominee or your doctor or a friend or colleague? No.

Your child has died tragically, Mrs Dorfling. Don't you need emotional support, or treatment for shock? No, I'm used to coping by myself.

He kept on and on. *Why, Mrs Dorfling? Where, Mrs Dorfling? When? Are you absolutely sure? Who else? What do you mean? What was the time? And after that?*

She was drowsy from the effects of the sleeping pill and felt cornered because she didn't understand where his questions were leading. An invisible hand tightened the knot in her stomach. Tighter, tighter. Something told her that there was more involved than just negligence. Somewhere something was wrong. Her instincts warned her not to let naivety or ignorance lead her into a trap.

'You must please excuse me now,' she tried again to escape from the man's relentless questions. 'I have phone calls to make, and before it's dark I must go to the township to see if Miriam is at home to tell . . .'

He lifted his hands as if to block her words. 'No, Mrs Dorfling, you are not going anywhere. Definitely not to Miriam.'

'Why not? Miriam has worked in this house for thirteen years and she was like a foster mother to Alexander.'

'Exactly, Mrs Dorfling. Miriam is a key witness in this investigation. What do you have to tell Miriam so urgently?'

Key witness. Investigation. Then her fears were not groundless after all: they were looking for a suspect.

'Miriam is part of this household. You have no right to forbid me to talk to her.'

'I do, Mrs Dorfling, and I will exercise that right. Any contact you try to make with Miriam will be seen as interfering with a witness.'

She was annoyed by his arrogance. She wasn't going to allow them to restrict her movements. If they wanted to see ghosts in what had been a tragic accident, then let them. 'I must go now. You can come back in the morning if you have more questions.'

She picked up the car keys where they were lying next to the bread bin. Turned her back on them and started walking away. She'd gone barely two yards, when he blocked her way. From the corner of her eye she noticed the woman moving towards her, soundlessly, like a cat.

'Mrs Dorfling, you are hampering our investigation and undermining the law. It's a criminal offence . . .'

'I'm undermining nothing! It's *you* who barged in here, showing no respect for my privacy and grief!'

'Mrs Dorfling ...' In a low voice.

She pushed the key ring on to her forefinger. 'I'm leaving now. I'll be available in the morning.' Then she tried to get past him.

As quick as a striking snake he grabbed her arm, twisted it downwards so that a sharp pain shot through her shoulder.

'Handcuff her, Captain.'

She heard the metal clink of the handcuffs and wrenched herself free. She scrambled towards the kitchen, trying to get away from them. She managed to dodge the man and ran to the bedroom. They followed with the handcuffs. Instinctively, she tried to ward them off. Her hand struck the man's upper arm. His flesh was hard as rock. In a flash he had forced her to her knees. Then she heard the sickening click of the handcuffs.

Merciful God, how could she be caught in this nightmare?

Time slipped away into a bottomless black hole.

He bombarded her with the same questions, over and over again. Her brain felt frozen. The sleeping pill, and an overwhelming sense of fatigue, dragged her down, down, down. Her tongue refused to form words while she was handcuffed like a criminal. Because she was not a criminal. She realised that resisting had been a mistake. But she simply couldn't surrender passively.

Was the child's life insured? Yes, Dawid took out an insurance policy for Alexander's education shortly after his birth.

Where is the documentation? I think it's in the study.

Are you currently having financial problems, Mrs Dorfling? My finances have nothing to do with Alexander's death.

How was the relationship between you and your colleagues? Normal.

Are you happy in your work? Under the circumstances, yes.

What do you mean by under the circumstances? My life is in chaos. I get hardly any sleep at night and during the day I work under pressure.

Are there any known cases of mental abnormalities in your or your husband's families? Not as far as I know.

Did you keep a record of your child's medical history? Mostly. The file should also be in the study.

I'm asking you for the last time, Mrs Dorfling: are you having financial problems? It has nothing to do with the issue.

He got up. 'You refuse to cooperate, Mrs Dorfling. You leave us no choice.'

He turned to the woman. 'See that she packs the essential stuff, Captain,' and with a nod he gestured to the woman to escort her to the bedroom. 'We're taking her to the Murder and Robbery offices for questioning. I can't waste time struggling with her here all night.'

16

SHE IS GRATEFUL THAT her in-laws live only a short walk from the church, in the patch of bluegum trees. On the truck her legs had felt like jelly from trying to keep her footing. From fear too. They would never manage a long walk. And on top of her arthritic legs was a tired body. The heavenly Father knows, she had had a rough week with Lexi. It's always like that when the air is heavy with rain.

On Monday he was in a blood sucking mood. She did everything in her power to prevent him from scratching himself or sanding down his skin with a stone. On Tuesday he walked down the passage with his forehead pressed against the wall until the blood ran. And then suddenly, when she thought he was still walking in the passage, he was gone. Must have slipped out the door right in front of her eyes.

Every available person in town helped search for him for the rest of the morning. It was just like Lexi to disappear like that. If she had used her common sense, she would have found him before lunchtime. Because there was a funeral at the white church and experience should've told her that he had heard the bells and taken the road to the church. It was after three o'clock when she found him curled up on the coir mat at the side entrance to the white church, fast asleep, his legs blue from the cold. When she woke him up his eyes were motionless, as if he had already ascended to the angels. He took no notice of her, so that she had to *abba* him on her back and carry him home. He wouldn't hold on around her neck and kept tipping backwards. The only solution was for her to walk bending forwards, her arms cramping from clinging on to his legs. Luckily, the butcher's delivery boy came by on his bicycle and he let her put Lexi in the basket for the rest of the way home.

On Wednesday he sat in front of the piano all day long, pressing the one black note over and over. Every now and then he jumped up and stormed through the house flicking the light-switches. To make matters worse, he also broke two plates that day.

On Thursday morning he had a bad fit, and in the afternoon the rain started sifting down. And rainy weather always brought out the worst in Lexi.

For a while now she has wanted to talk to Miss Ingrid about her legs that are slowly but surely giving in. She has shooting pains in her knees and groin, as if something is out of joint. And the pains move up into her buttocks and coccyx so that she finds it hard to bend. But she cannot scrape the courage together to talk to Miss Ingrid, because she doesn't want to load yet another burden on to Miss Ingrid's shoulders. Miss Ingrid has enough worries as it is.

'See how badly your feet are swollen,' Jeremiah badgered her the previous week while she was soaking her feet in a bowl of wild dagga water. 'Katrien has a good job, Miriam, she can look after us in our old age. It's about time you retire.'

She didn't want Jeremiah to know that she'd been thinking about that for a long time. Instead, she flew at him and told him it was foolish even to think Katrien could take care of everybody's mouths and stomach and backsides on her hairdresser's salary.

'I'm still strong, Jeremiah. I'm not like you who are satisfied spending your days sitting in the sun against the wall and letting the flies walk over your face. Struggling up now and then to shoo the chickens or collect the eggs isn't work.'

'Can't Miss Ingrid fetch you in the morning and bring you home in the afternoon? At least your legs would be spared the walk.'

'Walking keeps me strong, Jeremiah. It's sitting in the sun on your backside all day that makes you act like a scabby donkey. You can't even pick up a bag of chicken food without it sounding as if death is descending upon you.'

'Oh, *Jissus*, Miriam, I'm not talking about chicken food!'

She decided that silence was golden.

When the scent of bluegum tree resin comes drifting towards her on the afternoon breeze, she stops under the shade of a thorn tree to rest for a while. No, she could never upset Miss Ingrid with this thing about her sore legs. Who else would be patient with Lexi? Who would know all his hiding places? And Lexi wouldn't allow anyone else to build puzzles with him in his tablecloth house. Who would leave the ironing and polishing for later when the ice cream cart passed by? Or stand patiently at the ice cream cart for half an hour so that Lexi could ring the cart's bell?

Lexi might think she doesn't love him any more. Everybody in town thinks that Lexi's head is useless. But *she* knows he can understand every word. Just the other day she was talking to herself, saying she must remember to switch the oven off at three o'clock, before the meatballs baked dry as bone. At exactly three o'clock Lexi switched the oven off. And what about the day when Miss Ingrid told her to collect the meat order from the butchery at half past ten. At half past ten sharp Lexi combed his hair and pulled her by the hand to the door. Like always, she had first to comb the back of his hair because he only combed the front. Like he only towelled the front of his body. If a mosquito bit him behind the knee, he scratched his kneecap. It's as if he's unaware that his body and head have a back part.

Those people who think that Lexi is stupid must think again. He can tell the time and count money. Take the day Miss Ingrid left her purse on the kitchen table and asked her to go and pay the electricity and water account. When it was time to go, the purse was missing. She searched everywhere. Couldn't find it. And all the time Lexi was sitting in his tablecloth house with the purse; the money counted out to the last cent in front of him on the carpet, exactly the amount Miss Ingrid said.

For a long time she's believed there's just a tiny wire that's loose in Lexi's head. One day the loose end of that wire is going to connect again. Like the youngster living two streets away from her in the township. For many years he couldn't understand anything or help himself in any way. Then he slipped and tumbled down the front steps and hit his head on a stone. Today he has a wife and three children, and a decent job at the abattoir.

One day Lexi will come right. Long ago she asked Miss Ingrid if the clever doctors in Cape Town couldn't perhaps put Lexi's head into a machine and send a shock through his brain to connect the loose wires. But Miss Ingrid said it didn't work that way. She pleaded with Miss Ingrid to give it a try. Then Miss Ingrid started crying.

Her heart felt so bad that she never spoke to Miss Ingrid about it again.

She's glad when she nears the patch of bluegum trees and the children come running along from the house to meet her. To carry the suitcase home. Always hopeful for a present hidden in the suitcase, something sweet or shiny.

Would Jeremiah have remembered to put the bread in the oven before the dough rose too high? It would be his own fault if he had to eat bread that's full of holes.

'What did Aunt Miriam bring us?' the children ask excitedly, dancing barefoot around her on the carpet of bluegum seeds.

'Beautiful things. But they're right at the bottom of my suitcase.'

'Aunt Miriam will be sleeping with us in the back room. Mama put Dicker's mattress in the sun and she put his sheets in the blue, specially for you, Aunt Miriam.'

'If you're good and play outside while I'm having an afternoon rest, we can take those beautiful things out of my suitcase when I wake up.'

She's just going to give her in-laws Jeremiah's greetings. Then have something to eat and take a nap. So that she can release her body from the fear of speeding through the kloof, and rest her legs. Tonight will be the preparatory service for *Nagmaal* and she doesn't want to sit in church with a tired mind when it's time to lay Evert and Miss Ingrid and Lexi at the feet of the Lord.

Her own sins too.

And Jeremiah's. No matter if her prayers over the years haven't made any impression on him. It's true what the evangelist said: if a drop of water drips on the same spot on an ironstone for thousands of years, it will eventually eat a hole through the stone. Not that she has thousands of years in which to convert Jeremiah. But for her remaining time on earth, she'll stay on her knees.

17

SHE COULDN'T COMPREHEND that they were going to take her away.
Handcuffed. In a police car. As she stood on a chair to take a bag
from the top of the cupboard, she was overcome by fear and
dizziness. She dropped the bag that Dawid had always used for
golf on the bed.

What do you pack when you are taken into custody?

Tracksuit. Socks. Flannel pyjamas.

Since when do the police have the right to walk into your house,
make false accusations against you and handcuff you? Should she
seek legal advice? No. It would just be an extra expense. If she had
had anything to hide, she would have made use of the free legal
aid provided by the state that the man mentioned earlier. But she
had nothing to hide. No matter what sinister ideas were skulking
in the man's mind, and no matter what the findings of the post-
mortem report were, she would stick to the truth. Keep her mind
off the unsettling idea of lawyers and gaol and arrest.

The woman stood right next to her; checked every item that
went into the bag.

'These are personal things, could I please pack in private?'

'Hurry up, Mrs Dorfling, Colonel Herselman wants to leave.'

Underwear. Hair brush. Talcum powder. Perfume.

'You can leave the perfume,' the woman told her. 'Glassware

isn't allowed in the cells.'

'Cells? Surely, I'm coming straight home after the questioning?'

'Interrogation can take up to forty-eight hours. In the mean time you have to sleep somewhere.'

Toiletries. Shampoo. She unpacked the hairdryer when the woman said there were no power points in the cells. Nail file. Not permitted, the woman said. Warm jacket. Tissues. Purse.

'You can take the purse,' the woman said, 'but it'll be useless to you and will be kept in safe custody anyway.'

She'd be home before Teresa and Zettie arrived that night. She must stop being scared. Pack and go and get it over with. The sooner she left, the sooner she'd be back. They had nothing against her. She zipped the bag. Picked up her handbag.

'I cannot carry everything while I'm handcuffed.'

'Put your handbag into the other bag, or leave it behind. You won't be allowed to keep it with you in the cell.'

She unzipped the bag and stuffed the handbag into it. Walked over the soggy passage carpet. Outside she pressed the bag against her chest, hiding her handcuffed hands beneath it. Nobody in town must witness this moment of disgrace. She got into the back of the police car with the woman next to her. The man said he had to stop at the local police station to drop off the house keys; something about an investigation team staying behind and needing access to the house. He was gone for a long time while she remained half asleep in the police car with the woman. She was grateful it was a rainy Saturday afternoon and the streets were deserted. Nobody must see her. Not like this.

Nervously, she sat up when the man slammed the car door.

She bade farewell to the church steeple; the red roof of the hospital; the high cypress trees behind the town hall; the pine trees at the school; the gravel street where she lived; all the chimneys of all the houses.

She said goodbye to the damned town.

Without reading a word, she signs the form the man pushes across the desk towards her and hands back the sticky pen.

'Let's go,' and he uses his elbows to push his way through the drunkards.

She struggles to walk in her unlaced shoes. Squeezes her toes right up to the front to get a better grip. Through barren and cold passages with open barred ceilings through which the rain sifts down, over wet cement floors. Past sewerage pipes stained black at the musty joints, damp corners covered in dark green moss.

If one stays here long enough one will die of cold.

No, she won't die.

If she has survived the past nine years, she will survive this night too. Just keep walking. Don't be weak; don't give way to fear. They *will* take her home and she will sleep in her own bed tonight. When she wakes up in the morning she will be able to clear from her memory the image of barred ceilings through which she can see the grey clouds. Filthy sewerage pipes; voices sounding from the depths of the dark cells.

She doesn't want to be one of the many faceless rats locked up in those suffocating depths. She wants to go back to her own house. Even though it is quiet and lonely.

Because she needs time to mourn.

She knows that hundreds of times she had felt like throwing the chisel over the edge of the world. But she also knows that for the rest of her life she will wait for the rhythmic sound of the chisel at night. Chipping, chipping, chipping. The scraping sound of Alexander dragging the wooden chair over the floor; the creaking of the chair when he got on to it to reach another brick.

She knows many things. And yet, she knows nothing.

Turn right. Turn right again.

Can't the man see that she is struggling to keep up? Walk slower, she silently begs his back. Please, let God turn her into a nymph tonight. A fearless nymph who is not afraid of diving into troubled waters. Keep her strong and alert, so that she can swim safely through the turbulent waters.

Left. Past an inner court where the drizzle wets her cheeks and the wind pierces her to the marrow of her bones. It's going to be a bitingly cold night. She tries to mark the route in her head but realises that she's hopelessly lost. Too many passages and barred doors that look the same.

Will she have a decent mattress, clean blankets and towels? Toilet paper? Did she remember to pack bath soap? She must bath, because she had never got around to bathing the night before.

When she woke up on Thursday morning, the town was veiled in a curtain of rain.

Since Monday Alexander had sat hunched up in the broom cupboard, rocking, his legs pulled up tightly against his chest, his arms wrapped around his legs. He always went to hide there a few days before the weather turned bad. If he closed himself up in the broom cupboard, it was a sure sign that cold or rain was on its way.

'Lexi loves his own shadow. His shadow is his best friend, because his shadow does everything he does,' Miriam explained. 'When it rains, his shadow is gone. Then he's confused and thinks the world has turned upside down. Miss Ingrid must leave him to sit in the broom cupboard, because he cannot hear the rain when he's in there. Maybe the rain hurts his ears.'

So many things she had learned from Miriam. Miriam's instincts for Alexander's needs were sharper than hers. She also had far more patience. She would follow him for hours, making sure that he did not chew on nails or throw apricots over the fence into Aunt Betty's yard. She would open his fingers and remove the stone from his hand before he could break Aunt Betty's windows.

'Miss Ingrid, it's when the sun shines on the windows that he wants to break them. It's not that he means to break them; it's just that he cannot understand why the sun is reflecting so brightly into his eyes, and he wants to get rid of the brightness. Before he picks up a stone, I always see him putting his hands over his eyes to block the sun. Heaven knows, Miss Ingrid, we don't understand Lexi's burden.'

Miriam.

Miriam, who had insight where her own maternal instincts failed. Who sang *Gentle Jesus meek and mild* a thousand times, then started from the beginning and sang it another thousand times. Who knew all Alexander's hiding places in the house and in the town. Who even got him as far as eating with a teaspoon. Who rolled metres and metres of toilet paper back on to the empty roll; only to find it unrolled again in an hour's time. Up the street, down the street with the pushchair until he slept, never complaining about her arthritic legs. She sat with him in his tablecloth house building puzzles. When he rocked, Miriam rocked with him. When he spun lids, she also spun lids. When he smacked his cheeks in excitement, she also smacked her cheeks.

'You give him his way in everything, Miriam. You mustn't complain if he rules you.'

'It's easier this way, Miss Ingrid, it changes his anger into goodness.'

Conditioning. Repetition. Of all the vague advice she had been given by experts, that was the one solution they had all believed in: repetition, repetition. The day would come, they assured her, when he would brush his teeth and comb his hair automatically. Go to the toilet. Eat with a spoon. Even though he might not understand why he was doing it, the processes would have been drummed into his head. Don't give him his way, they recommended, otherwise he will never learn.

'Miriam, if you imitate him, you will make him understand that he's doing the right thing. We *have* to teach him, over and over, that certain things are wrong.'

'Who are we to say what's right and what's wrong, Miss Ingrid? How can he love me if I always prevent him from doing the things he likes to do?'

She was caught off guard. 'How would you raise your own children, Miriam?'

'With the love of our Lord, Miss Ingrid. If I can do something to change Lexi's anger into goodness, then it is the love of our Lord. The Lord understands that Lexi's world is different from ours.'

For a split-second a shutter opened in her brain and she was convinced that all the experts were wrong and Miriam was right. Because so often when Alexander was with Miriam he was calm, content. He giggled mechanically while they spun lids. Stayed in the bath longer when Miriam imitated him by hitting on the water. Copied Miriam and closed his ears when the train rattled pass.

Perhaps they were all wrong, and Miriam was right?

'Miss Ingrid mustn't buy the old type of puzzles. They confuse Lexi and he chews them up. Miss Ingrid must rather buy those with the knobs. He likes them very much.'

Often, while she watched Alexander putting puzzles together, she knew with a mother's instinct that there was not a world of emptiness locked up in his head. If his head was filled with emptiness, how would he be able to tell the time? If his brain registered nothing, how was he able to understand the notes that she left for Miriam on the kitchen table when she left for work? *Put the bread bin in the sun.* Next thing, the bread bin was standing in the sun. *Defrost the fridge.* When Miriam went to the kitchen to have her ten o'clock tea, the contents of the fridge had been packed in the cooler bag and the fridge door was open. *Dust the cobwebs on the stoep.* Alexander fiddled with the duster on the stoep for the entire morning. Certainly he couldn't *hear* what she wrote. Give him five mixed-up puzzles, and he knew exactly which piece belonged where. Took the little knob between his thumb and forefinger, whirred it around, and put it in place. In less than ten minutes, all five puzzles were done.

'Well done, Xander!'

She crept closer on her knees to stroke his hair in praise. All the experts told her to applaud each little thing that he did right, and also for everything that he did not do wrong. Repetition. Repetition. Repetition. The day would eventually come when the heavy curtain would be pulled aside. One day he *would* have understanding. Even if it had to be hammered in by endless repetition.

'Xander . . .' He scurried away like a lizard and hid under the table. She followed him to his tablecloth house. He growled like a dog that smelled danger. 'Come, Xander, let Mommy show you the daddy bear and the duckling with the yellow feathers and the rooster standing on the church steeple. Come, show me what you have built.'

He growled again. She lifted the edge of the tablecloth and pointed to the puzzles. Unexpectedly, he leapt forward and grabbed her forearm, sank his teeth into her soft flesh.

Aghast, she wrenched her arm free and slapped his leg. 'Don't bite, Alexander!' He lunged at her again. 'No, Alexander! Why don't you listen to me?'

Again she slapped his leg. But he did not blink an eye, or rub his leg. Nothing in his body or heart felt pain. His growls only intensified. Until eventually they subsided and turned into a soft whining lament. *Mimmi . . . Mimmi . . . Mimmi . . .*

A few days later she came home from work and found him and Miriam playing in the tablecloth house. She listened to them communicating. Alexander laughed, and although it sounded mechanical, he at least did not growl at Miriam.

Show me the daddy bear, Lexi? Silence. *Good for you, Lexi! And the yellow duckling?* Silence. *My goodness, Lexi, you really have a clever head on you! And the rooster with the red tail-feathers? Yes, Lexi, yes!*

His giggles filled the room and he called out: *Mimmi! Mimmi! Mimmi!*

Why could Miriam so effortlessly penetrate the walls that were too thick for her? Was there an evil in her that Alexander could sense? Or was she simply an irritating obstacle barring his way to freedom; forbidding him those things which gave him pleasure? Opening taps, slamming cupboard doors, unrolling toilet paper. Flushing and flushing the toilet, holding his ear to the cistern to listen to it filling up. Cutting pillows, scattering the feathers. Chiselling plaster off the walls when everyone else was trying to sleep. Sitting on the stoep for days on end, spitting on his palms;

forming bubbles between his thumb and forefinger, holding them against the sun, ecstatic about the coloured reflection. Biting on nails and screws. Running round and round the house endlessly when the north wind blew.

Maybe he saw her as the arch-enemy who served up peas and rice and a tiny piece of meat on his plate. If only he knew what it would mean to her if he ate one single pea. Or flung his arms around her neck, just once, and looked at her with recognition in his eyes.

So many nights she sat cross-legged next to his bed, watching his sleeping face. Sometimes when she saw him digging his nails into the pillow and mattress she yearned to comfort him; to hold his fragile body against her, without him yelling and pulling away from her.

But with Miriam he laughed his mechanical laugh in the tablecloth house. Showed her the duckling and the daddy bear and the rooster on the church steeple. Miriam's arms were never bitten or bruised. Miriam sat with him under the wild olive tree, singing and rocking him to sleep. *Gentle Jesus . . . In the kingdom of Thy grace, give a little child a place . . .* If Alexander was capable of loving, it was Miriam he loved. Not her, his own mother. He scrambled away from her, pulled back when she wanted to hold him, bit her hands when she tried to play with him.

In nine years he learned to say only one word: *Mimmi.*

Perhaps he was simply not interested in saying anything more. Perhaps there were many words in his head, strung together like beads, but his tongue could not manage to unstring them. Yet, if his tongue could form one word, why couldn't it form others? For there was a time, long ago, when he could speak. Many words, all at the right time and place. Tata, mommy, coffee, book, bed, don't, please. Though he never spoke in sentences, he knew many words. Until she and Dawid took him to the Children's Hospital in Cape Town for a series of tests. He was about three and a half then.

It had started with a simple hearing test.

'He could have a hearing problem,' Old Doctor said. 'I think you should have his ears tested.'

By that time she went to see Old Doctor with a heavy heart because all he could offer was the same old senseless speculation, over and over. Change from one medicine to another. Vitamins, sedatives, magnesium supplements, speculation about a shortage of iron in the immune system. Old Doctor did not seem to understand how she battled to get medicine down Alexander's throat. Yet in a strange way she found consolation with Old Doctor. At least he seemed to listen and to care.

'What if it is not a hearing problem, Doctor?'

'Then we'll take it from there.' There was a silent plea in his voice to give it a chance. 'I know Dawid is fed up with specialists, but I am convinced you should take Alexander to an ear, nose and throat specialist. Just to be sure.'

A light of hope flickered briefly. Maybe, just maybe, the specialist would come up with a solution. But darkness returned when she contemplated the journey. 'I'll talk to Dawid, Doctor. I'll phone you in the morning.'

Dawid refused to go. She insisted. They had a huge row about it. Yelled at each other like lunatics. About money and wasted time and trivialities.

'For God's sake, Ingrid, we've been going from doctor to doctor for more than three years! You listen to all sorts of crap, and month after month I am the one who has to crawl at the bank manager's feet asking for a bigger overdraft!'

'But you're never short of poker money.'

'Shut up about my poker! With my winnings I could buy the child a horse! What have we gained from the quacks you believe in?'

'We are his parents, Dawid, and I'll keep searching until I find answers.'

'Or until your bloody search forces me to cash in another insurance policy?'

She felt as if she had been struck blind. Cash in an insurance policy? Had Dawid really done that? 'Are you out of your mind, Dawid? Don't tell me you've been such an idiot . . .'

'What the hell was I to do? Or do you think money grows on trees?'

'Dawid, I cannot believe you were so short-sighted . . .'

'Short-sighted? Who's short-sighted? It's because of your stupidity that I owe the bank! And not just the bank, I owe my father too. And the chemist account is underlined in red! Have you not noticed how far in arrears our rates are?'

They railed at each other until late that night.

But she refused to bend the knee.

Another day off work. Petrol expenses. Arrangements for Miriam to stay with Teresa and Zettie until they got back from the specialist. The exhaustion of coping with Alexander's wild behaviour in an unfamiliar environment. She pleaded with Dawid to keep an eye on Alexander while she slipped away to buy something for Teresa and Zettie. Even if it was just a key ring or a hair clip. She couldn't bear to arrive home empty-handed.

She prayed that a hearing problem would be diagnosed. At least it would be a starting point.

If she had known beforehand what a battle it would be to attach the testing apparatus to Alexander's head, and how he would fight it with the strength of a lion, God knows she would have stayed home.

'No.' The ear, nose and throat specialist shook his head. 'His hearing is one hundred per cent.' Her hopes fell through the floor. She could see a dark cloud of discontent moving over Dawid's face. 'What concerns me, is his peculiar behaviour.' He pointed to Alexander who was sitting on his knees in the corner of the room, rocking. 'My advice is to get him to the Children's Hospital in Cape Town.'

Children's Hospital? Cape Town? Merciful God, did the man have any idea of how far that was? Dawid would never agree.

'But . . .' She glanced at Dawid. He was pale as death; clenching and unclenching his hands tensely. 'We . . . it's just that . . .' She wanted to explain that they did not have the money for petrol and accommodation; that they had used up all their leave. And that they were both drained beyond belief.

'There's no urgency, Mrs Dorfling. Physically there's nothing wrong with your child, but just by watching him for a short period I've picked up a very odd behaviour pattern. It would be best to get the opinion of an expert in behavioural problems. The Children's Hospital is very well equipped for that.'

A cold hand clutched at her throat. God, please don't let them find anything wrong with Alexander's head. Don't let them go all the way to Cape Town only to be sentenced to damnation. Rather try to stem the tide. 'Financially, we're going through a tough time . . . this is very unexpected . . .'

'I'll contact your family doctor, and he can arrange accommodation for you in Church House. Although it's not free, it's cheap. Or otherwise . . .'

Dawid put his hands on his knees and stood up, hunched over like an old man. 'Make the appointment, Doctor. The arrangements at Church House too. We'll go.'

And right there, in front of a strange doctor, she burst into tears. Tears that she had bottled up for months.

Afterwards she could recall little of the long trip to Cape Town. What was etched most clearly in her mind was Alexander sitting on the back seat, blowing spit bubbles. And the deathly silence between her and Dawid. Chilly, like a winter's wind.

'A penny for your thoughts,' she tried to make conversation when Alexander fell asleep. She opened the coffee flask and balanced the cup on her lap.

Silence. Dawid gripped the steering wheel tighter.

'A cup of coffee?'

'No, thank you.'

Silence. She sipped a mouthful of coffee. It was a long way to Cape Town, almost like going round the world it seemed. Her bladder was full but she was too scared to ask Dawid to stop in case Alexander woke up. 'Dawid,' she pleaded, 'I need your support desperately. Especially in the days to come. It's as if I'm losing my grip on life. I'm light years behind at work and I'm . . .'

He struck the steering wheel with his fist, interrupting her. 'And me? And my job? How the hell do you think I'm coping, Ingrid? I'm running out of money at a frightening speed! And you,' and she saw the speedometer needle climbing, 'you expect me to have an inexhaustible supply of money! It's driving me round the bend, Ingrid, completely!'

She had no answer.

At some stage while they were travelling through a landscape of green vineyards, she put her hand on Dawid's leg. A tiny gesture of reaching out to him. But he stared at the road ahead like a sphinx.

When they eventually reached Cape Town, they drove up and down for what seemed an eternity, looking for the entrance to Church House. The three-storey cement brick building, with its high wall and barbed wired, was next to the highway, but they could not find the entrance. Dawid swore. It was hot in the car and they were soaked in sweat. When at last they found the entrance hidden away in a side street, she prayed that Dawid would calm down.

'It *this* Church House?'

He frowned. On the back seat Alexander sat up, growling, his eyes wide open.

The building looked like a deserted school hostel. Barren, square, ancient. As if the rules and regulations of decades ago would still be pinned up behind the doors. No garden. Just a black tarred courtyard from which heatwaves rose.

'It looks like it.' The dreary building reflected the greyness in her heart and mind.

They took the luggage out. Locked the car. Took Alexander's hand firmly. He pulled and tugged, resisting obstinately. She tightened her grip on his hand. Took a deep breath. Walked across the hot tarred surface, begging God not to let Alexander get hold of something with which to ruin Church House. A sour-faced woman awaited them at the door like a watchdog. Notices on the wall screamed: *Children must be kept quiet at all times as ill patients awaiting therapy are staying here.*

Startled, she and Dawid looked at each other. Alexander covered his eyes with his hand and with a squeaking yell tried to break away. The sour-faced woman jumped up and pointed at the notice board, commanded him to be quiet.

How could she explain to the woman that he didn't understand instructions? She saw the disapproval on the woman's face and felt a coldness run down her spine when Alexander started yelling in a high-pitched tone. Determined to shut him up, the woman came from behind the counter, going straight towards him.

'No, son, no!' and she gripped him by the sleeve. 'Stop making a noise! This is a place for sick . . .' She flinched when he removed his hand from his eyes and hissed in her face.

She knew that she had to defend him. But she felt paralysed. Clutching at straws. 'He's deaf.' No matter that it was a lie. 'We have brought him here for tests.'

'Well, he is definitely not allowed to make such a noise. This is a place for seriously ill cancer patients.'

If she had never in her entire life felt like a pauper, she felt it then. Dawid took the key for the room and picked up their suitcases. With drooping shoulders he started walking up the stairs.

Second floor.

Room number seventeen.

Narrow single beds. A thin pillow on each bed. Threadbare bedspreads. Brown curtains. Ancient bedside table, stained with coffee rings. The smell of moth balls and floor polish and disinfectant hung in the room. She walked up to Dawid and stood close to him. 'It's not luxurious, but at least it's clean. And not too expensive. Fortunately, it's only for a few days.'

Then suddenly Dawid turned around and embraced her. Buried his face in her hair and spoke in a smothered voice. 'Ingrid, oh my God, Ingrid . . .'

Lonely and bewildered, they held on to each other while

Alexander tested every tap in the gloomy bathroom, and bounced the linen and mattresses off the beds.

Neither they nor Alexander wanted to be crammed into the dingy brown room at Church House. But they had nowhere else to go.

She has lost her sense of direction completely; cannot for the life of her remember where they turned left or right. The bag hanging from her shoulder feels like a rock. Her toes cramp from trying to keep the unlaced shoes on her feet. The after-effect of the sleeping pill leaves her mouth sticky and dry. But despite all the aggravations of this godforsaken hour, she is grateful that they removed the handcuffs in the charge office.

'Did you discuss the case with the district surgeon, Colonel?'

The woman's voice behind her sends a shock through her body.

'No, but I sent a police representative to attend the post-mortem. I've received his report and will discuss it with the district surgeon by telephone.'

Where do these people find the strength to stay up all night? Why does the man want to phone the district surgeon in the middle of the night? After all, what is there to say other than that Alexander drowned?

She must not be scared.

When, for the umpteenth time, they reach yet another intersecting passage, they turn left into an office. It's a relief to put the bag down. There are two policemen in the office. One of them closes the drawer of a filing cabinet and comes towards them. They converse in a technical language that she finds hard to follow; something about cell registers and registrations. One police constable lists her particulars in a thick blue-bound book. They instruct her to hand over all her possessions. Even her purse and toothpaste.

'My toothpaste . . . I have to brush my teeth . . .'

'No, Mrs Dorfling. What if you decide to eat the whole tube and we have to take you to hospital at the state's expense? And at the same time you might be hoping for an opportunity to escape. We're not that naive, Mrs Dorfling.'

'I have no intention of escaping, I only want to brush my teeth.'

'You can have some toothpaste under supervision when you need to brush your teeth.'

She swallows her frustration and humiliation.

The police constable puts her toothpaste, purse and handbag

into a bag and locks it away. He hands her a receipt and tells her not to lose it and afterwards claim that she did not receive one. She puts the receipt in the side pocket of the carry-bag. She can see the time on the police constable's wristwatch: five past ten. She must keep herself together and stay strong. The detective's eyes are bloodshot. Maybe he is also tired and wants to get the questioning over and done with.

Where are Teresa and Zettie now? What if they have trouble with the car? Perhaps they managed to leave earlier than planned and have already arrived at the empty house. What if they are starving? There's not much food in the house. Bananas, mashed pumpkin, cheese spread, frozen chicken. Maybe some stale bread and a few tomatoes and eggs. When they come home, Miriam always cleans their windows and puts fresh linen on their beds. Tonight they'll face closed rooms and bare mattresses. A house in chaos. If the detective gets the questioning over and done with quickly and they take her home within the next hour maybe there will be enough time to bake scones.

No. It'll take three-quarters of an hour to drive home. And just to get out of this labyrinth of passages will probably take more than fifteen minutes. Teresa and Zettie will definitely arrive home before she does.

'Listen,' and she steps forward, 'my daughters are on their way home from college. They should arrive at about midnight . . .'

The man interrupts, talks over his shoulder to the woman. 'Contact the investigation team and tell them to put a local police constable on guard at Mrs Dorfling's house. When her daughters arrive they must question both of them immediately, and fax the statements to me.'

For heaven's sake, is he really going to ambush Teresa and Zettie in the middle of the night and have them questioned by Murder and Robbery detectives? Why? What could they possibly tell anyone? 'My daughters have nothing to do with this. They were hundreds of kilometres away and . . .'

The hardness in his eyes almost shreds her to pieces. 'Mrs Dorfling, I am the investigation officer, and I will determine who is to be questioned and who not.'

'But they . . . they weren't even at home when . . .'

'There are many years prior to today about which I need details. Since you have apparently forgotten so many things, your daughters could be an excellent source of information.' He turns to the woman. 'Please find out from the investigation team how far they have progressed with the questioning of Miriam Slangveld. I urgently need a report on the information they have been able to get from her so far.'

So then, Miriam knows.

Perhaps Miriam was already with her in-laws in the kloof when the police arrived, giving her the fright of her life. And if Miriam is going through one quarter of the hell she's experiencing, she can forget about the *Nagmaal* service. They must be gentle with Miriam; she's old. And she will be heartbroken about Alexander's death.

The man closes the blue-bound book and checks his watch. 'Get the keys so we can take her to the cell,' he says to one of the police constables. 'I have phone calls to make.' He turns to her. 'Walk, Mrs Dorfling.'

She picks up the bag. The cuff of her tracksuit top scratches the abrasions on her wrists like sand. When the police constable unlocks the first heavy metal door and the shadowy passage stretches ahead of them, the musty stink of gaol hits her in the face. Bodies, smoke, urine. Through the windows situated all along the sides of the floor she can see into the illuminated cells on the floor below. One prisoner sits on his bed resting his head in his hands. Another reads from a Bible. Another stands in the corner of his cell and bangs his head against the wall while howling like a wolf. Another is standing naked under the shower. One is urinating in the wash-basin and he swings around when they walk past, squirting urine on the floor. She catches a glimpse of his genitals, and her hair stands on end. As sure as God is alive, tonight she will be raped or killed in this place.

As they walk down the passage, she hears the murmuring of bass voices. The further they move down the passage, the louder the voices become. At first she cannot make out their words, because her heart is throbbing in her ears with fear. But soon the words become distinguishable as they are passed on from prisoner to prisoner: *Herselman has brought in a white woman!*

Flabbergasted, she peers over her shoulder at the woman. 'I'm scared.'

And for the first time since they knocked on her door earlier that afternoon, she senses compassion in the woman's voice.

'Don't be scared. This is the maximum security section and you'll be in a single cell. It gets locked from outside, nobody will be able to get near you.'

She can only manage a dry whisper. 'Will the lights be on

through the night?'

For a fleeting moment the woman's fingertips touch her shoulder. 'Yes. Later on they will be dimmed, but it will never be completely dark.'

She utters another hoarse whisper. 'Are the women detained separately from the men?'

'Separate cells, yes, but in the same section.'

'How many women are here?'

'At the moment, only you.'

Her stomach turns. 'And what if something goes wrong? What if . . .'

'A guard comes round every hour. Just indicate through the catwalk if you need something,' and she points at the windows near the floor.

Does this mean she will have no privacy at all? Not even while she sleeps? Catwalks to spy on her while she uses the toilet or puts on her pyjamas. She forgets to grip her shoes properly and trips over her own feet while her body is shaken by a coughing fit.

Herselman has brought in a white woman! The bass voices echo the message down the gloomy passage.

The procession comes to a standstill and she hears the metallic sound of keys. With a squeaking sound the barred door of the cell swings open and the woman urges her from behind. When she takes the first step inside, she knows that she's entering a place where fear and desperation cling to everything like old rottenness. To the bundle of grey blankets on the filthy mattress. The dripping shower. The graffiti on the walls. The cigarette butts on the rough cement floor. The permeating smell of sunlessness.

'Are the blankets clean?'

The woman's eyes avoid her. 'They supply clean blankets every tenth day.'

Every *tenth* day? Good God. Surely they can see the cell is filthy. They really cannot expect her to sleep under someone else's dirty blankets.

'Good night, Mrs Dorfling,' the man says. 'Maybe it'll do you good to be alone to do some serious thinking.'

When they walk out and lock the barred door with a grating sound, she wants to call them back and plead with them not to leave her alone. But only a dry silence comes from her mouth. Shattered, she watches them disappear.

During the three days that they spent at the Children's Hospital in

Cape Town Alexander behaved like an animal caught in a snare. He hated the white hospital bed with the railings. Kept on trying to climb over and trample his way to freedom. Tried to tear the bedding with his teeth. Did not eat a crumb. When the staff strapped him to a trolley to take him for tests, he tried desperately to break free from the straps and buckles holding him down; his eyes distended as he looked for a hiding place or an escape route. He disconnected the sachet with which the urine test had to be monitored, squealing like a stuck pig while holding the sachet as far as possible from his body. The urine test was a disaster.

Merciful God, her energy and courage were depleted. Dawid hardly lifted a finger to help. He passed the long hours sitting in the reception area reading magazines. She had to do all the running and rescuing. She prayed that the nursing staff who were pumping Alexander full of sedatives would realise that the medication was increasing his energy levels, rather than calming him down. She pleaded with them to give him a mashed banana instead of porridge.

Only at night, when the buzz in the building subsided and the dimmed night-lights were switched on, did he sometimes calm down and rock himself to sleep. She put her hands through the railings and rubbed his tiny ribcage.

Child of darkness. With his head buried under the pillow, where people and objects did not pass him like shapeless whirlwinds; where colour and light and sound did not explode in his brain.

'He's sleeping,' she told Dawid who was waiting at reception. 'Won't you please stay with him for an hour or two?'

'No. Before we left home I told you explicitly that I'd come on condition that . . .'

'Please, Dawid, I need to sleep in the car for a while.'

'Just leave him. Let's go home, if one can call that miserable Church House home.'

She looked at him with emptiness in her heart. 'You can go home if you want to. I'm staying here. What if he has an epileptic fit?'

He flung the magazine on to the pile on the table and got up, stretched his arms. 'All right, I'll see you in the morning.'

Her vigil began. Why could she not abandon him as Dawid had done?

She placed a chair next to the bed. Pushed her hands through the railings and placed them on Alexander's body so that she could be alert to every little movement. To be ready when the gasp from his throat scared the hell out of her. She rested her forehead against

131

the cold iron of the bed frame and was drawn into sleep for a few restless minutes.

But she could never really sleep. Subconsciously, she watched. She dreamed about the parable of the ten bridesmaids with the oil lamps, that she was one of the foolish ones. Teresa and Zettie were also amongst the bridesmaids. They kneeled in front of her and begged for some of her oil to keep their own lamps burning. She refused. Because there was barely enough oil in her own lamp. When they turned around and walked away, their backs were hunched and their lamps burning low.

In the dead of night she woke up. Her feet were frozen; her legs tingling. She tried to recall where she had put her Bible; when last she had held it in her hands. She could not remember. It did not make any difference anyway. All that mattered was that the oil in her lamp had to last until the final hour.

Daybreak.

The staff changed shifts. Trolleys with coffee and breakfast moved along the passages. Another frightening day had begun. Alexander sat with his legs through the railings, kicking furiously. He screamed like a whistle and knocked the bowl of porridge out of the nurse's hand. Arched himself backwards and buried his head under the pillow.

Never in her entire life had she seen Alexander more panic-stricken than that morning when they forced his head into a machine for a CAT scan. She wanted to grab the staff by their ears and shout in their faces that it was useless to keep pumping him full of sedatives; that their commands and instructions made no impression whatsoever on him; to him everything was a haze of meaningless sounds. But she held her tongue since nobody would listen to her anyway. For all she cared, they could put him in a straitjacket and seal his lips with tape. Just as long as this hell came to an end. So that she could go back to Church House and pack her bags and go back to her own home.

'Come, Xander, Mommy will stay with you. They're going to take pictures.' He kept on battling to get his head out of the machine. 'Come, Xander, lie still, we're almost finished. Mommy's not going away. Mommy will stay with you. It's all right . . . it's all right . . .'

The technician who performed the CAT scan was short-tempered. He told her irritably that her child was uncontrollable and that she should stand at the top of the bed and hold his head still, because any movement would produce faulty results.

'He's terribly scared,' she said defensively. The man carried on setting the machine as if she had never spoken. 'Couldn't we try again later in the day?'

'It's out of the question. We work strictly according to a schedule.'

Children's Hospital. Meant for children. To her it seemed as if every patient was just a number. Nobody had time to stop and listen. Nobody could go to the kitchen and mash a banana. Mighty medical machine that kept rolling on and on. An ant's nest of white uniforms, hurrying from one case to the other, overloaded with schedules. Nobody was rude or unprofessional. But there was little time for compassion. A doctor was not a psychologist. A nurse was not a confidante. A machine operator was not a comforter to the sick.

Case number twenty. Case number one hundred. Case number one thousand.

While her oil was burning away.

'Would you *please* stand at the top of the bed and keep the patient still?'

She tried. Out of desperation, she started singing. *Old Macdonald had a farm . . . And on the farm he had some ducks . . . and on the farm . . . and on the farm . . .* Until her tongue stuck to her palate and there was not a single animal left that she could think of.

When she went to the bathroom afterwards she realised that she must have been crying, because her eyes were bloodshot and her face was puffy.

Some time during the course of the afternoon she looked around from her vigil at the white bed and saw Dawid standing behind her. Unshaved. Eyes sunk into the sockets. He fetched a chair and sat down next to her. Just sat there. Silent. Until night fell and Alexander buried his head under the pillow.

'Let me take you to Church House, Ingrid, to sleep.'

'I cannot.'

'You can,' and he combed his fingers through his hair. 'I'll stay with him tonight.'

He went looking for a nurse to stay with Alexander while he took her back to Church House. The nurse said they were not very busy and assured them that they could both go home and return in the morning. Yes, she was absolutely sure. And yes, there was an assistant nurse who would check on the patient regularly.

It was a small mercy. Although everything in her resisted leaving his bedside, she had no choice but to accept it. If she did not turn her wick down, her oil would be finished before the final hour arrived. Because with the coming of the new day, the lumbar puncture awaited her like a mountain. And her reserves were running on empty.

In her restless sleep on the creaking bed at Church House she dreamed about the song. *And on the farm . . . and on the farm . . . and on the farm . . .*

'I hope this will be over soon,' she said some time around midnight when she heard Dawid's bed creaking in the dark. Her mattress was thin and lumpy and every time she turned the bed rocked under her. Her body ached with fatigue. The day behind her had been long and stressful. She had had to comfort and soothe and sing and hold on for dear life. So that Alexander did not go over the edge. And thousands of questions had to be answered on endless questionnaires.

Please tick one answer for each question.

Was the child given oxygen in the first week after birth? No. *Did the child reach out or prepare himself to be picked up when the mother approached?* No. *At what age did the child learn to walk alone?* Approximately 20 months. *Did you ever suspect the child was deaf?* Yes. *Did the child rock in his crib as a baby?* Yes. *Does the child 'look through' or 'walk through' people, as though they aren't there?* Yes, always. *Does the child have certain eating oddities?* Definitely. *Does the child deliberately hit his own head?* Yes. *Is it possible to direct the child's attention to an object some distance away or out a window?* No. *Does the child take an adult by the wrist and use the adult's hand to open doors or cookie tins or to turn on the TV?* Yes. *Does the child look up at people and meet their eyes when they are talking to him?* Never. *Is the child interested in mechanical objects such as the stove or vacuum cleaner?* Yes, but only when he is in control. *Does the child like to spin things like the lids of jars and coins?* Yes.

She was tempted to lie and tick an answer she preferred to the truth. There were few questions that did not scare her. Just about every question that had to do with behavioural patterns seemed to refer specifically to Alexander. But there was one question that haunted her all night while she tossed and turned on the rickety bed at Church House. And she knew that the answer to that question carried the key to the riddle.

Would you describe the child as often seeming to be in a shell, or so distant and lost in thought that you cannot reach him?

Yes.

Almighty God.

Yes.

'Come to me, Ingrid,' Dawid said in the dark.

She threw the blankets aside and went to his bed; lay close to him. His skin felt unfamiliar against hers, as though she had forgotten how close they had once been. Yet, as much as he was a stranger to her, the warmth of his fingers softly stroking the flesh of her upper arm was an anchor in the loneliness of the bleak room.

'Tomorrow it'll all be over, and we can go home,' he said softly in the dark.

For a long time they just lay close to each other. Then Dawid lifted himself on to his elbow and brought his face close to hers. 'Ingrid, I don't know where you find the strength to do what you do. How do you bear all the suffering, Ingrid? How?'

There was nothing she could tell him but the truth. 'I love him, Dawid. Regardless of everything that's so awfully wrong with him.'

God alone had witnessed the many nights she stood next to Alexander's bed while he slept. She watched him wrestle with the blankets. Heard him calling for Miriam. Watched him getting off the foot of the bed, passing her as if she was invisible. Going straight to the chisel.

Dawid bent his head and rested it on her chest; she could smell his hair. 'I don't love him, Ingrid,' he said in a muffled voice, 'and I hate myself for it.'

What comfort could she offer him? 'You don't have to love him, Dawid, and you don't have to hate yourself for it. But I beg you, Dawid, love *me*.'

He held her so tightly that she struggled to breathe. 'I *do* love you, Ingrid, I do.'

Dawid. Her husband. Her shield and protector who had crumbled to pieces. She wrapped her arms around his shoulders and pulled him closer to her.

'Come to me, Ingrid.'

'I am with you.'

They fell asleep on the hollow single bed. Woke when daylight began filtering through the brown curtains. She got up and walked down the dreary passage of Church House to the primitive kitchen, furnished with little more than a kettle and a fridge. She made coffee. Prayed.

Last day.

Lumbar puncture.

They were both shaking with fatigue. If Dawid had not helped her, she would never have been able to keep Alexander lying on his side. He kicked, hit, bit, swung his arms like a windmill. His eyes protruded. He yelled: *Mimmi! Mimmi! Mimmi!* Inserting the needle was the least of it. It was as if he was not aware of the pain at all.

They waited a long time for the doctor to come and speak to them. Sat motionless on the upright office chairs, listening to his clinical conclusions. She had to concentrate because the foreign terms flew through her head like arrows.

Severely incapacitating lifelong developmental disability; neurological disorder that affects the functioning of the brain. As research has not yet excluded the possibility of heredity it's recommended that you don't have any more children.

As if it was a mere formality, the doctor said that he would send a copy of his report to their family doctor.

Three days of hell were over.

They put Alexander's suitcase into the car and sat him on the back seat. Went to Church House to pack. Before they finally drove away from Church House, she looked back at the sombre cement building and prayed that God would never send her back there again. And in the middle of her prayer she burst into tears of fatigue. Dawid held her to his chest. When she looked up through a veil of tears she saw that Dawid was also crying. But there was too little oil left in her own lamp to bring light to the dark sorrow in his heart.

All the way home Alexander vomited. When he was not vomiting, he sat on the back seat apathetically, with the cheese spread jar on his lap, but eating nothing. He had only a few mouthfuls of coffee. He vomited again and again, until everything in the car was a sweet-sour mess. When they stopped along the road, he got out of the car dragging his feet.

'That goddamned Church House,' Dawid erupted, drumming his fingers on the steering wheel. 'It's a *donnerse* pauper's nest. Everything in the place looks like the leftovers from a charity auction. Good God, Ingrid, what does the church do with all its money?'

'Church House is at least some kind of shelter for people who can afford nothing else. A roof and a bed and . . .'

'Do you imagine for one moment that a dominee with cancer would stay there? No, Ingrid, never. He'd use the interest on his investments and book into an air-conditioned hotel with room service and a view . . .'

She kept quiet, letting him spit out the venom bottled up inside him.

'What is the church all about, Ingrid? What is the church supposed to be about? The more I think about it, the more convinced I am that it's a money-making racket for dominees. Men of the cloth. With evil and greedy hearts. They rule and run the Church Council, and in the end they rule and run everything. They feather their own nests, Ingrid, and they feather them thoroughly. Look how things are getting out of hand in town! Pensioners on the street corners on Saturdays, selling hotdogs and curried chicken, and on Mondays the church secretary sets off to the bank to deposit the proceeds. But there's no money to fix the crack on the steps to the gallery. No money to smoke out the beehive in the steeple. The first thing the council budgets for, is the dominee's package. And to every salary increase proposed by the national Synod, the council members nod their heads and say: *approved, approved*. They are too shit scared to hold a different opinion, because a lot of things can go badly wrong if you dare to tarnish the image of the man of the cloth . . .'

Before they had left for Cape Town, she saw the letter on Dawid's desk: . . . *nominated for the office of deacon* . . . On the tear-off section at the bottom he had declined. It made her uneasy, because Dawid was right about one thing: many things could go wrong for you in a small town where everybody had a vested interest in everything . . .

'The other day when Andrew and I were talking at the post office, he told me that the manse kitchen caught fire because a pan of oil was left on the stove.'

She had heard clients at the bank talking about it. A huge sum of money had been claimed from the insurance company. It was paid out to the last cent and deposited in the church's bank account.

'Andrew is highly upset because the Building Committee accepted his quote for repairing the damage, but when he arrived at the manse to do the job it had already been done. They hired a handyman from the township who did it for next to nothing. But the insurance cheque went into the church coffers. When Andrew confronted the dominee, the dominee asked him to keep quiet about it. He said the money would be used for a good cause. The Building Committee had agreed that the balance of the insurance money would be used to erect a wall of remembrance for cremation urns. And to prevent gossip, the dominee asked Andrew to say that he subcontracted the builder from the township. Good God, Ingrid, that's fraud!'

'It's their sin, Dawid, not yours. One day they will pay for it.

Leave them alone, don't get involved . . .'

'Why not? No, Ingrid, it's about time people opened their eyes to the corruption in the church! And do you know what's worst of all? The funds to erect the wall of remembrance were collected last year when the old-age home sold raffle tickets for a Persian carpet. But then the Finance Committee "borrowed" that money to have the manse floors sanded and varnished to keep the dominee's wife happy.'

She had heard bank clients talking about that too. About the wall of remembrance, and about the dominee preaching against gambling, yet allowing the church's endorsement of the raffle lists. It was the same principle, they reasoned.

'And now they rob the insurance company, and Andrew too. *Bliksem*, Ingrid, I'm getting to the point where I won't be able to hold my tongue.'

It was a long drive home; the road seemed endless. Dawid said many bitter things about the dominee and the church which she wanted to forget, because the shocking truth of it scared her. If Dawid dared to repeat those things to anybody in town, there would be many townsfolk who would censure him. Even those who silently agreed with him. Otherwise they would be ostracised too. The thought of Dawid speaking his mind made her shiver.

Miriam and Teresa and Zettie were waiting for them at the front door. The girls went straight to Dawid, hugged him and asked if he had brought them presents. Miriam called *Lexi! Lexi!* and opened her arms to embrace Alexander. But he did not even notice her. He looked around anxiously, then tore all his shirt buttons off in one furious movement and started running around the house.

Around and around and around. Until it was dark and Dawid took Miriam home. Around and around and around. Until Teresa and Zettie went to bed. Around and around and around. Blindly. Dawid tried to catch him but he broke free and carried on running. She sat on the steps of the stoep, her mind a bundle of tangled wool. She sat there because she could not leave the running child alone and she did not know what else to do.

Lifelong disability . . . disorder that affects the functioning of the brain . . . I don't love him, Ingrid, and I hate myself . . . finally, it is most important that you love your child . . . it's fraud, Ingrid, that's what it is . . . come to me, Ingrid . . .

She was tired beyond belief.

Some time after midnight Alexander came tearing around the

corner of the house for the umpteenth time. Suddenly he stopped in his tracks, covered his ears with his hands and yelled shrilly. Then he turned towards the house and went through the front door backwards; lay down on his bed and fell asleep immediately.

She felt she could see the anger clinging to his whole being while he slept. It was almost as if he despised them for the bed with the railings and the agony which they had forced upon him. She sat down at the foot of the bed and placed his feet on her lap. Gently rubbed the dust off his feet with her dress. Prayed that he would be too exhausted to be woken by her touch.

A few days later he started whispering in a raspy voice, hissing words instead of pronouncing them. Bottle, book, cat, coffee. All in the wrong context. He pointed to the cat and said coffee. Reached for his bottle and said ta-ta. Less than two weeks after they came back from the Children's Hospital, he stopped talking altogether. As if he had become mute. And he no longer seemed to recognise the cat or his bottle.

It was a mystery to her, because all the thousands of advanced medical tests performed at the hospital in Cape Town had not revealed any physical abnormality.

'I don't understand what happened in that hospital in Cape Town,' Miriam said, 'but since Lexi came back he's different.' She dried her tears with her apron. 'He doesn't listen when I sing to him. It seems to me he's forgotten all the tunes.'

She would clutch at anything. 'You must keep talking to him, Miriam. Show him the different colours and get him to count. Don't stop singing, even if it seems as if he isn't listening. We must never think that he doesn't understand what we say.'

. . . *lifelong disability* . . .

'I do that every day, Miss Ingrid. I've done it for years already. If there's one person on earth who knows that Lexi *can* understand, it's me, Miss Ingrid.'

Why did he stop talking?

Nobody could ever give her an answer.

When the report from the Children's Hospital arrived a month after their visit, she could hardly make sense of it. To her it was just sheets of paper containing incomprehensible words. Indecipherable medical terms; unpronounceable names of recommended medication. Nowhere did it offer her guidance. Nowhere was a final diagnosis spelled out. Nowhere was it stated exactly what was wrong. The only paragraph which she understood, was the conclusion: *The whole family, but especially the mother, must receive psychological counselling and assistance. The possibility of enrolling him at a special school for autistic children, or of institutionalising him, must be investigated.*

Autistic. What did that mean? She looked it up in Teresa's dictionary: *isolation from the outside world, excluding interest in the ego.*

Meaningless words that left her with no more insight than before their visit to Cape Town. She phoned the doctor in Cape Town, but could not elicit any more information from him. Apathetically, he just said that the child's behaviour had to be monitored over a period of time before a final diagnosis could be made.

Institutionalisation. Over her dead body. Then and there, she swore to God that she would search for answers. Even if she had to work her fingers to the bone. Even if she and Alexander were eventually rejected by the whole world. But institutionalisation, never. Somewhere in the world there had to be someone who could help her solve the riddle.

18

'AUNT MIRIAM! AUNT Miriam!'

Why don't the children leave her alone to enjoy her Saturday afternoon rest? Why do they wake her up just because they are curious about the presents in her suitcase? She had battled to fall asleep. Just as she was drifting off, she dreamt that she was travelling in a black hearse without brakes. And Lexi was sitting behind the steering wheel and driving so fast that the wind pushed her against the back rest. And when they reached the top of a hill the road ended and the hearse began to glide through the air like an eagle. It was too terrible for words. When the hearse hit the ground, she woke with a dry mouth and her heart beating in her throat.

'Aunt Miriam! You must wake up!'

Why couldn't the children have left her in peace until it was time to wash and dress for the evening's preparatory service? A hand pats her shoulder. She lifts her head from the pillow and stares into the shadowy room. Now why would everybody be standing staring at her while she sleeps? As if they had never seen her sleep before. Even Jeremiah's sister and her husband are leaning against the doorpost.

'Why are you bothering me?'

'Aunt Miriam must get up! The police are here in a red car and they are looking for you, Aunt Miriam.'

This frightens her feet right out of bed and on to the goatskin lying next to the bed. 'What did you say?'

'The police are here, Aunt Miriam. They're waiting outside and they said we must wake you up and ask you to come out.'

Merciful God in heaven, something terrible has happened to Jeremiah! That's why the second sight in her stomach warned her so strongly this morning. And that's why she dreamt she was travelling in a black hearse without brakes.

'The police?'

'Yes, Aunt Miriam, three of them.'

'Tell them I'm coming. Close the door so I can get dressed.'

The Heavenly Father must rather let Jeremiah be dead than in gaol. She prays that he has not handed his soul back to the devil in his old age. Since that time many years ago when he lost his job and landed with his backside in gaol for two years because he stole yellowwood planks from the furniture factory, she had firmly believed that Jeremiah would never write in his old sinful book again. Not even page through it. For two fear-stricken years he had almost choked to death in the crammed cell. As thin as a fishbone the day he was released. It took months before his eyes came out of their sockets again.

She sips water from the glass on her bedside table to relieve the dryness in her throat. The police? In a red car? None of the police in town have a red car. Maybe something is wrong with Evert. No, the police are used to Evert's drinking and troublemaking over weekends. They would not drive all the way to the kloof because of Evert's nonsense. It *must* be Jeremiah. What if he committed a shameful sin with the money from her sacred bottle that she had left behind for him? Then it will be her punishment because she bribed him with money that belonged to God.

She ties her headscarf. Puts her shoes on. Dresses slowly to gain time. The police will know that she's old and cannot hurry.

For years now, ever since Jeremiah came out of gaol with his eyes sunk deep into their sockets, she has stayed on her knees, begging for the day when Jeremiah would meet God face to face and take Him into his heart. All in vain. And now the police were breathing down her neck just when it's time for *Nagmaal*. Did all her prayers disappear in the wind? No, God would never let her stay on her knees for so long and then be deaf to her pleas. And He knows He shouldn't place unnecessary obstacles in her way now. She cannot keep her protective wings over Jeremiah *and* Evert *and* Miss Ingrid *and* Lexi.

She bends forward and smooths the seam of her dress, shifts her belt. Takes another sip of water. Then she walks past the astonished family in the kitchen, out into the long afternoon shadows hanging over the kloof. There are two strange policemen in civilian clothes and one policeman from town standing next to the red car. There is a hard knob where her liver should be.

'Good afternoon,' she greets them.

The policeman from town steps forward. 'Good afternoon. Are you Miriam Slangveld?'

How can he ask such a silly question? He sees her every day when she and Lexi go to the shop to buy fresh bread. He has helped her search for Lexi on more than one occasion.

'How can you pretend not to know who I am?'

'Aunt Miriam, these people are from the Murder and Robbery Squad, and they want to question you.'

Robbery? Merciful God. Then Jeremiah had fallen deeper than she could imagine. Maybe worse, because he also said murder. 'Question me about what? Is Jeremiah in trouble?'

'No, Aunt Miriam, there's nothing wrong with Uncle Jeremiah. We went around to your house and he told us that you were here in the kloof for *Nagmaal*.'

Then, after all, God is a merciful God. 'What else could be so bad that you followed me to the kloof?'

'These people want to talk to you about the woman where Aunt Miriam works. Actually, not about the woman, but about her child.'

'You mean Lexi? My Lexi, and Miss Ingrid's?'

'Yes, Aunt Miriam.'

One of the strange men leaning against the car walks towards her, but she keeps her eyes on the man she knows. 'What do they want to know about Lexi?'

Then she recalls the picture of Lexi flying between the host of angels around the truck this morning; how he drove right over the top of the mountain in the black hearse. Why is an invisible hand suddenly knotting her gut?

'Is he lost again? Have you looked in the pine trees behind the school? You know you shouldn't look in the lower branches, he always climbs right to the top.'

'No, Aunt Miriam, he's not lost.' He rubs his forehead and looks at the ground. 'He's dead.'

The mountain peaks around her turn flat, distorted by shock. It's as if her eyes cannot focus; her ears are ringing. A sharp pain shoots across her ribcage. She's thirsty.

'You are lying to me!'

'Aunt Miriam, why would I come all the way into the kloof to lie about death?'

There's a throbbing in her head. 'How can he be dead? Yesterday afternoon . . .'

No, God, no. It must be a lie. She mustn't cry in front of these strange people. God must be with her in this black hour; help her to push the tears back into her head, until she's alone.

'He drowned in the bath just before daybreak this morning, Aunt Miriam. These people are from Murder and Robbery and they want to question you about . . .'

Then one of the strange men walks up to her and talks to her gently, as if he senses the sadness in her heart. 'Get your luggage, Mrs Slangveld. We need you to make a statement and we have to do that at the police station in town. We'll bring you back here as soon as we have finished.'

She is about to argue with him; tell him about the preparatory service and tomorrow's *Nagmaal* for which she had risked her life. But something inside her starts bleeding. Dear God, how can Lexi be dead? She turns and walks back into the house, takes her church dress off the hanger and closes the suitcase. She braces herself against the sadness that threatens to choke her.

And she longs to be with Jeremiah, even if it's only for ten seconds. So that he can put his sinewy arms around her and assure her that the police are lying about Lexi.

19

PETRIFIED, SHE RUNS HER eyes over the graffiti on the walls. Some are desperate pleas to a faraway God; others are crude and abusive. Dates. Rough sketches of genitals.

Her legs tremble, a splintering headache pounds rhythmically in her temples. She cannot possibly stand on the ice-cold cement floor the whole night. She will have to sit down or she's going to fall over. But there is no chair. Only the toilet and a cement slab with a stained foam mattress on it. The disgusting state of the cell makes her shudder. It stinks of unwashed bodies and damp cement. Strong tobacco. Cheap soap. The voices shouting midnight conversations drift towards her through the barred door. She puts her cold hands over her ears to block the noise. Her head throbs against her frozen fingers.

She will have to start at the beginning, and reflect on the happenings of the past few days. Clear her mind. Tomorrow morning when the man questions her again she must be sharper, more responsive. Get the questioning behind her as quickly as possible, and get back home. Teresa and Zettie are waiting. She certainly cannot expect them to arrange the funeral.

What can possibly be in the post-mortem report that is so damning? How does the man know she's in financial trouble? What did Gunter tell the police? She must think, because if she concentrates properly she will know what Gunter would have told the police, and what he would not have told them. The last time she spoke to him on the phone, she was explaining why she wanted to sell Lucy. But then Alexander opened the tap in the kitchen and a stream of water hit a spoon in the sink. A fountain of water spouted on to the floor. She heard Alexander gasping and knew he was going to have a fit. She hastily told Gunter she'd phone back in the morning.

But when morning came, everything had gone wrong. Everything.

Perhaps the detective thought that she wanted to sell Lucy because she was planning to drown Alexander. No, he could not think that. Or, yes, maybe it was an obvious deduction. But she's too confused to know whether she's right or wrong. Yet, if she looks at the events through the man's eyes, she can hardly blame him for suspecting her. Her ears are buzzing. A cold sweat spreads over her forehead and down her neck. If only the mattress wasn't so filthy. Perhaps she should take it off the cement slab and sit on the slab. It would be cold, but it would be cleaner than the mattress.

How can the man claim that Alexander was dead before he got into the bath? She must calm down and get her thoughts straightened out. She *must*.

On Thursday afternoon it started raining. A misty drizzle that left a fine spray on the windows of the bank. The clients who entered the bank shook the mist off their jackets and jerseys and closed their umbrellas. Stood at the cashier's counter with their hands in their pockets.

When was Thursday? The day before yesterday? Indeed. Yesterday was Friday. Yesterday after work she took Miriam home, leaving Alexander locked in the broom cupboard. Put Vivaldi's *Four Seasons* on repeat so that he would think she was somewhere in the house. Nothing could happen to him in the broom cupboard. She could have taken him with her, but she wanted to keep him as calm as possible, because the hairdresser said she could bring him in for a haircut after business hours. He would get hysterical in the car because of the rain on the roof. In any event he would go berserk on the way to the hairdresser. And two bouts of hysteria in one day would finish her.

They were always exhausting, those trips to the hairdresser. Miriam could not take him there during the day because the hairdresser refused to cut his hair during business hours. She always had to take him when there were no other clients who would be upset by his behaviour; no hairdryers and noisy hand showers that would scare him out of his mind.

If only she had the money, she would pay Miriam triple wages to stay in on a rainy weekend, because coping with Alexander on rainy days was worse than the worst. When she managed to get him out of the broom cupboard, he scurried from light-switch to light-switch, giggling incessantly, flicking the lights on and off, on and off. The perpetual flashing between light and dark exploded in her brain. But for the sake of peace she left him to fiddle with the light-switches; at least it was not vandalistic or noisy.

'Miss Ingrid must understand that Lexi's head works differently to ours.' Miriam always stood up for him. 'We keep shunting him here and there and everywhere. Everything he does is always wrong. By playing with the light-switches he feels that *he* is in charge and *he* can do the shunting. Maybe he has the idea that the light-switches are obeying his commands.'

On other days he would walk up and down the passage with his forehead pressed against the wall, his fingers entwined behind his back. Walk, walk, walk. In a strange ritualistic pattern that he carried out with precision. Shifted his left foot sideways. Dragged the sole of his right foot over the carpet with a scouring sound until it was level with his left foot. Shift, drag, shift, drag. To the bottom of the passage. Then he reversed the pattern, worked his way back to the other end of the passage. On and on and on. Never taking his forehead away from the wall. Until his skin was grazed and the blood trickled down the sides of his nose; over his lips, dripped from his chin.

Telling him to stop had no effect. She reprimanded him loudly; in desperation she started yelling. He seemed deaf. She grabbed him by the shoulders and pulled him away from the wall, but he stared at her with no recognition in his eyes, as if she did not exist. In her despair, she hoped he would stop when the bleeding wound became too painful, but she had slowly realised that he was immune to pain.

And so the rainy weekend lay ahead of her like a steep mountain. All alone with Alexander. With a deficit of seven hundred and ninety-two rand at the cashier's counter preying on her troubled mind.

'You must enjoy your weekend, Miriam,' she said in the car on the way to the township, 'and you must tell Jeremiah I say thank you for the seed potatoes he brought me. And he must work out a quote for plastering the wall in the dining room.'

After Dawid's death Jeremiah walked up to her house at least once a month. As if he felt the need to keep an eye on her and Alexander. He always brought her a sweet potato slip or a few oranges; a bunch of tied fowl feathers for Alexander. Sometimes he stayed the whole day, helping to mend the fence so that stray dogs could not get into her yard to scavenge in the rubbish bin. He never wanted to accept money for his work.

'I'll tell Jeremiah about the plaster job. Tonight I must hang out my jacket and iron my church dress, Miss Ingrid. On Sunday it's *grootkerk* at my in-laws in the kloof and I'm going there by truck. We'll be leaving early tomorrow morning, and tomorrow evening I'll attend the preparatory service. It's a long time since I've been there for *Nagmaal*. I've set this weekend aside for that.'

She knew that Miriam deserved a weekend off, but at the same time she wanted to plead with her not to go away.

'When will you be back, Miriam?'

'God willing, I'll sleep in my own bed on Sunday evening. Will Miss Ingrid manage with Lexi in this wet weather?'

Exhausted, she looked at Miriam and forced a smile. She felt like bursting into tears and telling Miriam that she was almost eight hundred rand short at closing time; that the bank manager had called her in, that she'd never seen him so upset. He had raged about reports on deficits at the cashier's counter that had to be sent to head office. That it was the umpteenth time that this had happened, and that neither he nor the accountant could afford to monitor an experienced cashier.

She wanted to lay her head on Miriam's shoulder and tell her that the day was dangerously close when she would lose her job. Not because she was careless, but because she was perpetually exhausted and couldn't concentrate. And that would be the end of a long and weary journey. Then she would also jump off a bridge. Or take out the revolver from its hiding place among the pillows in the linen cupboard.

But she needed to keep her anxiety about the deficit to herself. Maybe, just maybe, the accountant would pick up a simple error.

'I'll be fine, Miriam. But I'd be grateful if you could come to work a little earlier on Monday morning. I need to be at the office early. If it's raining, I'll come and pick you up.'

'I'll do that, Miss Ingrid.'

When she got home, she was met by Alexander's penetrating screams. Standing in the rain she dug frantically in her handbag for the front door key. Breathless, she unlocked the broom cupboard.

He was sitting there, plastered from his neck down in his own excrement. Eyes pinched closed; face distorted; revolted by the stench.

And despite her weariness and anxiety, her heart went out to him. Her child on his far-off planet. A desolate patch on earth where he had not chosen to be. Only God knew why that lonely planet had to be his world. She bent down, spoke to him gently. 'It's all right, Mommy will help you.' In her mind she was anxiously working out how much time she had before they had to be at the hairdresser. 'Come, Xander, let's go to the bathroom. Mommy will clean you up, then we will put your blue jersey on, the one with the four boats on the front. Come, Mommy will help you . . .'

Mimmi! Mimmi! Mimmi!

Fiercely, he wiped his hands on the front of his shirt, trying to get rid of his own dirt. Ripped his shirt open so that the buttons rolled in all directions. Then tore the shirt off and bundled it to his chest. Smelled the revolting stench and threw the bundle aside.

Mimmi! Mimmi! Mimmi!

'It's all right, Xander, it's all right. Mommy won't go away. Come, let's run some hot water and . . .'

For more than half an hour she battled to get him clean. He broke loose from her grip and raced through the house, around and around the dining room table, his arms stretched out stiffly in front of him. As though he was trying to get away from the reek on his hands.

She was ten minutes late at the hairdresser. The woman had already closed up and was locking the door.

'I'm sorry I'm late, but . . .'

The woman did not even greet her. Just pushed the door open again and stepped inside. 'Why is his hair dry? Didn't you wash it at home?'

Everything on him had been a mess, except his hair. And in the race against time she forgot to wash his hair. There was no chance in the world that they would be able to wash his hair at the hairdresser. He would tear the salon apart rather than allow a hand shower near him.

'No, I forgot. But I'm sure you can cut dry hair . . .?'

'Goodness, Ingrid, you know that I don't cut dry hair.'

'It's been such a rush . . .'

The hairdresser was exasperated as she moved the high stool into position and told her to put Alexander on the stool and keep him still. It wasn't easy. He grabbed at the scissors, struck his reflection in the mirror. Turned his head from side to side and called *Mimmi! Mimmi! Mimmi!* Flapped his hands as though he was trying to shake them off his arms. Jumped off the chair, scraped together a handful of the dry hair cuttings and scattered them over the hairdresser's jersey.

The woman clenched her teeth. 'Come on, Ingrid, try to control him!' She was on the verge of exploding with impatience. 'How can I cut his hair if he jumps up and down like this?'

'I'll try again.' She stood behind him, pressed her forearms on his shoulders, planted her thumbs firmly behind his neck, all eight remaining fingers tightly on his throat. 'Sit still, Alexander!'

His response was obstinate resistance. She tightened her grip. Damn, she would force him to sit still! She heard him choking under the pressure of her fingers and slackened her grip slightly. But he felt it and grabbed the opportunity to try to wriggle free. Quickly, she tightened her grip again. She was desperate for the clip-clip sound of the scissors next to her ear to stop. There was a roaring in her head; she didn't know whether she was more angry with the muttering hairdresser or the writhing child. Damn his tantrums! He would sit still! The hairdresser struggled to reach his head over her back. Again she tightened her grip on his throat until she heard him choke.

When eventually she paid and walked out, her body was numb with exhaustion.

It was always the same, everywhere they went.

Uncontrollable little wild animal who demolished other people's possessions. Ripped their flowers; strangled their cats. Not because he meant to harm the cat, but because of the astounding miaow the cat uttered. It was music to his ears. Music he wanted to hear again and again. Jiggled the door of the parrot cage open, unmoved by the fact that the parrot had already bitten off a chunk of flesh from his finger. When she found it, the parrot was already lying on the ground. Dead. Mirna burst into tears about her expensive parrot which could say so many words, and now the clever parrot was dead, his beautiful feathers scattered all over the stoep.

'Mirna, I am so awfully sorry . . . I don't know what to say . . .'

She was truly sorry, heaven alone knew how sorry. Not because of the parrot, but because she was watching the burning of a bridge behind her. She was no longer welcome anywhere in town. She was rejected and ignored. Sometimes subtly; sometimes rudely. Mirna's house had been the last safe harbour where she could throw down her anchor when the seas in her own home became too rough. A last refuge against the hostility of the community; where she could rest and have a cup of tea when Alexander's flapping and yelling and chiselling overwhelmed her. Apart from superficial conversations with bank clients it was the last place where she could communicate her distress and hopelessness.

The parrot was dead. She couldn't bring it back to life again. She looked at Mirna's shaking shoulders as she wept for her parrot, and she felt paralysed as she watched the last bridge burning to ashes.

She grabbed Alexander by his puny shoulders and gave him the hiding of his life. She hit him until she was out of breath and her hands felt bruised. Until she became scared that she was not going to stop until he was dead too, like the parrot.

He was unaware of the blows raining down on him. Didn't even try to dodge them. Just stared at her with blank eyes. Unmoved. She kept on hitting him until Mirna intervened and tried to catch hold of her hands.

'Stop it, Ingrid!'

She pushed her aside and grabbed Alexander by the sleeve.

'Please, Ingrid, I beg you to stop!'

Afterwards her mind was a blank. She could not remember what she had said in her uncontrollable rage. But what would stay with her for ever was the expression of aversion on Mirna's face. And she couldn't work out if it was because of Alexander, or the dead parrot. Or maybe because of her.

Another day when she needed somewhere to retreat for a while, Mirna was unfortunately on her way out. Had a doctor's appointment. Was preparing the agenda for a meeting. Desperately needing to make good the loss, she bought a new parrot on Dawid's overdrawn cheque account. Dawid was beside himself with fury about the waste of money.

'For heaven's sake, Ingrid, we have barely enough money to pay the electricity account, and you spend money on a *donnerse* parrot! Are you out of your bloody mind? I feel like cancelling your signing powers on my cheque account!'

'Please, Dawid, don't make it worse than it already is. What else was I to do?'

'If the goddamned bitch is angry about a bloody parrot, let her be angry!'

'Dawid, I . . .'

'Did you see this month's chemist account? Pills and pills and pills! And each pill is worth less than the next! You must put an end to this insanity, Ingrid, or we are going to be in the shit!'

Three weeks later the expensive parrot died from some kind of infection.

At night she sat cross-legged on the dining room floor with Alexander, trying to prevent him from cutting himself and sucking his own blood. Her mind went round and round in endless circles. She couldn't understand why the parrot, which was just an animal after all, could speak. And her child, who was a human being, could only growl.

Her concern about Dawid was eating at her like a cancer. Day after day, hour after hour, Alexander's strangeness was clearly getting too much for him. Their finances were in chaos and Dawid's drinking was getting out of hand to an extent which scared her. He stopped playing tennis. She could not remember when last they went on a camping weekend, let alone a proper holiday. They seldom had a normal conversation, and their love life was non-existent. Apart from going to Gunter's farm on Sundays, Dawid refused to go anywhere. The zest for life that had once sparkled so brightly in him turned into a handful of cold ashes.

Day after day she battled to coax him away from the cocoon he was weaving around himself. She talked. She pushed. She pulled. Because she dared not let him slip deeper into the blackness of depression.

'What do you hear from your parents?'

His forehead wrinkled in a frown. 'Bugger all.'

'Why don't you phone them?'

'To say what?'

'Just to talk . . .'

He snorted disdainfully and got up to fill his brandy glass.

How are things at work? *All right.* What kind of shaving cream must I buy you? *Any kind.* Miriam says Jeremiah's going to have a good crop of runner beans this season. *Oh.* Do you have any books to be returned to the library? *No.* I believe the mayor is threatening to resign because of conflict in the council offices. *That's his business.* Who do you fancy to win the Rugby World Cup this year? *No idea.*

After the dominee came to see them about Alexander's disruptive behaviour during services, Dawid stopped going to church altogether. She would willingly have stayed at home with Alexander while Dawid went to church, but he was furious with the dominee.

'He's a man of God who is supposed to have humanity and

compassion in his heart. His attitude stinks! Why should you have to sit in the appalling chaos of the mothers' room and listen to the service over a distorted microphone system? There's not even a carpet in the mothers' room, and the place is stacked to the ceiling with boxes and ancient church registers and all sorts of other crap!'

'Dawid, we must try to understand why people complain. Traditionally, a church service is meant to carry an atmosphere of . . .'

'But when it's time for the fund-raising fête, or time to collect the monthly pledges, *then* they don't push us into a poky little room. No, then we must dig into our pockets for a so-called good cause. Do you know what the *real* meaning of that good cause is, Ingrid? Do you?'

She shook her head, amazed at his fury.

'*Money*, that's the name of the so-called good cause. The dominee sends deacons from door to door to wheedle money out of pensioners and extort people into tithing. And all the while, he's filling his own pocket! Buys a mansion at the sea and goes on holiday four times a year! Sends his children to the best schools and drives around in an expensive car. But there's not a penny in the coffers to fix the mothers' room!'

She left him to blow off steam, hoping that he would get rid of his bitterness.

'When the deacons do their rounds again to collect baking ingredients and second-hand clothes and all sorts of crap for the church fête, you give nothing, Ingrid, nothing! Not one single crumb! I have no intention whatsoever of stuffing the pockets of a money-grabber!'

Sometimes she felt that she took Alexander to church intentionally. An intention born of a burning desire that people would take notice of her hapless situation. They did not have to pretend that Alexander was the best behaved child in town. Not at all. But at least they could show compassion and concern, ask questions about autism. Offer to take care of Alexander while she went to the hairdresser. Pop in for a cup of tea, even if they didn't linger.

Something. Just something.

'Bloody two-faced hypocrite.' Dawid sat back in his chair, picked up his brandy glass. 'But church or no church, the day is fast approaching when I'm going to reach the end of my tether with the child, so help me God. One talks and talks and pays and pays. One tries and tries, but it's as if he has no conscience at all. He

153

keeps on taunting and provoking me, and one day he will do it once too often.'

She wanted to shake him until something got through to his brain. But his face was covered in a veil of weariness, and she knew it was not the right time to rage at him.

'I do understand how you feel, Dawid,' and she sank on to her knees in front of his chair. 'And I'm grateful to you for continuing to take him riding on Sundays.' She leaned forward and rested her face on his chest. 'I love you, Dawid.'

'What good is love when things are the way they are?'

She was too emotionally drained to get into a pointless argument with a man who was not sober. 'What would you like for supper?'

'I'm not hungry.' He stood up and filled his glass again.

They couldn't take Alexander anywhere. And they were invited nowhere. For he opened taps; flushed toilets. Unrolled toilet paper. Switched on empty kettles. Slammed cupboard doors. Turned on stove plates. Ran madly around the tennis court, dragging his hand over the diamond-mesh fencing. Grabbed the spare tennis balls and threw them over the fence at the players. When they hid the spare balls, he used stones or clods of earth, giggling ecstatically when the clod hit the court with a thud. He stood on the other side of the fence with his fingers woven through the diamond-patterned wire, plucking and plucking. Threw the chalk from the score board into the puddle under the tap and struck his cheeks in excitement when the water changed colour. Until the chairman of the tennis club came to see her about the disruption Alexander caused.

'I'm sorry I can't offer any solution, Ingrid. But the hard facts are that some of our best players are threatening to resign and join the bowls club instead. As I said, I wish I had a solution . . .'

She forced a smile. 'I can see your point. I'll make a plan.'

Sometimes she left him with Miriam when she went to tennis on Saturdays. But she felt guilty asking Miriam to stay at weekends. Miriam had her own household to take care of, and enough troubles with her own children. In the end she stopped playing tennis altogether. For the sake of peace. Sometimes, after Dawid's death, when her frustration became intolerable, she took her racket and hit balls against the practice wall with all the strength in her body. But that was only when there was no one near the tennis courts who could be disturbed or annoyed.

In the years after Dawid's death she learned that keeping to herself caused the least hurt. As time went by and the community's eyes became colder and harder, she slipped into a lonely world of rejection. At night she lay in her bed staring at the ceiling, a heaviness in her chest. She listened to the never-ending rhythm of the chisel and wondered if she too had become autistic.

In the middle of the night she climbed on to a chair and checked whether the revolver was still between the pillows in the linen cupboard. She took it out. Ice-cold metal under her fingertips.

She had a recurring nightmare that Dawid was throwing her off a bridge. When her tumbling body hit the river bed she sat up, trembling and terrified. And from somewhere in the house she could hear the rhythmic hammering of the chisel. She turned her face to the wall and covered her head with the blankets. The drought in her soul had dried all her tears.

Her only desire was to sit on the kraal wall for ever, surrounded by the comforting scent of camphor bush drifting on the breeze.

20

As the red car drives past the patch of bluegum trees, she looks back and sees the children waving at her. But her arms are paralysed and she cannot lift her hand to wave back at them.

Dear God, how can Lexi be dead? What is she going to do on Monday when she gets to Miss Ingrid's house and sees Lexi's clothes and puzzles? Even if she lives to be a thousand, she'll never be able to look at the ice cream cart again without going a little insane. What about Lexi's blue corduroy pants lying in the laundry? She'd only had time to let one seam out before she left on Friday. And Jeremiah is more than halfway with a beautiful toy for Lexi, made from the tail feathers of the red rooster that he had slaughtered the week before. He'd drilled lots of tiny holes into a piece of wood with the hand-drill. Lexi would sit for hours arranging the feathers in the holes. She told Jeremiah he must not use a single nail, because Lexi would pull it out and bite it. Now Jeremiah would just have to stop making the toy.

Nagmaal will also have to wait until next time. She's not going to come all the way back to the kloof. When they have finished talking to her at the police station she's going to go to Miss Ingrid's house, no matter what time of night it is. Just to make Miss Ingrid a slice of toast and a boiled egg, and see that the house is tidy. See that Teresa and Zettie's beds are made. Surely they will come home?

And if the angel of goodness tells her to do so, she'll stay with Miss Ingrid right through the night.

Heaven knows, her heart is bleeding for Miss Ingrid. Since Master Dawid's gruesome death Miss Ingrid has turned into a walking skeleton. No friends. Nobody to love and comfort her. The only place she ever goes is the farm where Lexi's horse is kept. Strange man, the owner. Seldom comes to town. One day when she and Lexi were on their way home from the shops they sat down under the pepper trees opposite the butcher to rest and she heard one of the man's labourers gossiping that the man talked to the trees on the farm. And at daybreak he lit a candle as thick as a grown-up's arm on the window sill. And when the sun rose behind the eastern mountains he walked into the veld to pray. She told the labourer that he was a busybody and that *he* should rather concern himself with prayers instead of selling stolen chickens in town.

How can Lexi possibly be dead?

He wasn't even ill. How could he have drowned in the bath? She cannot understand it, unless he had a fit in the bath. She cannot for one moment imagine that Miss Ingrid would leave him alone in the bathroom. And Lexi was never a child who played in the bath. He went completely off his head with his fear of the bath plug. One had to finish bathing him and lift him out of the bath and take him to his room before one could dare remove the plug. Perhaps he was scared he'd be sucked down the outlet.

There are many questions she wants to ask the policeman sitting next to her in the red car, but her tongue feels numb. Besides, he seems to think himself very important now that he's with strange police. She will rather keep her lips sealed until they reach town.

Halfway down the kloof she remembers that she didn't take the children's presents out of her suitcase. Beautiful pencil boxes that Jeremiah had made from tomato tray planks which he painted with redberry juice. Keeping his hands busy while he watched over her chickens. Never mind, when auction time comes again she'll send the presents to the children with the sheep truck.

When the red car crosses the low-level bridge just past the halfway mark to town, she turns her head away and wipes the tears from her cheeks.

Child of her heart, with the bright blue eyes. He always tilted his head sideways and listened in fascination when she sang *Gentle Jesus meek and mild, look upon this little child* . . . Why had God not rather taken Evert?

21

Time to think.

She wonders if the accountant had come across an error. Maybe she entered the figures incorrectly. Yet she knows she did not.

'Exactly seven hundred and ninety-two rand,' the accountant said and seemed puzzled. 'Let's check everything once again.'

Merciful God, she was finished. Her back was aching. All day long she stood on her feet; bent to put down the heavy bags with the coins; bent again to pick them up. Stood up straight. Bent down. Up. Down. She tried to push the frightening thought of the rainy weekend without Miriam's support out of her mind. Alexander's hair had to be cut. She had to buy bananas and cheese spread; a pair of pants and a jersey for Alexander, as he did not have enough winter clothes.

And then she had to have the damned deficit of seven hundred and ninety-two rand.

'You don't concentrate, Ingrid!' the manager said impatiently, pushing his fists into his pockets. She could hear the suppressed rage in his voice. 'You cannot handle large amounts of money when your attention is divided!'

'Sir, when it rains, Alexander is . . . he's always . . .'

There was no compassion on his face. Only dissatisfaction.

Devoid of all desire to defend herself, she wished she could give Alexander to *him* for a month to look after, night after exhausting night. Then he'd change his tune. Yet she could not blame him for being furious, because he'd given her a fair number of chances in the past. Not just with deficits and calculation errors, but with many other things too. He gave her time off to take Alexander to the doctor. A week's leave at short notice during peak times when the office could barely operate without every available pair of hands. Often, when he could see she was at breaking point, he took her off the counter. Or made arrangements with the accountant to reduce her duties. Discreetly, so the other clerks wouldn't notice and start complaining.

During the first months after her return from maternity leave, the other clerks still had empathy with her and took on much of her tedious routine work so she could go home early. But later it was a case of everyone for himself. And anyone with a screaming or sick child at home, had to make their own plans.

Every time the bank manager or accountant was transferred she prayed that the replacement would be understanding. It was not that she wanted special favours. She just needed an extra bit of compassion. Fortunately, her prayers were answered. Each new manager made allowances for her circumstances. Allowed her to make long distance calls from work without making her pay for them. Agreed that she could go into overdraft until payday. And when Miriam phoned to say that Alexander had disappeared and that they had searched the whole town but could not find him, they let her go home.

'I'm going to ask the police to help me search, Miss Ingrid. But I don't want you to hear it from other people and worry yourself sick.'

Later on, it no longer frightened her when he disappeared. Because she knew they would find him. Hiding in a storm-water pipe or high up in the pine trees behind the school. Sheltering behind the saddles and bridles in the farmers' supply store. Curled up in a tiny bundle on the coir mat at the church door. It was just a matter of looking in the right places.

No, this time she could not blame the manager for being angry. Seven hundred and ninety-two rand was a lot of money.

'Let's go into the office.' He walked ahead of her. 'Sit down,' he said grimly, closing the door behind them.

'I am very sorry, sir. I'll repay the deficit.'

He looked at her in amazement. He spread his hands on his

desk, as if to say: enough is enough. His voice was icy. 'And how do you propose to pay it back, Ingrid? Your cheque account has been overdrawn since a week after payday, without my permission. You know the bank's policy about staff members overdrawing their accounts.'

He was harder than she had thought he would be.

'Look, Ingrid, I realise that Alexander is difficult. I know you're having a hard time financially and that you don't get enough sleep. But you must remember that the bank is a business that has to be run on disciplined lines and the aim is to show a profit. There is no way the bank can afford to waive . . .'

She longed to retreat to a dark and silent place far away, where nothing he said could hurt her. No reproaches. No reprimands. Nothing. All she wanted was to go home and be alone.

'Would it be possible for you to extend my overdraft limit a further eight hundred rand, sir? Just for two weeks?'

'You don't *have* an overdraft facility, Ingrid. It's a concession as it is.'

'Sir . . .?' Would the revolver have rusted? 'Please, sir. Just temporarily . . .'

'And then, after two weeks?'

She would make a plan. Even if it meant selling the cupboard in the spare room, and the carpet in the sitting room.

Or the horse.

Yes. When she got home, she'd phone Gunter and ask him if he would buy Lucy from her. If he asked awkward questions, or mentioned Alexander's love for the horse, she would tell him the truth . . . No, she had no idea what she would tell him. But she'd think of something.

And suddenly, as she sat in the bank manager's air-conditioned office, she longed for Gunter with an intensity that was different from the way she had ever longed for Dawid. She recalled the serenity of Gunter's face in the fading light of the setting sun. The way in which he cupped his hands over his knees. Knelt next to Alexander with his pocket knife. How he lifted the sleeping child from the horse's back and carried him on his shoulder to the car. Like the reopening of a painful wound, she remembered the day when she cried on his back. How he had stroked the soft flesh of her upper arm.

Man with the khaki shirt, holding his hand out for her to use as a step to get on to the kraal wall. Who wiped the horse sweat off his hands on his khaki pants. Who gave her a little stone in which she could save her prayers. How often she woke up, trembling, and prayed in the dark that the primeval woman in her would slumber a little longer.

'Sir, I will make a commitment to settle my overdraft within two weeks.'

Tensely, his fingers closed into a fist; he shook his head in disbelief. 'How, Ingrid, *how* are you going to do that?'

She'd tell Gunter the truth. Make a deal with him that she would buy the horse back from him one day. With interest. Stabling and grazing expenses too. 'I can only give you my word of honour, sir.'

Despondently, he covered his face with his hands and sighed. 'I'll agree this time, Ingrid. But this must never happen again. It's against the bank's policy and in the end I'll be the one in trouble. Next time I will be forced to act strictly according to regulations.'

'Thank you, sir.'

'Do you understand the implications, Ingrid?'

Dismissal. No job. No money. No Miriam.

'Yes, sir, I understand.'

'You have a weekend off, Ingrid. Perhaps you should think about discussing your situation with the dominee. Perhaps the church can offer assistance. Would you like me to phone him to make an appointment?'

Church? She wanted to laugh in his face. Which church?

In the days when, at her own expense, she had baked for their fêtes and manned their stalls, the church had acknowledged her and Dawid only too well. Before Alexander was born, and Dawid regularly gave their pledge money, the church was never slow to knock on their door. For money.

But when tragedy struck they showed no concern, offered no assistance. Shrugged their shoulders when she had pleaded for help in finding an institution or school where Alexander could be sent. In reply to her plea for a small monthly contribution towards specialised home teaching for Alexander she received a bleak letter on a church letterhead: We *regret to inform you that your request was unsuccessful. The current economic position of the church makes it impossible* . . .

But at the same time the Finance Committee approved an increase in the dominee's annual entertainment allowance, an amount that would have been enough to pay for two years' home teaching for Alexander. And at the same meeting they increased the dominee's monthly travelling allowance to an amount that exceeded her salary.

'I've heard bank clients discussing the church's financial dilemma,' she told Gunter one scorching summer afternoon. 'The Finance Committee is already digging into the investment that was made when the mission church closed and the mission manse was sold. At the time, the Church Council decided that the income from the sale of the manse was to be set aside for restoration of the church building.'

'Then what are they using the money for?'

'To pay the dominee the enormous salary prescribed by the Synod.'

Gunter suggested they move into the shade, or else they would get sunburnt. She drank water at the stable tap and sat down next to him with her back against the kraal wall.

'You know, Gunter, I still bear a deep grudge towards the church. There are many things I can't forget, especially things concerning Dawid. Did he tell you what happened?'

'Yes, he did.'

'I'm totally opposed to the dominee, Gunter, because . . .'

'Don't do this to yourself, Ingrid, you'll just damage your own peace of mind. Let the dominee account for his own sins. God will be his judge.'

'Every month the Roman Catholic priest comes to collect a provisional statement of his savings account. He receives very little each month. And yet he shares that with the poor and the needy. The other day when I went to the township to drop Miriam off, I saw him handing out groceries and bread to a bunch of township children in rags.'

Her words were like poison that refused to stay down any longer.

'Gunter, our Dutch Reformed dominee's monthly income must be about forty times that of the Roman Catholic priest. Add to that the respect and admiration he earns because of his position. And in the mean while the evening services have been done away with, because the congregation is so small, and his pastoral visits to the farms have been reduced to once every three months. The church garden looks like a desert because they have to save on water and the Sunday School books are ancient and falling apart . . .'

She started crying. Somewhere inside her she could hear the echo of Dawid's bitterness and rebellion.

His protests about the black woman employed as a cleaner at the church who walked a hundred kilometres to work and back every month, in rain or shine; no shoes or uniform or umbrella supplied. Not so much as a slice of bread or a cup of tea during the day. Not a drop of cough medicine during the wet winter months. She washed teacups every Sunday. Cleaned windows. Polished floors. Dusted rows and rows of pews. Vacuumed. Scrubbed stinking urinals. And was paid a shameful salary with which she could buy little more than four bags of bread flour. No yeast or salt. All approved by the god-fearing brethren on the Finance Committee. And if the cleaner was dissatisfied with the salary, they knew there would be many other hungry ones who would be grateful to have four bags of bread flour.

God, Dawid had been furious.

'How do you know all this, Ingrid?' Gunter asked.

'The cleaner at the church is Jeremiah's niece and Miriam knows everything about what goes on there. And I hear people gossiping in the bank about the dominee and the unfairness of it all, but nobody lifts a finger in opposition because nobody wants to be squashed like a flea. You know what happened to Dawid when he stood up to the dominee.'

'But, Ingrid, how is it possible? There is a law on minimum wages . . .'

'The church doesn't even obey the laws of God, let alone the laws of the country. And if the cleaner dared to lodge a complaint, she would be minus her four bags of bread flour.'

Gunter picked up a blade of straw and twisted it around his finger. 'The ward elder visited me six months ago. He asked me to donate a cow to be auctioned at the church's winter fête.'

'*You?* You're not even a member of our congregation!'

'I know.'

'Gunter, please don't tell me you actually donated the cow.'

He twisted the blade around another finger. 'I did.'

'But you owe the church nothing!'

'I know. I made an agreement with the elder: I would pick my best cow *and* transport it to the stock-fair, and I would do so every winter for the rest of my life, on condition that the proceeds from the sale of the cow were invested in a trust fund for Alexander Dorfling.'

She was stunned. Nobody from the Church Council had told her about a trust fund for Alexander. 'You're lying, Gunter.'

'Why would I lie?'

On the Monday morning she phoned the church office. No, the secretary said, she knew nothing about a trust fund. And yes, she was responsible for the church's banking business and all income from the fête had been deposited into the church's current account.

That night, after Alexander fell asleep, she took the Bible and sat down at Dawid's desk lamp. Searched. Read about false prophets long since denounced by God, money-grabbers whom God had condemned to perdition. She lowered her head on to her arms and prayed. If for nothing else, she prayed that Dawid's bitterness against the church would be filtered from her thoughts. And that the Church Council would vote money to renovate the mothers' room so that she could sit there with Alexander during services.

God knew, she needed to trust the church, to keep the umbilical cord between herself and the church intact. Because she could no longer allow herself to carry bitterness against the church in her mind. Yet, she knew that Dawid was right. Because the money from the sale of Gunter's cow had never been placed in a trust fund.

The manager must be bereft of his senses to think that she would reveal her personal affairs to the dominee.

'No, sir, I'd rather leave the dominee out of this.'

'As you wish. But do use this weekend to rethink your life and weigh up your priorities.'

'Yes, sir.'

'Perhaps you should see your psychologist again. Your medical aid will surely pay for it.'

Only partially, she wanted to say. And nothing for petrol or overtime pay for Miriam to stay with Alexander until she got back from the nearest town where a psychologist had a practice. 'Not at this stage, sir.'

Before she left the office she had decided that she would try to sell Lucy to Gunter. She had no other option.

She must have fallen asleep on her feet on the cold cement floor of the cell. She loses her balance and staggers when the guard knocks at the window of the catwalk. The man presses his face against the glass and holds up his thumb to ask if everything is all right. Her pride refuses to meet his gaze. When she eventually looks up, he's gone.

Goodnight, Mrs Dorfling. Maybe it'll do you good to be alone to do some serious thinking.

Time to think.

She does not want to think. She wants to go home and sleep.

For years. The ongoing drone of bass voices drifts down the dim passage towards her. Does this place never become quiet? Her bladder is bursting but the dirty toilet seat makes her shudder. No, she would rather hold it in.

She must get some sleep. Tomorrow morning, when she stands before the man again, her mind must be clear and ordered.

She lifts her knee on to the mattress, but retreats immediately. It's impossible to sleep on the filthy mattress. Or under the blankets where many unwashed bodies have slept. She'll stay on her feet. The whole night, the whole of tomorrow, until they take her home. Apart from the soles of her shoes no part of her body will touch anything in this cell.

And right at that moment, out of nowhere, it flashes into her mind what happened to the seven hundred and ninety-two rand. As clear as crystal, she recalls paying the church secretary for a petty cash cheque to the value of one hundred and nine rand.

One hundred and nine rand.

She remembers how she used her forearm to clear the counter of paper clips, and then counted the notes down. Nine blue hundred rand notes. And a one rand coin next to it. Nine hundred and one rand. Her exhausted mind had transposed the figures. And the difference between nine hundred and one and one hundred and nine equals the deficit.

Dear God in heaven.

And Gunter has already agreed to buy Lucy from her.

When they left the hairdresser, Alexander refused point-blank to get into the car. The rain was pelting down, her patience was wearing thin.

'Get in, Xander!' He slammed the palms of his hands on the roof and she gasped for breath as the water splashed in her face. 'Come on, we're going to buy bananas. Get in, Xander!' He curled his fingers around the metal edge of the roof and tried to shake the car. 'What's wrong? Get in, we're getting wet!'

Heaven knows, she often did not understand him. In fact, hardly ever. Why did he always get off the bed at the foot? Why did he turn his back and reverse in and out of doors? What did he see in his reflection in the mirror that made him shrink back in horror? Why did he wipe his plate clean with his shirt when he had finished eating? How would he know to arrange the dominoes from low to high before he set off the chain reaction? He could not count up to two, yet he could set out the letters of the alphabet in exact order. And it was not that Miriam or the girls had taught him how to do it.

In the weeks before his birth she and Dawid spared neither trouble nor expense turning the nursery into something special. It was painted blue. A life-size rugby ball hanging on a fisherman's rope above his bed. Dawid's cricket bat and boxing gloves from his high school years mounted on the wall. Teresa and Zettie made posters with figures from one to ten, then climbed on to the step ladder and stuck the letters of the alphabet, with illustrative pictures, on to the ceiling.

How old was Alexander when she removed the letters from the ceiling? Fifteen months? Two years? She couldn't remember. But what she did remember was that she removed the letters to wash the ceiling because it was a mess of mashed banana and lumps of pumpkin that he had thrown against it. Long after Dawid's death she was searching for something in the garage when she came upon the box with the letters of the alphabet. She left the box on the garage floor and forgot about it. The next day when she came home from work the letters had been stuck back on to the ceiling, in perfect order.

'It's Lexi, Miss Ingrid. He kept himself busy with the letters the whole morning. I was busy in the kitchen, and the next thing I knew he came in with the box. He went straight to Zettie's bottom drawer to fetch the glue. And he put the step ladder up himself. Does Miss Ingrid remember that the letters were stuck on the ceiling when Lexi was small?'

'Miriam, do you mean that he did this all by himself?'

'Yes, Miss Ingrid, all by himself.'

Day of hope! She clutched the end of the lifeline, believed that the missing link was slipping into place. Because if he lacked the ability to associate and remember, how would he know to use the step ladder and the glue? And somewhere in his memory the sequence of the letters of the alphabet must have been stored perfectly.

She went to bed with renewed courage. She lay awake in the dark long after midnight, wondering about the real child lurking behind the barriers. She turned her face into the pillows and prayed that the shadows would go away; that Alexander would return from the lonely island where he lived in bewilderment and distortion. She begged God to give her the chance to put her foot over the forbidden boundary of her child's lonely coastline.

166

The following day she tried to get close to him where he sat in his tablecloth house. She showed him the pictures of the Ape and the Bottle and the Cow and the Donkey and the Egg. She articulated the letters slowly and clearly. He growled at her and covered his ears with his hands, shut his eyes. Like he did when the midnight train rattled past. When he opened his eyes slightly, she smiled at him and held up the picture of the Fairy. She said f-f-fairy. He flapped his hands hysterically and grabbed the paper from her hand. Tore it into pieces and crumpled it up.

Disappointed, she crept out of the tablecloth house.

There were so many things she could never understand. Somewhere in Alexander's brain images and emotions became distorted. Nothing was what it should have been. Everyday events about which ordinary people would not blink an eye, caused enormous turmoil in him. If only she could look at the world from his perspective for one minute; if only she could sense how to reverse his distorted images so that they were normal.

Then she would be able to step ashore on his lonely island.

'Miss Ingrid must understand, God created some people totally different to others,' Miriam had said long ago. 'The evangelist also believes that. Just the other evening I walked over to the old woman living across the street to borrow a spoon of curry powder. She asked me why I didn't find another household to work for. I told her that God had placed me with Miss Ingrid because He knew that Lexi needed an angel. Then she said that if it was true that I was a child's angel, I didn't have to give the curry powder back.'

'Miriam, how do you manage with him all day long? You have the housework and the washing and ironing and many other things . . .?'

Miriam started putting away the clean dishes. 'It's just my legs that suffer, Miss Ingrid. For the rest, I cope. Miss Ingrid must keep in mind that us coloured people don't find it strange to have to cope with wrong-headed children. We never had special places where we could send our children when there was a screw loose in their heads. Let alone schools. All of us in the township are used to looking after children with a loose screw in the head. At night he sleeps in his own mother's house, but during the day he's everybody's child to look after.' She stacked the saucers and put them away in silence.

She didn't know what to say. But she knew Miriam was right about the bond between the coloured people living in the township. They had a hard life, a life lacking many privileges that the white people took for granted. But they loved. They belonged. They shared the little they had. Quite the opposite of the white community.

'Miss Ingrid mustn't worry about me and Lexi. We understand each other.'

What was wrong in Alexander's head? So drastically wrong and so against all normal rules of society that it had severed the bond between her and all the people she had ever cared about. Somewhere an important link was missing. Just missing. There was nowhere she had not searched for it. Nowhere. And the harder she searched, the less she could find it.

In answer to every question that she had asked up to that point, the doctors had shaken their heads. All their solutions and explanations were nothing but chaff in the wind. But in spite of the hopelessness of the situation, she kept asking. Not only the doctors, but herself too.

Why did he fear the sound of plastic and trains and rain, but listen to the church bells with a radiant face? What was hidden in the breath of the north wind that it chased him around and around the house, or in the south wind that it made him hide in the pine trees behind the school? Why did he yell when you put on his red jersey, but wore his blue jersey without complaint? What satisfaction did he get from lying dead still on the lawn for hours, watching the clear blue sky? And what caused him to roll over and turn his face into the lawn as soon as the smallest cloud drifted past?

Was it possible that he remembered the blue room, just like he remembered the letters of the alphabet?

The rain continued to sift down on them. Behind her she heard the hairdresser turn the key in the door. The missing seven hundred and ninety-two rand threatened to drive her insane. What if Gunter was not interested in buying the horse? No, he would not refuse. He would know she was in some kind of trouble.

'Come on, Alexander, damn it! Get in!'

It was only when she noticed the plastic shopping bag with his new pants and jersey lying on the front seat that she understood. She pushed past him and threw the bag on to the back seat. He yelled like a whistle and smacked his cheeks, then jumped into the car backwards. He immediately started fiddling with the radio, turning the volume up to an ear-splitting level. She switched the radio off, pulled it out and put it under her seat. He paid no further attention to the radio and started flipping the sunscreen up and down. He soon forgot about that too, and began slamming the lid of the glove compartment. Open, close, open, close. The louder the noise, the faster he flapped his hands and smacked his cheeks.

Drive fast, an evil voice inside her said; drive as fast as you can. Out of town. Don't think. Just step on the petrol. Faster and faster. Aim straight for the first telephone pole. Then you won't have to worry yourself sick about seven hundred and ninety-two rand. Or about selling the horse, or about the day when Miriam was too old to be Alexander's substitute mother.

What unsettled her more than on other days, was that it was Dawid's birthday. All day she had longed for him with painful regret in her heart. She caught herself yearning to turn the clock back to that last Sunday; to create an emotional barrier between him and the rail of the bridge. Why had she missed the signs of approaching tragedy? Why had she allowed their finances to spiral out of control to the brink of total collapse?

But what tormented her most of all was her inability to block the pictures of the past that flashed through her head.

Her Dawid. Young, strong, laughing. Beer in one hand, *braai* fork in the other. Waltzing her around the floor of the town hall, the sweat pearling on his forehead. Rolling up his sleeves and hooking up the caravan for a camping weekend. Standing on the rocks with a fishing rod. Rushing into the waves with a girl on each hand. Kneeling on the beach, helping them to build a sand-castle. Swinging his tennis racket back to serve an ace. Breaking kindling to light the fire on a cold winter's evening. Teaching Teresa and Zettie to wrap bread dough around a stick and make stickbread on an open fire. The sunlight reflecting on his hair as they planted anemone bulbs. How his naked buttocks tensed when he dried his back with the towel. His hand cupping her breast tenderly. Making love to her in the middle of the night, his skin warm against hers.

Her Dawid.

And a different Dawid.

Dear God, she did not want to remember.

If she could have been certain that both she and Alexander would die, she would have gone to look for the nearest telephone pole.

22

SOMETHING MUST BE VERY wrong. The police would never travel all the way to the kloof for an ordinary death. And why had they sent strange policemen?

Nobody in the red car says a word. The policeman steers the car smoothly through the sharp bends. Fast, but different from the irresponsible truck driver. There are butterflies in her stomach. It must be carsickness or shock. When they arrive at the police station, she must try to get a message to Jeremiah to go to Katrien's house and get her something to eat. And a bottle of sweet black coffee. He could send her food to the police station with one of the township children.

Dear Jesus.

No.

She cannot think of food now.

When the lights of the town appear in the distance, she gathers her courage and talks to the man next to her. 'What do these people want to know about Lexi?'

'I don't know, Aunt Miriam. Just something.'

'Something about what?'

'About the child. And about his mother.'

She's not going to lick his backside for information. They can ask her anything, she'll answer each and every question. Not that there's much to say. Lexi was just Lexi. She'll tell them that she taught him to eat with a teaspoon. Not that he ate with it every day, but still. And that she taught him to count his fingers and toes. Even though he could not say the answer out loud, he could show how much is seven and twelve and sixteen. Colours too. When she told him to hand her the green block, he knew which one it was. Red and blue and yellow too. But not the black blocks. He refused to play with them. She'll tell them about the puzzles that he could sort and put together so quickly. And that she doesn't know how he was able to, but he could read.

She'll tell them whatever they want to know.

But they must not lock her up in gaol tonight. It would destroy her dignity to sleep in the cells. When they have finished questioning her she'll go to Miss Ingrid's house. It doesn't matter if it's after midnight. Even though Miss Ingrid was sick with a tight chest, and even though her patience had been wearing thin during the last few weeks, Lexi was her child. And in the stillness of night a mother's heartache is deeper than when the sun is shining. At night you don't have to break kindling and knead dough and feed chickens. There is lots of time for the pain and sorrow to prey on you. Like the chicken eagle circling in the sky all day long watching the chicks. Waiting for the moment when one of them wanders away from the hen. And in the twinkling of an eye it dives down and grabs a chick in its claws. Tonight the chicken eagle will surely be circling over Miss Ingrid.

She knows the heartbreaking hell of losing a child.

Between Evert and Joseph she also had buried a child. Little Leth. Named after Jeremiah's grandmother who was struck to ashes by lightning while she was gathering firewood in the veld. Beautiful child, Little Leth. Dimples in her plump cheeks. She could not walk yet, but she could sit firmly. She was slaughtering a chicken behind the woodshed, and had put a huge pot of water on the stove to dip the chicken into before she started plucking the feathers. And she didn't know that Evert had pulled the pot with boiling water off the stove, while Little Leth was sitting right in front of it. Instead of calling her where she was busy chopping off the chicken's head, Evert ran off into the street like a wild horse.

It was only when she went into the kitchen to dip the headless chicken in the boiling water, that she saw Little Leth. She dropped the enamel bowl with the chicken on the kitchen floor and ran. One big stride down the front steps. Fright and panic made her jump right over the fence between her yard and Aunt Maria's, and she heard herself shouting at Aunt Maria to call the ambulance. She yelled to the children playing in the street to go call Jeremiah where the lazy bastard was playing dominoes on a five-gallon drum with her hard-earned bread money.

God knows, that day was the closest she had ever come to insanity. Jeremiah had to drag her off Evert, because in her madness she would have killed him with her bare hands.

For three weeks every living soul in the township prayed and sang for Little Leth while she was lying in hospital bandaged from head to toe in sterilised dressings. Nobody, not even she, was allowed to enter the room, in case Leth picked up a germ. The closest she could get to her child was to look at her through the little round window in the door. But the whole township sang and prayed. From Aunt Maria right down to Uncle William, whose clever brains eventually pushed him off the rails and who lived in an old car wreck at the far end of the township. Everybody.

Sang. Prayed. Sang. Prayed.

On the twenty-second day when God came to fetch Little Leth to become one of His angels, she refused to let go of her child. Raged at God and accused Him of stealing from her.

And to this day the chicken eagle still dives down on her. And his favourite time is in the small hours of the night.

It will be best if she stays with Miss Ingrid the whole night. Your child remains your child. The colour of your skin does not change the depth of your pain. There is no difference whether you sit behind the chicken run in the light of the moon, crumpled up and torn by sorrow, or whether you lie on a soft mattress under a mohair blanket, hunched by grief and sadness. The burden is equally hard to carry.

Miss Ingrid will need her tonight.

23

A SHADOWY FIGURE UNLOCKS the barred door with a clattering sound. Perhaps she was right after all: they are taking her home. She can recall the man saying that he had phone calls to make. Perhaps at last he has realised that she is innocent. She puts her hand out to pick up her bag.

'Come,' the police constable says. 'Colonel Herselman is waiting for you in the interrogation room.'

The flicker of hope dies immediately.

'He said I could sleep.'

'He changed his mind.'

She feels nauseous with disappointment. Not just because her hopes have been dashed, but because the man with the beady eyes is waiting for her. To whom has he spoken? What sinister information can he possibly have? Have they treated Miriam with respect? Have they also asked Gunter the same questions, over and over again?

Uncertainly, she takes her hand away from her bag. When she walks down the cold passage ahead of the police constable her feet feel like chunks of ice. She cannot stay on her feet the whole night *and* the next day. She'll either collapse from exhaustion, or she'll freeze from her feet upwards.

They walk past many cell doors; the bass voices fade away

behind her. She longs to touch her personal belongings in her bag. Will somebody bring her a cup of coffee and a headache tablet? Have Teresa and Zettie arrived yet? Did the police give them the key to the house?

The interrogation room is stuffy and smells of dust and pencil sharpenings. The woman pushes the steel door closed. There are carpets against the walls. No windows. A bare light bulb shines sharply into her eyes. The man sits down behind the desk and uses a ruler to tear a lengthy fax into individual pages. The woman sits down on a creaky upright chair in the corner of the room.

There is no chair for her and she remains standing, acutely aware of a shooting pain in her bladder. The man's mobile phone rings and he converses in police jargon, but she understands enough to know that he's discussing her. Something about an insurance policy; seven hundred and ninety-two rand; a final warning.

So they have spoken to the bank manager; they know she's in financial trouble.

'Mrs Dorfling,' the man switches the mobile phone off and arranges the fax copies into a square pile, 'let's start right from the very beginning.'

Ta-tate-ta, ta-tate-ta.

'You were alone at home with the child. There are no signs of unauthorised entry to your house. No unidentified fingerprints. All the keys are there. Mrs Dorfling,' and he walks around the desk, entering her personal space, '*what* really happened in your house this morning?'

What can she tell him other than the truth?

'Nothing happened. I've already told you that I lay down on the bed while I was waiting for Alexander to finish his cheese spread. I did not intend to fall asleep. I just wanted to rest my feet. It wasn't Alexander's habit to leave a jar of cheese spread half finished.'

A master of precision, Alexander. Everything was done with passion. When he tore up a magazine, he tore it frantically until there was not a shred left to tear. When he broke a toy truck, he carried on until it was nothing but an unrecognisable piece of metal. Then he buried it, as if to make absolutely sure it couldn't be seen. When he ate, he'd stuff everything on the plate into his mouth and then wipe the plate with his shirt. Smashed the plate to smithereens if she or Miriam did not catch it in time. Chiselled right through the night, until he could see the bare rectangular form of the brick. Stared into a candle flame without blinking an eye, until the flame went out. Squeezed Dawid's shaving cream from the tube until it was completely empty. Destroyed Dawid's cufflinks with a stone. Switched on every piece of electrical equipment that produced a sound. Hairdryer, kettle, vacuum cleaner, fan, radio, microwave oven, washing machine, tumble dryer. Then stood listening to the bedlam of clashing sounds, flapping his hands in ecstasy.

No, Alexander would never put the cheese spread jar down until it was empty. And then he would spin the lid for hours.

'At what time did you lie down on the bed?'

'I don't know, but it must have been before daybreak; it was still dark outside.'

'How do you know that it was still dark?'

Is he going to start splitting hairs again? 'I went out on to the stoep to check whether the washing was dry. It was pitch dark outside.' The pain in her bladder shoots like needles through her abdomen. 'Can I please go to the bathroom?'

Behind her the wooden chair creaks as the woman moves. 'I'll take her, Colonel.'

'Three minutes.'

Three minutes is not a long time. She has to walk quickly. With every step the urine swishes in her bladder. What utter relief when her loin muscles relax and she can get rid of the shooting needles. In her heart she blesses the woman for closing the door.

She washes her hands. Drinks some water. Back down the passage, to the stuffy interrogation room where the relentless man is waiting.

'Who ran the bath water?'

'I did.'

'And then you lay down on your bed and left your autistic child unattended?'

Her muscles tremble with fatigue. Like thousands of butterfly wings fluttering in her flesh. The phlegm rattles in her chest. If only the man would stop asking the same questions over and over.

'I have already told you: I never meant to fall asleep.'

When she got home from the hairdresser she yearned to crawl into bed and cover her head; to sleep until the end of time. Without coughing herself awake. Without dreaming that Dawid had taken her by the hair and was swinging her over the rail of a bridge. Without waking up, drenched in sweat, panicking about money to pay for Teresa and Zettie's expenses during the coming semester. Sleep. Sleep. In a haven of green pastures where her cup runneth over.

But experience had taught her that Alexander would never allow her that sanctuary of goodness and mercy.

Ten o'clock. Midnight. The small hours.

The rain started falling heavily on the roof. Alexander's anxiety grew more intense by the minute. His eyes bulged and he scurried from light-switch to light-switch. Flapped his hands wildly and dived head first into the ragbox. Turned the television volume to its loudest. There was a distressing noise in her mind, like many songs playing simultaneously in different keys. She needed to think about the seven hundred and ninety-two rand. And about many other things. About Gunter, who had agreed earlier that evening to buy Lucy from her.

'Lucy is worth more than eight hundred rand, Ingrid.'

'Eight hundred rand is enough.'

'I'll give you two thousand. And Alexander's right to ride Lucy for as long as she lives.'

'Please, Gunter, don't make it more difficult. You know that the horse is not worth that much.'

'To me Lucy is worth more than any sum of money.'

'Why? I mean, she's old and weak.'

Silence. A distant noise on the line, or was it the sound of the rain on the roof?

'Are you still there, Gunter?'

'Yes, Ingrid, I am. And I will always be.'

Specks of light danced before her eyes. Tiny white angels with silver wings fluttered through her mind. What did Gunter mean? No. She must stop cherishing the memories of an afternoon long ago when she put her face on his back and cried. Or the day when she fell asleep on the straw in the stable and he covered her with his jacket; stayed close until she woke up. Or the previous Sunday when he washed her feet.

'Eight hundred rand is enough.'

'That's not what I was talking about.'

'Gunter, I . . .' She stuttered.

'Are you in trouble, Ingrid?'

'Yes. When I cashed up this afternoon, I was nearly eight hundred rand short and I have to pay it back within two weeks or else . . .' Before she could finish the sentence, she heard the gasp behind her. She knew what was coming. 'I'll phone you in the morning. Alexander is having a fit.'

Panic-stricken, she slammed the phone down and rushed to where Alexander was lying next to the pot rack, his back arched, his eyes turned back. She kneeled and supported his head with her hand, blew in his face. *It's all right, Mommy is here. Come back, Xander, come back! Look at Mommy. Don't sleep. Come, we're going to listen to the church bells. Mommy loves you . . . Don't sleep . . .*

No doctor believed her when she told them that she could talk him out of an epileptic fit. Impossible, they said. But she knew: if she heard the gasp in time, she could get him back. She called and called to him; brought him back to the surface of his sinking world without breaking the ampoule.

Kneeling with her child next to the pot rack, fighting to open his clenched fists. Desperately calling him back from the depths of his murky ocean. *Love you . . . love you . . . Mommy's going to make you some sweet coffee . . . Look at Mommy, Xander . . . Come on, open your eyes . . .*

Then he sighed and his eyes turned back. His fingers relaxed.

In astonishment he looked at her, recognition in his eyes. Hesitantly, he put his hand out and touched her cheek with the tips of his fingers. And for that fleeting moment he allowed her to step ashore on his lonely island. In her heart she believed that he was grateful to her for pulling him out of dangerous waters.

But then the whistling of the midnight train destroyed the precious moment. He rolled over and jumped up. Gave a piercing scream and headed for the sitting room. Scurried up the curtains like a cornered cat. Before she could get to him, the pelmet came loose from the wall and fell to the floor with a thundering crash.

Dust. Cement powder. Bundle of curtains.

She yearned to call back the tiny white angels with the silver wings. Send them flying to Gunter's farm to ask him what he had meant. But the silver-winged angels had disappeared.

Her chest was tight and she took three drops of eucalyptus oil on a teaspoon of sugar. It was a remedy that Miriam had taught her. It was bitter, but it opened her chest, and saved her from having to buy expensive medicine on the chemist account.

'Come lie with Mommy, Xander. Let's go to sleep.'

He ignored her. Just kept tossing feathers up in the air. Giggled.

'Let's lie on the bed and look at your horse book.'

He spun the plastic lid. Faster and faster. Flapped his hands. Grabbed the lid before it could stop spinning. Spun and spun and spun it again. When he eventually missed it and it touched the ground, he lost interest; jumped up and began hammering with the chisel.

Just one hour of sleep would save her.

She sighs and suppresses a coughing fit.

'I swear I never had any intention of falling asleep.'

'What woke you up?'

'I don't know, maybe the silence in the house.'

'How could there be silence if the bathroom taps were turned on full?'

'Maybe it was the sound of the water that woke me up. I was very tired and disorientated . . .'

'What was the first thing you did when you got up?'

She feels faint, as if she is being sucked into a world of nothingness; the walls of the interrogation room seem to close in on her. She must stay strong. 'I ran to the bathroom. Alexander had all his clothes on and he was floating face down in the water.'

Everything becomes distorted. The man seems to have four arms and far too many fingers. 'I called him and turned him over. Then I picked him up out of the bath and carried him to my bed. Or, no, I first closed the taps. Then I ran to phone the ambulance . . .'

'Was he already dead?'

'I've never seen a dead person, but the water was streaming from his mouth and his eyes were . . .' The walls start tumbling in around her; she feels as if she's sitting in an upside down funnel.

'If you've never seen a dead person before, who identified your husband's body?'

Yet another contradiction giving him reason to accuse her of lying. 'I identified Dawid's body, but Dawid was . . . he was . . .' she whispers. 'I didn't recognise him. I only knew it was Dawid from his wedding ring and the shape of his nails.' She swallows the lump in her throat.

'Let's get back to my original question. Was the child dead when you lifted him out of the bath?'

'I think so.'

He leans forward and hisses in her face. 'How, Mrs Dorfling, *how* did he die?'

She moves her feet wider apart, trying to keep her balance. 'He must have fallen into the bath and then drowned.'

He frowns and pages through the faxes on the desk, pulls out a few stapled pages, flutters them in front of her face.

'No, Mrs Dorfling, you are lying.'

'I am not lying. I wasn't with Alexander all the time so I can't say exactly what happened. But how else could he . . . I mean . . .?'

'This,' and he waves the faxes at her again, 'is a report by the detective who attended the post-mortem. Your child, Mrs Dorfling, did not drown. Definitely not.' He lowers his voice to a menacing whisper. 'If he had drowned, there would be water in his lungs.'

Black and white spots dance in front of her eyes. She hears herself cough. 'But that's impossible . . . that's just not . . .'

'Your child was dead before he landed in the bath, Mrs Dorfling. Somebody put his body in the bath. And you were the only person in the house.'

Her legs give way under her. The floor comes closer and closer like a heaving ocean, the spots coalesce into a pitch-black blur. Her voice sticks in her throat. While her tongue struggles to form words, she dives head first into the pitch-black blur. She becomes a nymph dwelling in unknown waters. She swims around in circles, looking for hidden treasure. But she has lost her sense of direction in the dark stream that pulls her down, down, down.

A voice like a ringing bell calls her back to the surface. *Mrs Dorfling! Mrs Dorfling!* From far beneath the dark waters she hears a phone ringing, a voice speaking in short abbreviated sentences. But she cannot hear what the voice is saying. The bell-like voice speaks close to her; it sounds like tiny bubbles shooting to the surface of her black ocean . . . *give her time to sleep . . . protracted interrogation . . . blue circles under her eyes . . . back to her cell . . . good cop tactics . . . persuade her to make a confession . . .*

The one with the bell-voice supports her head and holds a cup of water to her lips. She grabs the cup with both hands and empties it. She asks for more. The bell-voice fills the cup again.

Then, suddenly, the dark stream spits her out into the harsh glare of the bare light bulb.

'You are going back to your cell, Mrs Dorfling.' The man hooks his mobile phone on to his belt. 'You must sleep. We cannot stop questioning you every time you faint.'

She doesn't want to go back. The mattress is filthy and it's cold. She'd rather sleep against the wall of the interrogation room. They can lock her up in here if they think she has the strength to try to escape.

'The mattress is filthy, I can't sleep on it.'

'Unfortunately, it's all that's available.'

'I want my toothpaste.'

'Get the toothpaste, Captain. Come, Mrs Dorfling, let's go.'

Down the passage with her unlaced shoes. Voices calling from the dark cells. Will the voices drone on all night? Or is the boundary between day and night meaningless to all those who are lost down here?

Will Gunter miss her tomorrow?

If there was no water in Alexander's lungs, she can hardly blame the man for suspecting her. She must stick to the events as they happened, as they are engraved in her mind. Sooner or later the man will be convinced of her innocence.

The cell door swings open. The woman pushes her in the back. She's glad to see her bag. At least it belongs to *her*; something that does not stink. A scrap of humanity to which she can cling in this labyrinth.

'Hold out your toothbrush,' the woman says and unscrews the top of the tube. 'Are you sure you don't want legal assistance? You do have the right.'

'I need to think about it.' Hannah's husband is the town's lawyer. Perhaps he could assist her. 'I'll tell you in the morning,' and she watches the woman putting the toothpaste back into the pocket of her jacket.

Maybe she should phone the dominee. Tell him that the brat who caused so much disruption during his services has died. That she needs help, because Murder and Robbery is keeping her in custody in a disgusting cell, because they say there was no water in Alexander's lungs. Ask the dominee to go to Hannah's husband and ask him to arrange legal assistance.

No.

Hannah's husband was a member of the church's Disciplinary Committee which lashed Dawid. Lashed him until he was a broken man.

Maybe Gunter will know of a lawyer.

'I don't understand the townsfolk, Gunter.'

It was a rainy Sunday. Misty and bleak. And even though the weather was too bad for horse riding, she still went out to the farm. Sat peacefully under the corrugated iron roof of the shed, watching Gunter working with Alexander's feet. Listened to the soothing music of the rain on the roof. Wondered why it was the only place where Alexander seemed unaware of the rain on the roof. Why did he, who was so frightened by the presence of people and their touch, lie so still while Gunter cleaned his feet? Why was he always obedient and motionless in the car when they drove out to the farm? No screaming or jumping or fiddling. He just stared in front of him. Giggled excitedly when they reached the turn-off to the farm.

'What don't you understand about the townsfolk?'

'Before Alexander's birth, our family was an integral part of the community. Dawid had lots of friends and was a member of every committee and commission and board. I was too. But soon after Alexander's birth we became bad eggs and were pushed to the edge of the nest. Dawid must have told you about that.'

'Yes, he did. That's human nature, Ingrid. People tend to shy away from things they don't understand, or for which they're not prepared to take responsibility.'

'Christians too?'

He looked back over his shoulder, straight into her eyes, resting Alexander's foot in the palm of his hand. 'I don't understand Christianity, Ingrid.' He picked up a handful of straw to clean the knife blade. 'Don't ask me to explain Christianity to you, because I cannot. It's beyond my comprehension.'

Suddenly, a massive rage erupted in her. She had kept it dammed up for a long time, but on that overcast day the wall simply gave way. 'How many people live in this little town, Gunter? A couple of hundred! The same handful of Christians have a finger in every pie. Sunday after Sunday they listen to the Ten Commandments. Week after week they attend prayer meetings, support charity organisations, help the poor, send their children to Sunday School and God knows what else. Allegedly fishers of men . . .'

She kicked at the bundle of straw so that it scattered in all directions. 'Where were they during all those years when I needed support so desperately? They ran away. They hid. Turned a cold shoulder. As if we had a contagious disease. If that is the true face of Christianity, Gunter, then I refuse to be part of it any longer. When Dawid was still alive, he wrote a letter to the Church Council to ask the congregation to help us . . .'

She found herself unleashing frustrations and grudges, crushing handfuls of straw between her fingers until her hands were covered in red prick-marks that itched and burned.

'The school headmaster is the head elder, selected by the congregation to be our leader. He has a comfortable seat at the right hand of God. Because the playschool could not see their way clear to accommodating Alexander, I asked him to allow Alexander to sit with the grade ones for one morning a week. He refused.'

She scratched at the pricks on her hands until it felt as if she was going to tear through her own skin.

'Then I asked him if Miriam could take Alexander to school during break times, just to let him watch the other children playing. He refused. Came up with thousands of poor excuses about the policy of the Department of Education; about Alexander being exempted from school, about overcrowded classes and a lack of proper supervision during break times. Oh God, I don't even want to think about it.'

The itching on her fingers was getting worse. 'I sent him with Miriam to the *Kinderkrans* playgroup at the church hall on Wednesday afternoons, and told her to stay close to him, sit in the shade of a tree, or at the back of the church hall. It was important for his development that he should see how other children played.'

She was out of breath, her throat muscles tense from holding in her tears.

'After less than two weeks, the deacon in charge of the Youth Committee came to see me about the chaos Alexander created. He said the woman in charge of the *Kinderkrans* had threatened to resign because her nerves were at breaking point. She could not control the children any more; they all wanted to climb trees and chase hadedas and pigeons around the churchyard. Would I please take him out of the playgroup until they could think of a workable solution. Famous last words. That was more than four years ago, and they still haven't come up with a workable solution.'

The words flowed from her mouth. Jolting, gasping. But they helped to deflate the heavy bag of poison in her head. When once she looked up, she noticed that Alexander had fallen asleep flat on his back on the straw, without resistance. She sat with her head on her knees, sobbing like a child. Dispirited, she silently prayed that God would take Alexander in his sleep. If He could take Eliah alive, He could take Alexander alive too. And yet she knew that if God walked into the kraal at that moment to take Alexander, she would fight Him. In spite of everything.

'I'm tired of fighting, Gunter. Tired of doctors and questions and struggling. Tired of blaming myself for Dawid's death. Of being alone in the world. Tired of every damn thing.'

When she lifted her face from her knees, he was sitting on his haunches in front of her with the tin of milk ointment.

'Hold your hands out, Ingrid, let me rub ointment into them.'

She was scared that she would give more than her hands. But she needed his touch. She held her hands out. Warm fingers moving over her own cold fingers. Every joint, every knuckle. Around the cuticles. Following the lines of her palms. In the sombreness of the cold winter afternoon she was overcome with peace. A strange painlessness. Release. Her crying subsided and her mind became still.

Very still.

'I'll be back soon, Ingrid,' he said gently, placing her hands back on her lap. 'I'm going to put Lucy in the stable before it gets dark.'

When he walked away, she crept close to Alexander and nestled next to him on the straw. Slipped into a dreamless sleep. She was unaware that Gunter had come back and covered her with his jacket.

It was almost dark when she woke up.

Gunter and Alexander were sitting close to a fire in the corner of the stable. Alexander was sitting on his haunches wrapped in a horse blanket, staring into the flames. Motionless. The light of the fire glowed on their faces. She sat up and pulled the jacket tightly around her shoulders. And she could smell Gunter in the jacket. Man. Earth. Horse.

'Gunter?'

'It's cold, come sit with us at the fire.'

The rain was still pattering on the corrugated iron roof. The evening smelled of wild herbs and winter rain and damp firewood. If she could have, she would have stayed in the stable for ever.

When night fell Gunter draped a hessian bag over her head and picked Alexander up, folding the horse blanket around him. 'You must go, Ingrid, it's getting late. Keep the jacket, you can bring it back next Sunday.'

She yearned for him to take her to his house.

But he did not.

In the four years after Dawid's death, all those times when she sought shelter with Gunter on the kraal wall, he never took her to his house.

It was better that way.

'What is the time now?' She holds the toothbrush tightly, scared that she will drop it on the dirty cell floor.

'Twenty past two.'

Way past midnight. Teresa and Zettie would definitely have arrived home. They must not badger her children by digging into the past. They had been burdened enough in their short lives. Would they allow Teresa and Zettie to visit her? Would they *want* to visit her? Perhaps it would be better if they didn't see her here. Would Zettie have enough money on her bank card for bread and milk and meat? Maybe they would start cleaning up the mess in the house while they wait for her.

'Have my children arrived yet?' she asks hesitantly when the man takes the bunch of keys from his pocket and starts moving towards the cell door.

'Yes.'

'You must tell them not to upset my children.'

'You don't have to worry about your children, Mrs Dorfling.'

'When can I go home?'

He unhooks his mobile phone from his belt and checks for messages. Puts it back. 'That depends on many things. The forty-eight hours we can detain you for questioning will only expire on Monday afternoon.'

She'll be home long before then. 'There's no towel in my cell. Could you please send . . .?'

'It's not standard issue, Mrs Dorfling.'

'How can I dry myself without a towel?'

'Use the blanket. Let's go, Captain, I have messages to follow up.'

They lock the cell door and disappear down the passage leaving her behind in a hell darker than she could ever have imagined. And she knows that nobody in town will pray for her.

Except Miriam and Gunter.

24

SHE CANNOT LEAVE Miss Ingrid at the mercy of her own thoughts on this night of grief. If *she* doesn't comfort Miss Ingrid, nobody will. There's not a single white person in town who will reach out a hand of goodwill to Miss Ingrid. She will lay her hand on Job and Habakkuk and swear to that.

It's strange, the way the white people live. As if they don't belong to the same town. Unconcerned about one another's sorrows and burdens. It's just everyone for himself. Feathering his own nest. They never consider that their fellow man might need a feather or two. They never borrow a spoon of curry powder from one another. Don't eat from the same loaf of bread. There's little warmth and forgiveness in their hearts. But they're good at making enemies . . .

Take this ugly thing with Miss Ingrid and Master Dawid. Before Lexi was born, they had many friends. Every week she and Miss Ingrid baked and cooked for visitors. Many mornings she arrived at work to find stacks of dishes and teacups, dirty glasses and ashtrays. She often had to clean the caravan and wash the sleeping-bags when Miss Ingrid and Master Dawid had been camping with friends. She'd prepared chicken pie and garlic rolls for them. Made ginger beer. Baked rusks. Cooked Sunday lunch. There were many weekends when she'd stayed with Teresa and Zettie while Miss

Ingrid and Master Dawid went to a dance in the town hall. Tennis dance. Rugby dance. Hospital dance.

Church events too. Miss Ingrid was always one of the church's most willing helpers. She was always in charge of the pudding stall at the church fête, helped Miss Hannah to bake unleavened bread for Holy Communion. Took the lead at the women's Bible study group. Sewed for five nights in a row making the angels' white costumes for the nativity play. When the church had a fundraising event in the church hall, Miss Ingrid always asked her to give a hand in the kitchen. The church paid her a few cents, and sometimes gave her a plate of leftover food. Not that she was hard-up for leftover food and a couple of miserable cents. But her heart bled for Sally who did all the dirty work at the church. After all, Sally was Jeremiah's niece, and she earned a pitiful salary. One night, close to midnight, while she and Sally were washing up piles of greasy dinner plates in the church kitchen, something happened that made her to think long and deep about the church's unfairness towards Sally.

While Sally was busy at the sink, she went into the hall to collect more dirty plates. The fête-goers had left. The dominee and a few other people were sitting at a table, sorting and counting the money. As sure as heaven, it was more money than she had ever seen in her whole life. Piles and piles of hundred rand notes tied together with elastic bands. She really thought they would give Sally at least *one* of the notes. After all, Sally had arrived before midday to make a fire outside and bake hundreds of ash-breads on the coals. It was hard work, baking ash-bread. Sitting on her haunches in the sun next to the hot fire, turning the ash-breads one by one with her bare hands, slowly, so that they wouldn't burn. When the kitchen was spotlessly clean at last and Miss Ingrid was ready to take her and Sally back to the township in the early hours of the morning, the dominee gave Sally a crumpled ten rand note. And a paper plate with leftover meat smeared with potato salad.

God of all gods.

She had sat behind the chicken run for hours afterwards, trying to understand how a man of God could have so little respect for Sally's dignity. The only answer that came clearly to her was that the dominee was not a true man of God.

One Saturday, a couple of weeks later, Miss Ingrid and Miss Mirna went to the neighbouring town to do their Christmas shopping. Miss Ingrid came back with a white blouse and a black pleated skirt for Sally. An outfit for the church choir, Miss Ingrid said, and added that it was a Christmas present from the white church.

But she's no monkey. She could see the lie in Miss Ingrid's eyes.

And what about the time when the white people's church hall needed repairs? One Saturday morning all the white people arrived with scrapers and paint brushes and ladders. Miss Ingrid and Master Dawid too. Miss Ingrid took her along to serve tea and cooldrinks, and to keep an eye on the children playing in the churchyard. When afternoon came and everybody started packing up their tools and paint brushes, the dominee gave her five one rand coins and said thank you for serving the tea.

When Miss Ingrid dropped her off at her township house, she opened the boot of the car and took out a sealed tin of white paint and a brand-new paint brush. She said the dominee had sent it for Jeremiah to paint their house. Again, she could see the lie in Miss Ingrid's eyes.

White people.

She didn't understand them at all.

There's no doubt that Miss Ingrid had been one of the town's most willing workers. She was always there. Always willing to pull more than her weight. But when Lexi arrived and yelled blue murder, they had all left Miss Ingrid and Master Dawid out in the cold. Just the opposite of what had happened with Little Leth.

And take Aunt Rosie's Tompy. Born dull in the head. Half blind too. Drags his feet everywhere he goes. Pees on anyone's doorstep. But Aunt Rosie goes to work without a worry in the world. She stands behind the school hostel's hot coal stoves during the day; delivers babies at night. Because Aunt Rosie knows that every single soul in the township will keep an eye on Tompy. For more than thirty years now. At breakfast time he gets his bread and porridge wherever he finds himself. At dinnertime too. There's always somebody to tie his shoelaces or blow his nose. Not a single dog in the township barks when Tompy opens the yard gate. On Sundays Tompy has a regular seat on the front bench in the township church. And even though he farts like thunder during prayers and sings his psalms from flyers that he picks up in the street, he's accepted and loved by all the people in the township. They protect him as if he was their own child. When evening falls and Tompy finds himself dragging his feet miles from home, there's always someone to take him home. When his shoes are worn out or he needs a new pair of pants for the Easter service, and Aunt Rosie's budget is running short, they all club together to help. Because you can be sure: when the day comes that your purse is empty, everybody will club together to pull you through.

But it's different with Lexi. Altogether. The times when he disappeared from under her nose and wandered into other people's yards they chased him away like a scabby dog. It was too much trouble to tuck his shirt in or give him a sandwich. Or to phone her to tell her where he was. But they were quick to phone Miss Ingrid to report what he had broken, or for how long he'd left their garden taps running. Master Dawid was always shelling out money to replace broken windows. Or for a parrot whose neck Lexi had wrung. After Master Dawid's death Miss Ingrid had to dig deep into her bread money to pay for the damage Lexi caused.

No forgiveness. No tolerance.

One night when the chicken eagle was pestering her, she woke Jeremiah and asked him why the white townspeople treated Miss Ingrid and Lexi with such ungodliness.

'White people are not used to hardship,' Jeremiah answered in the dark. 'When the seas are calm, they can cope. But when the seas get rough, they are quick to show their teeth. Bite one another's heads off all too easily.'

'Lexi is a small child, Jeremiah. Why can't they show a little bit of understanding for the strange way his head works?'

'White people are not used to wrong-headed children, Miriam. To them it's shameful. Maybe they find it easier to send a child like Lexi away to a special school or a home where there are many wrong-headed ones like him.'

'Miss Ingrid will never send Lexi away. Besides, she says there are no places in our country where children like Lexi can stay for ever. What do you think, Jeremiah, what's going to become of Lexi when Miss Ingrid is old and weak?'

'*Jissus*, Miriam, are you going to keep at this until daybreak? I need to get some sleep; tomorrow I have to go down to the river to cut reeds for the runner beans.'

She got up and went outside into the stifling summer night, the chicken eagle following her. She sat down behind the chicken run and stared at the bright silver speck of the morning star. Prayed that the man who looked after Lexi's horse would have a heart for Miss Ingrid; that he never pushed her to the edge of the nest like the heathens in town.

Because, whatever the man might be, on Monday mornings Miss Ingrid's eyes shone with happiness and contentment. Like a woman cherishing a secret.

When the red car stops at the police station, she is overcome with nausea.

'Take her to the office at the back,' the policeman says.

A sharp pain shoots through her guts. She takes her handbag and opens the door of the car. She'll tell them everything they want to know. But she will never tell them about the day, long ago, when Miss Ingrid's spirit was lower than low and she pressed the pillow over Lexi's face. That was between her and Miss Ingrid. Not even Master Dawid knew about it. Besides, Miss Ingrid lifted the pillow in time. And the next day she emptied her purse to buy Lexi two pairs of blue corduroy pants. Must have been out of remorse for the dreadful experience with the pillow.

25

FORTY-EIGHT HOURS is a long time. Monday afternoon seems a lifetime away. She won't be able to stay on her feet until then. But she won't think ahead; rather try to anticipate the man's tactics. Strengthen herself against his onslaught.

Hesitantly, she walks to the washbasin to brush her teeth. The small stainless steel hollow built into the wall of the cell is revolting. There's no plug. A greasy layer around the base of the single cold tap, the smell of wet tobacco. But it's a relief to brush the bad taste from her mouth. She dries the toothbrush on her tracksuit top; puts it in her bag. Looks around for a hook on which to hang the bag so that it will not touch anything.

She examines the shower. It has a bare cement floor, mossy growth in the damp corners. A dripping shower-head. No door or curtain for privacy. She picks up the bar of red soap, smells it. It stinks. She walks back to her bag and searches for soap. Dear God, she has forgotten to bring soap. The idea of washing with stinking red gaol soap makes her sick. She will just let the water run over her body; rub her skin with her hands; dry herself with a bundle of toilet paper.

But when she crosses her arms to slip off her tracksuit top, she freezes.

No. *No.*

She will not undress. The graffiti-covered walls will not see her naked. Not now, not ever. She lowers her arms, pulls her top back down over her hips. Takes the facecloth from the bag and holds it under the cold tap at the stainless steel basin. Washes her face and neck. Presses the cold cloth over the abrasions on her wrists. Takes the enamel mug from the window sill and fills it with water. Squats in the narrow space at the foot of the cement bed where the walls have no eyes. She washes herself without soap.

Gently. Softly. Because it's shockingly cold. And because her soul is bleeding.

Brushes her hair. Mutters a prayer. Puts her warm fleecy jacket on over her tracksuit top and sits down on the toilet seat in the corner of the cell. Rests her shoulders against the wall. Despite the bitter cold of the wall, the toilet seat is preferable to the stained mattress and musty blankets. The winter cold creeps through the soles of her shoes and gnaws at her ankles. She rests her head against the wall, pushes her clenched fists into the pockets of her jacket.

And sleeps.

26

'Have a seat, Mrs Slangveld.'

She sits down on the edge of the chair. Her stomach rumbles; she didn't eat much at dinnertime. A piece of cold mutton and a small helping of cooked mealies. But it's all right. When they have finished here she'll make herself a sandwich and a cup of tea at Miss Ingrid's house.

'Mrs Slangveld, how long have you been working for Mrs Dorfling?'

'Let me see,' and she counts the years on her fingers. She must be accurate because the man has a pen and paper to write down whatever she says. 'Must be about thirteen years.'

'So, you were working there when the deceased was born?'

She was a fool not to have asked the policeman who sat next to her in the red car whether these people were colonels or lieutenants or sergeants. They mustn't get the idea that she's stupid. The man is not wearing a police uniform, maybe it's better just to call him sir.

'Are you talking about Lexi, sir?'

'Yes.'

'I've been working at Miss Ingrid's house since long before his birth, sir. And apart from the time when I went to hospital to have a gumboil cut out, I've not missed a single day of work.'

192

'Do you know that the child was autistic?'

Heavens, he must not think she's a baboon. Or that Lexi was a baboon. 'Yes, sir, Miss Ingrid explained his illness to me. I was used to Lexi's ways. But Lexi was a clever child, although the townspeople thought he was a cabbage.'

'Did you and Mrs Dorfling get on well?'

He's talking too fast for her liking. 'Very well, sir. We've never bumped heads. Miss Ingrid is a kind-hearted woman. When we're finished talking here I want to go down to her house and stay with her until morning.'

He glares at her and she sees a bad colour in his eyes.

'Mrs Slangveld, you are not allowed to have any contact with Mrs Dorfling. And under no circumstances may you enter the house. It's locked anyway.'

'Locked? But where's Miss Ingrid?'

'She was arrested this afternoon, and she's being held in custody at the city head-office of Murder and Robbery.'

Jesus of Nazareth, what is the man talking about? 'Do you mean Miss Ingrid is being kept in gaol, sir?'

'In the police cells, yes, temporarily. For questioning.'

'You cannot put Miss Ingrid in gaol, sir! What for? Lexi was her own flesh and blood! Can't you imagine how her heart is bleeding for her child!'

He seems untouched. 'Mrs Slangveld, the child apparently drowned in the bath. You knew his habits well. Why do you think Mrs Dorfling bathed him at that hour of the morning?'

His eyes are like muddy water. A shiver runs down her spine. Is she reading the colour in the man's eyes correctly? Jesus knows, it gives her the creeps. They're evil, like those of a cat stalking a bird.

'Maybe Lexi was dirty, sir.'

'What could make him dirty at that ungodly hour of night?'

She swallows. The man taps his pen on the desk. 'Lexi did not know the difference between morning and evening, sir. Sometimes he was too slow to get his pants down in time. He refused to touch his pants. He stood at the toilet and wriggled his bum until his pants fell off. But when he could not manage to wriggle them down in time, there was often a little mishap.'

'Do you think he would have got into the bath by himself?'

'No, sir, not Lexi. He was frightened of water. Often when he saw water, he went into a fit.'

'A fit?'

'Miss Ingrid called it epileptic seizures. I told her Lexi was afraid of being sucked down the plug, that's why he flapped his hands so wildly and pulled his breath in too deep. And in the blink of an eye he would be lying on the floor with turned-back eyes and an arched back. And then you had to run . . .'

He rushes into the next question without giving her time to explain about the syringe.

'Are you absolutely convinced he would not get into the bath by himself?'

'Yes, sir. Not Lexi.'

He turns the page and starts writing on a clean sheet of paper. 'Did Mrs Dorfling ever act violently towards the child?'

Instinctively, she picks up the direction in which he's trying to steer the wind, and it scares her. God must tie strong wings to her shoulders tonight, so that she can fly over this evil-eyed man. Because he's a sly fox. She must play for time. Act stupid. 'What do you mean by violent, sir?'

'Did she beat him a lot, or handle him roughly?'

'Sometimes she gave him a hiding, like any mother would.'

'Did she ever lose control when giving him a hiding?'

'No, sir. Miss Ingrid was always soft-hearted. Towards Lexi too. She just gave him a little slap or two on his hand to teach him. There were many times when she sat with him on the dining room floor all night long while he chopped at the wall plaster with his chisel. There were many nights when Miss Ingrid never got near her bed . . .'

'Mrs Slangveld, the child was nine years old, but he had the body weight of a four-year-old. Why was the child so small for his age?'

Low bastard. Suggesting that they neglected Lexi.

'It's true he was a frail child, sir. But if you could have seen how little he ate, you would realise that it's only by God's mercy that he did not starve to death. Sometimes ten days would pass without him touching his food. I often cooked a big pot of pumpkin only to have it go stale in the fridge . . .'

'Do you mean that he went for ten days without *any* food?'

'Nothing, sir.' She clicks her fingers. He must not misunderstand her. 'Only sweet coffee. At other times he . . .'

He holds his hand up to stop her; writes for a long time before he speaks again.

'Mrs Slangveld, the child's body was covered in sores and scars. There's a raw wound on his forehead and fresh bruises on his neck.

Who abused the child so badly?'

Let God give her the wisdom to tread carefully. 'If he was abused, sir, it was because he abused himself. He used to bang his head, sir. Against the floor and against the walls, but the place he loved best was Miss Ingrid's shins. You'd never see Miss Ingrid wearing shorts. Only long dresses and pants, to cover the ugly bruises on her legs.'

She can see him drawing breath to fire a new question at her. She must get her thoughts lined up quicker. 'And he bit himself and sucked the blood out. He has the sore on his forehead because he walked with his head pressed against the passage wall when it rained. He always did that. And this week, with the bad weather, he did it again.'

'And the bruises on his neck? Did he strangle himself too?'

Heavens, how should she answer? 'It's . . . it's . . .'

'Answer yes or no, Mrs Slangveld. Did he strangle himself?'

Then God's angel of goodness places the answer on her tongue. 'No, sir, he did not strangle himself, but . . .'

'Thank you. Did you ever suspect that Mrs Dorfling . . .?'

'Sir!' This time she's not going to let him shut her up. The matter of the strangling cannot be recorded as if there's nothing more to it. 'I want to explain something about the bruises on Lexi's neck. I don't want you to have the wrong idea, sir.'

'Yes?'

'Lexi's neck was always bruised after he visited the hairdresser. You must understand, sir, Lexi was scared to death of the hairdresser. It's the mirrors and the hairdryers and the water pipes. Miss Ingrid had to hold him by his neck and force him down on the chair, otherwise he would have jumped up and run into the street.' She must press on before he interrupts. 'And just yesterday Miss Ingrid took him for a haircut. So I'm not at all surprised that his neck is bruised. It would be a miracle if his neck was *not* bruised.'

'If Mrs Dorfling herself took him to the hairdresser, how could you know what happened there?'

'Katrien, that's my eldest daughter, is the assistant at Miss Mari's hair salon. Every time Miss Ingrid had an appointment for Lexi, Katrien had to stay behind after closing time, because Miss Mari has only two hands and actually needs ten hands to cut Lexi's hair. Katrien often told me how they battled to get Lexi to sit still. But because it was raining yesterday, Miss Mari told Katrien she could leave at closing time or else she would miss the township taxi. But it was always the same story, sir.'

'This Katrien, please give her surname and address.'

She tells him. They can visit Katrien at any hour of the day or night. Her township house shines like a mirror. Just last month she had new linoleum laid on the kitchen floor. And brand-new pine skirting along the edges.

'The name of the hairdresser, as well as the name of the salon.'

She tells him.

He turns to the policeman sitting quietly in the corner of the room. 'Send someone to get a statement from this Katrien and from the hairdresser. Immediately. I want to know exactly what happened in the hair salon yesterday. Colonel Herselman will want the information as a matter of urgency.'

He writes for a long time.

Then: 'In the past few days, did you notice whether Mrs Dorfling was more impatient or tired than at other times?'

He doesn't have to know what she's thinking. 'Not more than at any other time, sir. Sometimes I was amazed at Miss Ingrid's patience with Lexi. Must be because she's so soft-hearted.'

He keeps asking and asking.

Why? When? What do you mean?

And although he's rushing her, she keeps up with his pace. Her mind is at ease, because she knows that the angel of goodness has gathered more angels to form a protective circle around her. To see that she does not put her foot into a trap. A trap that may not even exist. Slowly, she feels her breathing ease; the rapid beating of her heart slows down. She sits back on the chair and rests her hands on her lap. Now she must keep calm. Keep steering in the right direction. Never change her route. Whatever happened in Miss Ingrid's house this morning, she'll carry her to the very end.

27

She awakens from a world covered in misty layers. Drowsiness. Thirst. Fear tightening her stomach. From inside the foggy layers a distant voice calls her. *Mrs Dorfling!* Keys clatter. *Come on, Mrs Dorfling, get up!* She recognises the woman's voice.

A warm hand pats her cheek. As she turns her head, a stinging sensation shoots through her neck. The warm hand pats her other cheek. Her eyes refuse to open. The man said she could sleep; why don't they leave her alone? The hand tugs at her tracksuit top. *Wake up, Mrs Dorfling! Colonel Herselman is waiting for you!*

She stumbles up from the toilet seat, her feet frozen. Stiff knees. Bone-dry throat. She starts coughing and with each hollow bark the pain explodes in her head. She rubs her eyes to get rid of the grittiness. The woman comes into focus; she's wearing different clothes, her French plait is neat, her make-up fresh.

'I'm thirsty.'

'Have some water from the basin, then we must go. Colonel Herselman is waiting.'

Merciful God. He knows she's at the end of her tether. What difference would it make if he left her to sleep and carried on in the morning?

'What's the time?'

'Twenty-five to three.'

Middle of the night. It's bitterly cold. Like a sleepwalker she drags her feet along the gloomy passage. It doesn't matter that her shoes slip off her heels. Nothing matters. Maybe she should phone Gunter in the morning to tell him that, if she ever escapes from this nightmare, she's going to jump off the same bridge as Dawid. She's not scared any more. In her dreams she got used to Dawid throwing her off the bridge because she could not shut the goddamned child up. Gunter must see that the house and the furniture go to Miriam and Jeremiah. Certainly Teresa and Zettie will not want the house of grief with its bare bricks and the smell of stale pumpkin clinging to the ceilings and woodwork. No. Nobody will inherit the house. The bank will have to sell it to settle her debts. The chemist account, bank overdraft. Rates in arrears. The service station for fixing her ramshackle car. Alexander's funeral costs. Teresa and Zettie's study loans.

What was left, anyone can take.

The man must have showered because his hair is still damp. He's shaved and he's changed his shirt. Then they do rest, after all. Hot shower, clean clothes, a meal, coffee. Lie down so that they are rested before they bombard her again.

'Mrs Dorfling, I find it rather strange that, apart from your daughter, you made no personal phone calls after your child's death.'

Ta-tate-ta. Ta-tate-ta.

'Everything was in shambles and I was terribly confused. And besides, there was nobody in whom I had any confidence ...'

The first time she experienced explicit coldness and antagonism towards her, was on Hannah's daughter's birthday.

How old was Alexander then? Five months?

'I've had a rough time since Alexander's birth,' she told Mirna on the night of the last pre-school committee meeting of the year. 'Maybe I should resign from the committee and pay more attention to my family.' They were having tea on the stoep of the church hall halfway through the meeting. The summer night was stifling; the mosquitoes buzzed around their ears. Everybody in town was short-tempered after a hectic year. It had been a year of crisis for the town because, financially, the church was on its knees. And when the church was on its knees, it was a reflection of many other catastrophies as well. Throughout the year there had been one church meeting after the other. To discuss survival, and to make plans. The Church Council sent out numerous newsletters calling the congregation to action; urging them to increase their offerings and become more involved with fundraising activities.

One Sunday after church while they were having tea in Mirna's garden, she heard Dawid talking to Mirna's husband.

'I have a feeling,' Dawid said in a quarrelsome tone, 'that the financial affairs of the church are going horribly wrong. The congregation is small. Only two hundred members, of whom barely half are actively involved. People in the countryside don't have the same business opportunities and income as those in cities. I can't for one moment see how a handful of people can maintain the huge salary prescribed by the Synod for the dominee. Plus fringe benefits, plus a car allowance, plus an entertainment allowance.'

Mirna came through the patio door with a tray. She frowned in their direction. Somewhere in the garden Alexander started screaming. In less than a minute Zettie had pushed the pram back to her. They were playing hide-and-seek, she said, and she could not keep him with her when he was making such a noise; there was no point in playing hide-and-seek with him around. Then she ran off. Needless to say, she and Mirna could not hear each other speak. They finished their tea in silence while Mirna looked at Alexander with irritation. It was only when she pushed the pram under a tree and Alexander noticed the leaves moving in the breeze, that he calmed down.

'Hannah and I are painting tablecloths to sell at the church fête,' she told Mirna as she got up to pour herself another cup of tea. 'But I haven't been able to help her for days now. I must plan this week better, and help her to get finished.'

For some inexplicable reason they had nothing to talk about. Mirna seemed like a stranger.

'The fête is almost here, you'll have to hurry up. Fortunately, I've finished crocheting the doilies which I promised.'

'My life is in chaos, and I am awfully tired.'

'Hannah said she visited you last week and Alexander has . . .'

Mirna swallowed the rest of the sentence. She had said too much. To gain time in which to change her words, she bent over to chase a fly from the edge of the milk jug.

'Hannah said that . . . that . . . Alexander has grown so much.'

How ridiculous. They saw Alexander every week. In fact, Mirna had seen Alexander less than five minutes ago. She knew then that they were talking behind her back.

'It seems to me that he's not growing at all, Mirna. He eats very badly.'

Silence. Mirna chased the fly again. The uneasiness between them grew. In the background she could hear the two men arguing. The tone of their voices told her that they were at loggerheads.

'I hope the church's problems will be solved soon.' She could think of nothing else to say.

And she really did hope that. She could not work a full day *and* see to Alexander's needs *and* handle Dawid's discontent *and* help to prevent the church from running aground. Every week there were new demands from the Church Council. If it was not selling hotdogs on street corners to raise funds, it was staging a variety concert in which everyone in town had to participate. Takeaway meals to be delivered on Friday evenings. Ongoing meetings to discuss a new concept for each ward setting and reaching its own financial target. And more. And more.

'By implication the church is just a building of bricks and cement, Ingrid,' Mirna answered in a chilly voice. '*We* are the church, and *we* must take responsibility for the situation.'

There was an almost tangible nuance of animosity in the air. Before it could explode into something that everyone would later regret, she and Dawid and the children left.

At the last pre-school committee meeting of the year, a letter from the chairman of the church Youth Committee was on the agenda. It informed them that the church could no longer make a contribution towards the running of the pre-school. God alone knew how they were going to keep the pre-school going without the financial support of the church. All evening the committee members were irritable, snapping at one another. She would really rather not get involved. Her own problems at home were more than she could deal with.

'Teresa and Zettie finished pre-school years ago and yet I am still serving on the committee. I'm sure there are many other mothers who would be willing to take my place,' she told Mirna as they stood on the stoep having their tea.

'I suppose so.' Mirna's voice was cold and sharp. 'But bear in mind that we are a small community and everybody must help wherever they can. But if you feel it's the right decision to resign from the committee, then do so.'

'It's not that I *want* to resign, it's just that I'm already involved in so many activities in town. Dawid gets irritable when he has to look after Alexander in the evening. He's a real handful.'

Mirna did not answer. Just looked at her without emotion. Sipped her tea.

Two weeks before the whole group of friends had gone camping at the sea with their caravans. They were looking forward to a weekend of fun. But it didn't turn out that way. It ended on a distinctly sour note. Not openly, but simmering under the surface. Alexander got on everyone's nerves. He cried and moaned and kept them all awake. Went crazy if somebody dared pick him up. Dawid became annoyed on the Saturday morning while they were preparing breakfast on the open fire, and one of the men jokingly suggested that they put a double shot of brandy in Alexander's bottle. His face pale, Dawid threw the egg-lifter down on the tomato wedges in the pan and walked off to pick up Alexander who was lying whimpering on a bamboo mat in the shade of a tent. He walked to the beach with the screaming child, only returning long after breakfast was over and everything had been cleared away.

By Saturday evening the tension was palpable. A small space inside her was filled with a sense of relief. Somehow she was glad that her close friends were witnessing what a hard time she had with Alexander. And yet, that same space was filled with sadness and pain. When they woke up on Sunday morning, everyone started making lame excuses to leave, and one by one they packed up, hooked up their caravans and left for home. It didn't have to be spelled out to her that everyone blamed her and Dawid for the fiasco.

'Do you think Alexander spoiled the weekend?' she asked Dawid on the way home. She desperately needed his emotional support and comfort. Just a little bit of compassion.

'*Bliksem*, Ingrid!' he exploded. 'You must be a bloody fool to think otherwise!' He accelerated. She could feel the caravan swaying behind them.

'Next time I'll take Miriam.'

'Next time, Ingrid, I stay home. Or the damn child can stay home with Miriam!'

'Alexander will eventually settle down, Dawid. And we can't afford to cut ourselves off from our friends.'

'Oh? And how exactly are you going to force them to put up with the child's tantrums?'

'Maybe we're just being oversensitive, Dawid.'

He gave a sarcastic little laugh. '*You* may be stupid and naive, Ingrid, but *I* am not!'

They did not say another word to each other the rest of the way home.

Mirna finished her tea and clattered the cup back in the saucer; looked over her shoulder to see if the other committee members were gathering to continue the meeting.

'Ingrid, I know it's none of my business, but what on earth is wrong with Alexander? I've never seen him smile.'

She heard the question. She wanted to believe that it expressed concern. She desperately wanted to talk about the anxiety in her heart. But somehow the words got stuck in her throat. Because hidden under the well-intentioned question, she detected the cutting edge of an extremely sharp blade.

'I don't know, Mirna. We've tried everything.'

'Have you been to see a paediatrician? Or a specialist physician? Your marriage won't be able to take the strain indefinitely.'

'We've used up all our leave to consult specialists. Any time we take off now is unpaid leave.'

Behind them they could hear the scraping of chairs as the other members of the committee settled down for the second half of the meeting. 'Anyway,' Mirna said as they walked inside, 'I'll see you on Saturday at Hannah's for Caroline's birthday party.'

Birthday party? Why hadn't the girls mentioned anything about a birthday party? And she had seen Hannah in the bank the day before; why hadn't Hannah reminded her? As she put her teacup down, the truth hit her like a blow to the stomach. 'I don't think so,' she almost whispered.

She had not been invited. Nor had Teresa and Zettie.

On the Saturday morning she bought a present for Caroline and went to Hannah's house before the party was due to start. There was no reproach in her heart. Just a painful feeling of rejection. But when Hannah took the present hesitantly, the words tumbled over her lips. 'Is it because of Alexander that you did not invite us, Hannah?'

Embarrassed, Hannah fiddled with the wrapping paper. 'No, it's just that I . . . it's just that we . . .'

'We've never lied to each other, Hannah. I'm asking you a straightforward question: is it because of Alexander?'

Hannah held the present against her chest like a shield; she looked at the ground evasively. 'I didn't know what to do, Ingrid. You must understand that my sitting room is small and there are a lot of us. If Alexander cries all the time, we won't be able to hear ourselves . . .'

Her pride refused to allow her to stand there listening to the feeble excuse. She turned and walked away. At the garden gate she wiped the tears from her cheeks. On the way home she stopped at the café and spent every cent in her purse on sweets and cool drinks for Teresa and Zettie.

Offerings.

But nothing could compensate for the tiny space that died in her heart.

When Dawid came home from the golf club late that evening, she told him that she had sworn to herself that she would find out what was wrong with Alexander.

From that day she had spent three weary years of wandering in endless circles and mazes before she found the turn-off to the ultimate destination. And even then she was never able to unravel the frightening riddle completely.

'A whole town full of people, Mrs Dorfling, and not a single person to whom you wanted to make a phone call?'

'I've lost trust in other people. I was going to phone Gunter at daybreak but I never got that far. Apart from Miriam, he was the only person who ever tried to give meaning to Alexander's life.'

He pins her down with unblinking eyes. 'Mrs Dorfling, were you having an affair with this Gunter?'

'No.'

He licks his middle finger and pages through the docket. Pulls out a couple of stapled sheets from the stack. Reads. Highlights something with a neon marker.

'Considering that you were not having an affair, he knew an awful lot about your private life.'

There's no doubt, they have been to Gunter.

'It's true, I often discussed my personal problems with Gunter, if that is what you mean.'

Arched eyebrows. 'Even before your husband died?'

'I only met Gunter after my husband's death. Sometimes I saw him passing through town in his truck, but the first time I ever spoke to him was that last night when Dawid did not come home.'

In the beginning, Gunter was nothing more to her than the Samaritan on whose farm Alexander's horse was stabled. But later she thanked God for Gunter. Because every time Dawid seemed headed for a breakdown, after a Sunday on the farm, he seemed more tranquil. Better control of his tongue. Less aggressive.

On that last disastrous Sunday it was Dawid's turn to lead the deacon's duties during the church service. To ring the church bell; count the collection money; lock up afterwards. An hour before the service was due to begin, Dawid was still sleeping like a log. She took him a cup of coffee and woke him up. Told him that he had better hurry or he would be late for church.

'I'm not going to church,' he said in a numb voice.

'But, Dawid, you're in charge of the deacons today and . . .'

He flung the blankets off and jumped out of bed. She was frightened by the wild look in his eyes. 'I told you, I'm not going to church! Let the bloody money-grabber count his own collection money and lock up his own church. There are lots of other toadies to help him. And for God's sake, stop nagging!'

He threw the cupboard door open and grabbed a shirt and pants. Not church clothes. He dressed and drove off without shaving or combing his hair. She was glad that he had gone to Gunter, because she knew that he was perilously close to emotional collapse.

But she never imagined just how close.

Alexander was almost four and a half when she went to see the dominee after work one day. It was six weeks before Christmas. It would be a poor man's Christmas for them. No Christmas tree, because Teresa and Zettie had hardly put up and decorated the tree than Alexander had torn it down. Once more they would eat their plain Christmas meal at their dull Christmas table. The only people who would knock at their door to bring them a message of goodwill would be Miriam and Jeremiah. They'd have a bunch of rooster feathers for Alexander. Bracelets of strung redberries for Teresa and Zettie.

The six weeks to Christmas hung on her shoulders like a heavy wet coat. God knows, she hated the loneliness of the festive season. All day at work she had felt faint and her bruised body was aching. Bruises inflicted by Dawid. But she could not confide in anybody. Her body hurt when she lifted the heavy bags of coins on to the scale. Every time she stamped a cheque it felt as if her ribcage was tearing. As the day progressed, her anger towards Dawid intensified. Her hands were counting money and stamping deposit slips, but in her mind, she was getting on to a chair and taking the revolver from the linen cupboard; pressing it against Dawid's head where he lay snoring in front of the television.

She could not afford to have such evil thoughts.

For that reason she went to the manse after work, quite spontaneously, without making an appointment. She hoped the dominee would be able to explain to her what God expected of her when Dawid took his frustrations out on her. Dear God, she thought she was doing the right thing. Barely a month before that Dawid had been inducted as deacon. It gave her hope. Never in her wildest dreams had she thought Dawid would be elected. Especially not after the previous year when he had turned his nomination down with such bitterness. And never in her wildest dreams did she think he would accept.

But he did, and she felt sure that the trust shown by the Church Council would help Dawid back on to his feet.

But then he used his fists on her again. Because the creases in his trousers had not been properly pressed.

She did not go to the dominee to lay accusations against Dawid, or to disparage him. She went there to save herself, because she could not live with the picture of herself cocking the revolver; pointing the barrel at Dawid's head. God, it terrified her.

At first they just talked about generalities. He did not mention Alexander, as if he was a ghost who did not exist. A small part of her brain warned her not to trust him. But she tried to ignore it. He nodded his head. Yes, Ingrid. No, Ingrid. Would you like some tea, Ingrid? Served on a silver tray. The finest porcelain cups. Sugar crystals. She could not help imagining *their* Christmas menu, served while they enjoyed the blue ocean view from their holiday home. At the back of her mind she saw the Roman Catholic priest who had come to the bank that morning for a provisional statement of his savings account. It was a meagre balance. Simultaneously, the contents of the latest newsletter from the church flashed through her mind. The church's financial crisis was once again rammed down the congregation's throats; they were encouraged to pay their monthly offerings by debit order and to keep inflation in mind.

Her instincts told her not to trust the dominee. But she had no money for a psychologist. What other option did she have?

'Dominee, I need to talk to you confidentially about . . .'

'Everything you say here is confidential, Ingrid. Of course!'

She sat opposite his desk, pouring out all the sorrowful and shameful things in her life, until evening fell. Revealed her bitterness towards the community. Wept.

For weeks afterwards she was left with a gnawing unrest. At night while she sat on the dining room floor with Alexander, she recalled the dominee's eyes. Hard and cold as iron. No compassion.

He quoted her soothing words from the Bible. Honey in the mouth; sting in the tail; the velvet glove on the iron fist. *If you are slapped on one cheek, turn the other too . . . Never avenge yourself, leave that to God, for He has said that He will repay those who deserve it . . . Happy are those who strive for peace, they shall be called the sons of God . . .*

The following February, at the annual budget meeting of the Finance Committee they reviewed a circular from the Synod dictating an obligatory ten per cent increase for the dominee.

Perhaps things would have been different if Dawid had not been a member of the Finance Committee. Perhaps the abyss would have been avoided if Dawid had not proposed that the Church Council reconsider the dominee's annual package, as well as the contract they had signed with him. If they did not, it was a certainty that the congregation would bleed to death financially. In accordance with church policy, the dominee was asked to recuse himself while the issue was discussed. In his absence, the Church Council gave their full support to Dawid's proposal.

Perhaps, if they had shot the proposal down there and then, instead of only later revealing their duplicity, the storm of hatred and revenge would never have broken loose. But because they did not have to look the dominee in the eye when they cast their votes, they were unanimous in their support of Dawid.

For the first time in the history of the congregation, it was officially recorded in the minutes that the regional church authorities be called in to analyse the church's financial situation and to advise on a drastic decrease in the dominee's annual package as a means of balancing the books. At last it seemed as if justice was going to prevail.

But then, driven by anger, the dominee began his persecution of Dawid. And soon a hungry pack had joined him in the hunt.

The dominee hastily called a meeting of the Disciplinary Committee at his office in the manse. He told the committee about the dishonourable deacon who abused his wife while holding a respectable position in God's house. Who failed to attend each and every service, which amounted to indifference towards the church. Who bet on horses and played poker, ignoring the fact that gambling was an unbiblical practice. In his capacity as dominee, he went to see the regional manager of the post office to have a so-called heart to heart talk about the embarrassment of having an alcoholic in charge of the post office in town. He underlined everything with quotes from the scriptures.

He was merciless.

For once she stood up for Dawid. Very determinedly. She went to the church office and asked the secretary for a photocopy of the church regulations regarding disciplinary procedures. She sat with the copies on the dining room floor at night, while Alexander chiselled away. She understood everything. And yet, she understood nothing.

Ecclesiastical discipline should be exercised: to the glory of God, for the benefit of the church, for the salvation of the sinner. Since ecclesiastical discipline carries a strong religious character, the officials must, in the exercising thereof, avoid any actions that could leave the impression of civil administration of justice.

Civil justice. God of all gods.

They may never consider themselves judges, but rather as fatherly elders. Through humility to God, sincere empathy and true brotherhood in Christ, they must attempt to lead the sinner back from his wrongdoing.

Fatherly elders. Humility to God. Sincere empathy. Brotherhood. The discrepancies between man's will and God's will made her shudder.

She went to see each member of the Church Council. Begged for justice and humanity from each one. And each one promised her his wholehearted support. Each one spoke about unfairness and scapegoating. But at the next Church Council meeting they sat like brainless cabbages. Yes, Dominee. No, Dominee. It's true, Dominee. Approved, Dominee. She spent hours with the dominee of the neighbouring town, begging him to intervene. She appealed to his integrity and his Christianity. But he just stared at her with sheep eyes. She borrowed money for petrol from Miriam and drove all the way to the regional chairman. But it was all in vain.

She lost the battle.

Dawid too.

And so, deep down, she was at peace when Dawid decided to forsake his deacon responsibilities on that last Sunday. She was convinced that he would find more solace on the farm with Gunter.

By sunset he was not yet home. By ten o'clock, she was sick with worry. She looked up Gunter's phone number in the directory and called him. No, Gunter said, Dawid had not been to the farm that day.

Then she knew.

It was after midnight when Gunter knocked at the door. His ashen face told her that he had the same suspicion.

Shortly after sunrise he knocked at the door again. Shock visible on his face.

Afterwards, her biggest task was to try to erase the gruesome picture of Dawid's bodily remains in the drawer at the mortuary.

'Gunter had nothing to do with my husband's death. He was my husband's best friend. In fact, I think Gunter was my husband's only friend in the last year of his life. Even his old poker friends deserted him.'

'Earlier you mentioned that you and your husband had once had many friends and acquaintances. What happened to change that?'

Is he never going to stop repeating his questions? Her legs are numb. For a few seconds the walls of the room seem to topple towards her. 'I have already told you: after Alexander was born my husband's personality underwent a radical change.'

'Mrs Dorfling, your husband possessed a firearm licence for a .38 Smith & Wesson revolver. It would have been much easier for him to shoot himself than to jump off a bridge. Why do you think he chose such a dramatic option?'

If only she could understand why the man wanted to link Dawid's death to what had happened to Alexander. 'Because I hid the revolver.'

'The investigation team found the revolver in the linen cupboard. Did you suspect your husband was going to commit suicide? Is that why you hid the revolver?'

A painful cough rips through her chest. Her head feels like an over-inflated balloon. 'Could I please have a chair; I cannot stand any longer.'

Ta-tate-ta.

'I will see if I can find an extra chair somewhere in a little while.'

For a couple of seconds they measure each other in silence. Then she sinks down on the floor, cross-legged. Presses her ice-cold hands against her forehead to soothe the throbbing headache.

'Answer my question, Mrs Dorfling.'

Please God, let him stop this inquisition. Her head is too sore to think; her emotions too raw to bear digging into the painful past. 'I cannot remember your question.'

'You're wasting my time, Mrs Dorfling, and you're stretching my patience. Did you suspect that your husband was going to commit suicide? Is that why you hid the revolver?'

'No. I hid the revolver long before my husband's death. Suicide never entered my mind as a reality. I just felt uneasy. My husband was very unstable, especially after the diagnosis of autism was finally confirmed. His instability increased with the catastrophe with the church and his work.'

'Do you suspect that those factors were the cause of his suicide?'

'Whatever I think or suspect, is nothing more than speculation. I cannot answer your question.'

Behind her the wooden chair creaks; she can hear the woman turning the page of her notebook.

Perhaps it was the humiliating drama with the church that drove Dawid over the rails of the bridge. Or the investigation at the post office. Social rejection. Estrangement from friends. Financial disaster. Perhaps the culmination of all of it. Through sleepless nights she wrestled with her own part in the tragedy. Because, if she and Dawid had not lived in separate emotional worlds, light years apart, she could have been an anchor for him. She could not help wondering if her endless journey in search of answers had driven him over the edge.

From doctor to doctor. Second opinion. Tenth opinion. One refers her to another. That one refers her to the next. No, she often found herself saying, we've already been to that one, he could find nothing wrong. Another prescribed a diet that they could not get down the child's throat for anything in the world. And yet another came to the harsh conclusion that the child sensed a lack of motherly love.

God, it almost destroyed her.

Everyone gave it a different label; some were more vague than others. Feeding problems. Birth shock. Chronic colic. Emotional distress. One called it *global delay*. Another spoke of *developmental disorder*. Every time she left a specialist's room her faith in the medical world diminished. And so did her instinctive trust in her own capability as a mother. Every doctor, as well as Dawid, wanted her to find acceptance and carry on with life. But she couldn't. Wherever she perceived the tiniest glimmer, she followed the road in the hope of finding the light.

Doctor, he's six months old, why does he never smile at me? Doctor, he's eight months old, why can he roll over and push me away, but makes no attempt to sit? Why can he knock the bowl of porridge out of my hand, but cannot hold his rattle? Why does he not see when I roll the ball to him? Why does he never put his arms out to be picked up? Why does he never look me in the eye when I talk to him? Why does he seem frightened when I enter his room? He eats virtually nothing. Bath time is a nightmare. Why does he rock for hours on end?

Evasive answers were all she got.

It came as a terrible shock when yet another doctor told them to have a brain scan done. 'Doctor, are you implying . . . do you suspect that . . .?'

He must have sensed her defensiveness because he held up his hands to stop her. 'All I am saying, ma'am, is have it done. Then you can be certain that brain damage has been excluded.'

They took time off work and had it done.

The result: normal.

On the way home Dawid got stuck on a tune that she knew off by heart.

'You keep driving me, Ingrid. Your obsession is breaking me. Do you realise how high our medical expenses are? You should check the bank statement and see how my overdraft has sky-rocketed. We cannot afford to take a day's leave every week. All you can think about is a diagnosis. In the name of God, I beg you to think of Teresa and Zettie for a change. And of me too.'

He banged his fist against the steering wheel and drove far too fast. She could not find the words to explain to him how she tossed in bed at night, worrying about Teresa and Zettie. And about him.

'The zip on my jeans is broken and I've been asking you to fix it for weeks now. Teresa's fringe is hanging in her eyes; I swear I'm going to take the kitchen scissors and cut it myself. And when do you ever plan to invite people for dinner again?'

She knew all that. And more. But until she knew what was wrong with Alexander, she would find no rest.

She visited the library in town. Read the few available books on babies. None of them mentioned the unnatural behaviour that she noticed in Alexander. When Alexander was eighteen months old and had still made no attempt to walk, she went to see Old Doctor again. He shook his head helplessly and made an appointment with an orthopaedic surgeon. It was an exhausting day, battling to get him to lie still for the X-rays. He yelled and growled and hit out wildly. Dawid refused to help. He said the drama was driving him insane and he was going to find something to eat. The specialist seemed nervous when he tried to examine the raging child. Alexander kicked him in the stomach and grabbed his glasses from his face. The man was pale, his hands were trembling.

The X-rays showed no abnormalities. Perhaps the child doesn't *want* to walk, was the only solution he could offer. She went home, none the wiser.

'Miss Ingrid, it's the soles of his feet,' Miriam said. 'I've noticed for a long time that Lexi gets very cross when I wash his feet. He kicks and refuses to let me bring the sponge near them. Miss Ingrid must have his feet checked.'

She did. Miriam was right.

She made an appointment with a dermatologist. Dawid could not get leave because a team of auditors were doing a general audit at the post office. Driving a long distance alone with Alexander in the car was impossible. She had no option but to try to find someone to go with her. The bank manager's wife was unfortunately attending the flower arrangement classes at the garden club. If it weren't for that, she would definitely have gone with her. The nursing sister at the psychiatric clinic said she could not be absent from the clinic for a whole day. In any event it would take days for her leave to be approved. She swallowed her pride and knocked at Hannah's door. What a pity, Hannah said, trying to conceal her uneasiness behind a thin smile, if she had not already cut crosses on the flower-ends of the green figs and put them into lime-water to make preserves the following morning, she would definitely have joined her. She went to the secretary at the church office to ask if she knew of anybody in town who would be willing to go with her. The secretary promised to find out and call her back. But she never did.

The only solution was to take Miriam.

The child has exceptionally sensitive soles, the dermatologist said. It was rare; something he seldom came across. She must rub the soles of his feet with spirits, three times a day. Massage his feet regularly with a shoebrush. Use a soapy seaweed sponge in the bath. He gave her an expensive tube of ointment to anaesthetise the soles of his feet. But immediately added that she would have to pay cash for the ointment, because it was not on the list of medication approved by the medical aid. She had Dawid's cheque book in her handbag. It saved her dignity, even though she knew the bank would bounce the cheque.

It had been a long journey there and back. She'd humiliated herself begging for someone to go with her. Such a huge effort, for a mysterious shake of the head and a tube of ointment that would not last longer than ten days.

It was getting dark when she arrived back in town. She took Miriam straight home to the township. When she arrived at her own home she was met by an almost insanely angry Dawid. He shouted and waved his arms, stuck his finger in her face. Raged about dirty dishes, unmade beds, no food. And also because she had made a fool of him by not sending the promised plate of tea-time snacks for the auditors. Teresa and Zettie disappeared into their rooms like shadows. Only the ray of light beneath their doors was silent witness to the fact that they were in the house.

After what felt like hours, she fled from Dawid's fury and threw her exhausted body down on the bed and fell asleep immediately. She didn't care if Alexander destroyed the house. In the early hours of the morning she woke, cold. Alexander was not in his bed. She found him buried in the ragbox. She fetched a blanket and wrapped it around herself. Sat down next to the ragbox with her back against the wall, and went back to sleep.

She woke at daybreak, stiff and cold, her eyes raw. She went to the kitchen and fried the last six eggs for Dawid and the girls. Put them on toast and scattered cheese over them. Made coffee. Took them breakfast in bed.

A peace offering.

She had a disastrous day at work. She cashed a post-dated cheque; printed the wrong provisional statement for an important client. And when she balanced the cashier's counter at closing time, she was more than a hundred rand *over*. A shortfall could be paid back. *Over* implied that she had accidentally cheated someone. An unforgivable sin.

That night she placed her hand on Dawid's stomach. Caressed him with her fingertips. Softly. Lower, lower, lower. But Dawid did not wake up.

It was an empty offering.

A few weeks later a bank client told her enthusiastically about a homeopath in a neighbouring town who was brilliant with children. Dawid refused to go.

'I'll go on my own.'

'Then go! You are driving me off my damn head, Ingrid! Here, take my cheque book and my wallet!' He slammed them down on the kitchen table and switched the kettle on for coffee. 'Spend whatever you want! Bankrupt us! Drive the car into the ground if that will put an end to your itching!'

'Dawid, I'm just as sick and tired as you are. My purse is probably emptier than yours. I have no desire to make us bankrupt.'

God, he was angry. 'What the hell do you want then, Ingrid?' With a wild movement he spooned coffee powder into a mug and flung the teaspoon into the sink.

'There must be someone somewhere who can make a diagnosis, Dawid. We must persevere until we find that person. Alexander will always be our responsibility. He's a child and he cannot make decisions for . . .'

'Child? Did you say *child*?' and he squeezed the milk carton so hard that the milk spurted over the floor. 'No, Ingrid. As far as I'm concerned he's a monster who's brought chaos to my life! Take my wallet and my cheque book, spend what you like!'

The day before her appointment with the homeopath, Jeremiah was waiting for her on the stoep when she arrived home from work. He had a bunch of beetroot in one hand, and a peculiar contraption of leather and buckles and straps in the other hand.

'Miriam says you have a hard time with Lexi in the car, Miss Ingrid. One of my neighbours in the township helped me make this strap-in device. It's a present for Lexi, we don't want money for it. The people in our church pooled to buy the cured skin and the buckles. Let's go to the car and I'll show you how to strap Lexi in.'

The gesture of goodwill hit a painful spot in her heart. When Jeremiah's back disappeared down the street in the soft glow of evening, she put her head on the bonnet of the car and sobbed like a child.

The homeopath was a waste of time and money. And on the way home Alexander destroyed Jeremiah's strap-in contraption. Broke the buckles off; tore the leather straps between his teeth. It was yet another excursion that left her drained. And without answers. While she was preparing supper that evening, Teresa and Zettie stayed behind their closed doors. As she stood at the stove in the kitchen, she knew that she could no longer deny that the havoc created by Alexander was destroying the bond between her and her daughters.

'When are you going to bake us a cake again, Mom?' Zettie asked one Saturday afternoon while she was mixing a concoction to soothe Alexander's nappy rash. Vaseline, calamine lotion, talcum powder, friar's balsam. Miriam's recipe.

'Ask Teresa to come and help you, and the two of you can bake a cake.'

'She won't. She says the kitchen stinks of pumpkin.'

'It doesn't stink, Zettie, it just smells of pumpkin.'

'She says pumpkin stinks worse than cat shit.'

She rested the egg-beater in the bowl and embraced Zettie.

Her back was rigid, her neck stiff. 'Alexander is your brother, Zettie. He's a confused little boy and we don't understand him, but we know he loves pumpkin.'

'And we love cake.'

God, she was tired of making excuses. Tired of being the lightning conductor, always in the middle, never knowing what was going to hit her next. Why should she have to deal with a silly issue like the smell of pumpkin?

Mashed pumpkin for breakfast, lunch, supper. Sometimes he switched to cheese spread or bananas for short periods, but always reverted to pumpkin. Plates stacked with the orange mash. If the pumpkin was too watery, he threw the plate against the wall. If it was to his liking, he would dig into it as if it was the only thing in the world. Saw nothing; heard nothing. Did not blink an eye when a door slammed or when the telephone rang. He arranged the pumpkin in a perfect circle with his forefinger. Divided it precisely into six equal parts, like slices of a tart. Always ate them anti-clockwise. She found consolation in the fact that he knew what a circle looked like, and that he possessed a definite sense of proportion.

'Tell Teresa to help you to take the cake pans off the pantry shelf.'

'She won't. She's sulking because she had to stay behind for detention on Friday.'

Her heart skipped a beat. 'Detention? What for?'

'Her school books weren't covered in time.'

She felt as if cold water had been thrown in her face. Teresa had been nagging her for two weeks to buy plastic and help her cover the books. And for two weeks she'd been making promises. Detention. Dear God. Was living in this house not punishment enough? She finished mixing the ointment and went to Teresa's room, sat down on the bed.

'Teresa, I promise that I'll buy the plastic on Monday and before you go to school on Tuesday every single book will be covered.'

Teresa swung herself around and pulled the bedspread up to her chin. 'Forget it, Mom. Dad's already done it for me. Rather go cook Alexander's pumpkin. After all, he's your darling.'

Dad.

The strongest anchor they had. The only anchor. Regardless of his weaknesses and flaws, he was theirs. Until that dreadful Sunday when he walked out the front door and never returned.

Teresa was sixteen then. Zettie was fourteen. Alexander was five. And she felt older than the mountains.

28

IT MUST BE ABOUT time for the evangelist to be saying the last amen at the preparatory service in the kloof. Ever since she was a small child, she has always been deeply touched by the preparatory service. White candles burning on the window sills casting a warm orange light on people's faces; shadows on the high white-washed walls. Altogether different from the church in the township. In her times of sadness she always felt closer to God in the kloof church. Maybe because she grew up in the protection of the kloof. Jeremiah too. It was only when they finished at the kloof's primary school and had to go to high school in town, that they had learned about a bigger world and another church. But they always went back to the kloof to visit. Her heart would always belong there.

After Jeremiah finished school, he got the job at the furniture factory in town and they decided to make their vows in the *grootkerk* in the kloof. And every child that was born to them was baptised there. But when Little Leth died she could not bring her child's soul back to the kloof. She was too blinded by sorrow. That was why Little Leth was laid to rest in the cemetery in town. Perhaps it was a good thing. It was easier to visit the little grave to keep it weeded and to lay a fresh wreath. Much closer to walk to when the chicken eagle was haunting her and she needed to cry her heart out.

Tomorrow she will miss *Nagmaal*. No matter. It is God's will.

At daybreak she will go behind the chicken run to pray for Evert's soul. God listens everywhere. And the time has come for her to lay her feelings of guilt about Evert at the feet of the Father. Now that she's older and her soul can see more clearly, she believes that Evert's sinfulness and carelessness came from her. Because she always treated him differently to her other children. She could never erase the picture of Little Leth lying in hospital, wrapped in bandages. Night after night the chicken eagle kept telling her about Little Leth's agony and suffering. That's why she was always so quick to bare her teeth at Evert.

She had put this weekend aside to clean the backyard of her mind. And now she is sitting at the police station. All the singing to call the angels to the truck was in vain. Why hadn't she listened to the second sight in her stomach and stayed home? Maybe she would have been able to stop the police from locking Miss Ingrid up. Heaven knows, gaol food is worse than dog food. Although Evert says that nowadays they eat from a menu. But Evert talks lots of nonsense. Nevertheless, it's winter, and who knows whether Miss Ingrid will have a clean blanket? And cough medicine? What if they put Miss Ingrid in the back of the police van and drove through the town for everybody to witness her disgrace?

Dear Jesus, no.

And she has forgotten to ask the local police to get a message to Jeremiah or Katrien to bring her something to eat. Even if it's just a sandwich with apricot jam. The rumbling in her stomach is getting worse.

'Mrs Slangveld, did the child attend school?'

She must stop thinking about Evert and food, and pay attention to what the man asks her. Or else she'll choose the wrong words. 'No, sir, Lexi did not go to school. It's not that he had a stupid head, it's just that he couldn't speak. How would they be able to understand him?'

'Couldn't he speak at all?'

'No, sir. The only word he could say was my name. And he had his own way of saying it. He said *Mimmi*. He called everything Mimmi. When he wanted something, he ran through the house and called *Mimmi-Mimmi*. Even when I wasn't there.'

'How did you know what he wanted?'

'He pulled us by the arm, and then we had to guess. And he became very upset if we guessed wrong.'

'Did Mrs Dorfling consult specialised teachers? Did she make any attempt to let him mix and play with other children?'

Her heart so often bled with pity for Miss Ingrid and for Lexi because the townspeople, and even the church, pushed them to the edge of the nest. They were dud eggs. Sometimes they got pushed right over the edge. Master Dawid and Teresa and Zettie too. After Lexi was born, everybody stopped inviting them to birthday parties. And Master Dawid, who had always been so fond of lighting a fire and having a *braaivleis* and going camping, became a quiet man. It was almost as if he had lost his tongue. He never went to the tennis courts on Saturdays. Never went to a dance in the town hall; never hooked up the caravan. His soul seemed to have been extinguished.

There were seldom any visitors at Miss Ingrid's house. Not even Miss Mirna, who used to come so often. Poisonous woman, Miss Mirna. The second sight in her stomach told her that Miss Mirna's eyes could look in different directions at the same time. Squint-eyed soul, running with the hare and hunting with the hounds. But never mind Miss Mirna right now.

What about the time when the headmaster at the school refused to let Lexi attend the grade one class once a week, because he would cause havoc? It's true, he would have. But how did the townspeople expect Lexi to get a bit of knowledge into his head if he was never allowed to mix with other children? Surely he wouldn't become clever by running up and down the yard all day long; looking into the sun; blowing spit bubbles; throwing stones at old Miss Betty's windows.

Then Miss Ingrid went to Miss Lida and offered to pay her to teach Lexi. At least Miss Lida was the one person in town who understood how to work with wrong-headed children, as she taught the special class at the school. No one would know the ropes better than Miss Lida. Miss Lida agreed, on Wednesday afternoons after school. On one condition: she, Miriam, must come too and stay with Lexi all the time.

She could not help but feel sorry for Miss Lida. Wholeheartedly sorry. Because Miss Lida could not keep up with Lexi. Not a single thing could she teach him. She just ran after him all over the schoolyard until her tongue was hanging out with fatigue. It lasted for three weeks only. Because when Miss Lida pulled Lexi's head against her chest so that he could listen to her heartbeat, Lexi ripped her white chiffon blouse apart. Miss Lida wrote a letter to Miss Ingrid to say that she no longer wanted to try to teach Lexi;

that they should stop the lessons.

Heaven knows, she would never forget the dismay on Miss Ingrid's face when she read the letter.

And then the catastrophe with the *Kinderkrans* followed. Perhaps Miss Ingrid had thought that the playgroup was less formal. Just play, and learning to know the Bible. Not on Sundays, but during the week. And not in church where everybody had to be quiet. They used the church hall, and Sally always had to serve them cooldrink before they went home. Why they had not left Lexi to run around the churchyard and climb trees, she would never understand. Even if it meant he just sat in a tree and watched the other children playing oranges and lemons. But instead they forced him to sit on a chair and gave him a pair of scissors to cut out a paper lantern. They told him the lantern was a symbol of light; that his light must shine for Jesus.

Sally told her the story afterwards. One moment Lexi was looking at the shining pair of scissors in his hand; the next moment he flew up and started snipping the other children's hair and clothing. Really, she could not understand how their brains worked. If they had allowed her to stay with him all the time, it would never have happened. But because it was the white church, and her skin was brown, they told her to wait outside in the shade of the jacaranda trees until they were finished with the afternoon's activities.

While she waited under the tree, she thought about the story that her mother had told her many years ago about a brown heaven. Long ago, her mother said, an old woman who lived in the kloof died. But when she arrived at the gates of heaven the Lord told her that it was not quite her time yet, and that she should go back to earth until He called her again. The old woman told of the brown heaven she had glimpsed, where all brown people were turned into brown angels. Complete with paraffin lamps and bumpy streets and skinny dogs and ramshackle cars and patched-up chicken runs. Not that she ever believed her mother, or the old woman's story. But her eyes had not seen what the old woman's eyes had seen, and so she could not contest it. Still, she often wondered . . .

White church. Brown church. White heaven. Brown heaven.

Good children. And wild children, like Lexi.

God gives, and God takes, so the evangelist always preached.

In her mind she could see Tompy standing next to Aunt Rosie in church, singing hymns from the flyer in his hand. Farting loudly during the prayers. But the evangelist would never chase him out, or reprimand him in front of the other churchgoers. Everyone showed tolerance towards Tompy. And she decided that if the old woman was right, she would prefer to go to the brown heaven when her time came. Especially since she has to try to keep a seat there for Jeremiah too. Even if it meant hiding his dominoes under his hat. And if Lexi was not allowed through the gates of the white heaven, he would definitely be taken into the brown heaven.

But before she could wrap up her thoughts, a terrible screaming broke loose in the church hall. And within seconds all the children came running out the door, pushing and scrambling, like when you step on a spider and hundreds of tiny spiders burst from her swollen stomach.

That was the end of Lexi attending the *Kinderkrans* playgroup.

The next Saturday she allowed herself to become annoyed by deliberately listening behind the sitting room door when the white church's deacon came to speak to Miss Ingrid about the havoc Lexi caused at the *Kinderkrans*. And for Tompy and Aunt Rosie's sake she was glad that God had given Tompy a brown skin.

'No, sir, teaching him or playing with other children did not work out with Lexi. Miss Ingrid tried it many times, but in the end she gave up hope.'

'And toys? It doesn't seem as if he had many toys.'

That was one thing about Lexi that she could never understand. He broke everything. To play meant to break. All his little trucks; plastic animals; even the little toy soldiers that Master Dawid had bought him for Christmas. The only toys he left in peace were the Lego blocks and the puzzles. He even managed to break things that were unbreakable. Sat for hours with a stone hitting a plastic bowl until it was completely flattened. She would bet every chicken in her chicken run that one could not break a tennis ball. Lexi could.

'It's true, sir, Lexi did not like toys. His favourite toy was Miss Ingrid's old hairdryer. Even when all the inside parts were missing, he kept dragging it behind him. Sometimes he even took it to bed with him.'

Astonished, he stares at her; then writes it down.

'There is a broken bicycle hanging from the beams in the garage, whose was it?'

'It was Lexi's bicycle, sir.' No need to answer more than he asked.

'How did it get into such a bad state?'

She'd have to spill the whole bag of beans.

It's impossible to explain to anyone how furious Master Dawid's father was about the bicycle. They arrived with the beautiful little blue bicycle for Lexi's birthday. But Lexi's head could not tell him it was a bicycle. Teresa and Zettie tried to show him. Zettie's knees were higher than the handles but she kept riding the little bicycle up and down the street for Lexi to see. Teresa rang the bell. They tried to pick Lexi up on to the saddle. He refused. Master Dawid said *he* would teach him. He forced Lexi on to the saddle and pushed the bicycle down the street. Lexi yelled as if he was being murdered. It was too terrible. One would swear he thought the bicycle was going to bite him. Even old Miss Betty came out her front door and stood on her stoep watching the commotion in the street. Master Dawid got very annoyed. He uttered a string of swear words, picked the bicycle up, grabbed Lexi by the arm and carried the whole caboodle back to the yard. The next day Lexi danced around and around the bicycle, flapping his hands. Turned the bicycle upside down and started spinning the wheels. The faster the wheels spun, the more excited he became.

He did this for months on end.

When the Old Master and Old Missus came to visit again, there was just about nothing left of the bicycle. Only broken spokes and bent metal. Saddle, wheels, everything, destroyed. It was at this time that Miss Ingrid had the fallout with the two old people. It was the last time they ever visited.

'It was Lexi who broke the bicycle, sir.'

Don't let him ask anything more. Let the angels seal his lips.

'Mrs Dorfling's late husband,' and he stops and drinks half a glass of water, wipes his lips, 'did you know him well?'

Huge relief that he's going to let the matter of the bicycle be. 'Very well, sir. Master Dawid was . . .'

'Was there a close bond between him and the child?'

Dearest Jesus, how can she tell him the truth? What difference does it make now whether Master Dawid loved Lexi, or not? Lexi never opened a door to his heart to let Master Dawid in. Instead, the strange things he did irritated Master Dawid. And a man's patience does not stretch as far as a woman's. That's why Master Dawid and Lexi kept bumping heads; rubbing each other up the wrong way.

She stares at the half glass of water. She's thirsty. 'What kind of close bond do you mean, sir?'

'Was he fond of the child? Did he love him and care for him?'

She swallows the dusty taste in her mouth. 'I think so, sir.'

His evil eyes pin her down. 'You *think* so?'

'Yes, sir.'

He jumps up so quickly that she thinks he is going to knock the precious glass of water over. Thumps his fist on the book; the pen rolls against the glass with a tinkling sound. 'You are talking crap, Mrs Slangveld! Don't take me for a fool! I can see in your eyes that you're lying! You had better tell the truth! Don't waste my time with bullshit!'

Fright glues her lips together. Her knees feel weak.

'You'd better understand me, Mrs Slangveld, if you don't cooperate I'll lock you up until you change your mind!'

She's not going to be intimidated by his shouting. 'I am a Christian woman, I won't let anybody swear at me. Not even a policeman.'

He inflates with fury. 'And I, Mrs Slangveld,' and he stabs his chest with his finger, 'won't tolerate your lying to me!'

Bloody drop of piss. Who does he think he is? Thinks because he has the law on his side, she's got no law on her side. Damn him. 'I find it hard to understand when someone shouts and swears at me. That's not how I was brought up.'

He sighs heavily and sits down again. 'Mrs Slangveld, I'm investigating a murder case, and you . . .'

A whirlwind reels through her stomach. And simultaneously a swarm of blueflies buzz in her head so that she can hardly hear what the man is saying. Murder? Then *that's* why his eyes have such an evil light in them? God of mercy. All the time she thought he was working his way towards proving that Lexi died because of Miss Ingrid's negligence. What now? How can they possibly think that Miss Ingrid *murdered* Lexi? If Miss Ingrid had any such plans in her head, why did she talk just yesterday on the way to the township about buying Lexi new clothes before the shops closed? And cheese spread?

She mustn't antagonise the man. He mustn't get the idea that she's hiding anything or evading the truth. Tonight God's angels must put their fingers on her tongue and help her choose the right words. No unfair suspicions must be cast on Miss Ingrid.

'Could I please have some water, sir?'

He points to the plastic mug on the window sill above the basin. 'Get it yourself.'

When she gets up, her legs feel like dry firewood. The cool water runs down her throat. She fills the mug and places it next to her chair. She *must* get a message to Jeremiah or Katrien to bring her some food. Tonight she's going to need all the strength she can gather. And God must send His cleverest angels to her. And He must command them to stay with her until the very end.

Nimble-footed through the deep sea.

Him and her.

She holds the child and the pink starfish close to her heart. Because she fears that the dance in the blue-green water might be an illusion.

Gasping, she wakes up. What made that sound? What woke her?

She lies dead still on the floor, listens. No sound, no movement. The carpet in the interrogation room smells of dust. When she moves, the skin on her wrists feels dry like paper. Even though she is lying curled up on her side, the sharp light from the bare bulb scorches her eyes. She recalls the nimble-footed dance in the deep sea and blinks the tears away. They run from one eye over the bridge of her nose, into the other eye. Drain away into the thin carpet.

What woke her up?

She lifts herself on to her elbow; looks around to where the woman is sitting on the upright chair. The woman is asleep, the back of her head resting against the wall. In her sleep her knees have parted. The clipboard with the notebook has fallen from her hand and landed on the floor.

Quietly she rolls over on to all fours. Her eyes move from the woman to the docket lying on the desk. Can she risk it? Does she remember the man saying something about good cop, bad cop strategy? Is the woman really sleeping? Did the man say he would be back in an hour's time, or did she imagine it? How long has she been asleep? How much is left of the hour?

She watches the sleeping woman. Every time she breathes out, her lower lip trembles slightly. She is close enough to see the hands on her watch: twenty past four. In two hours it will be morning. It's the third night in a row that she has had to survive on fragments of sleep. How long can she go on? What is in the docket? Surely nothing that can incriminate her. Yet, there must be something that gives them grounds to suspect her.

If it is the last thing she does in her life, she must see who said what about her.

Quiet as a cat, she gets to her feet. The bones in her feet must not creak. Around the corner of the desk. Opens the front page of the docket. The paper must not rustle. From the corner of her eye, she watches the woman. Her heartbeat thunders in her ears when she reads the highlighted heading: *Medico-legal post-mortem.*

30

'Now, Mrs Slangveld, you'll tell the truth, the whole truth. No evasive answers; no dodging of the truth.'

She feels like attacking him with her bare hands. But she knows it is better to breathe calmly; act dumb. Because it's clear as daylight that cleverness and cheek will not get her anywhere tonight. 'I wasn't dodging the truth, sir, it's just that Master Dawid is dead and buried, and it's not Christianlike to sling mud at a dead man.'

'This has nothing to do with mud-slinging. I'm asking you a simple question: was there a loving bond between Mr Dorfling and the child?'

'You must understand, sir, it's not a matter of . . .'

'Just answer yes or no.'

'Then I'm telling you straightforward, sir, I don't know the answer. Whatever I say would be a lie. I can only tell you what I know.'

He rests his elbows on the desk. The evil colour in his eyes clears slightly. And she sees that, for once, he's going to listen to her. 'In my heart I'm certain Master Dawid did love Lexi, sir. But I think Master Dawid battled to understand the Lord's puzzle . . . You must understand, sir, white people find it hard to accept a wrong-headed child. They're not like us brown people who are used to raising . . .'

'White and brown have nothing to do with this. Don't drag politics in to suit your story.'

'I'm not dragging anything in, sir, I'm just trying to explain the matter the way *I* see it.'

The first thing that planted unrest in her heart was the number of liquor bottles in the rubbish bin. Master Dawid had always been a man for a drink. Before Lexi came into the world, there also used to be many bottles in the bin. Wine bottles, beer bottles, brandy bottles. But it did not worry her, because the pile of dishes on the sink told her there had been visitors. Dirty glasses, full ashtrays. House untidy from children playing with their dolls and tea sets.

But then it changed. Almost every morning there was an empty bottle in the bin, but only a few dishes in the sink. Then she knew something was very wrong. Because a man who drinks by himself night after night, is a man going downhill. And he would continue going downhill, faster and faster, until he tumbled head over heels and bumped his head very hard. Years ago, that same downhill road had overtaken Jeremiah. A handful of screws here; piece of leftover plank there. Before long it was wardrobe mirrors; copper handles for drawers. He sold it all for booze money and domino debts. But then they caught him red-handed with the stolen yellowwood planks.

Two years in a filthy cell. Trapped like a rat in a cage. Barely out, and he was up to his old tricks again. If he wasn't pinching from her sacred bottle, he stole the eggs from the nests. Sly fox, Jeremiah. But he minded his step because he knew she was watching him. The Lord knows, most of her married life, it took all her strength to keep him in check. The moment she slackened her grip, he began heading downhill again.

Day after day when she saw the empty bottles in the bin, she knew that there was no difference between Master Dawid and Jeremiah. Downhill is downhill. Whether your skin is white or brown, you're equally vulnerable to the devil. And neither Jeremiah nor Master Dawid were bad people, it was just that they had a weak joint in their souls.

She never said a word to Miss Ingrid. Better to stay out of it. Instead, she poured all her kindness on to Lexi. And at daybreak she kneeled behind the chicken run to pray for Master Dawid's salvation.

In vain. You can kneel until the cows come home, and God will carry you as far as He can, but if a man doesn't get up and walk the good path with his own two feet, then there is only one path: downward.

The day Miss Ingrid stayed in bed with two broken ribs and took sick leave for two weeks, she knew Master Dawid was going downhill faster than her prayers could keep up; he was surely going to bang his head against a solid wall.

'I slipped and fell against the edge of the bath,' Miss Ingrid explained.

Unnecessarily. She saw the hurt in Miss Ingrid's eyes, not in her ribs. Master Dawid slept on the couch for more than a month. For the first time in her life she kneeled behind the chicken run and pleaded with God to send a devil's angel to punish Master Dawid. Wring his balls right off. For goodness sake, how could he have done that? Miss Ingrid was so fragile and defenceless.

Before Easter that year, she went behind the chicken run to withdraw her plea for the devil's angel. Because one Saturday morning when she was coming into the house with a pile of dry washing in her arms, she saw the syringe lying on the passage floor. She threw the washing down and rushed inside. A fit was not a joke. She found Master Dawid and Lexi asleep close together on the double bed, Master Dawid's hand cupped over Lexi's head. She fetched the blanket that Old Miss Betty had crocheted from odd pieces of wool, and covered them. Because the Saviour of all souls on earth and in heaven knew how her heart ached for Master Dawid that Saturday morning.

'As I see it, sir: I have no doubt that Master Dawid loved Lexi. But Lexi did not love him in return. I think Master Dawid simply gave up all hope.'

'Why didn't the child love him?'

'It's always like that with autistic children, sir.' He mustn't think she's stupid or uninformed. 'They are born without a conscience and with no love in their hearts. That's why they don't like other people to come near them or touch them.'

'Did the child have pets? A cat or a dog maybe?'

'Master Dawid bought Lexi a little white dog, but Lexi squeezed it to death.'

A bad mistake to mention that, but it's too late now to withdraw her words.

'Squeezed it to death? How?'

'With his hands, sir,' and she clamps her hands around her leg to demonstrate. 'I was busy taking the washing off the line, and I have only two eyes.'

'How old was the child when this happened?'

'He must have been about four, sir.'

'Did the child have an aggressive temperament?'

Tread cautiously. 'It's hard to say, sir. I don't think he meant to kill the dog, I guess he just wanted to hear if the dog would make a sound. Lexi always wanted things to move and to make sounds.'

'How did Mr Dorfling react when the child killed the dog?'

It had been a day of rage that she had chosen to forget. When Master Dawid came home at five o'clock, she showed him the dead dog where she had put it in the laundry. He asked what had happened. She was scared to tell him but there was no way other than the truth. Where's the child now? Master Dawid asked. He's in the broom cupboard, she said, and she was filled with fear when she saw Master Dawid's eyes bulging in their sockets.

Holy heaven, even now her knees become weak when she thinks back to that day. Master Dawid hauled Lexi out of the broom cupboard and bashed the stiff dog against Lexi's stomach. Swore like a heathen. Hit him again and again. In his fury he trampled on the dead dog. And the longer he carried on, the harder his blows became. Lexi did not cry or blink an eye or try to escape Master Dawid's hands. He had no understanding of what was happening. Teresa and Zettie stood in the kitchen door, crying hysterically, pleading. But Master Dawid seemed blind and deaf. Thank God, Miss Ingrid arrived at that moment and grabbed Master Dawid by the sleeve and yelled in his face. He would otherwise surely have carried on like someone possessed by the devil until Lexi too was dead.

'Master Dawid fetched the spade and carried the dog to the back garden to bury it in the rose-bed, sir.' That was the truth, after all.

'And Mrs Dorfling, what did she do?'

'Not much, sir. She took the girls to her room and let them lie down on the double bed with her. She stayed with them for a while, then she went to the back garden and sat with Master Dawid while he buried the dog.'

It is not necessary to tell him everything. Of how her stomach had told her not to leave Master Dawid and Miss Ingrid alone. She finished all the ironing and hung around until the sun disappeared behind the mountain. It was getting dark when she went outside to say goodnight. Miss Ingrid sat with Master Dawid next to the rose-bed, stroking his back, her head on his shoulder. There was a lump in her throat as she watched them because it was the first time she had seen a white man crying. And she wondered if Master Dawid was crying about the dead dog, or about his own inevitable fate. For all she knew, in the blackest depths of his soul, Master Dawid was wishing he could bury Lexi with the dog. Because as sure as there were millions of stars in the sky, Master Dawid loved and hated Lexi simultaneously.

The next day she started spring cleaning the house. It was all she could offer Miss Ingrid. She washed curtains, polished brass-ware, oiled the furniture, shone the mirrors, tidied the cupboards. She had to use the cleaning materials sparingly as most of the bottles were almost empty. On the fourth day she found the gun between the pillows in the linen cupboard. Her heart almost jumped out of her throat with fright. Not because of the cold metal in her hand but because she knew Miss Ingrid had hidden it there. For a reason.

When the man looks up she can see he's ready to pepper her with his next questions. She must speak before he does. 'Sir, is it possible to send someone to my house in the police van to fetch me something to eat? I feel faint with hunger.'

He nods and sends for someone to pass the message on. Then he turns the page of the notebook. 'Mrs Slangveld, do you know whether Mrs Dorfling had financial problems?'

Damn, he keeps snapping at her heels with tricky questions. 'Not that I know of, sir. She never discussed money matters with me.'

'Did you receive your wages regularly?'

'Like clockwork, sir.'

It's not necessary to mention all the times she's received almost double her salary, because Miss Ingrid had borrowed a couple of rand here and a couple of rand there during the month. She always paid it back. And she says nothing about the time Miss Ingrid sold a whole lot of things to the school hostel kitchen staff. For a few pennies. Pots and glass bowls, blankets and sheets, Master Dawid's clothes and shoes, cups and saucers, odd cutlery, tapestries, pictures.

And as the money arrived in dribs and drabs, Miss Ingrid put it in a canned-fruit bottle. When there was enough, she filled the car with petrol and took Teresa and Zettie shopping. They bought shoes with thick soles, stretch denims that made their legs look like bicycle spokes. Baggy shirts that hung down past their buttocks. School bags. Silver chains with a row of tiny friendship rings on them. A radio for Zettie. She'd never seen the girls so excited.

They strutted like peacocks on their thick-soled shoes. Listened to the radio all afternoon. But that's none of the man's business. No need to give him a cane with which to whip her.

When she finishes the second cup of water, he's still asking about money. Strange questions. Until she has bad heartburn. But she manages to steer her way safely past the traps. Did she know if Master Dawid had perhaps left bad debts when he died? Is the grocery cupboard empty or full most of the time? Did Miss Ingrid take out an insurance policy for Lexi? Did she build up debts at the shops in town?

An angry swarm of bees buzzes in her head. But the clever angels smoke them out. Not once does she fall into a trap. Never lies; just acts stupid. No, Miss Ingrid never discussed those things with her. No, she knew nothing of Master Dawid's business. No, the food cupboards were never empty. It's true. Empty is *empty*. Even if there was just a packet of salt or ten teabags or a jar of cheese spread and half a tin of jam in the cupboards, it would have been a lie to say they were empty.

When she fills the cup for the third time, someone knocks at the door and says her food has arrived. She feels like kissing the man's feet in gratitude when he puts the pen down and says she can go and eat now. But she must hurry up, and she mustn't leave the police yard.

31

IF ONLY SHE KNEW how long she had slept. Perhaps the man had also gone to lie down for an hour to replenish his energy. He must not catch her reading the docket. Her fingers tremble while she scans the first page of the post-mortem report. Difficult medical language in single spacing. Thank heavens the man had used the neon marker.

Death register number. It's gruesome and unreal. Her emotions must not take over now. Turn the page quietly; the woman must not wake up.

Page two. Cause/causes of death: *possible suffocation or dry drowning*. Don't try to analyse the words. As long as she knows what's written in the report.

Page three. Height. Mass. Tattoos. Stains. Tears. Next to *scars* is a detailed list. It doesn't upset her, she knows every mark and scar on Alexander's body. Nothing that she can't confirm.

Page four. Nothing is highlighted.

She glances to check if the woman is still sleeping.

Page five. Mouth, tongue and pharynx: *hyoid bone fractured*. Something in Alexander's pharynx was broken or cracked. Don't try to determine what, just remember the facts. Still on page five. Muscles of the neck: *bleeding into the soft tissue of the neck*. Damn. It's incriminating. The man has no option but to believe she strangled Alexander. It must have happened at the hairdresser when she held him so tightly.

Page six. Pleura, lungs: *no water present in lungs*. So, the man is not using scare tactics on her.

She holds the post-mortem report between her thumb and middle finger, poised to close the docket if there's the slightest sound at the door. She will immediately put her head down on her arms and pretend to be asleep. After all, she *did* ask for a chair and he never brought it. And regardless of what the man might think, he won't have any *proof* that she has read the docket.

Statement by Aunt Betty. Ancient events. No need to waste time on that.

Miriam's Katrien. *Did not stay behind on Friday . . . child was frightened by the hairdryers and mirrors . . . Mrs Dorfling always had to use force to keep him on the high stool . . . yes, she held him by his neck . . .*

She starts when the woman sighs and licks her lips.

Mirna. Non-committal. Yet eloquent. Although she expected no less, the critical undertones pierce her to the quick. Why did Mirna have to mention the parrot? Why give a detailed account of how Alexander had thrown buckets of sand into her swimming pool? Dawid, drunk at work. Miriam, running through town searching for Alexander. How they found him in the pine trees behind the school, in the middle of winter, wearing a short-sleeved shirt in an icy south wind.

Dear God, if there's one person who won't be praying for her tonight, it's Mirna. By now she has probably told everyone in town that the detectives from Murder and Robbery have been to question her. As if it would enhance her status.

The bank manager. The first two pages are work-related events: taking leave at short notice, sick leave, impaired concentration, repeated mistakes. Page three is almost entirely highlighted. *Arrears at the municipality and chemist . . . serious financial trouble . . .* It hurts her. *Deficit at the cashier's counter . . . seven hundred and ninety-two rand . . . undertook to pay it back within two weeks . . . impossible undertaking . . .* But what hurts most of all, is the information about Alexander's policy. *Increased premium . . . adjusted two months ago . . . death coverage increased to the maximum . . .* Attached to the page are printouts of bank statements for the past six months, debit orders and overdrawn balances are highlighted.

The changes to Alexander's insurance policy must cast suspicion on her. And yet, as God is her witness, she made them with the best of motives. Gunter advised her; he said she should think of the future; that the policy would be worth less than nothing if she did not adjust it regularly.

She had washed her hair with bath soap and mixed her cereal with water to be able to afford it. Drank bitter coffee. Used a thin strip of toothpaste. Had not used the heater once this winter. Went to work without stockings. But in the circumstances, her well-intentioned sacrifices can only appear accusatory.

No point in fretting about water under the bridge.

Cautiously, she changes her grip on the stack of papers. Quickly looks up at the woman. Her head has turned slightly, but she's still fast asleep.

The dominee. His duplicity scratches at old wounds. *Invited the child to attend the activities of the* Kinderkrans *playgroup.* Blatant lie. *Regularly paid pastoral visits to the Dorfling family . . . child was fully accepted in the community . . .* Shameless two-faced old fraud. *Broke all ties with the church after her husband's suicide. Efforts to involve her were fruitless. Refused to have her husband buried from the church.* Why didn't he mention the mothers' room that looked like a pigsty? Or the letters she had written to the Church Council, begging for their assistance? What about the Youth Committee's stillborn plans to accommodate Alexander at the *Kinderkrans*? Or how Dawid was unjustly dragged in front of the Disciplinary Committee? Why didn't he mention his despicable part in the scandal at the post office which resulted in a final written warning being issued to Dawid?

Turn the page. *Turn* it. Don't waste one more second on the dishonourable hypocrite.

Jeremiah. Not a single word of criticism. Tells about the feathers that he tied in bunches for Alexander. How he kept an eye on her yard. *Yes,* he states, *Lexi's mother adored him. Just the previous day she sent a message to ask him to come and plaster a wall at her house.*

Old Doctor. *Yes, the deceased was a patient of his. He delivered the child. No, as far as he knows, Mrs Dorfling wasn't on sedatives or antidepressants. Yes, she saw a psychologist from time to time. The deceased was a poor eater and poor sleeper. Underweight since birth.* No. Yes. Unsure. No. Yes. Possibly. Nothing damning; but nothing in mitigation. Not a word about broken ribs or swollen green-blue eyes. Clinical, without being unethical.

Her left arm is numb from trying to keep the papers in a neat stack. The lack of ventilation in the interrogation room has produced a layer of sweat on her forehead and temples. She wipes the thin layer of fog from her eyebrows, momentarily overcome by nausea.

Lida. Explains how she took Alexander for remedial classes on Wednesdays. *Yes, she stopped the lessons because they had no purpose, and she could not look on while Ingrid wasted her money.* Nothing about how Alexander bit and kicked her, how he tore her blouse. *Very fond of Ingrid Dorfling . . . friendship gradually deteriorated . . . Unbearable situation. Still carries a sense of guilt. No doubt that the church and the community shunned the Dorflings. She was a deacon when the decision was taken to deny Alexander's participation in the Kinderkrans playgroup. Yes, she's aware of the dominee's involvement in the drama at the post office. Outrageous lie that the family received regular pastoral visits from the dominee. No, the mothers' room was not suitable for . . . Yes, for understandable reasons the pre-primary school could not accommodate Alexander . . .*

Tears fill her eyes. She sniffs and swallows. Maybe Lida will pray for her tonight. Tomorrow as well. Because when it was time for the truth, Lida had not turned it back to front, nor had she glossed over it.

Hannah. Not even half a page. Just a few highlighted sentences. *Mrs Dorfling would definitely not harm the child on purpose. Admirable that she could stay strong up to now. Irrespective of the circumstances she did her best to maintain a loving relationship with her two daughters . . .*

The Indian man. *Yes, it's true that Jeremiah Slangveld asked him to bury magic medicine at the house to drive the devil out of the child. Buried a meercat's tail in the garden . . . hung a chicken's gall bladder in the wild olive tree . . .*

May God allow the little bit of oil in her lamp to last until morning comes. May He give her sufficient time before the man comes back. And the woman must not wake up.

32

As SHE WALKS DOWN the passage, ahead of the man, there's a creakiness in her arthritic knees. This day has taken a heavy toll on her body. Risking her life down the kloof at the hands of a drunk driver. Barely arrived, when she had to come back into town in a police car. Sit up straight in front of the sneaky man and keep her ears open on both sides for help from the angels. On top of it all, she keeps seeing Lexi's heavenly blue eyes in front of her, and the sorrow sticks in her throat like a huge peach pip.

She knows she's no longer young. Jeremiah's been nagging her for ages to retire, rather to pay attention to her chickens and earn an income from them. Up to now she's managed to put him off, but now that Lexi is dead she'll have to find another excuse to satisfy him. The truth is that she has no desire to retire yet. It will kill her to have to witness Jeremiah's laziness and sluggishness day after day.

'Please stay inside the charge office, Mrs Slangveld, and don't talk to anyone about this matter; not until your statement has been completed and signed.'

'Must I tell the constable on duty when I have finished eating?'

'They're not blind, Mrs Slangveld, they will see when you have finished eating!'

Rude bastard. She was being polite, that's all. 'All right, sir.'

'We'll carry on in about ten minutes. You must eat quickly, I'm not going to wait all night.'

His bloody backside! She'll eat in her own time. Where does he get the right to tell her how fast to chew and swallow? If Jeremiah forgot to send a bottle of coffee, she can just say the bread wasn't baked through properly and that she was choking on it.

The door at the end of the passage feels like a thousand miles away. Her legs are aching and her head is dizzy from hunger. Maybe Jeremiah had the common sense to send someone to Katrien's house for cooked food. It's Saturday, and Katrien always cooks a decent meal on Saturdays. Meat, rice, vegetables.

The man leans over her shoulder to open the door.

And then she sees Jeremiah standing at the charge office counter. Jeremiah himself. Dripping wet. With a plastic food container in his hands. Dear Saviour, did he walk all the way to the police station in the dark and rain? For her sake? It cannot be true.

'*Jissus*, Miriam . . .?'

Then the tears stream from her eyes. Because Lexi is dead. Because of Little Leth; the shameful way she has treated Evert all these years. Because of Miss Ingrid sleeping in a cold cell tonight.

And because of Jeremiah.

The constable lifts the counter flap and as she walks through a raw sound escapes from her throat. Through the warm tears blinding her, she sees Jeremiah holding the container out to her in his knobbly hands.

'Aunt Miriam, you and Uncle Jeremiah may not talk to each other,' the constable says as he lowers the counter flap. 'Uncle Jeremiah is a witness; he's just allowed to hand over your food and then he must leave.'

She ignores him.

Dear Jesus, Jeremiah's hat and jacket are dripping wet. And is it an illusion, or is Jeremiah also crying?

'Jeremiah . . .?'

He sniffs and pushes the plastic container into her hands. 'I've brought you some food, Miriam.'

'You're wet right through, Jeremiah, and it's late . . .'

'I've been sitting behind the chicken run in the rain since this morning, praying for you, Miriam.'

Long after his bony shoulders disappear down the steps of the police station, she still sits on the wooden bench in the charge office; the unopened container on her lap. She looks at the tiny raindrops against the window; then at the burn marks on the wooden bench.

'You must finish eating, Aunt Miriam,' the constable says from behind the counter. 'These people from Murder and Robbery are not going to wait for you.'

She takes the lid off the container. Bread with apricot jam, pumpkin fritters and two chicken drumsticks. After all, Jeremiah *did* care enough to fetch something from Katrien's house. But suddenly her hunger is gone. She swallows at the salty taste of the tears in her mouth. 'Keep my food under the counter, I'll eat it later. Go tell the man I'm ready when he's ready. Tell him I'm old and tired, and I want to get this over and done with and go home.'

Nobody has to know her plans when she leaves here. Except Evert and Jeremiah. If Evert will lend her his car, she'll tell him that she'll cancel many of the debts in his book. Completely. If he's in a state of weekend drunkenness, Jeremiah can do the driving. He'll still know how. He often had to do deliveries with the furniture factory's truck. It's a skill you never forget. And she's not hard-up for petrol money. There's enough in the sacred bottle in her handbag to drive a long distance.

Then she lifts the counter flap with her own hands and steps inside.

33

WAS THAT A SOUND at the door? Petrified, she lowers the stack of papers; cocks her head to listen. No, there's nobody.

Her fingers are cramping, her arm is lame. She needs to read faster. Read Gunter's statement; then go back to the post-mortem report. Dry drowning? Suffocation? It makes no sense to her.

The town clerk. The pharmacist. All about accounts in arrears.

Miriam. Seven pages. Many highlighted phrases. Nothing undermining. No stab in the back.

The sister at the psychiatric clinic. *No, the child was not treated at the clinic . . . not a typical psychiatric case. Yes, on recommendation of the local doctor she assisted Mrs Dorfling to get help from a clinical psychologist.*

The clinical psychologist. Truly, they haven't missed a single soul. *Yes, Mrs Dorfling received counselling from him. Child about three years old at the time . . . asked advice on institutionalisation . . . she herself was dead against it. Cancelled all further appointments. Resumed treatment after her husband died. Welfare of the child a great priority to her. Obsessive in her search for solutions . . . very protective of the child. Discontinued further treatment due to the expense.*

She changes her grip and turns the page. Gunter's statement. She's too scared to read it. She looks up to make sure the woman is still asleep. The woman is sitting like a statue, watching her, unblinking. Terrified, she closes the docket and suppresses the impulse to vomit all over the desk.

Caught red-handed.

'Tidy up the docket,' the woman says in a soft voice, 'and lie down on the floor like you were when Colonel Herselman left.'

'I . . . I . . .' Her head feels like an echoing cave. 'I thought . . . you were sleeping.'

'I was never asleep. When I dropped the clipboard on the floor for the fifth time, *you* woke up. Close the docket and lie down before Colonel Herselman comes back.'

She lowers her tired body on to the dusty carpet. The woman gets up from the creaky chair, walks around the desk and arranges the docket into a neat pile.

'You've been sleeping the whole time, Mrs Dorfling. Agreed?'

'Yes.' She longs for a pillow. It feels as if her head is tilting downwards and the blood is gathering behind her eye sockets. 'I have a splitting headache.'

The woman unzips her handbag and breaks two headache tablets from a sheet. 'There's no more water and I'm not allowed to leave you alone. Swallow the tablets dry or chew them.'

'Thank you.'

The tablets are revoltingly bitter.

'You know nothing about headache tablets, Mrs Dorfling. Agreed?'

'Yes. What is the time?'

'Four o'clock. Colonel Herselman should be back any moment.'

Before the man comes back she must ask the woman something. 'Please tell me: what is dry drowning?'

'Probably a single drop of water that blocked the airway and caused suffocation. Exactly the same as choking on a grain of rice or a breadcrumb.'

The woman sits down behind the desk, rests her elbows on the surface. 'Mrs Dorfling, as a woman I can imagine what hell you've gone through the past nine years. I honestly admire your perseverance and persistence. Your courage too.'

Can it be that one person has compassion and understanding?

'I've worked with Colonel Herselman for many years. He's a hard man and he won't stop until he knows the whole truth. Up till now he's been gentle. It makes me shudder to think what's coming when he starts turning the screws. As soon as he's back, I'll see that you get a chair. It's inhuman to leave you sitting on the floor.'

She lifts herself on to her elbow. Is it possible the woman realises that she's innocent?

'Nobody can blame you for killing the child, Mrs Dorfling. Your circumstances were quite untenable and I admire your endurance. I understand your situation, and I want to assure you that the court will take into consideration . . .'

'I did not kill Alexander.'

'There is incriminating evidence in the docket, as you probably noticed yourself. Mrs Dorfling, listen to me . . .'

Her head resting in her palm, she listens to the woman. She speaks gently, and with profound insight. About the tragedy of autism and how a mother and her autistic child become outcasts, left to their own fate. Rejection by the community and, in her case, by the church too. A desperate moment in which the last straw broke the camel's back. How pressure and fatigue can push you over the borders of sanity. Extenuating circumstances. A voluntary confession will count in her favour.

'If you want to make a confession, Mrs Dorfling, you don't have to make it to Colonel Herselman. You can confess to me. We can talk woman to woman . . .'

She looks into the woman's eyes and sees that they are not speaking the same language as her tongue. And then she knows: it's a tactical game. Good cop, bad cop.

'I have nothing to confess.'

When the key grates in the lock, she puts her head down on the carpet and closes her eyes. The steel door squeaks open. And she is thankful for that moment in which she read the truth in the woman's eyes.

When the man prods her in the side with the tip of his shoe for the fourth time, she opens her eyes and turns her head to escape the harshness of the electric light.

'Sit up, Mrs Dorfling. Let's carry on.'

34

SHE PAUSES WITH HER fingers on the cold door handle.

'Don't you dare eat my food.'

'I've got my own food, Aunt Miriam.'

'I'm just warning you.'

Then she pushes the handle down and starts the journey down the passage to where the light spills from an open office door right at the end. This endless questioning must come to an end now, she's in a hurry to get to Evert. If Jeremiah is asleep when she gets home, she'll wake him up and tell him to wash the sleep from his eyes so they can walk to Evert's house. Get his car and go to the petrol station.

The man points to the chair. She has barely sat down and smoothed the wrinkles from her skirt with her hand, when he starts bombarding her again. Some questions are easy; others make her feel as though she's being chased barefoot down a narrow path strewn with devil's thorns.

What types of medicine was the child taking?

She tells him about the syringe and the medicine that had to be injected into Lexi's bum. And that the police should rather send someone to check in the medicine cabinet in Miss Ingrid's house, because she cannot remember all those difficult names. There was medicine to stop Lexi from flapping his hands and hitting his ears.

Medicine to make him look one straight in the eye. Another to stop him from biting on nails and screws. Yet another to stop him from sucking his own blood.

The man stares at her as if *she* has a screw loose.

'Did Mrs Dorfling ever talk of having the child admitted to an institution?'

'I don't know about that, sir. But before Master Dawid died, I heard him talking to her about Lexi going to a special school. Master Dawid often spoke about sending Lexi to a special school where the teachers were trained to understand his strangeness.'

'Did they ever send him?'

'No, sir.'

'Why not?'

Please, let the angels put the right words on her tongue. Because she would rather die than tell the man about the morning when she was standing in the laundry and heard every word that Master Dawid shouted in his drunkenness. Terrible things. About how Miss Ingrid had to choose between Lexi and the revolver, and that Miss Ingrid should have Lexi locked up in a madhouse, or else Master Dawid himself would batter some sense into Lexi's head. Heaven knows, she was so frightened that she almost vomited on the floor of the laundry. Not just because of the terrible things Master Dawid was shouting, but because he was dead drunk so early in the morning. It didn't matter that he was on leave. Morning is morning, and no right-thinking person should be drunk at breakfast time.

'I really don't know, sir. But Miss Ingrid explained to Teresa and Zettie that there were special places in our country where just about all kinds of disabled people could stay for ever, but not a single place of safety for autistic children like Lexi.'

A week after the fight between Master Dawid and Miss Ingrid, she was making meatballs in the kitchen when Zettie came in. The girls often came to the kitchen to seek comfort from her. She gave Zettie a bowl and told her to roll the meatballs in flour so they didn't stick to the pan. Then Zettie told her that mankind was clever enough to fly to the moon, they'd done that long ago, and that nowadays they can produce two exactly similar sheep from one single sheep, without a ram in sight. But they could not be bothered to build places of safety for children like Lexi.

She tells the man: 'Miss Ingrid said there were a few schools for autistic children in the country, but they were in Cape Town and Pretoria. Too far to drive month after month to fetch and carry Lexi. If I remember correctly, Miss Ingrid said the school rules said that they had to take Lexi home at least one weekend every month.'

He writes for a long while. She gets up to stretch her legs and fill the cup with water. Will Jeremiah remember to hang his wet clothes in front of the stove? If Miss Ingrid is locked up in gaol, who's going to have the presence of mind to go to the municipality on Monday to pay for the digging of Lexi's grave? The municipality will not bury anybody unless it's paid for. Only when you have put down the very last cent, will they instruct the grave-diggers to pick up a pickaxe. Not long ago, Henry Adrians's coffin had to be carried back to the mortuary, and all the funeral-goers had to go home and save their tears for another day. Henry Adrians's family could only scrape together half the fee, so the municipal grave-diggers dug only half the grave. But in all fairness to the living and the dead, the municipality also had to make a living.

If only she could think of a way of sending Jeremiah to a few trustworthy people to ask them to club together for the digging of Lexi's grave. Maybe she should try to send a message to the evangelist in the kloof. The people of the kloof had enough kindness in them to donate tomorrow's collection money.

'Did Mrs Dorfling ever speak about the child's future?'

'Yes, sir.' He did not ask *what* Miss Ingrid had said.

He glares at her, his eyes filled with the dirty colour of annoyance. 'Do you want me to smack the information out of you?'

Act stupid. 'What information must you smack from me, sir?'

He turns red in the face and points his pen at her. Almost in her eye. 'Don't waste my time, Mrs Slangveld! *What* did Mrs Dorfling say about the child's future?'

'I'm sorry, sir. I must've understood you wrongly. Lexi's future was a big worry for Miss Ingrid. She was worried about the day when he would be a grown-up man. But the biggest of all her worries was that the day would come when she would be too old and weak to look after him.'

One afternoon, a long time ago, she had picked fresh green beans from the garden and was busy slicing them when Zettie came into the kitchen and took a paring knife to help her. Zettie cut the beans thick and unevenly, but she did not reprimand her, because she knew Zettie was gathering her courage to tell her something. Often, when the girls had something on their minds or when things in the house were tense, they came to the kitchen or to the laundry and pretended to help her. But she knew it was because they felt safe with her. And before long they would tell her what was worrying them. Then she waited for the right time to let Miss Ingrid know the secrets and sorrows of her daughters' hearts. It worked well. Because the next morning when she tidied the house, she usually saw that the troubled one had not slept in her own bed, but on Master Dawid's side of the double bed. Then she knew that her pain had been soothed by the warmth of her own mother. The Lord knows, she felt sorry for the girls. They suffered greatly.

However.

While they were slicing the green beans, Zettie told her about a woman overseas whose daughter suffered from the same strange illness as Lexi. But then the daughter grew big and became too strong and wilful and obstinate for the mother to handle. So the mother made the daughter climb on to a chair and she tied a rope around the daughter's neck. Jump, she told the daughter. The daughter knew no better. She jumped. And before long, the mother was in gaol. The police, and the clever doctors who understood how to read a wrong-headed person's thoughts, said the girl did not have the ability to contrive such a plan.

Another time Zettie told her about an old man, well into his eighties. He was just skin and bone when they discovered him in the locked cellar of an old farmstead. Matted bush of grey hair hanging down to his calves. Stale brown bread lying on the floor of the cellar, a hubcap containing slimy water. His clothes in tatters. Could not speak a single word. Just flapped his hands wildly and screamed like a pig being slaughtered. If the farm workers had not thrown bread through the tiny window of the cellar every now and then, and stuck the hose pipe through to fill the hubcap, he would have died long ago.

'You've made that up, Zettie.'

'I have not,' Zettie replied sharply. 'It's the holy truth.'

'Says who?'

'I read it in a magazine in the school library.'

'Show it to me, Zettie, then I'll believe you.'

Two days later Zettie came home with the page that she had torn from the magazine. In black and white.

It took her the whole afternoon to wash and dry Zettie's long hair. Make two beautiful plaits. It was the only kindness she could offer Zettie to ease the fear and uncertainty in the child's heart.

'Miss Ingrid did not speak about Lexi's old age often, sir. But she always used to say that the same God who gave Lexi to her would help her to live to a hundred and twenty. And He would keep her fit and strong until the end.'

He turns the page again. It must be about the fourth page. Then he puts the pen down and leans back in the chair, folds his hands. Stares at her with a puzzled expression.

'Mrs Slangveld, why are you defending Mrs Dorfling so strongly? What are you hiding from us?'

He's guessing. There's no way he can see into her brain. 'Good gracious, sir! Why should I hide anything from you? I'm just giving you the facts as I understand them. If you bring a Bible now, I'll lay my hand on it!'

He rocks in the chair; twists his fingers. There's a cynical smile on his face. 'Why did Mrs Dorfling murder the child?'

Almighty God. 'Murder, sir? *Miss Ingrid?*'

He rattles off a string of facts. About the doctor who examined Lexi's body. Dry lungs. About strangling and a fractured bone in Lexi's throat; that Lexi was murdered and put in the bath after-wards to make it appear as if he drowned.

'You've got it all wrong, sir! Never! Miss Ingrid would never murder Lexi! I can promise you that! God can let my tongue fall off if I'm lying!'

He moves the chair closer to the desk and starts writing again.

Good heavens, *murdered*? What if Miss Ingrid's patience and tolerance finally came to a dead end last night, and she lost her reason?

What then?

Then the police will not get a single piece of evidence from *her* mouth. Not now, not ever. Not even if they drag her to court and put her in the witness box for ten days. Jesus of Nazareth be her witness, she'll raise her hand and take a false oath.

35

She sits up, wipes the dust from her cheek. The bitter aftertaste of the tablets clings to her teeth and tongue. Her hands feel sticky and dry.

'I'm thirsty.'

'Would you like some water, Mrs Dorfling, or coffee?'

Amazed, she stares at the woman. Maybe she has misjudged her motives.

'Coffee, please.'

'How many sugars?'

'One, thank you.'

'I'm leaving the door open, Colonel, I'll be back in a few minutes.'

The woman returns with a jug of water, a cup of coffee and an extra chair. She closes the steel door and sits down on the chair in the corner of the room; picks up the clipboard and puts it on her lap. The man is quiet. Head bent, neon marker in hand, he concentrates on the docket. She sips the warm coffee and longs for home. Her own sheets and pillows; the smell of smoke from a damp wood fire clinging to Miriam's clothes. Gunter walking in the twilight with the tinkling stirrups in his hand. Where is she going to find the money to pay for Alexander's funeral? Perhaps the bank manager will extend her overdraft. He can use the insurance policy as security.

The man puts the marker down, plants his elbows on the desk and resumes his interrogation. Old questions. New questions. He chops and changes and confuses her. Emotionally, she's still battling with one question, and he's already on to the next one.

Why did you ask the Indian man to bury magic stuff in your garden? It was Miriam's idea. I don't believe in magic, but I did not want Miriam to abandon hope.

Why didn't you make an effort to restore the friendship between you and your friends? I did, but the alienation between us seemed insurmountable.

Why did your husband never seek professional help from a psychologist? He was convinced that I was the core of the problem. He said if I accepted Alexander's disability, and stopped spending money on useless visits from doctor to doctor, everything would change for the better.

Where did the child get the chisel from? I cannot remember. It belonged to my husband, maybe Alexander found it in the garage.

Why did you never take it away from him? We did. But he found something else to replace it. We often tried to stop his obsessive behaviour. When Dawid put a lock on the lid of the piano, Alexander developed an obsession for breaking everything that had a lock. The lock on the piano too. That's why we left him to chisel as he pleased.

Your husband had a serious drinking problem, Mrs Dorfling. Why did he never book into a clinic or get help from your family doctor? He denied he had a problem. Nothing I ever said or did could convince him.

Yesterday you had no money to pay back the deficit at the bank. But on the same day you had money to have the child's hair cut and to buy him new clothes and five jars of cheese spread. How do you explain that? I sold my pressure cooker and frying pan to one of the kitchen staff at the school hostel. She gave the money to me on Thursday. It wasn't enough to cover the shortfall at the bank.

Who was she? Rosie March. She is the cook at the hostel.

Why did you sell the stuff? I seldom used it and it was just taking up space.

On and on and on.

Until she felt as if an endless procession of train trucks was running through her head. Tock-tock, tock-tock, tock-tock over the joints in the railway line. Every now and then the man's mobile phone rang, or he opened the steel door to take a fax. Read it;

sorted it into the docket.

'The clinical psychologist from whom you received counselling, Mrs Dorfling, who referred you to him?'

'The nursing sister at the psychiatric clinic in town.'

'What led to that?'

Alexander had just turned three. She could not recall the exact order of events, but she remembered that he was walking. Actually, running. Storming at everything that got in his way. Coffee table, magazine stand, standing lamp. He never cried when he hurt himself. Never broke his stride, was unaware of the havoc he caused. Some days she regretted sitting with the shoebrush, massaging his feet for hours while he was sleeping, and wished that he had never learned to walk. The running child also got on Dawid's nerves. From one wall to the other, striking his palms against the wall before he turned. Around and around the dining room table. Up and down the steps. And it never exhausted him.

'It's impossible to study while Alexander is thudding over the floor like this, Mom,' Teresa complained to her as she stood at the stove frying sweetcorn fritters. 'I'm writing a maths test tomorrow, and my maths marks are pathetic already. Can't you please do something to stop him, Mom?'

'*What* do you want me to do?'

'I don't know, Mom, but I can't study while he's . . .'

She felt as if a tiny gasping frog was trapped under the skin at her temples. It throbbed and made the blood rush to her head. 'Teresa, if I knew what to do, I would have done it long ago.'

'But at the same time, I'm expected to pass my maths test. It's unfair to . . .'

The tiny frog throbbed faster and faster. It made her blind and unreasonable. 'Oh, for God's sake, Teresa! Why don't *you* stop him?' A thunderstorm roared in her head. 'Why do *I* have to do everything? I'm on my feet all day long, and at night while the rest of you are sleeping, I stay up to . . .'

She had not meant to yell at Teresa. If it were possible, she would have gulped the words back and swallowed them. As a peace offering she turned to take one of the cooked fritters from the plate to give it to Teresa. But then she saw Dawid in the kitchen door. Bloodshot eyes. Drunk. He took Teresa by the elbow and pushed her out of the way; came straight at her where she stood at the stove.

'Don't take your bloody moods out on the child!' His voice hung in the kitchen like a black cloud.

'It's got nothing to do with moodiness, Dawid, it's just that . . .'

He bent over and hissed in her face. 'Shut up, Ingrid, for God's sake, just shut up! Or else *I* will shut you up!'

The tiny frog grew into a huge monster that threatened to break through the skin at her temples. She put the egg-lifter down. In the background she could hear that Alexander had knocked something over; the sound of breaking glass tinkled through the house.

'Did you hear me?' The smell of liquor on his breath filled her with revulsion.

'Why the hell should I shut up! Why don't you switch the television off and lift your backside from the couch and help me to . . .'

He slapped her against the side of her head with such brutal force that she staggered against the fridge. God knows, she was frightened out of her wits.

'Stop it, Dawid! Have you gone out of your mind?'

He slapped her again and again. Against her head, in her face. She lost her footing and tried desperately to find something to hold on to. Her hip hit the stove; a red hot pain shot through her shoulder as she was flung against the crockery cupboard. Tripped over a kitchen chair. Landed on all fours next to the chair; blood streaming from her nose. Distantly, she heard the train rattling past and Alexander yelling at the top of his voice. Then Dawid's shoe hit her in the ribs so hard that it knocked the wind out of her. She rolled over, filled with pain.

Then her animal instincts took over. She forgot about the excruciating pain in her ribcage. Slid under the table and leapt out on the far side near the sink. Grabbed the butter dish and threw it at Dawid. He ducked and simultaneously charged at her. She knew she was looking death in the eyes; that his pent-up fury was enough for him to kill her with his bare hands. She jabbed her forefinger into his eye and with all her strength she lifted her knee into his groin. He bellowed like an ox and folded over. It gave her the chance to escape. Gasping for breath, she limped down the passage and locked herself in the toilet.

Soon she could smell burning oil. But she did not care if the whole house and all its contents burnt down.

It was an endless night. Cold and dark. The light-switch was on the wall outside the toilet. She could not see out of her bruised left eye; she made a compress out of toilet paper; dipped it in the toilet and tried to soothe the swelling. Moved the compress down to her left cheekbone. Made a fresh compress. Took shallow breaths so that she did not go insane from the pain in her ribs.

When the grey glimmer of dawn was visible through the toilet window, Dawid knocked at the door and asked her to open it. She refused. Then he started weeping bitterly and she struggled up from the toilet seat to unlock the door. He stared at her in horror, as if he was seeing a ghost.

'Oh, my God, Ingrid . . .' His cheeks were wet with tears, he shook his head in disbelief. 'Ingrid, I cannot tell you how sorry . . .'

'Get out of my way.'

She pushed him aside. Limped to the kitchen to make herself a glass of warm milk.

On the second day she could no longer bear the pain in her ribcage and called Old Doctor to the house. She would rather die in her bed than show her bruised face in town. Broken ribs, Old Doctor diagnosed. As soon as the swelling in her face subsided, she had to go to hospital for X-rays, he said. He gave her an injection for pain and did what he could to make her comfortable. Closed his bag and sat down at the foot of the bed, waiting for the injection to start working.

'I'll visit you on my morning rounds,' he said. At the door of the room he turned and asked if she would have any objection if he sent the nursing sister from the psychiatric clinic to visit her.

'I suppose it's all right,' she said, her tongue slurring.

What difference would it make? When the numbness in your soul is reflected in the swollen flesh of your eye and the throbbing in your cheekbone and ribcage, your dignity is almost nullified. Few other things matter.

Two weeks' sick leave. No one knocked at the door with a bowl of soup or even a single flower. She knew that everyone in town knew the truth.

Two weeks can seem like two hundred years when you have to battle to get out of bed to wash and brush your teeth. Shuffle to the bathroom, grunting, every muscle in your body aching. Appalled, you stare at your reflection in the bathroom mirror. And it is hard to acknowledge that the swollen face with the blue-green-purple bruises looking at you out of the mirror, is yours.

For a month Dawid slept on the couch. His remorse lasted for almost a year, but then he lifted his hand to her again.

'I went to the psychologist out of desperation. I needed a professional person to help me make sense out of my confusion, and there was nobody in town that I could trust.'

'How long did you carry on with the treatment?'

It had been a waste of money and time. Every Saturday. An hour's drive there; an hour's drive back. Petrol expenses. Miriam had to be paid extra to look after Alexander until she got home. Excess to be paid to the medical aid fund, because they only covered a certain stipulated percentage of the fee. She gained nothing from the psychologist. All he did was dig into the past. The past, which could not be changed; it was a waste of mental energy and time. She wanted to learn how to go forward; not keep circling in water that had already gone under the bridge.

'For about four months. Then I couldn't afford it any longer.'

'The dominee surely had the knowledge to assist you. Why didn't you confide in him?'

'May I have some water, please?' The chair creaks as the woman gets up to pour her a glass of water.

What could she say? Dawid could escape by jumping off a bridge. The doctors could shrug their shoulders. Miriam could retire one day. Lida could send Alexander home with a cryptic note. The pharmacist could draw a red circle around the outstanding amount on her account. Aunt Betty threw the green apricots back over the fence. The municipality cut off the electricity supply when the account wasn't paid promptly. The bank manager could report her to head-office. The dominee had the right of veto whenever it suited him.

But her hands were tied.

'Because the dominee led the Church Council in taking disciplinary action against my husband. *He* reported my husband to the post office authorities, and when a disciplinary hearing was held against my husband, *he* was quick to . . . then he was . . .'

She bows her head, lifts her hand to her face; bursts into tears.

Torrents of tears.

Tears for shattered dreams of what had been and what was and what would be. And what would never be.

36

ONE OF THE STRANGE policemen puts a cup of coffee and a sugar bowl on the desk in front of the evil-eyed man. They whisper to each other before the policeman walks out. She hopes the man doesn't take long to drink his coffee. Look at the time! And she must get to Evert's house. Please God, let Evert not be playing taxi-man tonight.

'Mrs Slangveld, do you know if Mr Dorfling had problems at work?'

She's not going to try and sidestep this one. Everybody in town knew that Master Dawid was skating on thin ice at the post office. If the police asked Jeremiah, he would tell them. 'It's true, sir. A team from the head-office arrived in town to inspect Master Dawid's affairs.'

'And?'

Heaven knows, it was a time of confusion and uncertainty. At night the chicken eagle pestered her and it did not help to sit behind the chicken run and plead with God to make things easier for Miss Ingrid. It was during that time that she woke Jeremiah up in the middle of the night and told him that she could not understand how white people's heads worked. Couldn't they see for themselves how Master Dawid suffered? Was it necessary for them to gang up against him? And why did the white dominee, who was supposed to be a man with clean hands, take the lead in the witch-hunt on Master Dawid?

It was totally different from how they lived in the township.

If you had to testify against somebody who had committed a dreadful crime, then it was your duty to do so, according to the Bible. If the evil-hearted person had to spend time behind bars because of your evidence, then it served him right. A trespasser is a trespasser. But when somebody's weaknesses lead him to a wrong turn-off in life, and he commits a forgivable crime, you don't kick him when he's down. Because, but for the grace of God, it could have been you.

Take the time when Jeremiah could not keep his hands off the yellowwood planks. Nobody in the township treated her and the children like dirt. When she visited Jeremiah in gaol to pass some of her strength and endurance on to him, the township people always sent him presents. A bar of soap. Socks. A comb. A domino set that they made from match boxes. During times of hardship they helped to keep her ship on the water. And she'd relied on the church and the evangelist to help her steer her ship safely through storms. And when Jeremiah walked out of gaol after he had paid for the yellowwood planks with his soul, nobody trampled on the bit of dignity he had left.

Master Dawid was not even close to gaol, but the white people had already trampled him into the dust.

One afternoon she sat behind the chicken run praying for Jeremiah's two cranky old legs, that they would carry him into the veld outside town to pick prickly pears. They had good rains that year, and the prickly pear trees were bearing delicious fruit. The shops in town offered a good price if the prickly pears were dethorned. She wanted to buy galvanised sheets for a new roof before the first winter rains fell. If Jeremiah would lift his backside and move his two cranky legs, the new roof could easily be on before the prickly pear season was over.

However.

She knew that Master Dawid was battling stormy waters and that he had lost both his oars, but she knew nothing about the disaster brewing at the post office. While she was praying behind the chicken run, Sonny arrived at her house on his delivery bicycle. At first she thought he was bringing her a letter, because he was the postman, after all. But he did not have his mailbag with him and his shirt pocket was empty.

'I need to talk to you, Aunt Miriam,' he said, 'but you must take an oath that you won't split on me.'

'You know me, Sonny, I'll never put up my hand to swear if I don't know what I'm swearing about.'

He squatted and stared at the ground. Picked up a splinter of firewood and scratched in the loose soil. 'It's about an ugly thing at work, Aunt Miriam, about Master Dawid.'

It made her blood run cold, and there and then she swore with her hand on her heart. Sonny would never pass on an untrue story to her. And in any event, she'd been expecting the devil to finish his dirty job at the post office for quite some time now.

Dusk fell and the chickens had gone to roost, and Sonny was still sitting with her behind the chicken run. Telling how he overheard the ladies at the post office gossiping while he was making tea in the kitchen. That apparently the path to the dominee's front door had been turned to dust because of the number of townspeople who had been to the manse to complain about Master Dawid being drunk at work. And that he heard with his own ears when they said that the dominee was going to write a letter to head-office to ask the big bugs in charge to come and have a look at what was going on at the post office.

'They're going to cut Master Dawid's throat, Aunt Miriam.' He got up and tossed the wood splinter to one side. 'You must think of a plan to warn Master Dawid. Being drunk at work is as good as firing yourself. Those people aren't coming all the way from head-office to play games, Aunt Miriam.'

For days she turned the matter over and over in her mind. But the angel of goodness refused to speak to her. Then Jeremiah said she should let it be. Master Dawid was a grown man, he said, and he had to take responsibility for his life.

Jeremiah's words were hardly cold, when the dominee arrived at Miss Ingrid's house on Sunday after church with his grand car and his shoes polished like mirrors. When she took the tea tray in, she noticed a dangerous light in the dominee's eyes. Like a polecat waiting for a chance to steal an egg from the nest. She put Lexi on the tyre-swing to swing himself asleep and stood under the sitting room window where she could keep an eye on him and at the same time hear what was being said in the sitting room. Listening to conversations that were not meant for your ears was a sin. But listening to a conversation because the angel of goodness told you to, was a different matter altogether.

When she went inside to check that the sweet potatoes weren't burning, she stood at the stove listening quite openly. Because the discussion in the sitting room was loud and heated. Heaven knows, Master Dawid gave the dominee a good piece of his mind. In choice language. Said the Church Council could stuff his certificate of membership up their backsides and that he wouldn't tithe one single cent, because without blinking an eye the dominee abused God's money on overseas trips and a luxurious holiday house. But there was never money in the church's coffers to pick up a telephone to find out about a home for the disabled where Lexi could go. Just as she was about to put the potatoes in the oil to deep-fry them, Master Dawid jumped up and opened the front door. Told the dominee that he had better leave. Immediately. Before Master Dawid *donnered* the shit out of him.

After dinner, when she and Miss Ingrid were alone in the kitchen, she told Miss Ingrid that she had to get something off her chest. And she told Miss Ingrid about Sonny's visit. That night she could sleep with a clear conscience. Nothing to explain to the chicken eagle.

Less than a month later the team of investigators from head-office arrived.

Afterwards Sonny told her everything. About the written warning that he read with his own eyes when he dusted Master Dawid's desk. According to Sonny, the letter said it was Master Dawid's final warning for arriving late at work and drinking on the job.

'Master Dawid tried his best to comb out the knots in his life, sir. But he became old within a month. Hardly ever spoke and just moved his food around on his plate. He turned into a walking skeleton and had to make two extra holes in his belt with the awl. I'm telling you, sir: to this day, I believe it was the humiliation of that final warning that drove Master Dawid over the rails of the bridge.'

'Did Mr Dorfling ever threaten to take his own life?'

Keep quiet about the gun in the linen cupboard. And about the times Master Dawid yelled that he was either going to go insane or kill himself. 'Not that I know of, sir.'

'You've been working for the Dorflings for thirteen years. The Dorfling girls . . .' and he stops to check something in the docket next to his arm, 'they were six and eight when you started working there. Three years later the boy was born. How did they handle this?'

Dangerous questions. Think before answering. 'Sir, do you mean how did they handle the people from head-office, or Master Dawid's death, or Lexi's birth?'

Exasperated, he throws his pen on the table. 'Are you doing this on purpose, Mrs Slangveld, or are you just plain stupid?'

'Neither, sir. But I'm quite mixed up by the many questions you're asking. I'm hardly halfway through answering one question, when you . . .'

'You are hiding things from me!' His cheeks are red with annoyance. 'You're going to lie yourself into a corner and *then* you'll be in serious trouble! Answer my question: how did the Dorfling girls handle *everything*, from the child's birth to this day?'

'Some days things were all right, sir; some days they were bad. They understood Lexi just as little as anybody else. He broke their things and made a noise when they were trying to study or sleep. And he buggered up their school books when they forgot to lock their rooms. Anyone would be cross.' A sip of water. 'But I can assure you, sir: they would never allow anybody to hurt Lexi; they would fight for him.'

His questions are unending. Later on she doesn't know the difference between up and down or back and front. Now it's Master Dawid, then it's the chisel. Back to the grocery cupboards. This about the bath plug; that about medicine and doctors. Asks where Miss Ingrid got the money to pay for whatever. Back to the bridge and the *Kinderkrans* and Lexi's fear of the sound of train wheels. It doesn't help that she tells him that he's repeating himself. He ignores her. Every little piece of kindling he can possibly pick up, he uses to add fuel. On and on. Until she's tired to the bone.

Then she realises that she won't get to Evert and his car before the new day dawns.

37

HER BODY IS CONVULSED with weeping. Nothing exists any more. Just the bitter grief of the loss of all that was precious to her.

'Come, Mrs Dorfling, we're taking you back to your cell,' the woman says and gently touches her shoulder. 'Come, get up.'

But everything inside her feels lifeless. They take her under her armpits and lift her up. The man kicks the chair aside and they support her until her legs are stronger. Slowly, her feet start moving. The key grates in the lock of the steel door. Through the east windows of the passage daylight streams into the building. It hurts her eyes and aggravates her headache.

So, after all, the sun had risen while she was in the oppressive interrogation room.

It's Sunday.

Kraal wall day.

If they took her home straight away, she could bath and go to Gunter. Lie down on the straw and hold out her arms to him, say: come lie with me, Gunter. Hold me until evening comes. Then take me to your house and shelter me. After the funeral I'll go back to my own house.

The woman pulls her by the arm. 'Come, Mrs Dorfling, I'll bring you a cup of tea.'

Good cops and bad cops. What difference did it make? Let them play their games with her; it'll change nothing.

Hunched by sorrow and fatigue, she shuffles down passages filled with the sour smell of unwashed bodies. Does the sun ever reach these dungeons? Or is it always cold and musty and damp down here?

There's a clatter of metal when they unlock the barred door. 'Have a shower,' the woman says. 'You'll feel more comfortable.'

Long after they have left, she remains standing in the same position, shivering. Then she slowly moves towards the bed, the unlaced shoes flapping at her heels, and sinks down on the mattress. It's like crossing an inconceivable boundary, but she's unaware that she's done so. She pushes the carry-bag under her head and pulls the coarse blanket over her trembling body. Draws her knees up tightly against her stomach.

It doesn't stink or make her shudder. Her body doesn't know that she hasn't had a bath since Thursday. The mattress and the blanket become her only boundaries. In the drifting moments before she's carried away by the weightlessness of sleep, she sees Teresa and Zettie's faces hovering above her. Soundlessly, their lips move as they call her. And she longs to escape from this hell. So that she can try to heal nine years of open wounds.

For a fleeting moment the sound of stainless steel dishes and a loud voice calling out in the passage brings her back to the surface. They mustn't bring her food; she'll vomit. She pulls the blanket over her shoulders and moves the carry-bag under her head.

Sunday.

Will Teresa and Zettie find something for lunch? Will Gunter miss her on this cold winter afternoon?

'I've become hard,' she told Gunter one autumn Sunday. It was a windless day bathed in sunshine, rust-coloured poplar leaves fluttering in the mild breeze. The western sun shone on her shoulder and hip, making her feel contented and warm where she basked on the kraal wall. The air carried the scent of cow's milk and wet soil and camphor bush.

'Take this.' Gunter held out the rake. 'Get off the kraal wall and help me rake the straw.'

She loved him so desperately. But she always had to hide it; push it aside. Surrender and forget. Because she carried the mark of Cain.

Sitting on the kraal wall on Sundays was the warm side of her life. Protection and comfort. Gunter must never know about the fire that burned in her heart and groin. Never. Because if he knew, he too would weigh anchor and sail to calmer waters, as everybody close to her had done. No sensible person would voluntarily and permanently tie himself to a living hell. And then there would be nothing left but darkness.

'I haven't always been so hard.' She started raking the straw in the corner of the stable into a heap.

'Rake, Ingrid, the sun is setting. Look, Alexander is asleep and Lucy's drawing in her circles.'

When she glanced over her shoulder, she saw that he was looking at her. Stooped, his hands resting on the fresh bale of straw that he was separating. His eyes glowed with yearning. She wanted to throw the rake down and run to him. Lay her head on his chest and plead: Show me where I can find a cave in the mountains, Gunter. Take me there and teach me to chop wood and make fire and pick berries. Tell me which veld fruits and tubers are edible. Show me how to set a hare trap and teach me how to read the time of day from the moving shadows of the sun. Take me away from town, Gunter. *You* don't have to take me. Just find me a cave where I can build a new kingdom.

For me and Alexander.

Then, sometimes, you can come to us in the mountains when it's full moon or dark moon or quarter moon. If you tell me beforehand at which moon you'll be coming, I'll sweep the floor of the cave and burn sweet-scented wild herbs. Wash my hair in a mountain stream and let the sun and the morning wind dry it. We'll wait for you at the mouth of the cave . . .

Alexander and I.

Because I cannot leave him behind. He's mine.

She gripped the rake and turned her eyes to the floor of the stable so that he could not read her emotions. It might frighten him away for ever. 'I'm not in a hurry to finish raking. What doesn't get done today, I'll do next Sunday.' She rested the rake against the kraal wall. 'Did you hear me when I said I haven't always been so hard?'

'Yes.'

'Before Alexander was born, I was sweet-tempered, obliging. My life was filled with peace and contentment. Completely different from now . . .'

Different . . . different . . . different . . .

The word echoes from the vent in the ceiling; ricochets around and around the walls of the bare cell. In her sleep she's aware of the coldness of her body and the coarse blanket covering her shoulders. She turns over. Glides back into the oblivious waters of sleep where she cannot recall the man's intimidating questions. Dreamlessly, she floats in one sun-drenched spot in the green-blue pool; does not return to the rocky bank where Alexander had earlier waited for her with the salmon-coloured starfish in his hand.

38

SHE MUST PUT AN end to the man's questions, if only to buy a little time; find a breathing space. If it is God's will that she should remain at the police station all night and only go to Evert's house in the morning, then she will abide by that.

'Mrs Slangveld, if the child was scared of water, why would he get into the bath?'

Now she's on a narrow footpath. Because she's convinced that Lexi would never have climbed into the bath himself. And if he did not get in by himself, how *did* he get into the water? 'I need to go to the lavatory, sir. My bladder is too full to think.'

He sighs and throws the pen down. 'Damn it, Mrs Slangveld! If you're not hungry or thirsty, then you have to have a darned piss! Do you think I can't see where you're heading? Answer my question!'

She puts her hands on her knees to get up. 'I'm an old woman, sir. You can work out for yourself when last I went to the lavatory. It was back in the kloof at Jeremiah's people.'

He glares at her as if he can smell the urine right through her skin. 'Go then. I'll give you three minutes.'

'Make it five, sir. My legs are stiff and I won't be able to get my step-in down and up, and pee, and walk back in three minutes.'

Halfway down the passage the angels give her the answer as to how Lexi got into the bath.

Years ago, before the huge rift between Miss Ingrid and Master Dawid's parents, the Old Master and Old Missus visited for a couple of days. It was always bad to have them there. They behaved as if the house belonged to them. The white sauce had to be done this way; the vegetables had to be cooked that way. She wasn't allowed to prick the sausage with a fork to let the fat cook out. Zettie had to sleep on a mattress on the floor in Teresa's room. And the Old Missus fiddled with everything. Checked for dust under the beds and greasiness around the kitchen taps. Forced Lexi to eat oat porridge. Didn't think twice about giving him a hiding with the wooden spoon when he growled at her. And when they were there, Lexi's tantrums and strangeness got worse. He broke the Old Missus's lipstick and scattered her face powder on the carpet. Bent the Old Master's sunglasses. Lay on the passage carpet and kicked against their door while they were taking an afternoon nap. Then they bitched in *her* ears about Lexi's naughtiness like a flock of mouse-birds cornered by a tree snake.

However.

This time when they visited, they brought Lexi a little blue portable swimming pool. They pitched it on the front lawn and filled it up with water. She watched them with worry in her heart. And then she told the Old Missus that Lexi wasn't fond of water.

'What do *you* know?' the Old Missus snapped at her. Old cow.

After dinner, while she was washing the dishcloths, she watched them through the kitchen window with a gnawing feeling in her gut. Forcefully, they picked Lexi up and tried to put him into the swimming pool. Lexi shouted *Mimmi! Mimmi!* Arched his back and kicked against the edge of the pool. The Old Master bent Lexi's toes away from where they were gripping the edge. Next thing they let go of Lexi and he landed on his back in the splashing water. The moment he touched the water, his neck became stiff and his eyes turned back in their sockets like white marbles. She dropped the cloth in the soapy water, grabbed the syringe and ran. Halfway up the front steps she shot past the panicking Old Missus with the syringe in her hand.

That same day the Old Master folded the swimming pool up and packed it back into its box. Somewhat spitefully, he said that he knew of another boy who would love to have the pool.

She rinses her face and hands. In less than five minutes she's back in the chair.

'If I have to guess, sir, I'd say that Lexi fell into the bath because the sight of all that water caused him to have a fit.'

'The doctor is absolutely convinced he did not drown, Mrs Slangveld. He died of suffocation. And there was nobody in the house except Mrs Dorfling.'

She mustn't mention the day when Miss Ingrid cried hysterically and covered Lexi's face with a pillow. Jesus knows, that will put Miss Ingrid straight behind bars.

'That same doctor, sir, will be clever enough to explain to you that having a fit and suffocation come to the same thing. If Lexi had a fit and fell into the water, he could very easily suffocate under the water.'

He glares at her distrustfully. Takes his mobile phone from his pocket and walks out the door. She can hear him talking in the passage. And although she cannot hear what he's saying, she instinctively knows that she played the dominoes' double six at exactly the right moment.

She fills the cup again; sits back on the chair.

Says thank you to the angels.

39

SOMEONE STRIPS THE BLANKET from her curled-up body. She shivers with cold. For a moment, she has no idea where she is.

'Wake up, Mrs Dorfling, your lawyer is waiting for you in the visitors' room.'

Lawyer? What lawyer?

When she lifts her head, the cell comes into focus. Air-vent in the ceiling, catwalk, cement block around the toilet, washbasin, bar of red soap, enamel mug on the window sill. Graffiti. Bare cement floor strewn with cigarette butts, covered in urine stains. It feels as if an invisible hand is cracking her head like a walnut shell.

'Get up, Mrs Dorfling, your lawyer is waiting.'

It's a good cop strategy. Probably a state lawyer primed to show compassion and encourage her towards a confession. Let them play their games, she has nothing to confess. Painfully aware of the stiffness in her body, she swings her legs from the bed and forgets that the foam mattress is wider than the cement block it's resting on. She loses her balance and lands on her knees on the cement floor. Struggles up, knocking over the mug of cold tea. 'What day is it, and what's the time?'

'It's Sunday morning, seven minutes to nine. Comb your hair and brush your teeth, and let's go.'

She couldn't have slept more than an hour. The sun was up when they brought her back to the cell. 'I'm hungry.'

'As soon as your lawyer has left, you can eat.'

If she hadn't seen the hardness in the woman's eyes earlier, she would have believed that the woman felt sympathetically towards her.

She washes her face and brushes her teeth at the small basin. Empties her bladder. Rolls down the last sheets of toilet paper. Pulls the brush through her crumpled hair. Puts it back into the bag and zips it closed.

It will be the first Sunday in many months that she won't be sitting on the kraal wall. She will have to use the two thousand rand that Gunter offered for Lucy to pay for Alexander's funeral. Teresa and Zettie will have to arrange the funeral on their own.

A police constable comes to fetch her. Down the passage yet again. She gets the fright of her life when a hand shoots through the bars and grabs her by the sleeve of her tracksuit top, pulls her sideways. A stinging pain shoots through her shoulder as she hits the bars. The face behind the bars grins at her; his stained teeth look like a row of worn-out piano keys. His crude words splatter in her face. The police constable forces the clutching hand from her sleeve and rages at the grinning face behind the bars.

'Stay in the middle of the passage,' and he pushes her, 'and walk faster.'

She cannot walk faster. She wonders how she manages to walk at all. On Thursday night she hardly slept. Friday night almost broke her back. Yesterday was sheer hell. If they're bargaining on exhausting her physically and emotionally and tricking her into a confession, they're misjudging her strength.

The lawyer waiting opposite the glass partition does not look like a set-up. He looks her straight in the eyes, indicates to her to sit down. The woman remains standing in the corner of the visitors' room, head tilted to listen to what they say. The man picks up the intercom phone and indicates to her to pick up the phone on her side of the partition. The mouthpiece is greasy and smells musty; it's damp from someone else's spit.

'I'm going to be your legal representative, Mrs Dorfling. It's important that you trust me and . . .'

'I have no money to pay you.'

'There will be no charge, Mrs Dorfling. It's to your advantage to have legal representation, and I will . . .'

No charge? Then he is a state lawyer. 'I've said everything that

I'm going to say. I'm too tired to repeat it.'

She is about to put the phone down, when he holds his hand up to stop her. 'Gunter sent me to you.'

A heavenly light seems to shine on her, veils her in unexpected protection. Then, after all, Gunter did remember. 'I'll accept your offer. But honestly, I'm too tired to talk now. I have hardly slept for three nights. Will it be possible to come back in the morning?'

'By all means. Don't hesitate to call me, day or night. My telephone number is available from the investigating officer.'

When the lawyer leaves, the woman steps forward. 'Colonel Herselman is waiting to continue with the questioning. If you want to talk to me alone, just say so.'

When she is faced once more with the door of the interrogation room, she feels as if an invisible hand is twisting her guts. Mercifully, the chair is still there; the water and the glass too.

'Mrs Dorfling, your child was diagnosed as autistic when he was three and a half years old, correct?'

'Yes, it was when we took him to the Children's Hospital in Cape Town. But nobody ever spelled out the diagnosis to us. After sifting through a vast amount of information, I came to the conclusion myself.'

Arched eyebrows. 'Without any medical knowledge?'

'In the report that arrived about a month after we came back from the Children's Hospital I saw the word *autism* for the first time in my life. From there on it was simply a matter of applying logic.'

'Mrs Dorfling, for five and a half years you were aware of your child's disability. Your family life and social life suffered. In fact, the quality of your lives deteriorated so badly that your husband committed suicide. What efforts did *you* make to improve the situation?'

What didn't she do? God knows, she was prepared to try anything.

For more than a month she mentioned nothing about the report from the Children's Hospital to Dawid or to anybody else. Emotionally, she was shocked to immobility. Before she discussed the contents of the report with anybody, she needed to mull it over; digest it; figure it out for herself. She took out the few available books on the subject from the library. Sat with Teresa's dictionary while Dawid was elsewhere, withdrawn into his own non-communicative world where nothing mattered. After reading a quarter of the first book she was one hundred per cent sure of the diagnosis. In fact, her maternal instincts had sensed the truth the day she completed the questionnaires at the Children's Hospital. But then she did not know *what* the truth was. Now she did. With every page she read the pieces of the puzzle fell into place.

Disturbances in the development of social and physical skills. Abnormal responses to sensations such as sight, hearing, touch, balance, reaction to pain. Abnormal development of speech, language and non-verbal communication. Abnormal ways of relating to people, objects and events in the environment.

Everything was abnormal, distorted. Contrary to accepted norms. Page after page she was confronted by the shattering sentence: *lifelong disability*. During lunchtime at work she made photocopies from the books before returning them to the library. Filed the pages. At night she woke up, gasping, in a cold sweat. Stumbled out of bed to check something in the file yet again.

There are no medical tests for autism ... problems in the way they see the world around them. People with autism perceive the world like an FM radio station that is not exactly on the station ... Inconsistency is a hallmark of autism ...

She made an appointment to see Old Doctor. For once in her life she would sit on the riempie chair until they saw eye to eye. He had a startled expression in his eyes; stuttered when she demanded an explanation. His knowledge of autism was shockingly limited, almost non-existent. Symptoms that she could recite off by heart seemed unknown to him.

Inappropriate laughing and giggling. Difficulty in mixing with other children. Physical overactivity or extreme passivity. Indicates needs by gestures. Not cuddly. No eye contact. Spins objects. Inappropriate attachment to objects. Crying tantrums. Extreme distress for no apparent reason.

'How is it possible,' she asked Old Doctor with impotent rage, 'that Alexander has been to so many doctors and specialists and medical experts, and not one of them had the slightest notion what was wrong?'

'Some of these psychological and mental disorders are hard to pick up, Ingrid. They are rare, and many of them remain a dark riddle to the medical world. If Alexander is autistic, as you suspect,' and suddenly he looked old and weary, 'it will be the first case I've come across in more than forty years of practising. Not even during my training did I encounter it ...'

'And the paediatricians? After all, they are *specialists* ...'

A sigh escaped from deep inside his chest; he brought his hands to his face. For the first time she noticed his knobbly fingers; the parched skin covering his bony hands. The crow's feet at the corners of his eyes.

'There are many kinds of specialists, Ingrid. Ophthalmologists. Neurologists. Cardiologists. Paediatricians. But unfortunately no autism specialists. And many of the symptoms of autism can be related to other disorders. It's extremely difficult to draw the line. I don't have the statistics, but the incidence of autism would be only a few cases in many thousands.'

He was right. Two to four out of ten thousand. Four out of every five cases were boys. And Alexander was one of them. Lonely child, on his isolated island. Where the prevailing wind was a whirlwind; where the rain sounded like rocks on the roof; where looking at colours caused severe pain to his eyes. Where cold was hot, and hot was cold. Where everything was distorted and dimensionless.

'Ingrid,' and he put his weathered hand over hers, 'I want you to know that I'm here for you. I might have insufficient knowledge about autism, but I'll do my best.'

From there she went to the psychiatric clinic. The sister made tea for her and stared at her as if she was hearing a ghost story.

Then to the manse. The dominee clicked his tongue and crossed his hands like a praying mantis. Man proposes, but God disposes, he said.

'Dawid doesn't know yet, Dominee. And I,' she swallowed to stop her voice trembling, 'I feel as if I'm in a vacuum. You must help me, Dominee. Up to now the community has believed that Alexander was just plain naughty and undisciplined, but now we know better. You are in a position to bring understanding to the community.'

'But of course, Ingrid, of course we'll support you and Dawid.' His lips uttered the words but there was no compassion in his eyes. 'As true believers in Jesus Christ, we must do as Paul tells us in his letter to the Galatians: Share each other's troubles and problems, and so obey our Lord's command.'

About a year later she sat at the same desk with an aching back, bruises all over her body. Little knowing that he would be the one to submit Dawid to ecclesiastic discipline. Or that it would be his signature on the letter of complaint that was sent to the regional head-office of the post office.

Obviously, he denied any intention to harm anybody.

But then Miriam told her about the day behind the chicken run when Sonny had been to warn her.

'As far as was humanly possible, I gave everything I had to give. To Alexander as well as to my family. Everything. And sometimes I gave more than everything.'

'Be more specific about what you did.'

Her legs feel like lead. 'It will take hours and I'm too tired to think straight. Can I please sleep until I'm rested?'

He runs his fingers through his hair. 'Don't talk to me about sleep, Mrs Dorfling. It's my job to find out what happened in your house yesterday morning. The incident involved a disabled child who was unable to speak for or defend himself. It's my duty to act on his behalf. So, answer my question: what did you do during the past five and a half years to improve your child's lot in life?'

Where does she begin?

Is there a beginning?

40

By this time Jeremiah will be lying under the warm bedclothes. Her body longs to rest on a mattress too. But the man is still standing in the passage, talking on his telephone. When he comes back, his eyes seem less evil.

'Where is Mr Dorfling's revolver, Mrs Slangveld?'

Nobody knows she found the revolver in the linen cupboard when she was spring cleaning the house. Except Jeremiah. And he won't remember, because the evening she told him about it, he was three sheets in the wind. It was a Friday evening, and shortly after sunset he had gone to Evert's house to listen to Evert's new guitar. Came home zigzagging through the township streets long after midnight, singing many muddled tunes.

'Master Dawid must've sold the revolver, sir, because after his death I never saw it again.'

'Why would he sell the revolver?'

Why indeed?

Now her foot was caught in a trap.

'I wouldn't know, sir, I'm just guessing.' She must stop fiddling with her hands, or her nervous movements will give her away. 'Maybe Master Dawid thought the revolver was useless, and swopped it for something useful.'

'Swopped? With whom would he swop a revolver?'

Deeper and deeper into the trap. If she isn't careful she might find herself having to cut off her foot to free herself. 'No, sir, now you've got me. I just thought maybe it was the same as the horse.'

'What about the horse?'

'Long ago Master Dawid scored Lexi a horse, sir. One of his friends owed him money for losing at poker, and the man couldn't pay. So Master Dawid took the mare in exchange.'

He pulls a page from the stack, reads through it. 'Are you referring to the horse on which the child rode on Sundays?'

Thank God he's letting the issue of the revolver go. 'The very same one, sir. Every Sunday Miss Ingrid took Lexi to the farm to go horse riding. When Master Dawid was still alive, he used to take Lexi.' Get it through his thick skull that Master Dawid was often kind to Lexi too.

'Why would Mrs Dorfling want to sell the horse?'

That's a bloody lie. It *must* be. Miss Ingrid would take the curtains off the rails and sell them for bread money; she would sell the frying pan and the pressure cooker to Aunt Rosie for a couple of pennies. Easily. But not Lexi's horse. Not in a thousand years.

'Miss Ingrid would never sell Lexi's horse, sir! I never saw him riding with my own eyes, but Miss Ingrid said that he was totally different when he they placed him on the horse. He even stood still and let them put a riding hat on his head.'

Motionless, he stares at her. The angels tell her that he knows all about the man and the horse. How else could he know Miss Ingrid wanted to sell the horse?

'Was Mrs Dorfling having an affair with the man?'

Dear Jesus, now he's chasing her barefoot into the devil's thorns. Out of the revolver trap and into an even more dangerous one. What if he reckons Miss Ingrid killed Lexi because the man wanted *her,* but not the child?

'What do you mean by affair, sir?'

'Were they lovers?'

In the early days after Master Dawid's death she never thought of Sundays as anything more than for Lexi and his beloved horse. That something special was developing between the man and Miss Ingrid did not cross her mind. But the day Miss Ingrid brought a plastic bag of camphor bush flowers home from the farm and put them in a brass bowl on the chest of drawers in her room, she knew Miss Ingrid was carrying a secret. A woman's secret.

She watched Miss Ingrid's eyes on Mondays. They sparkled with the silvery light of the morning star. She was touched to see the glow of life returning to a sad woman's eyes. She knew for sure that Miss Ingrid had dedicated a tiny room in her heart to the man. But at the same time she knew there were few men on earth who would have the courage to marry a woman if he knew that a child like Lexi was part of the deal.

Hardly a year after Master Dawid died, just when winter was turning and the flowers of the puzzle bush in the back garden changed from purple to white, Miss Ingrid put away the black mourning-band that lay on her bedside table. It was a mourning-band that Jeremiah had ordered from Aunt Maria and given to Miss Ingrid a week after Master Dawid's death. She never wore it, but perhaps for decency's sake she left it lying on her bedside table. Nowadays white people have little respect for the value of mourning. They don't weep or talk their hearts out, but bottle up their sorrows and mask their feelings. And before long, they are tripped up by depression. Black illness, Aunt Maria calls it. Because the light of the soul goes dark and blackness fills the mind.

But then Miss Ingrid put the mourning-band away. Finished mourning for the man who had almost dragged her with him. On Monday mornings her eyes shone. If she could, she would wish Miss Ingrid straight into the man's arms. After the long years of hell with Master Dawid and all the battering she took, plus Lexi's wrong-headedness on top of it all, Miss Ingrid deserved a little bit of love and affection.

One night when the chicken eagle was haunting her again, she woke Jeremiah up and told him that she'd never seen a person change like Miss Ingrid did after Lexi was born. In the winter when she went to hospital to have the baby, she was still the old Miss Ingrid. A happy woman. Laughed a lot. Picked bunches of flowers to fill the house with their scent. Sang while she prepared salads for friends. Danced over the kitchen floor with Master Dawid when a joyful song played on the radio. On hot days she ran through the garden spray with Teresa and Zettie.

But when summer arrived, she was not the old Miss Ingrid any more. By Christmas time she was a different woman altogether. Hardly ever laughed. Never played with Teresa and Zettie. Never switched the radio on. Seldom went to the shops with Miss Mirna and the others. Left the garden to go wild.

That time when Master Dawid's life was running downhill at top speed, she often sat behind the chicken run and begged God to sew wings to Miss Ingrid's shoulders. So that Miss Ingrid could learn to fly. Even if it wasn't higher than the church steeple or the pine trees behind the school. Flying is flying. And a woman who has forgotten how to use her wings to take her to her own places of peace and quiet, will battle to learn all over again.

And so she wished Miss Ingrid into the man's arms and heart.

It'll be best if the evil-eyed man knows nothing about the stars in Miss Ingrid's eyes.

'If there was something between them, sir, I wasn't aware of it. The man never came to Miss Ingrid's house and nor did he phone there.'

He finishes writing, tears the pages loose from the book and stacks them neatly. 'Thank you, Mrs Slangveld, that'll be all for now. Please read the statement and sign at the bottom.'

She finishes the last bit of water in the cup. 'Do you mean that we're done with each other, sir?'

'For the time being, yes. But you mustn't leave town, because we have the right to call you in at any time for further questioning.'

She reads a sentence here and there, signs her name at the bottom. 'We're taking you home now, Mrs Slangveld.'

'In the red car?'

He shakes his head, says that someone else is using the red car to get a statement from another witness somewhere in town.

'Do you mean they're taking me home in the back of the police van?'

'Yes.'

'I'd rather walk.'

'It's raining.'

'I prefer walking in the rain to being transported in the police van.'

Only when she passes the first streetlight, the food container, her suitcase and handbag clutched in her hands, does she realise that she has left her host of angels behind. Never mind, they'll follow her. She changes her grip on the suitcase handle. Her house is not just around the corner. And she's tired. When she looks up, Jeremiah appears like a ghost from behind a redberry tree and walks towards her.

'Jissus, Miriam . . . I thought they were going to keep you at the police station all night. Give me the suitcase, I'll carry it home.'

Then she knows that the angels have followed her through the window. Because Jeremiah is here to carry her suitcase. And the rain has stopped and she will get home dry.

41

How DOES SHE BEGIN to tell the man about the journey of the past nine years?

'My biggest problem was that the community showed no understanding. They avoided us like the plague. I think they did not *want* to understand, because showing compassion might imply the need to be involved and tolerant.'

It is not that autistic people do not relate, it is that they relate in peculiar ways. It is not that people with autism do not want to make friends, but often they do not know how. Thus it becomes critical to teach social skills . . .

She can't remember how many times she has read those distressing words in the last five and a half years. Hundreds of times. Until the corners of the pages were brown and dog-eared from handling. Any book or magazine article on the subject that she could lay her hands on, she read, again and again. Old Doctor often supplied her with information from medical journals and from the internet.

'Mrs Dorfling, I did not ask about the townsfolk. My question was: what effort did *you* make?'

On a Sunday morning, about a month after the report from the Children's Hospital arrived, she took the report and the photocopies and called Dawid to their room. Closed the door and asked him to sit down on the bed.

And to listen.

Please. Please.

Rebellion written all over his face, he stared at her while she explained the report, supplementing its contents with cross references from the photocopies.

'Ingrid, are you telling me that Alexander will never get better?'

'What I'm trying to tell you is that Alexander's behaviour now has a name: *autism*. Now we know where to begin and we have basic guidelines for the future.'

'Are you telling me that this is going to last for bloody ever?'

She read some of the highlighted parts out loud to him.

. . . once an autist, always an autist . . . at this point in time we do not know what specifically causes autism, so we cannot cure what is wrong with your child's brain. However, people with autism can and do get better. They can lead happy and productive lives when appropriate treatment is begun.

'What kind of treatment is involved, and what will it cost?'

There were no straight answers. All she could do was to cling to the information she had gathered. *There is only one treatment that has passed the test of time and that is structured educational programmes.*

Dawid was beyond despair. 'What are the implications of these structured educational programmes that you are talking about?'

'I'm not sure yet, Dawid, but I'll find out as much as I can.'

With a sigh he got up and walked out of the room, took the car keys from the key-holder in the kitchen. Left for the farm without Alexander. Came back with swollen eyes long after sunset.

From that evening she knew without a doubt: if she hoped to cross the ocean, she would have to do it on her own.

Breathe slowly. She must not let the man's harsh question throw her off balance. Nine years is a long time. It cannot be dispensed with in one or two sentences.

'My first priority was to gain knowledge. It was confusing because autism differs from child to child. Even the experts differ about the diagnosis and treatment . . .'

As the parent of an autistic child, you will constantly be bombarded by people who claim to be able to cure autism . . . In her mind she can picture the sentence on the page; even the colour of the pen she used to underline it.

'I received valuable help and information from the Autistic Society. But it was unreasonable to expect them to keep me up to date at all times. Later on, when internet facilities became available, the local doctor often gave me printouts of some of the latest information. I would have loved a personal computer, but I did not have the money. What little money we had had to be set aside for more urgent priorities.'

'Like what?'

'It was a priority to send Alexander to a school for autistic children.'

During the five or six months between the arrival of the report and the arrival of winter, she was distraught; she felt like a blind person forced to walk over unfamiliar territory without a stick to lean on. Her efforts to find help were for the most part fruitless, because help required money. A lot of money. Which she did not have.

In the autumn she made the exhausting trip to Pretoria in her unreliable car. There was a school for autistic children there and she needed to see with her own eyes and hear with her own ears. All the way there she prayed that Dawid and Miriam would be able to keep things together at home and that the school would offer a solution.

It was a long way to Pretoria. But the road home seemed ten times longer, because she knew then that her hopes were unrealisable. Alexander could board at the school hostel, but it was compulsory for him to go home at least one weekend each month. As well as every school holiday. Back and forth to Pretoria in an erratic motor car, a thousand kilometres there, a thousand kilometres back. Every month. It was impossible. The closest star seemed more reachable than the boarding fees. Add travelling expenses, school fees, clothes, unforeseen costs. The total seemed light years beyond the furthest star.

But during the two days that she spent at the school, she met and spoke to many knowledgeable people. She absorbed every grain of information; stored thousands of pictures and images in her mind. It scared her to death. And yet it also gave her the courage of a lion.

'If sending the child to a school was such a priority, why did you never do it?'

'I did.'

On the way home from Pretoria the car broke down. She was stranded on a sun-scorched Karoo road. Treeless. Shadeless. Waterless. She sat in the baking sun for hours, hoping that the message sent with a passing motorist had reached the service station in the nearest town. She had hours in which to think; to weigh; to try to balance her scales. Surrounded by the hot north wind and the flat expanse of Karoo bush as far as the eye could see. God alone knew how she feared the future on that desolate day.

The service station towed the car in and repaired it. Another cheque from Dawid's cheque book that would be returned, marked in red pen: *refer to drawer*.

In those six months of treading water, and swallowing many a mouthful, the fallout with Dawid's parents was merely an aggravation. Day by day Dawid declined. And when she saw that his emotional legs were going to give way under him, she stepped in and held him up. She never lost hope. Always believed that eventually there would be light. Just as long as she could stay strong.

She gathered her courage and drew up a list of questions. Used her lunch break to phone the school for autism in Cape Town from the bank's telephone. Spoke to the liaison officer. She did not know why she bothered to phone, because the car would never make it to Cape Town. Dawid had already threatened to set it alight to claim some money from the insurance.

'You're out of your mind!' she'd told him. 'How will I get to work when it rains, and how will we take Miriam home when she works late?'

'I don't give a damn who gets where, or when, as long as I don't have to cough up for it!'

'Be reasonable, Dawid . . .'

He threw the car keys against the bread bin and bellowed at her. 'We've become penniless paupers in less than four years! *You* tell me, Ingrid, or maybe a merciful God will tell me: where are we going to be in another four years' time?'

Her guess was as good as his.

But she was prepared to eat and drink and sleep hope.

The school in Cape Town was also beyond the furthest star.

'Why don't you try the Quest School for autism in Port Elizabeth?' the liaison officer asked. 'Although it's a small non-governmental school without boarding facilities, it's much closer to your home town. And the School Committee is currently negotiating with the Department of Education to have it registered as a government school. Apart from the schools in Cape Town and Pretoria, there are no other schools for autism in South Africa.'

'And . . . and . . . institutions?'

'Overseas, possibly, but not in South Africa.'

The voice was a lifeline. 'What do other parents of autistic children do if they live so far away from a school?'

'Many of them move to Cape Town or Pretoria. Then the child can be picked up and dropped off by a school bus every day.'

Miriam and Jeremiah would never move away from their children. No big city post office would tolerate a drunk postmaster. 'What about those who cannot move away?'

'Well, the parents follow a structured home teaching programme . . .'

It was as though her hands had been cut off yet again.

That night she went outside and sat under the wild olive tree in the hot north wind. Because she did not want Dawid or Teresa and Zettie to hear her cry.

The future seemed so bleak. No dreams. No hopes. No prospects. And yet, there *had* to be an answer. She could not let her child grow up like a wild animal.

'Ingrid?'

In the warm night Dawid knelt next to her. His breath smelled of brandy. He stroked her hair and pulled her head on to his knee. 'I love you, Ingrid,' and he sniffed, 'but I don't understand what is happening to us.'

What could she say?

'We can sell the caravan, Ingrid, and my hunting rifle and my fishing tackle.' His voice shook. 'Or I could cash in another insurance policy. Then we could use the money to send him to the school in Port Elizabeth.'

'Dawid,' and she rested her elbows on his knees and looked up at him, 'maybe we should sell all those things and move to a bigger centre with better facilities and doctors. Or maybe we should use the money to buy food and clothes; a few luxuries for Teresa and Zettie. And forget about autism. Let's just live our lives, and let Alexander live his . . .'

'I don't know, Ingrid. All I know is that life seems dreadfully wrong.'

For a long time they sat in the dark under the wild olive tree, her head resting on his knee, his fingers entwined in her hair.

'Let's go back to bed,' he said when the wind began to blow too strongly.

That June, when the new school term started, she took leave. Dawid hooked up the caravan and she and Alexander left for Port Elizabeth. They parked the caravan in the backyard of distant relatives of Dawid's. Money for a stand in a caravan park was out of the question.

It was worse than Church House. At Church House she at least had space and a bathroom. In the family's backyard she and Alexander lived like rats in a cage. During the mornings things were bearable, because she walked Alexander to school and waited there until school came out. Even though he fought the routine with all his might, she had a support system at the school. During the afternoons he almost drove her out of her mind. Ran round and round the caravan, flapping his hands, shrieking. When she turned her back for five minutes to peel a potato or put a pot of pumpkin on the caravan stove, he ripped the family's washing from the line and threw sand and leaves on the stoep. Chased their white Persian cat until the poor creature climbed on to the roof and refused to come down. Then he started throwing stones on the roof. When she walked down the street to phone Dawid from a public telephone, he broke loose from her hand and caused havoc in the street. During the freezing winter nights he fretted in the narrow space inside the caravan, searching for his chisel, calling *Mimmi! Mimmi! Mimmi!*

After three weeks she had no choice but to go home.

'He was four when I took him to the Quest School for autism in Port Elizabeth. The staff at the school taught me some valuable skills. But there were no boarding facilities and I had to stay in a caravan in the backyard of relatives of my husband's. I only had four weeks' leave, and it was coming to an end . . .'

The space inside the interrogation room shrinks and stretches as if it is filled with moving water. The man's face seems distorted. Vaguely, she can hear the woman telling the man to give her a break.

' . . . fetch her a cup of tea, Colonel. It's unreasonable to . . .'

When she looks up, she sees the woman winking at the man. They're playing a game.

'I'll just have some water, please.'

Good cop, bad cop. They're wasting their time.

'And after those three weeks, Mrs Dorfling, is that where the priority of your child attending school ended?'

She becomes incoherent, struggles to express her thoughts and to complete her sentences. Stutters, whispers. Sometimes she's in a time before Dawid died; sometimes after. The most important thing is that he should know she never threw Alexander to the dogs.

As if in a distant dream she hears herself telling him about the hyperbaric oxygen unit which she couldn't afford. It was a lot of money for each dive; many dives were needed over a long period to inhale oxygen that might possibly bring life to dead brain cells. Some children benefited, others showed no improvement. She didn't have the money to experiment.

'Even though I wasn't officially a parent, I attended the monthly meetings of the parents' association at the Quest School as often as possible. It was close enough for me to leave after work and get there in time for the meeting. And it was good to talk to the parents of other autists because they had valuable practical experience to share. But after each meeting I had to travel home through dangerous kudu territory. My car was old and unreliable . . .'

Is it *her* voice she is hearing? The man sits motionless, his hands clasped behind his head.

She hears herself talking about the frustrating weeks when she and Miriam forced Alexander on to a tartrazine and gluten-free diet. Other parents recommended it as an antidote against hyper-activity. Alexander's eyes bulged when they brought the spoon near his mouth. He vomited everything out and developed diarrhoea.

'Heavens, Miss Ingrid, we can't carry on like this! When a child starts wetting his bed, you must know there's a bad screw loose.'

She knew that Miriam was right. Switched back to pumpkin and cheese spread and mashed banana. But he'd come to fear food and the spoon; Alexander refused to eat for three weeks. Only drank cold coffee.

She can't stop talking. All the muddled thoughts in her head come spilling out.

Medicines that she could not afford. Naltrexone. Haloperidol. Dimethylglycine. The miracle cure, secretine, derived from the duodenum of a pig that reportedly helped mute autists to speak and brought composure to those who were confused. Imported at high cost and heavily taxed, there was no medical knowledge of its side effects or long-term success. Those who could afford it, clutched at it as a last resort. She was battling to pay her electricity account, let alone think of importing secretine.

She's unable to stop the flow of words . . .

About the cow and the trust fund. About the day she went to the manse, unannounced, to see the dominee face to face about Gunter's agreement with the ward elder. The dominee had shrugged his shoulders, said that people could not dictate how their donations and offerings should be utilised; whatever was given, should be given unconditionally.

How she and Miriam persevered with trying to teach Alexander to communicate in sign language. *Please*: rub the chest. *Where*: palms up and move in a circle. *Mine*: closed fists to the chest. *Hungry*: rub the tummy. *Well done*: thumbs up. *Book*: two hands open, like opening a book. Many other gestures. But he never took any notice or tried to imitate them.

Some parents engaged therapists or used volunteers to work through a fixed routine with their children on a daily basis. She could not even find a volunteer to accompany her for one day to visit a specialist. Dear God, how disappointed she was when Lida sent Alexander home with a note.

Other parents were able to try many things. She could do the bare minimum. Because when Dawid's estate was finally settled, she found that every single insurance policy had been terminated. *And* he had borrowed money in advance against his salary. *And* he had taken out a second bond on the house. She had to cover hair-raising debts from his pension pay-out. Then his poker cronies came to collect outstanding poker debts. Two wealthy farmers, both of them members of the Church Council, knocked at her door, claiming that Dawid had borrowed money from them. Show me the written agreement, she demanded. No, they said, it was a gentleman's agreement.

She had to cough up.

She couldn't care less into which bottomless pit Dawid had thrown the money. Betting on horses, untested medicines, poker, brandy, bread and butter, specialists, a dead parrot. The crux of the matter was that she had to plug all the gaps.

'When my elder daughter went to university, the bank manager approved a study loan. The agreement was that if I paid the interest promptly, he would do the same for my younger daughter.'

She's thirsty for tea from her own teapot; a cheese sandwich made in her own kitchen. And she yearns to wash her hands with her own soap.

'Your daughters have a second-hand car, Mrs Dorfling. Who is responsible for paying the monthly instalments?'

'The study loans included enough to pay a deposit. The monthly instalments, petrol and insurance they pay themselves. They both work as waitresses at night and during holidays.'

It was not how she had wanted life to be for Teresa and Zettie. But the years of hardship had made them resilient. She knew they would manage the instalments. 'I couldn't change the hard realities, I had to choose: keep searching for ways to improve Alexander's condition, or let it be and use the little money I had to see my daughters through university. For once in my life I tipped the scales in favour of my daughters. Until they completed their studies, Alexander's needs had to take a back seat.'

Ta-tate-ta.

'Mrs Dorfling, two months ago you changed the structure of your son's insurance policy. You raised the death coverage to the maximum, and adjusted the monthly premium accordingly. Why?'

It doesn't shock her, because sooner or later she was expecting the question.

42

IN THE YELLOW GLOW of the street lamp Jeremiah seems older than his fifty-eight years, his back bent like an overhanging branch. The result of sitting at a five-gallon drum for hours on end playing dominoes. Perhaps she's too hard on Jeremiah. Poor man. All his adult years he'd had a chip on his shoulder. Thief. Gaol-bird. And she never failed to rub it in. But one full moon night while she sat behind the chicken run trying to chase the chicken eagle away, the angel of goodness had given her a sharp rap over the knuckles.

Since then, she had tried her utmost to be more tolerant of Jeremiah's shortcomings. And it had borne fruit, because he spent today behind the chicken run, speaking to God on her behalf. Walked all the way in the rain to the police station. Waited for her at the redberry tree in the cold night with no guarantee that they would let her go before sunrise. He may well have stood there all night with his feet in the frosty grass. No, God could have cursed her with worse than Jeremiah. There are few women who can say that their husbands have never lifted a hand to them.

She's hungry for the bread and chicken. 'Do you know what the time is, Jeremiah?'

'The church clock has just struck eleven.' He moves the suitcase to his other hand. 'Miriam, I heard them talking at the police station. Teresa and Zettie are on their way home. They should arrive any time after twelve o'clock. They've sent someone with a police car to wait at Miss Ingrid's house. The Murder and Robbery detectives are going to question the girls when they arrive.'

It's like a bucket of icy water thrown in her face. 'Heavens, Jeremiah . . .'

There's nothing to fear from Teresa and Zettie. But if they don't shelter Miss Ingrid with their compassion, and they tell the naked truth, it's going to cause big trouble. Because such a depth of sorrows can easily create the impression that Miss Ingrid had reason to harm Lexi. She *must* get to the children before the police do. Tell them to spare their mother wherever they can . . .

'I'm going to wait for them at the stop street next to the pepper trees . . .'

'What for, Miriam?'

'Because she's their mother, and they must think carefully before . . .'

'You're a witness, Miriam! If anyone sees you near the children, you'll be in stinking shit! Leave the children, they *know* Miss Ingrid is their mother!'

'But still.'

He stops in his tracks and puts the suitcase down. In the light of the street lamp she sees him push his chin out; his face wrinkled in frowns. 'What are you trying to cover up, Miriam?'

There's not a soul on earth who knows her better than Jeremiah. 'Nothing. But Miss Ingrid doesn't deserve to . . .'

He comes right up to her, whispers. 'Miriam, tell me the truth: do you think Miss Ingrid killed Lexi?'

Nobody has to know what's in her mind. Not even Jeremiah. It's between her and the chicken eagle and her Saviour.

'No.'

Then she commands the host of angels to go and wait for Teresa and Zettie at the stop street. 'Pick up the suitcase, Jeremiah, my body is at the end of its tether. I want to get home.'

As soon as they have crossed the railway line and are almost home she'll tell him she wants to be up at daybreak. And before the sun rises from behind the mountain, she wants to be at Evert's house.

43

'COULD YOU AFFORD TO increase the monthly instalments on the policy?'

'It was in Alexander's interest.'

'That's not what I asked.'

There was a kraal wall day, not long ago. She was raking the old straw on the stable floor into a heap. The serenity of autumn lingered in the air and the afternoon breeze carried the medicinal fragrance of crushed camphor bush.

The camphor bush grew at the southern edge of the garden. Her eyes had wandered beyond the camphor bush many times, but not her feet. Often when she sat on the dining room floor with Alexander at night, she imagined the inside of the white manor house that sat so peacefully on the northern side of the garden. Surrounded by giant trees bearing bunches of red flowers in summer; casting their autumn leaves on to the lawns when the season changed. Green slate roof, green louvres. Bright pink bougainvillaea twining in abundance around the stoep pillars, tumbling on to the slate floor.

What did Gunter's bedroom look like? Did his blankets smell of man?

Long ago, in the first autumn after Dawid's death, she had asked

Gunter if she could pick some of the camphor bush flowers in his garden. By all means, he said, take as many as you want. He offered to stay behind at the stable to keep an eye on Lucy and Alexander.

She picked bunches of the white flowers and laid them on her jacket; carefully wrapped the jacket around them and took them home. Arranged them in a brass bowl and told the house that she had surrendered a tiny piece of her heart. When she came home from work on the Monday, the house was filled with the herbal scent of camphor. And she longed for the days to pass quickly until Sunday.

Was it possible that three years had passed since that autumn?

She gripped the rake. It made more sense to keep her hands busy than to dwell on the past. Forget the past. Don't think of the future. Today is today. The mulch on the stable floor was soft and warm under her bare feet. The autumn sun shone gently on her head and shoulders. Right at that moment nothing else mattered.

'Why are you raking?' Gunter was behind her. Too close. 'I put out fresh straw two days ago. Rather come and sit with me on the kraal wall.'

She put the rake down. Rinsed her hands at the stable tap. Found a foothold on the round stones of the kraal wall and hoisted herself up. Lifted her right knee on to the wall. As she lifted her other knee, she looked up at Gunter. He was smiling at her; a tender light in his eyes.

'What are you looking at?'

'Nothing, really. But you're getting too old to clamber on to kraal walls.'

She clicked her tongue at him and settled herself on the wall. Pulled one knee up and rested her foot on the edge of the wall. Moved her fingertips in circles over the fine layer of sand on the kraal wall. Next to her Gunter smelled of wet soil and camphor bush and horse. Or was it the smell of the earth brought to her by the afternoon breeze? She yearned to reach out to him, put her hand on his back, to feel his warmth just once more. But it was safer to tuck her hand under her thigh.

'I've picked you some camphor bush leaves,' he said. 'Use it to make a thick poultice and put it on Alexander's hands and legs. We're not even close to winter, and he's already developing a rough skin.'

So, after all, it was he who smelled of camphor. 'I don't know how to make a poultice.'

'Miriam will show you.'

'We'll try.'

'I picked you a bag of flowers too.' He broke a twig between his fingers into minute pieces. Put the pieces on his tongue and then spat them out. 'Long ago you asked if you could pick some camphor bush flowers. I thought that perhaps you might like some again.'

A palpable silence. And a tingling in her spine. It would be better to talk, anything that came to mind, before she took her hand out from underneath her thigh. 'Alexander has grown, his old winter clothes don't fit him. One of these days he'll be nine.'

He spat the last piece of wood from his tongue. 'Before you know it, Ingrid, he'll be a man.'

It was a frightening picture that often haunted her. 'I try not to think about it. The idea that he's going to grow hair on his legs and a beard and . . . and . . .'

She was embarrassed. These were sensitive matters that she hadn't felt able to discuss with anybody. Except Miriam, and once with a mother at a parents' meeting. Normal puberty, normal sex drive. But a total lack of inhibition. 'I once spoke to a mother whose son is twenty-three years old and still wearing nappies. They live on a farm, but when they take him for medical tests, the high buildings and the buzz of the city make him agitated and he develops an . . . an . . . erection.' Red-hot blush flaming down her neck. At the same time, it was a tremendous relief to get the words out; to speak to someone who didn't shrink back. 'Then he develops an obsession . . .' she swallowed, licked her dry lips. '. . . to masturbate.'

He had not stared at her in disgust like the sister at the clinic. Or suddenly changed into a holy saint with his hands folded like a praying mantis, quoting sweet verses from the Bible. He just sat there with her on the kraal wall in the lukewarm sun. 'She puts his nappies on back to front so that he cannot loosen the pin behind his back.'

For a long time they sat on the kraal wall in silence. Until Alexander fell asleep and Lucy started drawing her circles in, smaller and smaller.

'What financial provision have you made for his future, Ingrid?'

'Not much. When he was born, Dawid took out an insurance policy for his education one day. That's all. I can hardly afford to add to it.'

'You must have the policy adjusted regularly, Ingrid, or else it will be of little value when you need the capital.'

Then Lucy came to a halt and Gunter jumped off the kraal wall. Dusted his hands on his khaki pants and held them out to her.

'Come, let me help you down.'

Four weeks later, when the bank's broker sat opposite her with the forms ready for her to sign, she recalled Gunter's warm hands under her arms. How he had put her down in front of him; run his hand down her spine. Just for a fleeting moment. On that day, in the autumn light of the setting sun, death and insurance pay-outs and arranging a funeral were nowhere in sight, not even on the furthest boundaries of her horizon.

The upright chair creaks behind her. There's the sound of paper when the woman turns a page in her notebook.

'I asked the advice of the bank's broker and had the adjustment done because it was in Alexander's interest. I was prepared to cut expenses wherever I could to afford it.'

'According to the law, you could've made the adjustment when he was seven. Why did you wait an extra two years if you were so eager to protect his interests?'

'I don't know much about the laws on insurance policies. I would never have thought of adjusting the policy if Gunter had not mentioned it.' A coughing fit shakes her body; the phlegm in her mouth tastes of blood. 'I simply asked the broker's advice and trusted what he suggested. I had no hidden agenda.'

'Mrs Dorfling, what sort of relationship did you have with Gunter?'

'I've already told you.'

He pulls a couple of pages from the docket, shakes his head in disbelief while he reads through them again. 'I don't believe you, Mrs Dorfling.' He picks up the bunch of keys and pushes his chair back. 'You're going back to your cell now. We'll continue after lunch. Rest while you can; you're going to need it. When we start the next session, the game of hide-and-seek will be over.'

Her feet are ice cold in the flopping shoes.

She's thankful to see her bag. And to be alone.

Sunday afternoon.

She would by now have run her bath water and brushed her hair until it shone; driven out to the farm to find solace in the moist earthy smell of the stable; watched Gunter packing out fresh straw. Watched Lucy carrying the fragile bundle on her back. Come home after sunset and waited for the next Sunday. A life of tiny splinters of Sunday joy. No dreams. No beckoning horizons. Tied in invisible chains. Because she had to steer a riddle child through life, and he could see nothing but that which was contained within his own peculiar boundaries.

44

WHERE THE GRAVEL ROAD crosses the railway line, she tells Jeremiah to stop so she can rest her painful legs. Just to sit down on the soft grass next to the road for five minutes and eat a piece of bread. Heaven knows, her mind is troubled about Miss Ingrid. If only the police would give her a decent bed and clean linen; show respect for her dignity. And may Teresa and Zettie have the wisdom to weigh their words carefully.

'Do you think Evert will be at home?'

'He taxied today, but he should be back by now. Why?'

'I'm just asking.' She throws the chicken bone over her shoulder into the long grass. 'Jeremiah, do you think you can still drive a car?'

'*Jissus*, Miriam, what's brewing in your head?'

She feels like snubbing him for so carelessly taking the name of God in vain. But she rather bites her tongue. Evert might be incapable of driving and she'd be forced to call on Jeremiah. 'All I'm asking you, is if you can still drive a car.'

He utters a snort of contempt. 'How could you even *think* I cannot drive a car?' He takes the last sandwich from the container. 'But I'm asking you for the last time, Miriam: what's going on inside your skull?'

'As soon as day breaks, Jeremiah, I want to get up and wash

and dress. Then I want to go to Evert's house and ask if I can borrow his car. I'll pay him.'

'With money from where? Evert's not cheap in renting out his car.'

Funny how a man's head works. First thinks about money; not why she needs the car. 'I'll use the money in my sacred bottle. I cleared it with the Lord earlier tonight. I need the car to go somewhere, urgently.'

'Where to?'

'Just somewhere. But if Evert has a hangover, or he's cheeky with me, you must do the driving. I'll pay you.'

'First tell me where to.'

'I must still think a few things over. When I wake up at daybreak, I'll tell you. Pick up the suitcase, let's go. I'm tired and there's not much sleeping time left. You'll never understand the hell I went through on the truck this morning.'

When they arrive home, the chickens are asleep on their roosts. At least Jeremiah had kept his head and opened the chicken run, so they didn't have to fly into the tree to find shelter for the night. The bowl with Saturday's eggs is standing on the kitchen table. It's easily five eggs short compared with other days. She swallows her annoyance. It's a small sacrifice to make in exchange for Jeremiah's goodwill.

45

THE OVERWHELMING URGE TO sleep has left her body; her mind is sharp and clear. It's bitterly cold in the cell; she's thankful to be alone. She looks at the cockroach floundering in the spilled tea. They must hurry up with her lunch; there are many things she needs to tell the man. And she wants to phone Teresa and Zettie. The woman did say she would be allowed to make a phone call in the morning.

She brushes her teeth without toothpaste. Measures the cell by pacing from corner to corner. Three and half paces between the bed and the door; two and a half paces between the door and the toilet. Again. And again. Counts the cobwebs in the corners of the cell. Three big ones, lots of small ones. Focuses on counting the holes in the ceiling vent. Fifteen rows, alternately containing fourteen and fifteen tiny vent holes. Two hundred and seventeen holes in one vent.

Her feet are aching.

When will it be lunch time?

Why can't she recall Dawid's face? Have sorrow and guilt blocked it out on the film of her brain?

In the summer after Dawid's death she went to see the psychologist. She had grievances and self-recriminations to sort out; countless regrets to bury. For ever, if possible. And she was desperate for professional advice on how to handle Teresa and Zettie. But the one thing that she yearned for most of all, was to be able to erase the gruesome picture of Dawid's mortal remains from her conscious mind. Because it wasn't Dawid that she saw in the mortuary drawer, it was just a torn bundle of human remains that she had to identify.

A revolting sweet smell hung in the gloomy cold mortuary. Rows of drawers, each containing a label: *feet first*. Petrified with shock, she pointed at the label, stuttering a few incoherent words.

'The bodies are put in the drawer feet first, so that the arms don't get stuck when the drawer is pulled out. Sometimes, when rigor mortis sets in, the arms lift up,' the attendant explained dispassionately.

Dear God.

Then he pulled the drawer out.

She needed the psychologist to help her wipe that nightmare from her memory. Or at least to try and soften it.

He couldn't.

As time went by she managed not to recall it every hour of the day. But sometimes, when she sat on the dining room floor at night, watching the pieces of plaster thudding to the floor, she recalled the words on the label. And slowly, very slowly, it started growing inside her brain like a tapeworm. She tried to think beyond it; force her thoughts on to something more hopeful. She thought about how few clothes Teresa and Zettie had in their cupboards and tried to think of ways to buy them new clothes. Her mind searched every shelf of every cupboard in the house making a list of stuff that she could sell to Rosie and the hostel staff. Or maybe she should use the money to buy cement and ask Jeremiah if he could come and replaster the walls of the dining room.

The food arrives. A Sunday meal. Pale chicken with rubbery skin; more bones than meat. Overcooked rice drenched in a watery gravy. Dry pumpkin without cinnamon sugar. A slice of lukewarm tomato. She pushes the plate aside. Her stomach declines the Sunday meal.

She brushes her teeth again to get rid of the acid taste in her mouth. Someone knocks at the cat walk. She shows him the empty toilet roll. He nods his head, holds his thumb up. When his face disappears, she regrets not asking for a bucket and a scrubbing brush and a broom to clean the cell. It would help to pass the time. And to escape from Alexander's distended blue eyes staring at her.

She opens the shower taps to see if there's hot water. Miraculously, there is. If she takes her shoes off one at a time and stands on one leg so that she can hold each foot under the hot water, her feet might get warm. She can wear the clean socks in her bag over her other socks. It'll also make her shoes fit better.

The previous Sunday she had stepped on a thorn on the stable floor, and it broke off in her foot.

Gunter was saddling Lucy. Alexander lay on his back between the horse's legs; hoisted himself backwards on to his shoulders; pommelled his feet against her stomach. A couple of times he jumped up, screaming, and swung on her tail. Lucy stood dead still, did not even move her ears. Gunter spoke to Alexander as if he was a normal child. *Get away from Lucy's tail, Alexander, she's going to kick you.* Immediately, Alexander let go of her tail and lay down between her legs again. *Don't kick so hard, Alexander, you're hurting her.* Alexander stopped his kicking and rubbed the soles of his feet against the swollen, hairy curve of Lucy's stomach. *Come, let's put your riding hat on.* Alexander hopped up and down with excitement, flapping his hands wildly. He laughed out loud. But while he laughed, the tears were streaming from his blue eyes.

That was something she could never understand: when his mouth laughed, his eyes wept. When he needed the toilet, he slammed his hands against the fridge door. When he was hungry, he cupped his hands over his eyes. When his hands were sticky, he looked in the mirror.

The wrong way round. Everything. Always.

She leaned on the rake and watched them performing their Sunday ritual. Gunter held out his cupped hands to give Alexander a foothold. Alexander never thought twice, he trusted the foothold. *Put your feet into the stirrups,* Gunter said. Alexander did. *Take the reins and pluck them.* Alexander laughed and slapped his cheeks, then he took the reins.

Always obeyed Gunter's commands. Never did things the wrong way round.

As Lucy walked off on her journey of Sunday circles, Gunter put his fingers between his lips and whistled. Alexander looked back and waved. Every Sunday she watched the ritual, and it remained a mystery to her. Because at home she could wave until she was blue in the face, he wouldn't wave back at her. If Miriam took his hand and lifted it up to show him how, he threw a tantrum and hid his hands under his shirt.

Then she stepped on the thorn. She hopped on one leg into the shade of the shed, sat down and tried to remove the thorn. But she couldn't get hold of it properly and it was too painful to try and scratch it out.

'It's because you're always barefoot,' Gunter said when he came in and saw her sitting on the floor of the shed. 'It's winter and the floor of the shed is damp. And you have a bad cough already. I'll get some beech bark and make tea for your chest.'

She brought her face closer to her foot, pressed on both sides of the thorn. And in her heart she spoke to him: *Take me with you when you go to fetch the beech bark in the mountains. We'll build a huge fire. You and I.* 'Can I borrow your pocket knife?'

He opened the pocket knife and kneeled next to her. 'Let me take the thorn out.'

'I'll take it out myself. If I could just use the sharp point of the knife-blade to . . .'

He held his hand out to take her foot. 'Let me take it out, Ingrid.'

He removed the thorn painlessly. Went to fill the stable-pail with water and washed her foot. Rubbed it with milk ointment.

'Give me your other foot too.'

'It's all right, I . . .'

'Give it to me, Ingrid,' and he held his hand out, 'or else your feet are going to feel odd.'

While he washed and rubbed her foot, she prayed into the hazy air of the cold winter afternoon that God would give her the strength never to start a fire that would burn a treasure to ashes.

Can it be possible that only seven days have passed since then?

She holds her right foot under the hot water. For a long time. Dries her foot on the leg of her tracksuit pants. Puts a clean sock over the other sock. Then her left foot. It feels heavenly to have warm feet. Nobody brings the toilet paper. Nobody comes to fetch her for questioning. The plate with Sunday food remains untouched.

She measures the cell again and again. The distances remain the same. She blows the dust and tobacco flakes from the window sill. It becomes her kitchen. She arranges the enamel mug and the bar of red soap in one corner of the window sill. Rinses the tea mug and puts it next to the other mug. Talcum powder, deodorant and shampoo in the opposite corner. It becomes her dressing table. She uses the empty toilet roll to scrape the cigarette butts and rubbish on the floor to the corner of the cell. Her stomach starts to cramp. She holds the facecloth under the hot water of the shower and washes her face and neck; soothes the abrasions at her wrists.

She wishes that the overwhelming desire to sleep would come back. But it doesn't. Instead, her images and thoughts are crystal clear.

When are they going to bring the toilet paper? Her stomach cramps again. She lifts the mattress from the cement slab and puts it against the wall. Sits down on a reasonably clean spot on the bare cement. It is a huge relief to be off her feet.

She sits. She waits. It's Sunday afternoon. What is Gunter doing?

It feels as if there are air bubbles in her stomach. She bends forward to relieve the cramps. The cement is hard and cold under her buttocks. Will they ever bring the toilet paper? She gets up and digs in the carry-bag. No, the tissues are in her handbag which they locked away. She sits down again. Pearls of cold perspiration form on her upper lip and forehead.

When the next cramp grips her stomach, she stumbles to the funnel-shaped stainless steel toilet. Naked legs and hips. How far can she be stripped of her dignity in one day? And while she's sitting on the toilet, she feels a terrible itch in the crook of her arm. Without having to look, she knows. She rips her fleecy jacket off, pushes her fingers in under the cuff of her tracksuit sleeve and shoves it past her elbow.

There's a tiny circle of crawling pink insects.

She wants to yell and yell and yell. But her voice seems frozen.

Panic-stricken, she takes one shoe off and uses a sock to clean herself. The other sock must be kept in case the toilet paper never arrives. Bag. Shampoo. Facecloth. Opens the shower taps. Strips her clothes off. It does not bother her when a man's face appears at the bars of the door to ask if he can take the plate away. Take it, she indicates and turns her back on him.

She washes her hair; squeezes shampoo on to the facecloth. Rubs between her toes, behind her ears, in her armpits. Every fold where the lice could possibly creep in. Her teeth are chattering with cold when she dries herself off with the facecloth. Talcum powder. Deodorant. She takes the last clean clothes from the bag and puts her pyjamas on under them. As sure as God is alive, tonight she's going to freeze to death in this damp cell, because she can no longer wear her fleecy jacket. She bends over and fans her hair, trying to dry it. Uses the empty toilet roll to drag the infested clothes to the shower.

The door clatters open. It's the man and the woman.

'Come,' the man says. 'You have visitors.'

Whoever it is, she doesn't want to see them. And nobody must see her. 'I don't want visitors.'

'Come, Mrs Dorfling,' the woman says in a sweet voice. 'It's your children. We'll allow a contact visit, and I'll stay with you all the time.'

'My hair is still wet.'

'It's all right. Come,' and the woman touches her shoulder, gently steering her in the direction of the door. 'Your children have brought you bedding and towels.'

She walks ahead of them down the dreary passage. And she's filled with a deep thankfulness that she has showered and at least smells fresh. Thankful, too, that it's not Mirna or the dominee waiting for her.

46

WHEN THE RED-FEATHERED rooster crows to announce a new day, she wakes up.

It's Sunday.

Grootkerk day.

She lights the Primus stove to boil water for coffee. Today there's no time to start up the wood stove. Heavens, she has a bad night behind her. She arrived home shortly before midnight on two tired legs. Then she still had to boil water to wash, and sweep a layer of breadcrumbs from the kitchen floor. Hang her dress on a coat hanger so that it's not creased in the morning. After blowing out the candle, she tossed and turned, struggling to escape from the chicken eagle's claws. It was as if she could hear Lexi calling her in the quiet night. *Mimmi! Mimmi!* A thousand images rolled through her mind. Building puzzles with Lexi in his tablecloth house; his blue eyes laughing at her as he pointed to the rooster on the church steeple; his joy and excitement when he heard the ice cream cart coming down the road.

And to make things worse, Jeremiah snored like a pig, so loud that it felt as if the roof was rattling.

It's a battle to get Jeremiah out of bed. He grumbles about the cold and about having to get up so early. He turns on his side and grunts, complains that his back aches from carrying the suitcase all the way to the township.

'I'll fry you two fresh eggs before we leave,' she tries to console him. She is used to Jeremiah's excuses. And she ignores them. He must wash and dress and eat; she doesn't have all day.

'Fry three eggs, my stomach is hollow with hunger. And I'm telling you, Miriam, before I put a foot out of this bed I want to know where we're going with Evert's car.'

She puts the pan on the flame and goes to stand in the door of the bedroom. 'I want to go out to the farm where Lexi's horse is kept, and speak to the man.'

He throws the bedclothes off and swings his feet out of bed. '*Jissus*, Miriam, to do what?'

'It's *Nagmaal* Sunday, Jeremiah. Watch your words.'

'I'm asking you, Miriam: to do what?'

'I want to ask him something.'

'You're mad in your head, Miriam!'

'Then I am. You just get your backside out of bed.'

When they walk down the front steps, the morning star twinkles like a jewel in the black winter sky. The yard gate is frosty under her fingers. It's too early in the morning to talk to Evert about levelling their wrongs. At weekends Evert's brain can't think until the sun is high above the mountain. As it is, it will be a battle to wake him up and get him to listen to her.

'Where do you want to go with my car this time of a Sunday morning, Ma?' He holds his head and grunts.

'Just somewhere. Your Pa will do the driving.'

'Pa? Drive *my* car?'

He mustn't know that her nerves are on edge. It's mountainous country to the man's farm and it's a narrow gravel road. What if there are sharp curves or yawning abysses? What if there's on-coming traffic?

'Your Pa is a good driver, Evert. We'll be back before dinnertime. I'll pay you cash, here and now. And if the car doesn't give trouble, I'll have six brand-new strings put on your guitar before Friday.'

At first Jeremiah struggles to find the light-switch. Then to move the seat forward so his feet can reach the pedals. Twice the car jerks and cuts out. But the third time he revs it until petrol fumes hang in the air above them. Then the car rockets off over the potholes in the township street and she holds on to the dashboard with both hands to anchor herself.

47

'TEN MINUTES ONLY,' the man says.

Teresa and Zettie sit close together on the wooden bench in the visitors' room. Their faces are pale and weary, they wring their hands nervously. It shatters her to see their hunched shoulders, like old women carrying the world on their backs. Not even the Monday morning when she had to tell them about Dawid's death was worse than this.

Are you OK, Mom? Yes. *Is there anything we can do for you?* No, not really. *We brought you bedding and towels, Mom.* I'm glad, thank you. *They questioned us last night, Mom.* I expected it. *We told them that you loved Alexander more than anything in the world, and that it's absurd to think you would harm him.* You know it's the truth. *What really happened, Mom?* I swear to God, I don't know. *Do you need anything, Mom?* Perhaps you could bring me a box of tissues. It's best just to drop it at the charge office. *We don't know what to do next, Mom.* Go to Aunt Lida and say that I've asked if she'll help with the funeral arrangements. Tell her to ask the Roman Catholic priest to bury Alexander. *When will you be coming home, Mom?* I don't know.

Zettie starts crying. Teresa steps forward and talks in a trembling voice.

Do you have enough clothes, Mom? I don't think so. *What are they giving you to eat?* Ordinary food. *Are they treating you decently?* Yes. *We don't have much money left, Mom, and we still have to get back.* Phone Gunter, he'll help you with two thousand rand. *Do you have a legal representative, Mom?* Yes. *What happened to your wrists, Mom?* Nothing. *You're lying, Mom, look how bruised your wrists are. Don't tell me they handcuffed you?* Only while we drove here. *But, Mom . . .?* It's the law, Teresa.

The woman steps closer and interrupts. 'Visiting time is over,' and she taps her nail on the face of her watch. 'I've already given you three minutes extra.'

'I must go now.'

'Mom . . .?'

'Thank you for coming. You must phone Grandpa and Grandma to tell them about Alexander.'

'Mom . . .?'

Simultaneously, they embrace her and press their warm cheeks against hers, wrap their arms around her.

At the door she stops and looks back at them. Two old, frail little women. Waving at her like flags flying half-mast.

SHE DOESN'T KNOW WHAT'S worse: a drunk man who *can* drive, or a sober man who *cannot* drive. Jeremiah's neck is as stiff as a poker as he stretches to see the road. Behind the steering wheel his head looks like that of a small child.

'*Jissus*, Miriam, this car of Evert's is as powerful as anything,' he says and does something to the gears that makes the engine roar.

'Holy heavens, Jeremiah, lift your foot off the petrol! You're going too fast!'

'Relax, Miriam, I know how to drive.'

Jesus of Nazareth, please let Jeremiah realise his limitations. On the tar road her nerves could take it, but they're on the narrow gravel road now. One sharp, sandy bend, and the car will surely turn on its roof. And she has to get to the man's farm in one piece.

'Look at the speedometer needle, Miriam!' and she holds her breath as he takes his eyes off the road. 'I'd forgotten how exciting it is to drive a car!'

'Keep your eyes on the road, Jeremiah!'

'Don't you tell me where to keep my eyes, Miriam. I know where to keep them!' and he steps on the petrol.

Today she'll have to call on the powers of the salvation psalm to rescue them. Or else Evert can wave his new guitar strings goodbye. She shuts her eyes as Jeremiah speeds on the wrong side of the road. How does the salvation psalm start?

You are my fortress, Lord, the Man in whom I put my last trust today. Today You must cover me with Your wings. And be Jeremiah's shield . . .

'Get your foot on the brake, Jeremiah!'

The car swerves in a cloud of dust. Jeremiah utters the ugliest swear words he knows. But by the mercy of the salvation psalm they get through the sharp bend.

Don't let me be afraid of the arrow that flies by day. Don't let us fall like thousands of others, Lord, because Evert doesn't have insurance on his car. Prove to me today, Lord, that You can take us to the man's farmyard before we have bad luck, or terror strikes us. If You have an angel that can fly fast enough, send him to hold Jeremiah's hands and feet so that he doesn't crash into a krantz. There are no lions around here, Lord, but it's winter time and there are plenty of kudus. I beg You to keep them off the road, Lord.

'Take my false teeth out, Miriam, I'm scared I might crack them in two. This damn car of Evert's goes too fast for my nerves.'

'Don't take your hands off the steering wheel, Jeremiah, I'll remove your teeth.'

Lord, in all those days and nights of pleading behind the chicken run I have learned that You have set Your love upon me and You know my name, therefore I rely on You to bring me to my destination in one piece. And even though sometimes Jeremiah is a thorn in my flesh, Lord, rescue him too. Because I don't want to go into my old age without him. I call upon You, Lord, because my troubles are bigger than me. But not bigger than You.

She has just started the salvation psalm from verse one again, when Jeremiah steers around the last bend, and the white house with the green roof appears before her eyes. Jeremiah is too slow on the brakes and races past the turn-off. He has to make a wide turn through the bushes next to the road, because he can't find the reverse gear. When they reach the farmyard, Jeremiah comes close to uprooting the camphor bush. But a split-second before they smash into it the car stops dead, and she puts Jeremiah's false teeth in his hand.

So far, Lord, glory to You.

49

THE SHORT DISTANCE TO the interrogation room seems like a thousand miles. There's a dullness in her brain; emptiness in her heart. For nine years she fought like a tigress. There are times in life when you fight with every ounce of your strength, even though you don't understand why you are fighting. And there comes a time when you surrender, even though you have all reason to fight to the bitter end. She walks into the interrogation room, knowing that she has crossed the boundary to no-man's-land. Somewhere in the ten minutes that she spent with her aged young daughters, her back was finally broken; her fighting spirit killed. It's not important whether she eats Sunday food or Tuesday food. Because she has crossed that boundary.

The man runs his fingers through his spiky hair; paces around her in circles. His trouser leg brushes past her knee; his brown sharp-pointed shoes seem disproportionately long.

'Why are there so many half-empty bottles of medicine in the medicine cabinet, Mrs Dorfling? Surely it was meant to . . .' He pauses, looks at her with raised eyebrows.

'I began to believe that his medicines clashed with one another. They'd been prescribed by too many doctors. Alexander was better off without medicine.'

Brown sharp-pointed shoe. Trouser leg brushing against her

knee.

'I was his mother, I could see what it was doing to him.'

He keeps circling around her, invading her personal space. Spits out question after question, seemingly unperturbed by her answers. What is the name of the bank's insurance broker? Is it true that your rates and taxes are way in arrears? Why did you neglect your child by letting him wear a short-sleeved shirt in the middle of winter? What was your husband's reaction when the credit bureau blacklisted him and the bank summarily closed his cheque account?

God, if it would deliver her from this hell, she'd ask the woman to bring a sheet of paper, and she'd write a false confession. If only the man's voice would stop resounding in her tired brain.

'Can I please go back to my cell? And can I have the bedding that my children brought?'

'All parcels are searched at the charge office before they are given to detainees. I'll enquire about your belongings in the morning.'

In the morning. Her brain refuses to think so far ahead.

Why did you resign from the tennis club? What were your plans when Miriam Slangveld retired?

'The toilet paper in my cell is finished. They said they would bring . . .'

Sharp-pointed shoe. Trouser leg.

Why did you attempt to sell the horse, one of the few things your child clearly enjoyed, a few hours before he died?

'My cell is infested with lice, my fleecy jacket too. These are my last clean clothes.'

He's deaf to her pleas. His voice drones on and on with the monotony of a fly caught behind a wall picture. Somehow she gets lost in the mistiness beyond the boundary. She walks her no-man's-land in godforsaken solitude. Actually, she doesn't walk, she lies with her face to the ground. And she knows that her dreams and hopes are lying down beside her.

God alone knows how much she will miss the kraal wall.

And the scent of camphor bush lingering on the breeze.

50

THE FARMYARD IS FILLED with Sunday serenity. From the trees surrounding the white farmstead comes the sweet chattering of a flock of canaries, mingling with the deep resonant hooo-hooo-hooo of a rock pigeon. The front door of the house is closed. Perhaps the man is still sleeping and she should wait a while before knocking. If she could be sure there would not be a watchdog, she would walk round the house to inspect the backyard. It was true what her mother had taught her years ago about backyards: the way you care for your backyard is a reflection of how you care for the precious yard inside your head. If your backyard looks like a pigsty, then your thoughts will look exactly the same. That's why she's forever sweeping and raking her own backyard. When she had the chicken run put up, she refused to use second-hand scrap. She saved up for a couple more months and bought new chicken wire and galvanised sheets. Never mind Jeremiah, who almost had a fit about the expense.

It would ease her mind to see the man's backyard. But she's not going to risk her life against a watchdog.

'Go knock,' she tells Jeremiah who is still sitting behind the steering wheel with an ashen face.

'It's *you* who wants to talk to the man, not me! Why must I go knock?'

She's halfway up the broad stone steps when one of the farm workers comes around the side of the house, carrying a pail of milk. She turns around and stops him. No, he says, Master Gunter is not at home. At daybreak, when they started milking, he saw him walking down to the kraal.

'Show me the way to the kraal.'

He puts the pail of milk down. 'It's easy. Past the camphor bush, past the cement dam. Then Auntie just follows the veld path until Auntie sees the kraal on the sunset side of the path.'

Her legs will make it there and back, for Miss Ingrid's sake.

'Come, let's go,' she tells Jeremiah.

'I'll watch Evert's car. I'm not the one who wants to talk to the man.'

Past the camphor bush. Past the cement dam. Please, Lord, let the man listen to her. Let him reach down a helping hand to her. Down the veld path. The dewy grass along the path brushes against her legs, leaving the hem of her dress damp. How much will six new guitar strings cost? Last fifty yards to the kraal. If Jeremiah gets them back to town alive today, she's going to bake him raisin bread. And he can have a whole week's eggs without having to explain what he did with them.

The man is bending over a bale of straw. When she touches the latch of the kraal gate and it tinkles, he dusts his hands on his trousers and comes walking towards her.

'Good morning, sir.' She swallows, makes her back stiff to muster courage. 'My name is Miriam Slangveld. I work for Miss Ingrid and I've come all the way from town in a borrowed car to ask you something, sir . . .'

When the twelve o'clock sun is high in the heavenly blue sky, she kneels behind the chicken run. To glorify God who sent his angels to help Jeremiah get them back to town in one piece. For Evert's car which did not let them down. For the attorney the man sent to Miss Ingrid. And because he said she could go back to town with peace in her heart; he would stay by Teresa and Zettie's side through this sorrowful time. And he would pay all the funeral costs.

When she mutters her final amen and opens her eyes, Jeremiah is sitting on the threshold of the woodshed, his hat on his knee, his bowed head resting in his bony hands. She walks past him quietly, her head inclined out of respect. Because it's the first time in her entire life that she has seen Jeremiah talking to God.

51

She's lost all sense of time.

'What day is it, and what is the time?' she asks when the woman accompanies her to the bathroom for the third time.

'It's Sunday evening, twenty past ten.'

Then darkness has fallen over the kraal and the mountain. Gunter has put Lucy back into the stable without saddling her. 'When can I go back to my cell?'

The woman shakes her head. 'Mrs Dorfling, if anyone understands your position, it's me. Make a confession. The court will take all extenuating circumstances into consideration. I can guarantee you, you'll come off lightly.'

Her lips say one thing; her eyes another.

'I have nothing to confess, because I am not guilty.'

Back to the interrogation room. Ten thousandth pace down the passage with the flopping shoes. She no longer asks them for a chance to sleep. Somehow she doesn't need to rest any more. Her no-man's-land has no boundaries. She hears her own voice echoing about the sadness and tragedy that she had long ago buried in the deepest layers of her subconscious.

Past midnight.

Past the empty black hole that lies beyond midnight.

'Mrs Dorfling, you claim that the community had no compassion and that the church rejected you. But when the dominee expressed his willingness to conduct your husband's funeral service, you turned his offer down. Why?'

Trouser leg brushing against her knee.

'You should go back to the dominee and get the truth from him. Ask *him* why my husband was cremated without a memorial service. He knows all the answers.'

'I'm asking *you,* Mrs Dorfling.'

'And I'm telling you to ask him.'

He glares at her. Glares and glares. Picks up his mobile phone and walks out. In the distance she hears his endless voice. The woman hands her a glass of water and asks if her headache is better. When the man returns he says they're taking her back to her cell.

The black curtain of night covers the passage windows. From behind the barred doors of the dim cells the faceless voices communicate in their midnight language. They lock her up in the sleeping section of the cell, behind the heavy steel door with the porthole window. The thick double glass of the window is cracked, probably where a fist hit it, long ago.

She sinks down on the ice-cold funnel of the toilet; lays her head against the graffiti on the wall. And sleeps.

In the dead of night she is woken by a hollow sound rolling down the passage. It comes towards her, louder and louder. Closer and closer. Until it becomes a clear tune, harmonising into a perfectly blended choir of unaccompanied male voices. *Nearer, my God to Thee* . . . It sends shivers down her spine, until she feels as if her scalp has shrunk, and the skin on her arms too.

Cell-bound souls singing a hymn before a new day dawns.

As if controlled by a power beyond her, her voice rises with the other, invisible tones. *Though, like the wanderer, the sun gone down, Darkness comes over me, My rest a stone; Yet in my dreams I'd be, Nearer my God to Thee* . . .

A hand shakes her shoulder.

'Wake up, Mrs Dorfling!'

Through the misty shadows of sleep the man's face looms in front of her. He's alone and he is holding the docket under his arm. 'Pack your stuff, you're going home.'

It's a good cop set. She remains motionless.

'I'm in a hurry, Mrs Dorfling.'

She leaves the infested clothes in the corner of the cell. Empties her kitchen cupboard and her dressing table. Zips her bag. Hears the slamming of the barred door behind her. There is nothing but loneliness and emptiness inside her.

She walks in the middle of the passage.

Sunlight pours through the windows, its brightness blinds her.

In the office the man hands the docket to the constable on duty. 'We're releasing her, she's not going to be charged,' he says without expression.

The police constable asks for her receipt and she hauls it out the side pocket of the carry-bag. He takes the bag with her possessions from the safe, orders her to check the contents.

Handbag. Purse. Toothpaste. Shoelaces.

'Sign the register,' he says grimly. She signs.

'Lace up your shoes.' She squats and laces her shoes.

Don't let it be a game, God, please.

'Where is the woman, I want to say goodbye to her?'

'She went off duty.'

'Will you please tell her . . .?'

Rudely, the man interrupts. 'Someone else is taking you home. They'll pick you up in the parking lot. Will you find your way there?'

She has no idea. 'Yes.'

Turn left. Left again. A policewoman unlocks the last gate to freedom. One moment she's still standing on this side of the border. The next moment she crosses over to the other side. It wasn't a game. Two steps. Three. Twenty. Nobody calls her back, no heavy hand on her shoulder. The arrow on a green board indicates left to the parking area.

Her shoes fit tightly.

When she looks up, Gunter is walking towards her. The breeze tousles his hair and he holds his arms out. She drops the bag and runs to him. He picks her up and holds her tightly against the roughness of his khaki shirt.

Over his shoulder, through a film of tears, she sees Teresa and Zettie getting out of the car.

✳

The following autumn, the inquest was finalised. A concise ruling by a magistrate on a clinical piece of paper:

Cause of death: possible suffocation/dry drowning.

Could the actions of a person prima facie indicate a criminal offence? No.

On a morning bathed in yellow sunlight when the leaves were falling from the trees like rusty-coloured butterflies and the herbal fragrance of the mountain lingered over the farmyard, she walked around the white house with the green louvres to where Miriam was sweeping the backyard. Asked her to remember to put winter sheets on Teresa and Zettie's beds for when they came home for the Easter holidays.

Then she walked back into the house and opened all the curtains to let the light in. Through the open window Miriam's hallelujah song followed her. *Give to the wind thy fears . . . God hears thy sighs, and counts thy tears . . .*

Barefoot, she walked out on to the cool stone floor of the stoep, past the tumbling branches of the pink bougainvillaea. To the kraal. Alone. She found a foothold and hoisted herself up. Sat down on the kraal wall in the gentle rays of the autumn sun, staring at the place where Lucy always used to walk her Sunday afternoon circles.

And she gave the truth, the whole truth, as only she knew it, to the camphor-scented wind to carry away into eternity.